IN DEAD WATER

A British Murder Mystery

THE WILD FENS MURDER MYSTERY SERIES

JACK CARTWRIGHT

CHESTNUT PRESS

IN DEAD WATER

A Wild Fens Murder Mystery

PROLOGUE

The fading moonlight cast deep shadows across the sand and mudflats but barely lit the tall marsh grasses that seemed to reach for her legs as she ran. Twice she stumbled and barely stayed upright, but never did she stop. She couldn't stop.

Because he was out there somewhere, and he was mad as hell.

In daylight, she could have outrun him with ease. She could've been home and dry by now. In the darkness of the night, however, she had only her memory to guide her through the maze of streams and patches of deep, boggy mud.

But it was all so different. The little waterways she knew so well seemed to have moved with malice. The patches of soft, wet sand were the same shade of grey as the dry sand, and grasses seemed to have sprouted everywhere. Only the reflections from the brackish streams that spread like arteries throughout the mud provided any real contrast against the night, and her thudding heart was the beat to which her bare feet pounded.

She launched herself across one of those mirror-like obstacles, time seeming to stand still for the fragment of time she was airborne. Then she landed with a thud and instantly knew her mistake. Her feet sank deep into the wet, and the mud immediately began its campaign to claim her.

She took a moment or two to regain her senses. No bones were broken. Using the opportunity to gain control of her breathing, she listened hard for the sound of his footsteps somewhere behind her.

From where she stood, she had a clear view of where she had run – the tall marsh grasses, the arterial streams, and the beach beyond, framed by two large sand dunes. And beyond that, the inky mass of the North Sea, capped by the pale horizon, where, somewhere, the sun graced some other land with its light. Somewhere in Europe, she thought. Germany, or Holland maybe? Somewhere close, for the sky was warming and brightening, and the moonlight she had used to find her way to him was giving way to the power of the sun.

Surely if he was out there, she would see him against the sky? Like some wraith from hell trudging through the stinking mud and sand with a methodical purpose.

But there was no sign of him. No shape against the horizon, no sound of sucking mud. There was only that smell. That smell she would never ever be rid of.

How she wished she had just stayed at home. Why did she have to go out alone? Why didn't she listen to her father?

A shiver ran through her, marking her time there. The cool evening breeze licked at the layer of sweat on her back, and the idea of fighting against the sucking mud seemed beyond her remaining strength.

She could just sleep in the ooze.

He wouldn't find her. Not here, surely?

She glanced at the horizon again. An hour at the most.

If she really tried, perhaps she could crawl to the dry sand a few metres away? She could lie between the grasses out of the cool wind.

She scanned the desolate ground behind her again, finding nothing but stillness.

Then she made her move, or tried to, at least.

Her feet seemed to be stuck in the mud. She had been there too long. Panic set in and she struggled against the vacuum that held her, only to find that she sank further with the effort.

She reached for a tuft of those hardy grasses, but it pulled free, allowing the ground to inhale another few inches of her body.

The temptation to call out was overwhelming. But he was out there somewhere. Maybe he was watching? Maybe he knew the marshland better than her and had found a way to overtake?

Inland was a mass of black. She could just make out the ramp that emergency vehicles used to access the marshes. She had seen them once before, when a girl from her school had become stuck in the mud and died out here alone.

Then it dawned on her.

She was that girl from school. Hers was the name that would be on people's lips.

Have you heard about Hayley Donovan? Did you hear about the girl from Saltfleet? You'd have thought she'd have known better. Her family must be devastated.

She reached for another tuft of grass, and this time, its roots held fast. She fell forward to dig her elbows into the mud, to give herself every chance.

But it was no use.

A sob came from nowhere, a quiet whimper amplified in the still of the night. She sniffed, no longer caring if he found her. No longer caring what he might do.

"Help," she called out, crying now, openly venting her fears. "Please, help."

She laid the side of her face down in the mud, staring at the horizon. She could have sworn it was brighter than before.

Her dad always said that everyone should see at least one

sunrise and one sunset every year, just to remind them of their insignificance. She had seen the sunset only a few weeks ago.

And now she was watching the sunrise, as insignificant as could be.

The sunset had been beautiful. She remembered how fast the sun seemed to fall below the horizon, faster than she could comprehend. She remembered the hues of oranges and reds like watercolour paints leaking across the sea.

Now she stared at the onset of the day. There were no orange hues. The sea was not calm and inviting.

And his black shape lurched into view, like death himself emerging from the shadows, braving the looming sunrise.

She could call out for help, but nobody would hear. She fought harder to free her legs, but she only sank further. What would be worse, death by his hand or drowning in the thick mud?

He moved closer and she cried freely, no longer caring for silence or stealth, and praying for there to be some remnant of a heart inside of him.

But he stopped a few metres away, seeming to peer at her with a childlike curiosity.

"Please," she said. "I'm stuck. Please, help me. I won't say anything."

But he said nothing. Instead, he stepped closer, and his broad, black body blocked the promise of the last glorious sunrise she would ever see.

CHAPTER ONE

The hot summer sun burned fiercely on the Lincolnshire fields, but the air conditioning in DI Freya Bloom's Range Rover breathed cool air across her open-toed shoes. Even in the early morning, the heat was intense enough to raise a shimmer on the horizon.

Even the soil in the fields surrounding the little cottage she rented was dry. The straw bales that she always thought added beauty to the scenery had all been collected, only to be stacked to form a long wall near the three houses further up the track.

She reached the little junction in the tracks, where in days gone by the farm workers who rented the cottages, including hers, would have ventured straight ahead to be assigned a task for the day.

But instead, she turned left towards the main road. There was scant reason for her to take any other route anymore.

She joined the main road, enjoying the early morning light on the fields and the drip of weekend traffic. Today was a new day for her, a new start, in some respects, and it was liberating.

Her destination was Dunston, a small village just fifteen minutes from the city of Lincoln. Being a Lincolnshire resident for less than a year, Freya's knowledge of the local areas was centred around places she visited during investigations. The romance of the wild, open countryside and the lure of peace and quiet had combined with her desire to be part of something, part of a community.

She pulled up outside the cottage she had found on the internet, viewed twice before, and, quite simply, fallen in love with.

It was small, terraced, and offered no off-street parking, and that was fine. The road saw very little traffic, so parking her car outside would be no problem.

She greeted the estate agent, and, as the British so enjoy, discussed the fine weather for a few moments. But she wasn't really listening. Her eyes roamed across the stonework, the cottage garden, and the quaint porch, so much so that she saw herself sitting on the little bench beneath the window one day in the near future, with a cup of fine coffee perhaps or enjoying a book to the soundtrack of the birds.

"Shall we?" he said finally.

"I'm sorry, I didn't get your name," she replied. "It was a different guy last time."

"Greg," he said. The same name as her ex-husband, and her mind wandered to a past life. "Gregory Fell."

She let him lead the way so she could enjoy the wonderful front aspect for a moment longer, then followed him inside the house. He was a handsome man, she thought. Or at least he could be, if he only learned to relax. His features were sharp, his skin was flawless, and his hair a boyish blond. The cheap suit he wore, along with how he seemed to force proper pronunciation, belied his true qualities and gave Freya a sense of distrust. It was as if he was trying to be better, instead of being proud of who he was.

"You haven't been doing this for very long, have you?" she asked, when he began to tell her how she could position her furniture to make the most of the space.

"What gave me away?" he replied.

"A good salesperson waits for their prospect to speak," she said.

"Ah. You've got me bang to rights."

He gave a nervous laugh and then opened his mouth to say something about the kitchen. Then he paused when he caught Freya's questioning expression.

"Three weeks," he said.

"I thought so. Relax. Let the house do the talking. When I have a question, I'll let you know. Besides, I've been here three times now, my offer has been accepted and the searches are done. All we need to do is exchange. So, if you manage to somehow dissuade me from going ahead, then you should really look at a new career."

"Are you in sales?" he asked, to which she laughed out loud.

"No, I work with a different type of criminal. What did you do before this?"

"I was in prison," he replied, and for the first time caught Freya off-guard.

"Oh?"

"HMP Lincoln. Prison officer."

"Ah, I see," she said, relieved that she was not alone in a house with a convicted criminal. "What made you move?"

"I just want to be closer to home. More flexibility. You know?"

"I do. Sadly, flexibility is a rare commodity, despite what they tell you. We can work from anywhere now, yet I still find myself chained to this."

She held her phone up and rolled her eyes.

"I'd rather be chained to my phone than walking a landing. Most of the prisoners were okay. They just want to serve their time and get out. But you always get the odd one. Usually, it's a youngster who's yet to learn that there's always someone bigger and tougher than them. That's when the trouble starts," he said, then stopped and gave an apologetic look. "Sorry, I'm waffling–"

"No, it's fine," she said. "I understand. More than you might think."

"Oh really?"

"I'm a detective," she said. "Major Crimes."

"Very nice."

"Not really. The customers aren't always as courteous as I'd like them to be."

"I see it now," he said, appraising her from her shoes to her hair. "I should have spotted it. So, what do you think anyway?"

"Think?"

"The house," he said with a smile.

She studied him for a moment, noticing the way he seemed to have relaxed into the role. His smile was far more natural and his body language far less forced.

"That's better," she told him. "Less round peg in a square hole and more just a man presenting a house. Far more alluring."

He looked quite sheepish listening to Freya's honest appraisal. Then his eyes ventured across the room to the stairs.

"Do you want to see the bedrooms?" he asked, which took her back a little. "I mean–"

"It's okay. I know what you meant," she said, saving him the embarrassment. She swept her hand as if presenting the room. "Lead the way."

Freya was halfway up the stairs, admiring the view ahead of her, when a slight rumble from her bag interrupted her imagination as it ventured to places that no lady should ever verbalise.

Greg was on the small landing, bathed in sunlight from the rear window and waiting for her to choose which room she would like to have a look at first. She gestured for him to hold on for a moment and took the call.

"Ben?" she said.

"Freya. I've had a call from DCI Standing. We're needed."

"Oh no, not today."

"Sorry, are you busy?"

"I'm just with someone," she said, and her eyes tracked Greg's strong V-shape. "A friend."

"A friend?"

Hearing one side of the call, Greg demonstrated his impeccable manners once more.

"We can reschedule if you like. I'm around later," he said.

"Who's that?" Ben said.

"I told you, I'm with a friend," she said, then addressed Greg with her hand only partly over the microphone. "I'd love to see the master bedroom."

"Oh, I see. Well, you'll have to cut your romantic breakfast short. Standing wants us there in under an hour," Ben told her as she followed Greg into the master bedroom. It was bigger than she had initially expected with plenty of space. It was almost as if the previous owners had removed a third bedroom to create a larger master suite.

"Under an hour," she said aloud while checking her watch. "I think I can do what I need to do here and be there in time."

"Wow, there's nothing like a running commentary."

"I'll see you there," she told him. Then, just as she was about to end the call, she added, "Oh, and Ben?"

"Yes?"

"Grab some decent coffee from somewhere, would you?" she said. "It sounds like we're going to need it."

CHAPTER TWO

The incident room was empty when Ben arrived. He set his bag down with his coffee and put Freya's coffee on her desk before opening the windows.

"It's stifling, isn't it?" a voice said from behind him.

Ben turned to find the recently promoted DCI Standing in the doorway. He wore trousers and a light blue shirt, which was already damp beneath the arms.

"I didn't hear you come in, Steve."

"What do you reckon?" he said, and shoved the incident room doors open a few times, letting them close of their own accord each time.

"You've oiled the hinges?"

"I had maintenance do it. Do you know, when I was DI, sitting up there at that desk, it was like somebody had walked across my grave whenever these doors opened. I could even hear it over all the conversations. Now I'm stuck in my office out there, it's even bloody louder."

"Well, it was about time somebody did something about them, Steve," Ben said.

"And that's not the only change I've made," he replied.

"It's not?"

"I've ordered us a decent coffee machine."

"A coffee machine?"

"One of those fancy ones. You know? With the little pods you put in."

"Well, I'm sure that'll be a welcome addition," Ben said before the two fell into an awkward silence, which eventually Standing broke.

"Ben, I was wondering..." he began, and Ben made a show of being all ears. "I know we've worked together on and off for a long time."

"We have," Ben agreed. "On and off."

"It's just, well, the others..."

"What about them?"

"I don't want them all calling me Steve. I'm trying to make a go of this role and, well, I thought if you called me guv or boss, or whatever, then they'd follow. They respect you."

"You want me to call you guv?"

Standing nodded.

"I'm a DCI, Ben. I can't have everyone using my Christian name."

"Alright," Ben said, not really fussed about what he called the man. "If that's what you want."

"It is."

"Leave it with me," Ben said, just as they heard a familiar click of heels in the corridor.

Standing stepped to one side and let the doors close, presumably so that Freya would notice the oiled hinges. She burst through the doors, glanced at Standing, and then dumped her bag unceremoniously on her desk and collected her coffee in one swoop.

"Morning, Ben," she said, and he nodded a greeting, doing his best to hide the knowing smile that was forming.

"Morning, Freya," Standing said.

"You're right," she replied. "It is."

It was clear from Standing's body language that he was trying to engage with her. But Ben knew Freya better than that. When she had a bee in her bonnet, there was absolutely no way of getting through her defences.

"Well?" she said, when she found Standing staring at her little summer dress and open-toe shoes. "You called us in."

"Oh, right," he said. "I've got something for you both to–"

"What about the others?" Freya asked, cutting him off. "If we're going to be briefed, surely we should get the key members of the team in? Chapman, Nillson, Gillespie."

"There's no need for them to be here. Not this time," Standing said. "I need you both to report to Saltfleet."

"Saltfleet?" Ben said.

"Where's that?" Freya asked.

"I'll give you a clue," Ben said. "It has a beach."

"A beach?"

"They need a bit of help over there," Standing explained. "And, well, I've got the resources, so I said I'd send you both."

"They need help?" Freya said. "With an investigation?"

"They're a little thin on the ground, shall we say," he said, his Black Country accent adding highs and lows to his voice. "I said you'd pop over and lend them a hand. They've found a body, you see. In the marshes."

"You mean *on* the marshes, Standing," Freya corrected him.

"No," he said. "No, I mean in them. Buried. A girl. Late teens, early twenties. I'll send you the details. I've arranged for a local DS to meet you. She'll be able to give you any resources you need."

He wore his hair in a side parting and since his promotion to DCI a few weeks previously, he had opted for a moustache reminiscent of those that had been fashionable for middle-aged men in the seventies and eighties.

But like many things, fashion had moved on, and the addition of a facial decoration, in Freya's opinion, did little to aid any shortfalls he had in the looks department.

"How far is Saltfleet?" she asked Ben.

"An hour and a half," he said. "Two hours if we get stuck behind a caravan, which, given the time of year, is highly likely."

"Two hours? We're not going to get much done in a day before we have to turn around and come home. I hope there's budget for overtime on this."

"Oh, you won't need to come home," Standing said. Then he waited, watching Freya realise what he meant. He seemed to enjoy delivering the punchline. "I'll arrange some digs for you. Somewhere nice and cosy."

CHAPTER THREE

"It's an absolute outrage," Freya said, the moment Ben climbed into her car.

There was no point wasting his breath trying to calm her down; he might as well just enjoy the ride, tune her out, and make the most of a couple of days at the coast. He'd packed enough clothes for a week but hoped he wouldn't need that many.

He waved goodbye to Michaela, who was at the front door of his house looking less than impressed but more than a sight for sore eyes. He'd miss that view.

"Is she staying at your place now?" Freya asked when she'd pulled away.

"Only while her place is being decorated. We had a nice weekend planned, which is annoying."

"A nice weekend? What exactly does that entail?"

"Oh, I don't know. Get some dinner somewhere. Maybe a walk."

"So, you hadn't actually planned anything?" Freya said as she pulled the car out onto the road, heading towards Woodhall Spa. "You were just going to do what you always do and wing it?"

"What? No. We were just going to... Oh, forget it. You wouldn't understand."

"Try me."

"No, honestly, I can't be bothered. If all you're going to do is criticise me, I'd prefer if we spoke about something else," Ben said.

"Try me. I won't criticise, I promise."

"We were just going to enjoy each other's company," Ben said. "That was the plan. We actually planned on not having plans."

"You really like her, don't you?" Freya said, and there was a disappointment in her tone, though she'd never admit it.

"She's a lovely person, Freya," Ben told her. "We have a lot in common. Anyway, who's the lucky man?"

"Lucky man?" Freya said.

"Your *friend*," Ben said, gesturing with inverted commas as he did so.

"Oh, you know. Just somebody I met."

"Somebody you met in the past two weeks?"

"Let's just leave it there, shall we?" she said. "When I'm ready to talk about him, I will."

"Ah," Ben said knowingly.

"What's that supposed to mean?"

"Nothing."

"Ben," she snapped, and he laughed, knowing that would irritate her even more. "What?"

"It means he's nobody. Not yet, anyway," Ben said. "And you being coy is an attempt to make me jealous, although I can't think why."

"I do not play games."

"No? Of course not. You're perfect, Freya. A model citizen."

"If anyone is playing games, it's you and her."

"What games?"

"Standing at the front door, waving you off like a good little wife. I'm surprised you haven't bought her a pinny to wear."

"Now who's jealous?" Ben said.

"Oh, I'm not jealous, Ben. I've been there and done that. It's not for me."

"No? I wonder why?" Ben muttered, and he let the air cool for a few moments. "So?"

"So what?" she said.

"Where did you meet him? Online dating? Were you swiping left or right, or whatever it is, and then you saw him?"

"Not exactly," she said. "I've also been there and done that, if you remember."

"Ah, yes. Martin, wasn't it? Or was it Mark?"

"I can't remember," she said, and a wry smile crept onto her face.

"I tell you what," Ben said. "I don't want to argue. In fact, I honestly can't be bothered with it. Let's agree not to talk about our partners."

"Partners?" she said with a little laugh, then controlled herself. "Okay. We'll keep it purely professional. We'll only talk about work, politics, and sport."

"I don't know anything about politics or sport," he replied.

"Neither do I, Ben. But that's what people talk about, isn't it?"

"Yeah, people who read the papers."

"Like Michaela? She's a Sunday Times girl, isn't she?"

"Freya!"

"Okay, I was just playing," she said. "I do have something I would like to talk about though."

"Go on."

"Standing."

"Oh, here we go–"

"What on earth is that moustache all about, and what was he thinking of by sending us to Saltfleet? What if we're needed back home?"

"He's got Gillespie and Nillson. They're more than experienced enough to cover anything in our absence. I think you'll find he's obliged to help out when another station is in need."

"Helping out is one thing. Sending his two most experienced officers is another," she said, shaking her head. "He's up to something."

"Like what? Redecorating? Perhaps he's having the walls painted a different colour and wanted to get it done without you complaining."

"Or perhaps he's testing the ground to see how the team operates without us."

"Without you, you mean?" Ben said.

"Exactly. He's new to the role. He'll want to make a difference. He'll want to demonstrate to the powers that be that they made the right decision. He'll also want to put me in my place."

"So, he's a miracle worker now, is he?"

"He's a ruthless so and so, Ben, is what he is," she said, almost convincing herself as she spoke the words. "He's up to something."

"Well, I'm sure the team will keep us informed. It's not like he has any allies, is it?"

"Only one," she replied, and then turned to look at him and they both said the name.

"Gillespie."

"Do you think Gillespie would take sides?" Ben asked. "I mean, the man's a buffoon at times, but he's not a bad guy, and he does have morals."

"He's corruptible, Ben," she replied. "And DCI Standing is about as corrupt as they come."

CHAPTER FOUR

The sat nav led to a dead-end road, where a concrete ramp led up and then down to open marshland. But there was no questioning if they were in the right place. At least three liveried police cars were parked across the ramp to dissuade drivers from getting too close, and two uniforms performed the same function for foot traffic, opting to do so in the shade of a nearby tree.

Freya parked as close as she could, outside of what looked like a large holiday park.

"Here we go," she said. "A nice stroll in the heat of the midday sun."

"Not my idea of fun," Ben said, as he climbed from the car and stretched. "But a change of scenery might be good for the soul."

"Always finding the positives," Freya remarked, and she stared up at the two uniforms who watched them with disdain. "In a world of negativity. Look at those two. Just itching for us to get close so they can turn us away."

"They probably think we're rich tourists," Ben said, "come to explore the marshes in search of adventure."

"Why rich?"

Ben gave a little laugh and shook his head in disbelief.

"Not many police officers drive a Range Rover, Freya. Not the ones on the ground anyway."

"Well, then," she replied. "This should be fun."

They walked towards the ramp, feeling every degree the sun had to offer, and as she had thought they might, the two uniforms waited for them to get close before stopping them.

"Sorry, love," the first man said. He was small, larger than Cruz but still smaller than average. "No access today, I'm afraid."

Freya could feel Ben's stare; it always irritated him when she toyed with the people who stood in her way.

"Oh dear," Freya replied. "Don't tell me somebody has died."

"I'm afraid we can't share any details. But if you're looking for a walk, you could try a bit further down the coast road."

"That's very helpful," Freya said, fishing her warrant card from her pocket. "What if I were to show you this?"

He studied the card and then her face, perplexed but respectful.

"Why didn't you say?" he said and stepped out of their way. "Down the ramp, follow the markers."

"That was childish," Ben muttered when they were out of earshot.

"Ah, but was it?" Freya said. "To me, it was a test."

"A test?"

"Yes, I wanted to see who it is we're working with. As it happens, he was good. He didn't give anything away. He was courteous and polite. If he's anything to go by, we shouldn't have any trouble at all."

"You've done this before?" Ben said.

"Of course. You'd be amazed at the variation in standards across different stations," Freya said as they reached the bottom of the concrete ramp and stepped onto the sand.

"And here's me thinking you were just antagonising him for the sheer pleasure of it."

The marshland before them was perhaps eight hundred yards

deep and stretched as far as the eye could see in either direction. Beyond the marshes, a raised bank, presumably some kind of sea defence, ran adjacent to the coast. The only gap in the defence was directly ahead of them, where the water ran in and out of the marshes like veins, shimmering in the sunlight.

Tough, wild grasses grew sporadically throughout the open marsh, hindered only by the elements, as no man could pick a way through the maze of little streams without succumbing to, in the best case, a wet foot, and in the worst case, death, as was evidenced by the white tent ahead of them, some three hundred yards into the marsh.

"Something tells me there will be no pleasure in this case," Freya said softly.

They walked in silence, following the markers that had been placed in the mud to identify the safest route. The makeshift path zigzagged across artery-like streams and around the larger clumps of vegetation. Eventually, they reached the crime scene, where some aluminium steps had been laid down on the firmer ground to both prevent contamination of evidence and to provide a route around the crime scene.

"DI Bloom," Freya said, flashing her warrant card when one of the three individuals heard them approaching. "I believe somebody is expecting us?"

"We are, yes," the woman said.

She was, Freya guessed, in her early thirties, pretty, with a masculine jawline and eyes that some might have said were too close together. She stepped across a few of the platforms and came to shake Freya's hand. "DS Hart. I've been holding the fort for you."

"I see," Freya replied. "This is DS Savage. What do we have?"

Hart glanced over her shoulder at the two white suits crouching over the scene, which was nothing more than a patch of wet and empty mud and sand with a white tent draped over it.

But given the lack of a body, Freya surmised the tent had been left erected to provide some kind of shade.

"Female, late teens, early twenties. No ID, no possessions, no shoes or socks. She was there for some time."

"Some time?" Ben said. "A few hours? A few days?"

"At least a day. No more than two. We won't know for sure until the pathologist sees her."

"Without stating the obvious," Freya said, glaring down at the crime scene investigators, "where is she now?"

"We got her out. There was no sense in keeping her in there. She's on her way to Lincoln Hospital as we speak."

"Lincoln? Is there nothing closer?"

"We do have hospitals, if that's what you mean," Hart replied. "But a forensic pathologist? We're not that equipped."

"Has the FME been, at least?" Freya asked.

"He's been and gone. He had to come up from Norfolk."

"Peter Saint?" Ben asked.

"That's him. Do you know him?"

"I didn't know he covered this area."

"We don't have much call for him, if I'm honest," Hart said. "We see him a couple of times a year at the most. Although that number seems to be rising of late."

"Cause of death?" Freya said before they wasted any more time discussing Peter Saint.

"He couldn't be sure. There are no visible signs of injury, so it's likely to be either exposure or dehydration. Peter couldn't really do much with her in the mud. He recorded her temperature, checked for injuries, and gave her a once over, but the conditions are too harsh for him to provide anything of substance."

"Dehydration? That takes days," Freya said.

"It's been in the high thirties this past week," Hart said. "If she's been here for a few days—"

"Surely somebody would have seen her?"

"Not necessarily," Hart said, and she pointed back in the direction they had come. "There's a footpath that runs parallel with the coast, along that tree line, plus one or two safe paths that cut across the marshes. Nobody really comes out here. The ground is too soft and wet."

"She could have called out to somebody."

"Call out to who?" Hart said. "The closest homes are in the caravan park. That's too far to be heard."

"Well, who found her?"

"A jogger, and that was by pure chance."

"So, this could be an accident?" Freya said. "In which case, why have we been asked to attend?"

"I'll show you," Hart said, and she made her way across the network of platforms, around the pool of water where the CSI team were working, and then pointed down to the ground. A single, white flag bearing the number thirty-six marked the spot, which was nothing more than large boot prints in the mud that led off towards firmer ground.

"Is this all we have?" Freya asked, and Hart nodded.

"We believe somebody was here while she was still alive," she replied.

"They were watching," Freya said, thinking aloud. "Why on earth would somebody watch and do nothing to help her?"

"I don't think they did nothing exactly," Hart said, and she stepped across to the next platform, which was just two feet from the girl's body. "There's a single boot print here. Looks like it matches."

"That's at least a size eleven," Freya said. "Surely a man with size eleven boots would be strong enough to pull her out? How deep is this mud?"

"Not deep enough to swallow somebody whole, but deep enough that he or she might become stuck, especially if they went in with some force."

She pointed to another marker that indicated more footprints. These were made by bare feet and were much smaller than the boots.

"She tried to jump the mud?" Ben asked, to which Hart nodded.

"We're certain this wasn't an accident. We just don't have the resources to get to the bottom of it right now," Hart said, and she handed Freya a card. "Here's my details. Call me if you need anything."

"Is that it?" Ben said, as Hart squeezed passed them then stepped off the platforms onto the mud. "You're leaving?"

She stared at them both, eyebrows raised.

"Do I need to hold your hands?" she asked.

"Well, no–"

"Well, then yes. You're on your own," she said, turning to walk away. "Oh, and make sure you keep DI Larson in the loop, unless of course you want the grilling of a lifetime."

"Is he prone to tantrums?" Freya asked.

"No," Hart replied. "In fact, I've never seen him lose his temper. He has a way about him, though. He doesn't suffer fools."

"That's a good trait to have," Freya said. "I shall look forward to meeting him."

"We'll see," Hart said dismissively. "One more thing. We've got a lead for you."

"A lead?" Freya said.

"We've had a report of a missing girl. A Hayley Donovan. Eighteen years old. Her sister reported her missing this morning. I'll email you the details. It might be a good place to start."

Ben handed her one of his cards, which she pocketed without reading.

"Or we might just scare the hell out of a family for no reason," he muttered.

"I'm sure a couple of pros like you can handle it," Hart said as she walked away, raising her hand to bid them farewell. "Ask the sister about the tattoos."

"What tattoos?"

"The ones on the dead girl's back," Hart called out. "Peter Saint found them. An angel and a devil. Match those and you've got yourself a positive ID."

CHAPTER FIVE

"Well, that was unequivocal," Freya said, when they reached the top of the ramp where the uniforms were still standing. The men were leaning on a steel barrier that had been placed to stop vehicles from going any further up the ramp, and they both stood when Freya and Ben came into view.

"So, we haven't seen the body, our local support has gone, and any evidence, other than some rough boot prints, has very likely been washed away with the tide."

"The pathologist might find something. Fingerprints or DNA maybe?" Ben said, but even as he said it, he seemed to recognise the doubt in Freya's eyes, and the hope in his voice waned.

"The clock is ticking," Freya said, as they passed the uniforms. "We need information, and fast."

Ben nodded a thanks at the uniforms, hoping they might read an apology on Freya's behalf in the subtle gesture.

"What do you have in mind?" he asked.

"Well, first of all, we'll need to establish who she was, and as much as it pains me to be steered by somebody I've only just met, I suggest we pay a visit to the missing girl's house."

"Hayley Donovan," Ben said, recalling the name.

"While we do that, we'll need to understand who was in the area. Our problem is going to be gathering the information in a timely manner. We'd normally have an entire team to help us, but it looks like it's just you and me," Freya said, checking her watch. "Not to worry. It's one p.m. DS Hart suggested the victim had been there for at least a day, but no more than two, which means whoever those boot prints belong to could still be in the area."

She stopped where she'd parked the car and peered past Ben, making a point of avoiding his questioning glare.

"What?" he said.

"Call Gillespie for me," she said. "Ask him and Cruz to visit Doctor Bell on our behalf. We need them to attend the autopsy. I'm just going to pop in here for a moment."

"You want third-hand information from Gillespie?" Ben asked. "Are you sure that's wise? Has he even met Pip before?"

"I'd rather third-hand information than endure a telephone call with Pip," she said. "When you're done, meet me in there."

"In where?" he said, holding his phone up to find a bar of signal. But Freya had disappeared into the caravan site by the time he had dialled Gillespie's number.

Unable to move for fear of losing his signal, Ben clicked the phone onto loudspeaker and moments later, Gillespie's brash voice came loud and clear over the line.

"Benjamin Savage," he said. "What can I do you for?"

"I need a favour, mate."

"Don't tell me, you're having woman trouble and need some advice?"

"Technically you're half-right," Ben said. "But I don't need advice. I need your eyes and ears."

"Does that entail me leaving my sofa?"

"Not only does it require you to leave your sofa, but you'll need to get dressed–"

"I am dressed."

"Into something other than a pair of shorts and a t-shirt with takeaway down the front."

"Are you watching me or something?"

"No, Jim, you're just predictable. Do you want to know the good news?"

"Oh, there's good news, is there?"

"I need you to pick up Cruz."

"Gabby Cruz?" he said. "What the bloody hell do I need to get him for? You realise it's a Sunday and he'll most likely be arranging his sock drawer or whatever it is he does in his spare time?"

"I'll make sure Freya books the overtime," Ben said.

"Oh, aye. I've heard that wee little treasure before."

"I need you to go and witness an autopsy. DCI Standing sent Freya and me to Saltfleet this morning. The body is already on its way to Lincoln."

"Saltfleet? Why the bloody hell has he sent *you* there?" he said. "I'd have gone. A few days at the coast sounds nice. A wee bit of R and R."

"How about you get dressed, clean your teeth, and pick up Cruz, and then I'll fill you in on the details when we speak next? I have a feeling we'll be doing plenty of calls while we're up here."

"Alright, alright," Gillespie said, audibly shoving himself off the couch. "I'll get myself ready. What are we looking at anyway?"

"The victim is female, late teens to early twenties. Likely died of dehydration or exposure. The FME couldn't be sure."

"He couldn't be sure?"

"She was up to her waist in the marshes, Jim. There was no way he was going to examine her in situ."

"Jesus."

"However it was that she died, it was slow. Of that we can be sure. We need Pip to give us some facts. Right now, we've got next to nothing to go on. From what I can see, the only reason it's being treated as suspicious is a bloody boot print in the mud. We haven't even seen her."

"You haven't seen the body?"

"No, mate. They'd removed her by the time we got here. The local DS has buggered off somewhere too. It's just Freya and me, and not much to go on. We need all the help we can get."

"Aye, I've got you," Gillespie said. "Tell you what, I'll call you when we've seen her. Give me a few hours, eh? I'll have to drag the wee weasel out of his pit, I expect."

"The signal isn't great," Ben said. "If you can't reach me, send a text and I'll call you back."

"Leave it to me, Benjamin. I'll add it to the list of favours you already owe me."

"One more thing," Ben said. "Hart mentioned something about tattoos on her back. An angel and a devil or something. Take a look, will you? Get us some photos."

"Surely CSI took some photos?"

"I imagine they did," Ben said. "But I'm not sure how many hoops we'll have to jump through to see them."

"Not a problem," Gillespie replied. "Talk soon."

He ended the call and then entered the caravan park in search of Freya. The hunt didn't take long. A raised female voice could be heard coming from a small building on the left-hand side of the entrance, which was marked by a small sign that read, *Site Office*.

Ben strolled up the little pathway and identified the accent in question as north-eastern, somewhere in the Newcastle region.

He stopped in the doorway to appraise the situation before deciding to say nothing at all. Freya had clearly already made her mark.

"Who the bloody hell do you think you are?" the woman said, her hands firmly entrenched on her hips. "I can't give out personal information just like that. Haven't you heard of GDPR? Don't you have a warrant or something?"

"No," Freya said. "But I suppose I could get one, if you insist."

"I do insist," the lady said, as she lit a cigarette and settled back onto an extremely untidy desk.

"In that case," Freya started, "Ben, would you mind asking our uniformed friends to close access off from the main road?"

"You what?" the woman snapped, taking a long drag on her cigarette. "You can't close the road. I've got about two hundred guests arriving and another two hundred guests leaving. It's a Sunday."

"Well, I'm afraid we can't let anybody leave," Freya said. "As I explained, this is a murder enquiry."

"I couldn't care less if you'd found the bloody Mary Rose out there. If you close the road off, you'll have a bloody riot on your hands."

"Well, I'm sure we're equipped to deal with a few disgruntled holidaymakers," Freya said, and she turned to stare at Ben over her shoulder. "Could you make the arrangements for me? Nobody in or out."

"Hold on, hold on," the woman said, stubbing her cigarette out prematurely into an overflowing ashtray. "What exactly do you need?"

Ben watched with interest as Freya let the woman's temper fade and the balance of power fell into Freya's lap with relative ease.

"I just need a guest list," Freya said. "I need to know who was here on Friday night and Saturday night."

The woman nodded with clear reluctance.

"Okay."

"I see you have a camera on the entry barrier," Freya said. "The footage would be helpful."

"Is that all?" she replied.

"To start with."

"And you'll keep the road open?" she said. "This is our busiest time."

"I'll do what I can," Freya said. "There is one more piece of information that might aid our enquiries."

The woman rolled her eyes and steeled herself for yet another request.

"Where were you on Friday night?" Freya said.

"Excuse me? Are you accusing—"

"I'm merely asking where you were, Mrs Robinson, that's all."

"I was here. I worked until around nine p.m. then I had a drink at the bar and went to bed."

"Do you live here on site?" Freya asked.

"I don't live here. I've got a house nearby. I stay here when I need to, when I'm working late, which at this time of year is every day. I have a caravan across the way," she said, indicating the rough location with a flick of her head.

"Alone?" Freya asked, and Mrs Robinson's mouth hung open as if she was about to launch into a venomous rant at the line of questioning.

"Yes, alone."

"I see," Freya replied, and she glanced at Ben to make a mental note.

"What the bloody hell is that supposed to mean?" Mrs Robinson said. "There are plenty of people who can vouch for me."

"How're those lists coming along?" Freya asked calmly.

"I don't want you going around upsetting the guests," Mrs Robinson said, as she passed Freya two sheets of paper, which, from where Ben was standing, appeared to be printed spreadsheets.

"Oh, we'll try not to upset them," Freya said, and she met the woman's stare. "But if they do get upset, it's often a strong indication of guilt of some kind."

"I see," Mrs Robinson said, after a brief and uncomfortable pause.

"Don't go anywhere, Mrs Robinson," Freya said. "We may have further questions to ask you."

CHAPTER SIX

"Well, the sea air has certainly brought out the best in you, hasn't it?" Ben said as he climbed into Freya's car and peeled his damp shirt away from his chest then blew into the space.

Freya started the engine and set the air conditioning to full power then waited for the cool air to wash over her face before she replied.

"What's that supposed to mean?"

"We've been here less than an hour and you've managed to upset nearly everyone we've spoken to," he replied.

"Nearly everyone?" she said.

"Well, alright then, everyone."

"That's more like it," she said with a smile. She put the car into drive and rolled forward, checking her phone for an email from DS Hart. When she saw it, she handed Ben the phone. "Guide me in, will you?"

He said nothing, as he nearly always did when she had annoyed him, and the silence suited her. It gave her time to process what they'd learned so far.

"Left at the top of the road," he said, using the Maps app on his phone to locate the address on her phone. "Then it's the first turning on the right."

"She's definitely local, then," Freya said. "Let's see what the mother has to say for herself."

"Can we just..." Ben began, then stopped to take a breath.

"Can we just what?"

"Can we just see if we can get through a meeting without causing anybody any unnecessary upset?"

"What are you implying?" she asked, nearly laughing at the comment. The car came to a stop outside a semi-detached house, which looked perfectly respectable in every way, except for the disused sofa that had been placed in the front garden. "That I might purposefully antagonise the sister of a missing girl? What type of person do you think I am?"

"I often wonder," Ben said, and he winked to soften the blow. "Come on. Let's get this over with."

They walked side by side up the paved driveway and Freya grinned inwardly.

"It's nice, you know?" she said.

"What is?"

"Having you back."

"I didn't go anywhere," he said, as he reached for the doorbell.

"It's just nice to have somebody who knows me, on my side. Somebody who isn't trying to impress me or vice versa."

"You mean a friend?" Ben said, as if he was speaking to a child.

"I suppose I am," she replied. "I'm glad things didn't work out between us. In a nice kind of way."

"Wow," he said, as he pushed the doorbell and prepared his warrant card. "If that isn't a let-down, I don't know what is."

The door opened and a woman in her late twenties to early thirties stood in the doorway. Her eyes were red and swollen, her hair was a mess, and she wore a dressing gown over faded pyjamas. Behind the tired appearance was an expression of worry and anticipation.

"Mrs Donovan?" Ben said.

"Miss," the woman replied, and she stepped to one side to let them in. "Have you found her?"

"That's what we need to establish," Ben said, as he waved his hand for Freya to enter before him.

"You'll have to excuse us," Freya said, as Miss Donovan led them into an open-plan living space then gestured for them to sit on an ageing, floral-patterned sofa. "We've been called in from North Kesteven."

"From North Kesteven? That's miles away."

"It's just to help out," Freya said, as Ben took the seat beside her. "We understand you reported your sister missing this morning. Is that right?"

"Well, yes, of course."

"And her name is Hayley Donovan? Is that right?"

"You've found her, haven't you?" she said, but her tone lacked any real sign of hope.

"Can you tell me when you last saw Hayley?" Freya said.

"I told them on the phone. She hasn't been home for a few days now. Not since Friday."

"You're sure about that?"

"As sure as I can be. I work nights at the local Tesco. She was here on Friday when I left. I spoke to her."

"And when did you come home?"

"Saturday morning. Around sixish. We were doing a big stock take, you see?"

"Are you sure she wasn't home then?"

"I don't know. She might have been in bed. She doesn't normally get up until late at the weekend. You know what it's like."

"And what did you do when you returned home, Miss Donovan?"

"I'm sorry. I don't understand. Have you found her or not?"

"I'm sorry, could you please just answer the question? I can assure you, I have Hayley's best interests at heart. But that does entail us asking a few questions, none of which have any purpose other than to locate Hayley."

"Alright," she said eventually. "I had a cup of tea. It was a long night, see. This bloody heatwave we're having, you'd think people are planning for a disaster or something. There's barely a toilet roll left in the whole area, let alone bottled water."

"It was a busy night then?" Ben said.

"Sorry, yes, it was. I had my tea and went straight to bed. I normally take a sleeping pill to get off. But not Saturday. I was out like a light."

"And when you woke up?" Freya asked.

"Mid-afternoon sometime. Three-ish, I'd say. Trevor was home."

"Trevor?"

"Sorry, he's my partner. He was watching a film," she said, then leaned in as if to share a secret. "He doesn't do well in the heat."

"Was anybody else in the house?" Ben asked.

"Only Justin," she replied, flicking her eyes upwards to the room above them. Then her expression shifted, and she realised that comment required some kind of explanation. "He's my brother. In between Hayley and me. He doesn't get out much. He has some challenges."

"Physically?" Freya asked.

"Socially. It's his nerves, so the doctors say anyway. He doesn't come downstairs very often."

"Is he bed bound?"

"No. Well, he might as well be. But it's all in his head. I'd offer to take you to meet him, but..."

She hesitated, averting her gaze.

"But what?" Freya asked, and Miss Donovan relented.

"I don't want to upset him unnecessarily."

"And Hayley was out, I presume?" Freya said. "When you woke up, that is."

"That's right, yes. She's old enough not to tell me where she's going these days. She's a good girl. You know?" she said, tapping her temple with her index finger. Then she gestured at a small pile of books on a shelf. "She's not silly. Smart as they come, our Hayley."

Freya ran a trained eye across the book titles. They were non-fiction, not textbooks for studying but interest-based books on historical artwork, religion, and even symbology. There was also a small notepad with a scatter of coloured pens, all of which indicated that Hayley was comfortable in her own company and could while away the time curled up reading. Or keeping a journal, perhaps?

"And when did you realise that she might be missing?" Freya asked.

"This morning, I suppose. I got up around seven. Thought I'd go in and see how she is. We're quite close. I suppose we have to be. I took her a tea."

"But?"

Miss Donovan stared into space, reliving the moment in her mind, just as so many others had done before her.

"She wasn't there. Her bed hadn't even been slept in," she said. "Trevor said he hasn't seen her since Friday, and aside from a church function, he was home all weekend. So, that's when I phoned. You know? To report her missing."

"Have you tried her friends?"

"Of course, I have. I did that first. She doesn't have many, but the ones she does have are good. Reliable, if you know what I mean? If Hayley was in any trouble, they would have told me. No, she's out there, probably lost or something."

"Miss Donovan, we're not here in Saltfleet to investigate a missing person," Freya began, and the expression on Miss Donovan's face morphed into one of confusion. "We're with the Major Investigations Team."

"I don't understand. She hasn't done anything wrong, has she?"

"No," Freya said. "At least, not that we're aware of."

"There's something you're not telling me, isn't there?"

Freya agonised over the decision to divulge any more information. She was leaning towards keeping the body in the marshes to herself, but the woman's face told a story of absolute misery.

"Miss Donovan, I have to tell you, we found the body of a young girl this morning."

"A young girl?" she said, her voice quiet and disbelieving.

"In the marshes at Saltfleet," Freya said. "I'm sorry to ask, but if there's a chance it could be Hayley—"

"It's not Hayley. Of course it's not Hayley. She wouldn't go out there. Not on her own. She knows better."

"Miss Donovan, the girl we found has been taken to Lincoln Hospital. We have a forensic pathologist there who might be able to help us."

"I don't see what that has to do with me, or Hayley for that matter."

She stood and walked to the fireplace. A large mirror with a gilded-gold frame hung above a solid, oak mantle, on which were two photos, each bearing the images of two young girls and a boy with their parents. The mother was pretty. The dad was handsome, groomed, and proudly wearing the clerical collar of a vicar or reverend.

"Is there somebody else we should talk to?" Freya asked.

"No," she replied in an instant. "There's nobody else. Not anymore."

"The girl we found has tattoos on her back," Ben said, coming to stand beside Freya, who was studying the photos.

"Hayley doesn't have any tattoos," Miss Donovan said softly. She sniffed and checked her reflection once more. Then, deftly, she snatched up the two photo frames and peered at Freya and Ben as if they had just delivered a monumental insult. "So, you're not here to help find Hayley then?"

"We're investigating a murder, Miss Donovan," said Freya.

"We didn't mean any harm, and it doesn't mean we can't help you."

"There's no harm done. But, if you don't mind, I'd like to be alone. She'll come home. Of that, I'm sure. And when she does, I'll be here waiting for her. It'll be alright, won't it?" she said, staring Freya in the eye. "That's what you have to tell yourself, isn't it? That everything will be alright. We've been through enough, the three of us, we've had our share of it."

"Is there somebody that can come and sit with you?" Freya asked. "You mentioned a partner. Trevor? Was that his name?"

"He's at work," she said dismissively. "I'll be fine. She'll be back. You'll see."

"I hope so, Miss Donovan,' Freya said. "I really hope so."

"It's Deborah," she replied, with a smile that was as weak as it was brief.

"We'd like to speak to her friends, if you don't mind?" Ben said, and she found Ben in the mirror.

"I've already spoken to them, I told you."

"Still, they might have something to say. At this stage, any information is better than none," Freya said. But Deborah just kept staring at the photo. "Does Hayley have a boyfriend?"

She nodded, ever so slightly, but it was enough of a thread for Freya to pull on.

"She did have, but not anymore. You know how it goes. They split up a while back."

"Can you tell us his name, Deborah?"

"Vaughan," she said.

"Vaughan? Does he have a last name?"

"I don't know it," she replied, then turned to face Freya. "I never even met him, which meant that we never spoke about him. We just kind of brushed it under the carpet. It's hard, you know, being a sister and a parent. The lines you can't cross are different."

"Do you know where we might find him?" Freya asked.

Deborah shook her head.

"May I ask..." Freya began, then stared at the family photograph, hoping that Deborah would see where she was going.

Deborah inhaled, long and hard, then puffed out her cheeks as she exhaled.

"It was a car accident. Dad was driving. Apparently, he turned around to check on Justin in the back seat and swerved into oncoming traffic."

"But Justin survived?"

"If you can call it surviving," Deborah replied. "I'd call it existing myself."

Freya said nothing but read the horrors of what followed etched into the lines on Deborah's forehead, much as a book's synopsis might hint at the tragedy within without spoiling the story.

"I'd like to be alone now. She'll be here soon," she said, then turned to stare at Freya's reflection in the mirror. "I know she will."

CHAPTER SEVEN

"So, I said, why don't we have the beef? We rarely have beef. We could have chicken any day of the week. But beef is like a treat, isn't it?" Cruz said, as the pair walked along another long corridor within the sprawling hospital building.

The lady on the reception desk had told Gillespie to follow one of the coloured lines that had been painted on the floor, and at some point, they had to change and follow a different colour, but Cruz had been waffling on about God knows what, and all Gillespie had been thinking about was ways to shut him up without making him cry or causing a scene.

Now they were deep inside the belly of the beast with only the vague hospital signs to follow. The trouble was, there were thousands of them. Every intersection of corridors looked as if the council was planning roadworks and had utilised its full armoury of road signs.

"Hermione said beef gets stuck in her teeth," Cruz continued. "So, we settled for the lamb. Not as boring as chicken, not as chewy as beef, which I thought was a good compromise, as long as it came with mint sauce."

"Are you going to give me a rundown of your entire weekend so far?" Gillespie said.

"Eh?"

"At what point does this story end? Does it end when you actually eat the lamb, or when you go home? And are you actually going to acknowledge the fact that your face is redder than a baboon's backside? Have you ever heard of sun cream?"

Cruz looked offended, which was inevitable. He was bound to take offence at some point. If he wasn't so sunburned, Gillespie might have seen his face redden with embarrassment.

"So, you don't want to hear about pudding?" he said.

"No, Gabby, I do not need to hear about pudding. As delicious as it might have been, all I want to do right now is find our way through this godforsaken building."

"Even though I had sticky toffee pudding?" he said, as if the thought of such a delight might set Gillespie's taste buds alight.

"Gabby!"

"And Hermione had treacle sponge."

"For crying out loud–"

"You should have seen it, Jim. Honestly, I often wonder why they put the good stuff right at the end. I could have had about four bowls of the stuff if I hadn't stuffed myself silly with lamb."

Gillespie stopped at yet another crossroads. The lines on the floor gave no indication of where to go. If anything, there were more lines than he remembered, and the signs on the walls might as well have been written in Sanskrit.

"It was epic, Jim. You would have loved it–"

"Gabby, it's Sunday bloody afternoon and I am trying to navigate my way through this bloody place with all these bloody signs, and all I can hear is your tiny voice scratching away at my bloody soul."

"Where are we going?"

"To the morgue, Gabby. Where do you think they store the dead bodies? In the bloody canteen?"

His raised voice caused a passing lady to cover her child's ears as they walked, offering a loud tut and a shake of her head.

"Why didn't you say?" Cruz said, and he looked around as if familiarising himself with his surroundings for the first time. "It's this way."

"You know the way?"

"Of course. We came here before, remember?"

"Oh, aye, I remember," Gillespie said, letting Cruz lead the way. "It's just that the last time we were here, I must have forgotten to leave breadcrumbs to follow. Either that or somebody has hoovered them up in the last six months."

"It's through here," Cruz said, pointing to a set of double doors that led to a long corridor with windows on either side. "Yeah, this is it. You should have just asked. Whose dead body are we going to see anyway? I didn't think we had any open investigations."

"Oh, nobody in particular, Gabby. I was just going to ask if they had a spare scalpel I could borrow and room in the fridge for a five-and-a-half-foot detective constable who died from a terrible case of verbal diarrhoea."

"Eh?"

"Forget it," Gillespie said as they reached the entrance. He reached up and pushed the button to let the pathologist know they were there. "Just let me do the talking. You're here as a witness, that's all."

"A witness. What am I witnessing?"

The door opened and Doctor Bell looked up at Gillespie in surprise. Her hair was a natural blonde, despite him being sure it had been red the last time he had seen her. There were multiple piercings in various parts of her face that he didn't even know could be pierced, and a tattoo of a dragon was reaching up from the confines of her Led Zeppelin t-shirt.

"Doctor Bell, I presume," Gillespie said, finding himself staring.

"Yes?"

"DS Gillespie," he said, then tapped his pockets in search of his warrant card. A flash of memory hit him, and he saw it in his mind's eye, sitting beside the microwave in his house. "This is Cruz."

"I remembers," she said, and immediately he connected her Welsh accent to the dragon tattoo. "Well? Have you come to stare at me, or did you have something else in mind?"

"Oh, aye," he said. "Ben sent me. Ben Savage."

"Right?"

"You have a body, or something. A young girl? Late teens?"

"This is a mortuary, as it happens. If there's one thing I'm not short of, it's bodies."

"We need to witness the autopsy."

"Autopsy?" Cruz said. "We're not—"

"Shut up," Gillespie told him, his eyes never once leaving the doctor's.

"No Ben and Freya today?" she asked.

"They're in Saltfleet," he said.

"Saltfleet?" Cruz said. "What the hell are they doing there?"

"Tidy," the pathologist continued, ignoring Cruz and holding Gillespie's stare. "I thought they'd just had a holiday? Went to Paris, didn't they?"

"DCI Standing sent them," Gillespie said. "They're helping out another station. It's a resource thing apparently."

"In Saltfleet?" Cruz said.

"And they sent you, did they? Well, you'd better come in," she said, stepping to one side for them to enter.

The little reception was tidy and calm, exactly as he had expected the reception of a mortuary to be. There were a few comfortable seats for guests and a series of storage cupboards along two of the walls.

Doctor Bell pointed to a few of the cupboards in no particular order.

"Boots, smocks, gloves, and hats," she said. "Come and find me in here when you're all suited and booted."

She pushed through a heavy door which seemed to sigh with the effort and a blast of cold air cooled the sweat on Gillespie's back.

"A bloody autopsy?" Cruz hissed when she had gone. "You could have bloody warned me."

"Warned you? About what?"

"Well, it's not every day I'm asked to go and see a dead body, let alone witness one being butchered."

"She's not a butcher," Gillespie said, staring after her. "She's a pathologist, and need I remind you; you literally work with murders every single day."

"Yeah, I work with murders. I see bodies usually lying on the floor. That, I can handle. Bodies on the floor, fine. Stab wounds, not a problem. Strangled, fine by me. But watching them being opened up and..."

"And what?"

"Dissected," Cruz said, shaking his head. "I don't have a good feeling about this. I had porridge for breakfast, you know? Not to mention the bloody sticky toffee pudding at lunch."

Gillespie was partway through figuring out how to get into the smock. He stopped with one arm in what he was sure was the correct armhole and one foot raised, poised to slip into the garment.

"What does it matter what you had for breakfast, Gabby?" he said, utterly incredulous at the young detective constable.

"It doesn't matter," Cruz replied quietly, as he somehow managed to navigate his way into the smock and pull on his white Wellington boots. Eventually, he looked up at Gillespie, who was staring at him. "What?"

There were a number of things Gillespie wanted to say – a response to the whole porridge and sticky toffee pudding thing, about the fact that Cruz knew how to get into the smock and boots, not to mention a comment that with his white coveralls and red face, he now looked like a malnourished Oompa Loompa.

"Just give me a hand, will you?" he said.

CHAPTER EIGHT

Despite the long drive from Ben's family farm to Saltfleet and the icy yet stilted conversations with Freya, the car was, by far, the most pleasant place to be. The cool air conditioning belied the shimmer of heat coming from the tarmac road and the sagging shoulders of an old man out for his afternoon walk along one of the many narrow lanes flanked by seemingly endless fields.

The dashboard thermometer read thirty-six degrees outside and a balmy eighteen degrees inside when they pulled into a parking spot designated for visitors.

"Do you think we could conduct the investigation from in here?" Ben joked, not really expecting an answer but expecting Freya to at least acknowledge he had spoken. She simply stared through the windscreen at the local police station, which was a fifteen-minute drive away from Saltfleet.

"Are we back to square one?" she asked. "Hayley Donovan doesn't have tattoos, so all we have now is the body of an unknown girl that you and I are yet to see. We also have some boot prints which means pretty much nothing right now, and we don't even have a place to stay."

"We could go inside," Ben suggested. "At least we might be able to rustle up a few uniforms."

"Just give me a minute," Freya said. "I'm not walking into that station without at least having something to go on. A narrative, for example."

"A narrative?"

"How long was she in the sand?" Freya asked.

"We won't really know until Pip has had a look," Ben said, checking his phone for any missed calls from Gillespie but finding none.

"We need to see photos of the body," Freya said. "She'd been there longer than a day. That's what the FME told Hart, right?"

"Right."

"It's thirty-six degrees outside today, and if anything, yesterday was even hotter. If she was alive in the sun, she'll be sunburned."

"But if she's not burned, then we can deduce that she was killed during the previous night," Ben said, seeing where she was going.

"We can then use the guest list from the caravan park to work out who was in the area at the time she was killed."

"And if the photos show she *was* sunburned, we can eliminate anybody who left before the previous night. I like it," Ben said, reaching for the door handle. "Let's go and find Hart."

"Hold on," Freya said, reaching for his arm to stop him. "We need more than that."

"We do?"

"We need a plan, Ben. These people have asked for our help. The least we can do is demonstrate competence."

"Right," Ben said, nodding. "And how do you propose we do that?"

"We give them a list of resources we need to do our jobs. I'm not going to be pushed around, and I'm certainly not going to be shoved into a corner."

"We could have some uniforms go door to door in the caravan park?" Ben suggested.

"True," Freya said. "But what we really need is a Chapman."

"A Chapman? Since when did she become a noun?"

"Surely they can assign us a researcher," Freya said, almost convincing herself of what she needed. She shoved open her door. "Come on. Let's go and meet the team."

The heat was oppressive. From the moment Ben opened the car door, the sun weighed down on him and seemed to be forcing the sweat from his body, which then cooled the moment they entered the station. His damp shirt clung to his back as Freya approached the front desk, presenting her warrant card in advance.

"DI Freya Bloom to see DS Hart," she said.

"Hart?" the uniform behind the desk repeated, then reached for a button beneath his desk, and the double doors beside the reception desk clicked open. The uniform returned to whatever he was doing without so much as an indication as to where they should go. But in Ben's experience, Freya rarely asked for help.

She gestured for Ben to follow, and they walked through into a layout not too dissimilar to that of their own station. The long corridor ahead of them had a few doors off to the sides and a set of double doors at the far end, which Ben assumed to be the custody desk, gateway to the cells, and therefore kept as far from the public space as possible.

Ben peered through a window set into a door on the right-hand side. He saw a few people buzzing around and two men sitting on the edge of a desk discussing the piece of paper one of them was holding. It was like an eighties commercial for a recruit-ment drive. There was no shouting, no arguing, no messing about, just people cheerfully getting on with their jobs.

"CID," he said, reading the whiteboard fixed to one of the drab-coloured walls. "Burglaries, car thefts, and drugs."

"You don't suppose a place this small has a Major Investigations Team?"

"Only one way to find out," Ben said, taking a breath and shoving open the door.

Everyone in the room stopped what they were doing. Even the man holding the sheet of paper froze, the pen he had been using to point poised in the air.

"Help you, duck?" one of the men said, removing his glasses to study Ben.

"Any ideas where I might find DS Hart?" Ben said. "She said she'd help me with something."

"You'd better get in line," the man replied, much to the amusement of the other men in the room. "I should think every man in this station wants her to help him with something. Some of the women too, come to think of it."

It was at that point that Ben felt Freya nudge her way into the room. She flashed her warrant card and stared at the man who had made the comment with utter distaste. The laughter in the room fell silent in an instant.

"Detective Inspector Bloom," she said. "And you are?"

"Why do you want to know?"

"Because I'll find your superior and inform him of your inappropriate comment," Freya said.

The man stared at Freya as if gauging how serious she was, and Ben, knowing full well the potency of her mind, leaned against the doorframe, enjoying the lesson in manners.

"You're looking for DS Ivy Hart?" the man said finally, and Freya nodded. "Next room along. Major Investigations. You can't miss it."

"Thank you," Freya said, pocketing her warrant card. "And you are?"

"Oh, come on, I was only joking–"

"I don't joke," Freya said. "Name and rank."

"DC Butterworth," he said with reluctance. "Sean Butterworth."

"Good," Freya said. "I suggest you mind your manners for the few days we're here. Unless, of course, you'd like a lesson in exactly why you'll never reach the rank of sergeant."

"Ma'am," he said quietly.

"I need a map of every ANPR camera in a two-mile radius of Saltfleet."

"Hey now, hang on a minute," another man said. It was the man holding the sheet of paper, and he backed down the moment Freya glared at him.

"I assume your protest is based on resource allocation and reporting lines?" Freya said.

"Eh?"

"DC Butterworth reports in to you, and you would prefer him not to spend his time working on an investigation for which you and your team will receive no credit. Am I right?"

"Well, yeah," the man said.

"You have a decision to make then," Freya told him. "Either DC Butterworth here provides a map of every ANPR camera in the area, or I go directly to the top floor and make a complaint about sexual misconduct."

"Sexual misconduct?"

"I presume the superintendent's office is on the top floor?" Freya said, meeting him eye to eye for longer than was comfortable.

"I've heard about you. You're the lass from London."

"That's partially correct," Freya said with a smile. "But the fact is that you *have* heard of me, which tells me you're fully aware of who I am, and what I'm capable of."

The man peered over her shoulder at Ben, who simply shrugged, offering no opinion either way.

"Alright," he said, nodding at Butterworth. "Just the cameras. Don't go thinking he's working for you while you're here."

"A map of the cameras and a list of every car that passed through them between Friday morning and Saturday."

"You're pushing your luck, lady."

"It's a simple process. The ANPR system does all the hard work. All he'd have to do is export the list. I'd do it myself, but as you know, we're not local. We don't know the area."

She stood with her hands on her hips, waiting for an argument. But no argument followed, just a simple compromising nod.

"When he's done, he's done. You can get anything else you need from Ivy and George," he said.

"George?" Freya said, her head cocked to one side, waiting for him to explain.

"DI George Larson," the man said. "I'm surprised you haven't heard of him."

"I hadn't," Freya said. "Not until today, at least."

"Well, wouldn't I like to be a fly on the wall when you meet him," he replied, returning his attention to the man sitting beside him. "Your map will be ready in ten minutes. Not a minute before."

CHAPTER NINE

Finding Doctor Bell standing beside a stainless-steel bench wearing a perfectly clean, non-disposable smock over her Led Zeppelin t-shirt, Gillespie led Cruz across the room, drawn by her impatient glare.

"Ready, are we?" she asked, letting the R roll across her tongue like an aniseed ball.

"Aye," he replied. "Had a wee spot of bother with the smock."

"You're not the first," she told him. "They're not really made for larger men. Ben struggles too, truth be told."

She turned her attention to Cruz, who had the exact opposite problem to Gillespie, whereby he'd had to roll the sleeves and legs up to accommodate his smaller-than-average limbs.

"And what have you come as?" she asked.

"Me?" he said. "I'm Cruz."

"I know. Never forgets a face, I do. I was asking what you've come as," she said, her expression telling a story of complete bewilderment.

"I'd say he's either an Oompa Loompa or one of those weird aliens in the original Star Trek series. You know? The one with

William Shatner," Gillespie said, and she laughed, just once, but it was a laugh, and knowing how volatile the doctor could be, he'd take it.

"Right then," she began, and for the first time, they acknowledged the body beneath the sheet on the bench. "No ID as yet, but before we open her up, there are a few points worth mentioning."

Carefully, she whipped the sheet back to reveal the dead girl's face then pulled a pen from her pocket, and Gillespie noticed it was the type that had four different colours, like the ones the girls from wealthy families had when he was at school.

"See here?" she said, highlighting the girl's eyes. "The little, red dots are petechial haemorrhages."

"What does that mean?" Cruz asked, but Doctor Bell ignored him and waved a circle in the air above the girl's mouth.

"See these traces of blood?"

"Aye?" Gillespie said, leaning across the bench until he was almost cheek-to-cheek with the doctor.

"Pulmonary edema."

"I should have brought a bloody dictionary," Cruz muttered.

"Lastly," Doctor Bell said, moving down to the girl's feet and pulling back the sheet, "lacerations to the soles of her feet."

"I see," Gillespie said, waiting for her to make a professional evaluation. But she didn't. She covered the feet with the sheet and stood there waiting for one of them to say something. "What does this mean?"

The pathologist rolled her eyes and took a breath, as if everyone should know what the signs indicated.

"We don't normally do this," Gillespie explained. "We're normally knocking on doors when Ben and the boss come to see you."

"It's okay. You'll get to learn the signs," she replied. "The petechial haemorrhages—"

"The little dots in the eyes?"

"Yes, the little dots in the eyes. They, along with the signs of blood around her mouth, indicate asphyxiation. We won't know for sure until we see inside."

"Asphyxiation?" Cruz said. "You mean she was suffocated? What about the lacerations on her feet? What does that tell you?"

"That she ran across something sharp. Stones, I think. I've sent some samples to the lab already."

"Right," Gillespie said. "So, she was running from somebody, barefoot, for whatever reason, and then she was caught and suffocated?"

"She wasn't caught, as such," Doctor Bell said, as she carefully peeled back the sheet to reveal the girl's feet in full, along with her legs, all the way up to her waist. She was covered in what looked like a disgusting mix of sand and mud.

"What is that?" Cruz said.

"Sand," the pathologist said. "I've also sent a sample of this to the lab, not that I expect it'll help much. But if you want my opinion, this girl, whoever she was, was running from somebody. She was barefoot. Sooner or later, and for whatever reason, she fell into a bog or a pool."

"A pool?" Gillespie said. "What kind of pools do you go to?"

"You said Ben and Freya are in Saltfleet, is that right?" the doctor asked.

"Aye."

"Well, what is there in Saltfleet that she could have got stuck in?"

Gillespie shook his head.

"I've never been, if I'm honest. I prefer Spain."

"You've never been to Saltfleet?" Cruz said in surprise. "It's amazing. My auntie has a caravan up there. We went there a few summers back. Not that it was hot, not like it is now anyway. But when you're stuck in a caravan with half your family, it doesn't matter how hot it is—"

He stopped and met each of their stares.

"What?"

"We're talking about how the poor wee girl might have died, Gabby. When we want to hear about summer holidays of days gone by, we'll let you know, alright?"

"Ah, sorry."

"So?" Doctor Bell said, turning her attention to Cruz. He looked up at her, waiting for her to ask a question. "Saltfleet?"

"Oh, yeah. Saltfleet," he said. "The marshes. Dangerous place if you don't have your wits about you. I mean, it's easy to trace a path through them if you don't mind getting a wet foot every now and then."

"But if you were running through them in the dark, maybe?" Doctor Bell suggested.

"Then you could easily get stuck," Cruz said. "It's pitch-black out there. There aren't any streetlights either. Is that what we think happened here?"

"I think she was stuck at least up to her waist," the doctor said.

"So then how did she suffocate? I mean, it's not like she sank into the marsh, or else nobody would have found her. I heard of a few dogs that suffered that fate."

"They sank in the mud?" Gillespie said.

Cruz nodded.

"One minute they were running about on the old salt flats. The next minute, they're nowhere to be seen. Gobbled up by the loose sand."

"Well, our wee lass only went in up to her waist," Gillespie said, remembering what Ben had told him on the phone. "Which suggests third-party intervention."

"Third what?" Cruz said.

"Somebody else was there. They suffocated her. Her trachea is intact, so I'd suggest something over her head. A plastic bag or something similar," Doctor Bell said, as she rolled the girl onto her side, holding her head so it didn't roll with it. "And then there's these."

"Jesus Christ," Gillespie said. "Look at that bad boy. Is that an angel?"

"It is indeed," Doctor Bell said. "Bold for her first tattoos."

"Tattoos? As in plural?"

The doctor rolled her onto her other side to expose the other shoulder blade.

"Holy crap," Gillespie said. "An angel and a devil. Were these done at the same time?"

"They were, yes. In the last few months at least."

"How can you tell?" Cruz asked. "Is it the strength of the colouring?"

"No," the doctor replied, staring at him like the idiot he was. "In case you hadn't noticed, I have a few myself."

"A few?" Gillespie said, impressed.

"Twenty-four, to be precise," the doctor said. "So, I knows the signs and I'm familiar with the healing process. These are new."

"They must have hurt like hell."

The doctor then rolled the victim onto her back, covered her up, and handed Cruz a stainless-steel bowl that looked like the type a dog eats from.

"What's this for?" Cruz asked.

"You're on exhibits," she replied, and although he tried, Gillespie just couldn't hide his glee.

"What does that mean?" he asked, as Doctor Bell marked a Y-shape on the dead girl's chest with a marker pen. "What are you doing?"

"I'm just marking out the incisions," she replied.

"The what?"

"The incisions," she said again. "I'm going to cut along these lines, open up her chest, and then I'm going to hand you the organs, one by one, so you can weigh them and record the data."

Cruz said nothing. He seemed to rock back and forth on the balls of his feet, and even his sunburned face paled.

"You alright there, Cruz?" Gillespie asked, as Doctor Bell held up the scalpel. If anything, he paled even more, shaking his head in denial.

"Right then," she said, setting the tip of the blade down into the first arm of the Y-incision. "Are we ready?"

CHAPTER TEN

"Wow," Ben said, as Freya checked her appearance in the reflection of the window of the next room along the corridor. "The uniforms at the scene, the woman at the caravan park, and now the local CID. Are you going for some kind of record?"

"No, Ben, I most certainly am not going for some kind of record," she replied. "However, if you're asking whether or not I give a hoot about upsetting these people, then the answer is irrefutably no."

"Why?" he said. "I don't understand why. Isn't it easier just to try and get along with people, rather than rub everyone up the wrong way?"

"Tell me, Ben, when I first came to Lincolnshire, do you think I cared whether or not you and I got along?"

"No, you most certainly didn't care. In fact, as I recall, you were going to report me for touching your backside, even though I didn't."

"Well, you did, actually. But you're right, I couldn't have cared less about our relationship at that point," she said. "But ask yourself this, did I get the job done?"

"Of course, that was the girl found on the beach. What was her name?"

"Jessica Hudson," Freya said.

"That's right, but I still don't see how rubbing everyone up the wrong way helps at all."

"For God's sake, Ben. I am not going out of my way to upset people. But I'm sure as hell not going to bow down to them either," she said. "Why should I stand for comments like that?"

"Well, okay, but–"

"And why should I let a lack of professionalism give us all a bad name?"

"Right, I see–"

"And as for the cow in the caravan park, what do you think would have happened if I had done as she asked and actually requested a warrant to access the guest list?"

"Well, it might have taken a while–"

"A while we do not have, Ben," she said. "Now, I don't know about you, but I don't plan on spending a second longer in this place than is absolutely necessary, and if that means I put a few noses out of joint to speed things along, then so be it."

"Gotcha," Ben said. "I'm sorry I asked."

"I presume you want to get back to the delightful Michaela?"

"Of course I do," Ben said.

"Well then, perhaps next time you could offer me some support."

"Support?" He laughed as he rapped on the door and pushed it open. "Of all the things you need, Freya, support is not one of them."

They were greeted by five inquisitive stares belonging to five individuals, each of whom had stopped what they were doing to see who dared to barge into their office.

The first was a young, olive-skinned woman with hair as dark as could be, reminding Freya somewhat of Pocahontas. Beside her, a middle-aged man leaned back in his seat, twirling his pen between what appeared to be manicured fingernails. He had a thick, blond crop of hair pulled to one side and held in place with what Freya could only assume to be a large volume of hair product. But the icing on the cake was his whiter-than-white, perfectly aligned teeth.

He winked at Freya, which she ignored, instead moving on to the next person in the room, without a doubt the most senior in age and, more than likely, rank. The paunch across his stomach stretched his check shirt, and yet he didn't have the look of an unhealthy man, but rather somebody who had aged gracefully and was enjoying his journey to retirement. What little hair he did have was not styled in any way, and Freya guessed that, should he attempt to brush it, he would risk losing even more. He peered at her over round spectacles that could have been used as a prop in a Second World War movie.

"Now then," he said, his voice conveying a hint of authority and more than a hint of annoyance at the interruption.

"We're looking for DI Larson," Freya said.

"You found him," the man replied, removing his glasses and pinching the bridge of his nose for a moment. His voice was old, or ageing, yet still retained some element of strength.

It was then that Freya noticed DS Hart sitting at the rear of the room.

"This is DI Bloom, boss," she called out. "The one I told you about."

"I see," Larson said with renewed enthusiasm. He turned back to Freya. "You bring good news, I hope?"

"I don't bring any news, I'm afraid," she said. "I was actually hoping to use some of your resources."

"I see," he said again. "Well, there's coffee in the kitchen, but I wouldn't drink it, the printer is over there, but it's not great, and I believe there might be a few spare desks next door."

"I was actually looking for bodies."

"You already have a body," he said, at which the pretty boy smiled.

"Nice one, boss," he said.

"Live ones," Freya countered. "Preferably a DS, but I'd settle for a DC or two."

"If we had live bodies to spare, you wouldn't be here," Larson said. "You are up to the job, I hope? DCI Standing, isn't it? He assured me you were."

"Oh, we're perfectly capable–"

"So why do you need more bodies?" he asked.

"Well, she's a local girl. We were hoping that by having a local officer–"

"There's damn near two hundred thousand people in these parts. More if you count the Wolds. Do you think we know them all? I hope you don't think that just because we're off the beaten path we're a quaint little community where everyone knows everyone. This isn't Last of the Summer Wine, lady."

"Of course, I don't–"

"Well, then what use is a local officer? What difference does it make where they're from?"

"We haven't even seen the body–"

"But you will get a report from the pathologist?"

"Of course, but–"

"And you spoke to CSI?"

"Briefly, yes–"

"And the FME?"

"No, actually, we missed him," Freya said.

"But DS Hart filled you in, I hope?" He turned to face the only familiar face in the room. "You gave her all the details, Ivy?"

"Of course, boss."

"So, what else do you need?"

Freya took a breath, searching some hidden place within her for enough patience not to explode. She could feel her face redden, and her eyes watered as she restrained the anger she bore that this man, apparently, had under control.

"Maybe some uniforms to go door to door?" Freya said.

"Door to door? You mean, you want resources to go around the holiday park asking holidaymakers if they saw anything?"

"I don't think that's unreasonable given the circumstances–"

"It might not be unreasonable but I'm afraid it's just not practical, not to mention the subsequent media storm you'd cause. No way. You're not going door to door, not yet at any rate."

"What about the regulars?" Freya said. "You must have a few names you can call on in times like this."

"Regulars?" he said with a laugh.

"Recidivists," Freya explained.

"Our regulars, as you put it, are where they belong. Most of them anyway. Any that aren't are on their way in one way or another, and I guarantee you, none of them will speak to a member of the police force, local or not."

"So, what you're saying is we're on our own."

"That's about the size of it, yes," he said. "How far have you got so far? I understand you had a lead. Wasn't there a missing girl?"

"It was a dead end," Freya replied. "The girl in the marshes had tattoos. According to her sister, Hayley Donovan didn't. We'll check, of course, but I don't want to close off any other lines of enquiry in the meantime. If Hayley Donovan did have tattoos and the body is in fact her, then great. If not, we won't have lost any time. The clock is ticking, as I'm sure you're well aware."

"So, you're back to square one. What do you intend on doing next, and does it include a report of some sort?"

"We've got the guest list from the caravan site close to where she was found, plus the CCTV footage, and I've requested the details of every car that passed through local ANPR cameras from the estimated time of death to this morning. If the perpetrator was a holidaymaker, then statistically they'd move on as soon as they could."

"So, you're going to analyse every number plate that passed through ANPR in, what, a twenty-four-hour period, against every number plate on the guest list?"

"It's a start."

"It's a waste of time is what that is."

"Why would you say that?"

"Because in case you haven't noticed, there are more than a dozen caravan parks within spitting distance of the marsh. Who's to say our killer wasn't staying at one of the others?"

"I'll approach the other parks if the first guest list doesn't come up trumps," Freya said. "Every one of them if I must."

"That's a big job."

"That's why I asked for resources."

Larson leaned back in his chair, giving her plan some thought.

"And what if, by some miracle, you manage to identify a car on the guest list that also passed through the cameras? What then?"

"Then we'll run some background checks. We'll see if the owner checked out early, see if they have a criminal record. It's not rocket science, Inspector Larson."

He was a mature man who Freya guessed to be in his sixties. He bore the calm disposition that experience brings and the ability to make decisions based on merit. He was also blessed with the ability to disguise his thought process, remaining straight-faced and infuriatingly stoic.

"I'll tell you what I'll do," he said eventually. "You identify some persons of interest and I'll give you a resource to take it to the next level. Run a few names and the like."

"I can help out, boss," Hart said.

"There you go," he replied, offering her a curt nod of thanks. "That's my offer. Take it or leave it."

"I'll take it," Freya said, knowing when she was beaten. She gestured for Ben to back out of the room just as the young DC

Butterworth from the room next door handed him a file with an accompanying warning glare.

"I see you've already made some friends," Larson said. "How lovely."

"I wouldn't call it a friendship," Freya replied, and she nodded a curt thanks to Butterworth, who then retreated without uttering a word. She turned back to Larson and Hart. "You'll be hearing from me."

Then, just as the door was about to close fully, Larson called out, "DCI Standing mentioned you always have to have the last word. How right he was."

Freya stopped mid-step and Ben silently urged for them to leave. But she shook her head and pushed open the door again.

"Out of interest," she began, "did you request help from DCI Standing? Is that why we're here?"

"Request help?" He laughed. "God, no. He offered your services if you must know. I asked him to look into a few of our unsolved cases to help with our resourcing and he said he'd be more than happy to loan us two of his finest detectives."

"He offered us?" she said. "You didn't ask?"

Larson shook his head.

"We're all disposable, DI Bloom," he said quietly and with maturity. "And none of us knows all there is to know."

CHAPTER ELEVEN

Unlike during winter, when by four p.m. all that remained of the sun was a teasing orange slice of somebody else's joy on the horizon, during summer, the sun was still high in the wide expanse of sky when Freya and Ben left the station.

"You did well," he told her, as she unlocked the car. Then he waited until they were both inside, just to tease her. Freya closed her door, started the car to get the air conditioning working, and then leaned to one side to demonstrate she would do little else until he explained himself. "You didn't piss him off," Ben explained.

"I didn't need to," she replied. "In fact, had the tables been turned, I like to think I would have handled the situation in much the same way."

"Oh right. Admire him, did you?"

"Not so much admire him, but yes, I do see his reasons for behaving the way he did."

"And how was he behaving?"

"Like a schoolboy protecting his bag of sweets from a bully," Freya said with a smile.

"And you're the bully?"

"Why don't we see how Gillespie is getting on?" she replied. "I'd like to go over the facts tonight and get an early start tomorrow."

Ben fished his phone from his pocket, called Gillespie, and set the call to loudspeaker.

"Oh, aye, Ben. I was going to call you in a wee while," Gillespie said when he answered the call. "I'm just picking something up from the station."

"How did you get on?" Ben asked, feeling the burn of Freya's stare.

"With the wee girl, or with the pathologist?"

"Both," Ben replied with a laugh. He could picture him in the incident room with his feet up on the desk, leaning back on the chair with the phone on loudspeaker, freeing up his hands to rest behind his head.

"Well, she's a bloody nut job alright. But you can't fault her work."

"It's funny," Ben said. "I had an idea you two would get along nicely."

"Oh, I wouldn't say we got along, as such. But she did put Gabby on exhibits."

"How did he do?" Freya asked.

"Let's just say there were two outcomes of today's work experience," Gillespie said. "The first is that it's highly unlikely he will be putting his hand up to do that job ever again."

"And the second?" Freya asked.

"He won't be eating sticky toffee pudding for a while," Gillespie said. "I did find something out though. Our wee lass was asphyxiated."

"Strangled?" Ben asked.

"No. Not strangled. The trachea was intact. Pip seems to think she was suffocated, with a plastic bag or something. She showed us a few signs."

"Blood spatter around the lips?" Freya asked, at which Gillespie sounded surprised.

"Aye, actually."

"And dots in the eyes?" she continued.

"Bloody hell, boss. Have you thought about a career change?"

"Many times, Gillespie, but I can assure you, being a pathologist is not at the top of my list," Freya said. "Anything else?"

"Aye, the tattoos."

"The angel and the devil?"

"Aye, those. Pip said they were recent, and she should know, she's bloody covered in the things."

"How new?" Ben asked.

"A few weeks at least. A few months at the most."

Ben let his head fall back onto the headrest and then met Freya's wide-eyed stare.

"Are you still there?" Gillespie said.

"Yep, still here," Ben replied. "Sorry, we're just processing that information. What else did Pip have to say?"

"Ah, well, you know. She has a theory."

"A theory?"

"Aye, she showed us the girl's legs. They were covered in sand, Ben. Not the lovely, golden sand you might hope for on a wee beach holiday. I'm talking about the dirty, muddy sand you get in a dirty, muddy marsh."

"I told you she was found in a marsh," Ben said.

"Aye, you did. But I wasn't expecting what I saw. She has lacerations to the soles of her feet, too. Pip thinks she was running across the marsh barefoot, got stuck in the sand, and was unable to defend herself."

"She was being chased?" Ben said, for clarity.

"Looks like it. Her feet are ruined, Ben. It must have hurt like hell. Anybody else would have stopped and crawled or called for help or something. Either nobody heard her crying out, or she didn't cry out at all."

"In which case, it's possible she was trying to stay quiet," Ben agreed.

"That's a good theory," Freya said. "Now all we need to do is work out who was chasing her and why."

"Don't you need to work out who the lass is?" Gillespie asked.

"No. No, I think I've done that already," she replied. "Listen, Gillespie, I need you to do one more thing."

"I think you've asked enough already, don't you?" a new voice said, one with a strong East Midlands accent flavoured with malice.

A scrape of chair legs followed, and Ben imagined Gillespie scrambling to get his feet off the desk.

"Guv?" he said, and Freya mouthed Standing's name silently. "I didn't know you were in."

"Well, I am."

"I mean, I didn't hear you. The doors, I mean. They didn't–"

"I had them fixed," Standing said. "Just one of many improvements you'll be seeing in the coming weeks."

"Right," Gillespie said.

"Are you there, Bloom?" Standing called out.

"I am," she replied with enough courtesy to avoid being accused of insubordination, but no more.

"And you, Ben? Are you with her?"

"Yes, Guv," he replied.

"Good," Standing said, the volume of his voice altering as Ben pictured him pacing around to the other side of the desk where he could look Gillespie in the eye. "In case I didn't make it clear, while you're both in Saltfleet, any assistance you may require should be provided by the local team. DI Larson should be able to help."

Ben opened his mouth to speak but Freya placed her hand on his arm to silence him.

"Is that understood?" Standing said.

"Yes," Freya said, waving off Ben's silent argument. "What you're saying is we're on our own up here."

"I'm sure the two of you won't be feeling lonely anytime soon," Standing said, and even over the call, his smile was clear. "While we're on the subject of keeping each other company, you'll be pleased to learn that I've arranged your digs."

"I was wondering when we'd find out," Freya said. "I was beginning to think we'd be sleeping in my car."

"Oh, we couldn't have that, could we?" Standing replied. "But being holiday season and such, finding somewhere suitable has been somewhat of a challenge."

Ben glanced sideways and caught Freya closing her eyes in anticipation. He pulled his pen and notepad from his pocket.

"Go on, Guv. I'm ready," he said.

"It's the Beachview Holiday Park on Sea Lane. I had a nice wee chat with the manager earlier, a Sandy Robinson. They're fully booked, but when I explained who you were she said she had something that might be ideal. Nothing fancy but functional."

A silent interaction took place inside the car as Standing relayed the bad news. Ben mouthed the question of whether the caravan park was the one they had visited earlier that day, to which Freya nodded. He then mouthed the name Sandy Robinson, to which Freya shook her head in dismay.

"Are you there?" Standing asked.

"We're here, Guv," Ben said. "Just looking it up on the map."

"Oh, is that right?" he replied. "Well, it's getting late. I'm sure DS Gillespie will want to be off before the takeaways close and I expect you two will need to get some sort of provisions."

"We'll take care of it," Freya said, loud and clear. "Thanks for making the arrangements."

"Oh, you are more than welcome," he said slowly. "In fact, you might go as far as to say it was my pleasure to arrange it. Sleep tight. Don't let the bed bugs bite."

CHAPTER TWELVE

Not far from Mablethorpe Police Station, a large supermarket had been built to provide locals and tourists with all the supplies a family would need.

"This must be where Deborah Donovan works," Ben said as they made their way from the car to the main entrance.

"We need to hurry," Freya replied. "It closes soon. Grab a trolley, will you?"

Ben veered away from the doors to a small trolley park, grabbed the closest one, and set off in pursuit of Freya.

"We don't need one that big," she said when she saw him coming through the doors. "We're not staying for a month."

"Well, then we just won't fill it," he said.

"Can't you just get a smaller one?"

"What's the problem? It's a trolley."

"I know, but if you get a big trolley, you'll fill it. It's psychology. That's why there are always more big trolleys than small ones."

"Well, I don't plan on filling it," Ben said. "We'll call their bluff, shall we? Besides, all I need is a few packets of boil-in-the-bag rice, a jar of coffee, and some milk. I might get a loaf of bread and some butter for breakfast too, come to think of it. But that's not exactly going to break the bank."

"Ben!" Freya hissed, then checked to make sure nobody could hear. "Just because we are staying in a caravan, doesn't mean I'm going to slum it. I'm not a student."

"I had noticed that—"

"As it happens, and in case you'd forgotten, I'm a seasoned glamper. You'd be amazed at what I can do with a single gas burner, a microwave, and a kettle."

"Okay then," he said, and he shoved the trolley towards her. "You're in charge of food and drink. Let me know when you're ready and I'll meet you at the checkout."

"And what is it you'll be doing?" she asked.

He took a stroll over to the newspapers and books on a nearby rack and picked up the latest Kevin Banner crime novel.

"I'm going to give Michaela a call. You know? Let her know I'm okay and where I'm staying."

"You're checking in with the boss, you mean?"

"No, I'm making an effort to keep her informed, just as I would like to be if the situation was reversed."

"So, you're going to leave all the shopping to me?"

He hit dial on his phone and turned his back on Freya, calling over his shoulder as the call connected, "Knock yourself out, Gordon Ramsey. The menu is yours."

"Hello?" Michaela said, and Ben put the book down.

"Hey," he replied. "How's it going back there?"

"Oh God, it's hot, Ben. I was sitting in your garden earlier. You really should get out there and do something with it. It could be so nice."

"The key to the shed is in the kitchen. Feel free to have a go."

"Not likely, not in my bikini anyway."

"Your bikini?"

"It's thirty-something degrees, Ben. What do you think I was wearing, a bloody coat?"

"No," he replied, smiling to himself. "I was just picturing you in your bikini, cutting my grass and trimming my hedge."

A nearby woman in the queue for cigarettes must have heard what he was saying. She frowned at him and shook her head in disgust.

"Like I said, I was not going to do your garden for you. And if you need to know the details, I suggest you talk to your brothers."

"My what?"

"Your brothers," she said. "They popped round to invite us to a barbecue."

"My brothers saw you in your—"

"It's okay, Ben. I wear it on the beach. It's perfectly respectable."

"But you're going to a barbecue with them?"

"Only at their house. I'll take a stroll over there in a while. It's nearly four now, so I suppose I should think about getting dressed."

"Is this what they call FOMO?" Ben asked.

"Fear of missing out? I suppose so."

"Listen, whatever my brothers tell you, it's all lies. Don't listen to them."

"It'll be fine. Besides, your dad is going to be there. I'm sure they won't land you in any trouble in front of him."

"Don't count on it," he replied.

"How's it going there anyway? I hope your hotel has air-conditioning."

"Yeah, funny," he said.

"What's funny?"

"We don't have a hotel, Michaela. We have a bloody caravan."

"A what?"

"A caravan," he said glumly. "Not my choice, I can assure you."

"You're staying in a caravan with...with her?"

"I'm sure it'll have more than one bedroom, babe," he said.

"What do you mean, you're sure?"

"We haven't seen it yet. Standing just told us. We're just picking up some supplies for dinner."

"Oh, that sounds romantic."

"It will not be romantic," he said. "I've told her all we need is some boil-in-the-bag rice and some coffee. With any luck, we'll be home in a couple of days."

Michaela said nothing, but her silence was loud and clear.

"Babe?" he said. "Listen, there's nothing to worry about."

"I don't like it, Ben," she said eventually. "I'm sorry, but after everything that has gone on between you two, I really don't like the idea of you sharing a caravan with her."

"I don't have much choice," he told her. "Like you said, it's thirty-something degrees. Every man and his dog are here on holiday. That's all he could get us."

"Ben—"

"Trust me, Michaela," he said. "Listen, I want you. I want us to work. I'm not going to ruin what we've got. I promise."

He could hear her breathing over the line, and he pictured her standing in his kitchen, leaning against the worktop.

"Alright," she said. "But would it sound needy if I asked you to call me? Just in the evenings and mornings."

"I planned on doing that anyway," he said.

"Thanks," she said. "I suppose I'd better get dressed. I can't go to your brothers half-naked, can I?"

"No, you can't," he said. "And anyway, stop trying to make me jealous. This is hard enough as it is."

"I'll talk to you tonight?"

"You will, but before you go, I was wondering if you could help us out here."

"Will it mean you come home early?"

"It might do," he said. "We spoke to the local CSI team earlier. They didn't really give much away. I was wondering if you could find out who they are and get things moved along somehow. You know, pull some strings."

"Who were they?" she asked.

"I think they were down from Hull. We didn't even get to see the body."

"You what?"

"I know. They'd extracted her before we arrived. The local DS saw her, and we sent Gillespie and Cruz to Lincoln to witness the autopsy. The trouble is that resources up here are slim at the moment. I suppose because of the holidaymakers. The place is heaving. So, we don't really have any local support to speak of, which means we don't have any relationship with CSI."

"Leave it with me," she said. "I'll make some calls before I go to your brothers' house."

"Thanks," Ben replied, as he made his way along the checkouts looking for Freya, who should have easily picked up a few things to keep them going by now.

"Speak tonight, yeah?" he said.

"Miss you," she replied, and ended the call.

He pocketed the phone as he reached the end of the checkouts, and then turned back on himself, peering up the aisles in search of Freya. He didn't have to look hard. He found her in the wine section, adding a fifth bottle of Chianti to the already full trolley.

"A few bits?" he said, as he rifled through the shopping, finding things were way beyond what he would deem as supplies. There were packs of cured ham, chorizo, smoked salmon, eggs, and even two pots of fresh basil – to accompany the family-sized bag of pasta and block of cheese, Ben presumed.

"Like I said, I'm not a student," she replied, without looking up from reading the label on a bottle of white.

"Garlic-infused olive oil?" he said, reading the labels aloud. "And what's this? Greek yoghurt? What the bloody hell are you going to cook?"

"I don't know yet," she said. "But I'm sure I'll be able to knock something together with this."

"Did you get loo rolls?" he asked, to which she rolled her eyes.

"Barely, all the nice brands have sold out."

"Well, you'll have to mind how you go then, won't you?" he replied, but she didn't respond. "Biscuits?"

"Biscuits?"

"Yeah. Chocolate digestives to have with coffee. Shall I get some?"

"I was going to make some nice tuiles. I find them to be quite delicate on the digestive system."

"Tuiles? What on earth are tuiles?"

"They're like chocolate digestives," she replied, as she put the sixth bottle of wine onto the trolley and heaved it into motion. "Only they are different in every single way. How did the call with your mistress go?"

"I've asked her to contact the CSI team we met. I figured we're not going to get much help from Larson, so she might be able to speed things along a little."

"Oh," Freya replied thoughtfully, as she directed the trolley towards the checkout. "She might have some uses after all."

CHAPTER THIRTEEN

Gillespie ended the call and pocketed his phone before gathering his files into a single heap, as opposed to the many heaps that had formed over the course of the last week. He didn't bother sorting them. It was more for show than for organisational purposes. Despite the call being over, and despite Gillespie's obvious attempt to close off the day, Standing didn't budge an inch. In fact, he made his presence even more known by folding his arms and leaning on the desk.

"Are you alright, Guv?" Gillespie asked.

"I will be," he replied. "When I can whittle this team into something a little more workable."

"Right," Gillespie said, avoiding eye contact. He made a show of peering past Standing to check the weather, although there wasn't much point. The sky was bright blue, and even from inside, the streets looked hotter than the sun.

And still, Standing remained where he was.

"Something I can do for you, maybe?" Gillespie said, reaching for his bag, a move designed to prefix his retreat.

"In a word, yes, there is."

He stared down at Gillespie as if the answer had been written on his forehead in pink marker pen, along with a fake moustache and rosy cheeks.

Gillespie took the hint. He set his bag down beside his chair, leaned back, and interlinked his fingers across his waist to indicate he was all ears.

"Trust," Standing said.

"Trust, Guv?"

"That's what I want," he said. "Trust."

"Aye, well, you can trust me," Gillespie said.

"But do you trust me, Jim?"

There it was. Just like the old days, when Standing had been DI and Gillespie had been his DS. It was the use of his first name, and if Gillespie had been a religious man, he would have taken it as an omen.

"I think so, Guv," he replied. "I've no reason not to anyway."

"I need you to trust me, you see."

"Right," Gillespie said, unsure of where this was heading. But if there was one thing he could be sure of, he would be going home via the pub to order a stiff drink afterwards.

"I have a number of..." Standing began, as if searching for the right word. Then he found it and his eyes glazed. "Tasks, for you."

"Tasks, Guv? That sounds ominous."

"Not really. Ominous isn't really the word I would use. I would say intriguing or enticing, or even crucial."

He spoke slowly, pronouncing every syllable as if the sentence would be illegible without it.

"Crucial, Guv?"

"DI Bloom and DS Savage are in Satlfleet for the week, as you know. As it happens, DI Larson contacted me with a number of cold cases. Unfinished business."

"And you want me to work on them?" Gillespie said. "Is that it?"

"Oh, no. I wouldn't waste talent like you on unsolved investigations, Jim," Standing replied. "Not when we have Nillson,

Anderson, and the others on the team. Oh no, I have far more important tasks for you in mind."

"Such as, Guv?" Gillespie said, feeling extremely uneasy now.

Standing leaned forward, despite them being the only two people in the room, and he whispered, "Follow me," then straightened and made for the door.

Gillespie went after him, then as a second thought, returned to grab his bag so he could make a quick escape should the need arise. He slipped through the incident room doors and had to do a double take, as they closed silently behind him.

They had never closed silently, not in all the years he had worked there.

Things were changing, and not for the better.

"In here," Standing called from his office, and Gillespie found him sitting behind his desk, on which were two piles of files. "Take a seat."

Gillespie sat in one of the guest seats, which were little more than stackable chairs stolen from the custody suite. The force rarely splashed for luxury, as was apparent in the bland decor.

"I was hoping to grab a bite," Gillespie said, his polite way of saying he wanted to get away before, as alluded to earlier, the takeaways closed.

"This won't take long," Standing replied, slapping his hand on the first pile of files. "Unfinished business. This lot is for Nillson and the team, unless, of course, something new comes our way."

"I'm sure they'll be delighted, Guv," Gillespie said, as Standing teasingly slid his hand across the desk to the second pile, which was a little smaller than the first, though the difference was only marginal. "And these are for you, Jim."

"Me? Wow, how lucky I am," Gillespie said aloud, although he had meant to say it under his breath; the moment just kind of got away from him. "Unfinished business?"

Standing shook his head, grinning from ear to ear like the cat that had not only got the cream but found a big, fat mouse to dunk in it too.

"Oh, these are as finished as you can hope them to be," Standing said. "Closed, signed, and sealed, as they say."

"I didn't know they said that, Guv."

"They do now," he replied. "But I want you to think of these files as opportunities."

"Opportunities?"

"To progress, if you get my meaning."

"If you don't mind me saying, Guv, I haven't got your meaning during this whole conversation. What exactly is it you want me to do?"

"I told you. I want you to trust me."

"And say I did trust you, then what?" Gillespie said.

"Then I'd ask you if you wanted to go a little further in your career."

"Promotion?"

The word caused Standing to pull a face as if a bad smell had entered the room.

"Not so much a promotion. Not yet anyway. But if you helped me, I'd obviously consider you with high regard."

"And you don't already?" Gillespie said. "Consider me in high regard, that is?"

"I think we need to rekindle our relationship, Jim. It's been a long while since we worked together. But prove to me you're a team player, and maybe we can enjoy those benefits once more."

"So, the files are closed investigations? What is it you want me to do, Guv?" Gillespie said, his hands becoming tackier with every moment that passed.

"Not a lot, really. Just read through them with that scrutinising eye for detail of yours."

"You want me to read them?"

"I want to you find every fault in every one of these investigations, Jim. I want to know about every mistake, misjudgement, and miscommunication you can find."

Gillespie ran his eye over the spines, counting as he did.

"And would I be right in assuming those are every single one of the investigations DI Bloom has worked on since she's been in Lincolnshire?"

"Oh?" Standing said in mock surprise. "Well, I suppose they might be. I hadn't considered that."

"You want me to identify cases of misconduct," Gillespie said. "You're pushing her out."

"I wouldn't put it quite like that—"

"Guv, the team like her."

"I don't doubt that—"

"She's one of us now," Gillespie said.

"She's poisonous, Jim," Standing said, a little sterner than before. He shook his head as if to accentuate the point. "I won't have her destroy this team. Not while I'm at the helm. She has to go."

"And do you really think this is the right way to do it?"

"I'm asking you to carry out an audit, DS Gillespie," Standing said, matter-of-factly and with all the innocence of a saintly angel, only with stained teeth and breath that smelled like he'd lunched on coffee grinds and garlic. "I'm well within my rights to request an audit, aren't I?"

"Aye, I suppose you are."

"I know I am," Standing said. "And what's more, if we want this team to be the best in the region, then we need to make sure our Ts are crossed and Is are dotted, don't we?"

"Aye, Guv."

"You do want this team to be the best, don't you, DS Gillespie?"

"Of course."

"Then you'll understand the benefits of being credited with helping us reach that goal, won't you?"

Gillespie sat still, his sweaty hands flat on his lap. And then he shoved himself up from the chair, still pondering the task, along with the associated consequences of both doing as he was asked and not doing as he was asked.

He opened the door and stood in the doorway, then glanced over his shoulder at Standing, who watched his every move with kestrel-like eyes.

"You know that Granger asked me to betray her a few weeks ago, right, Guv?"

"I do," Standing said, and if anything, the statement only served to feed his magnanimous grin.

"What makes you think I'll do it this time?"

"Because when Detective Superintendent Granger asked you to report on DI Bloom, you didn't know what he was capable of," Standing said. "But with me, Jimmy boy, you know exactly what I'm capable of."

"Aye," Gillespie said, as he made to walk out of the room. "I'll see you tomorrow."

"Oh, Jimmy," Standing called out, before Gillespie had even taken three steps. He turned to face him and watched as the newly appointed DCI heaved the stack of files from the desk and held them out for Gillespie. "Don't forget your homework."

Gillespie reached out for them but Standing held them fast, meeting him eye to eye.

"Don't miss anything," he said with a wink. "I'll know if you have."

CHAPTER FOURTEEN

A sour-faced Mrs Robinson was locking the office door when Freya pulled into the little parking space. She glanced over at the large, rumbling Range Rover with interest that gave way to contempt as soon as she saw it was Freya in the car. She stopped what she was doing, entered the office, and emerged holding a small set of keys.

"You'll need to fill in a few forms," she said, as she approached the car and held the keys out for Ben to reach through the window and take. "But given the time, I suppose that can wait."

"Where's the pitch?" Freya asked.

"Follow the road, keep to five miles per hour, please. It's number ninety-eight. You'll find it in the far corner."

"Where the riffraff is kept, I suppose?" Ben joked. But the humour was lost on the site manager, who brushed it off with a statement that encapsulated everything Ben hated about caravanning.

"It hasn't been cleaned and it hasn't been used for a while. I'm not even sure if they are bed sheets, so you'll have to check and let me know."

"Sounds inviting," Ben joked again.

"I'm doing this as a favour to your boss. Steve Standing, isn't it?"

"He's not really our boss," Freya explained before Ben could say anything to the contrary. "He's more of a glorified secretary but thank you. We do realise it's short notice."

Mrs Robinson nodded towards the static homes.

"Well, like I said, if you can get through tonight, anything that's missing will have to be dealt with tomorrow."

"Thanks," Ben said. "I'm sure we'll be fine."

It was the time of day when, after spending a day at the beach, families had showered and were heading to the clubhouse for dinner and whatever entertainment the park had arranged. A few kids tore across the road on bicycles, disappearing between two caravans, while some parents with younger children strolled at a sedate pace pointing out wildlife around the pond.

Freya kept to the five-miles-per-hour speed limit, and they drove in near silence as they each anticipated their accommodation. They passed static caravans with verandas, potted plants, and even one with a hot tub to truly create the home-from-home experience. Neither of them had any doubt that their accommodation would provide a similar level of comfort to the ones they were passing. But all the same, neither of them was expecting what they found, as Mrs Robinson had suggested, in the far corner of the park was a static home bearing a sign that read, *Buttercup.*

Buttercup was like a caravan from the old Carry On movies Freya's father used to watch, where Barbara Windsor flirted wildly and Sid James laughed filthily at what many in the seventies would have called lewd and inappropriate behaviour.

Inside the caravan was no different. The decor was brown and yellow, the kitchen worktop was a peeling, unrealistic veneer, and the curtains were so yellow it was hard to tell if they were meant to be that colour or if they were nicotine-stained, probably from back in the seventies when everyone seemed to smoke.

"Bloody hell," Ben said, when he stepped into the caravan beside Freya. "Is this a joke?"

"Nope," she said. "This is Standing at his best. This is home for the next few days."

"I'm going to complain. Nobody should have to stay in a place like this."

"Or we could just swallow it," Freya said. "We could tell him our accommodation was wonderful, with a hot tub, barbecue, and even one of those verandas. Let's not let him win this."

"This isn't a game or a competition, Freya. I don't mind playing him at his own game, but if it means getting bitten by fleas or rats or something–"

"There won't be any fleas or rats," Freya said. "There are standards places like this have to follow. And if you think about it, how long are we going to be here? We'll be out all day and we'll come home, eat, and go to bed."

"Talking of beds," Ben said, and within two steps, he was inside the nearest of two bedrooms. "Oh my God."

"What?" Freya said, as she slipped in beside him.

The bedroom was filled by a queen-size bed, leaving a six-inch space along one side through which the occupant could crab their way to the tiny wardrobe at the far end. But the layout had not been the cause of Ben's exclamation. In the centre of the bare mattress was a stain so dark and ominous that no matter which angle Freya looked at it, she couldn't tell if it was blood or worse.

"You could always turn the mattress over," she said.

"What do you mean, *I* could always turn it over? This is *your* room."

"Sorry, but I'm pulling rank. I'm not sleeping in here. I'd rather curl up in the shower tray."

"We haven't seen that yet."

"It can't be worse than this," Freya said, as she stepped outside and poked her head into the next bedroom. "Yep, this one's mine."

Ben barged his way in beside her and sighed. The room was larger, featuring a six-inch space around three sides of the bed, instead of just one, and the wardrobe was double the width of what was provided in the first room. But most noticeably, the bed had sheets, a duvet, and four lovely, soft pillows.

"I think I'll be okay in here," she said.

"Do you want to check the mattress?" Ben asked.

"No," she said sharply. "I think, in this case, ignorance is bliss. Why don't you get the bags in and I'll make a start on dinner? I'd like to go through our notes and make a plan for tomorrow."

Ben did that thing he did when he couldn't be bothered to argue, even though Freya wished he would; he rolled his eyes, gave a little sigh, and then stepped outside leaving Freya to navigate the kitchen, which wasn't hard. There was a small sink and enough workspace for a single chopping board. Surprisingly, the appliances weren't as prehistoric as the rest of the place. The microwave was the type that doubled as an oven and could have been brand new. There were two gas burners and a shiny new kettle. A small fridge had been placed under the worktop, and after checking the drawers and cupboards, Freya was pleased she had all she needed to at least eat well.

The first of the bags were brought in by Ben and, hearing the chink of glass, Freya took the shopping off him so she could chill the white wine and refrigerate the necessary food. Naturally, she poured herself a glass before continuing, then set to work preparing dinner.

"Where do you want this?" Ben asked, as he heaved Freya's luggage set through the main door.

"Oh, just pop it on my bed, will you?" she replied, as she flicked the kettle on to boil. Then she leaned against the counter to peruse the guest list Mrs Robinson had supplied while she waited.

"What the bloody hell do you have in here?"

"Just a few things to keep me going," Freya mumbled without looking up.

Ben reappeared in the doorway a few moments later with his little sports holdall, which he tossed onto the couch.

Freya looked up from the sheet of paper, glanced at the bag, which, after a tantalising moment where she thought it a good throw, rolled onto the floor, and then stared at Ben.

"What is that?"

"My clothes," he replied.

"On the couch?"

"You don't think I'm sleeping in there, do you?" he replied, pointing to the soiled bedroom. "No chance. I'll be sleeping in here."

"But what if I..."

"What if you what?"

She took a deep breath and exhaled through her nose.

"What if I need to use the restroom in the night?"

"Then use it," he replied. "There is a door."

"I know, but..."

"But I might hear you?" he said. "Is that what you're worried about?"

She said nothing, turning away to check on the kettle.

"In case you haven't noticed, Freya, these walls are paper-thin. We'll both be hearing absolutely everything the other says or does for the next few days. If anything, me sleeping on the sofa works better. I'll be far enough away that I won't hear you snoring."

"I do not..." she began, then stopped herself when she caught his wry grin. She gestured at his bag on the floor.

"Is that it? Don't you have another bag?"

"Nope. Two pairs of socks, two pairs of boxers, and two changes of clothes," he replied. "Oh, and my toiletries. What's that you're reading anyway?"

"The guest list," she replied, and handed it to him.

"Judging by the look on your face, you've found something."

"Maybe," she replied, watching him scan the list of names.

"Vaughan?" he said, looking up from the piece of paper. "No surname. You don't think it's the same Vaughan?"

"It's not exactly a common name, and this place is a stone's throw from the Donovan house. We should at least check it out."

"Okay, we can give him a knock first thing in the morning."

Freya sipped her wine, waiting for him to spot her smile.

"What?" he said. "Tonight? You want to go there after dinner?"

Still, she maintained her grin, refusing to move until he had got the message.

"Now? He said and set the paper down on the table. "Oh, great."

"Dinner might be late," she said. "Come on, Savage. Let's go and pay him a visit."

CHAPTER FIFTEEN

"Bloody hell," Ben said, when they had navigated the maze of caravans and found the unit they were looking for. "And here was me thinking we had the worst plot on the site."

"We do," Freya said. "At least he doesn't have the communal bins outside his back door."

It was as they drew closer to the caravan that they heard a thumping noise above the sound of nearby families cooking, drinking, and laughing.

"True," Ben replied, and he reached up to knock on the door, giving it three hard raps.

The thumping stopped. Ben turned to Freya who accompanied her tired expression with an eye roll as the source of the noise became clear. Then the door was snatched open revealing a young, shirtless man with an array of crude and infantile tattoos across his chest and arms. His head was shaved, and his glazed eyes bore the red rings typically associated with smoking cannabis.

He lit a cigarette, gripped it between his teeth, then once he'd fastened his belt, he leaned on the doorframe, peering down at them with no evidence of shame or guilt. His sweat-covered chest rising and falling was the only sign of exertion.

"Now then," he said, and his voice was dry and cracked. He took a pull on his cigarette and flicked the ash in their direction.

"Vaughan?" Freya said, and she held up her warrant card, letting it fall open for him to see.

"Thought so," he replied. "It's the filth, Stella. Get some clothes on."

"Detective Inspector Bloom," Freya said. "This is Detective Sergeant Savage. Might we have a quick word?"

"Not from round here, are you?"

"Can we come inside, Mr..." she said, hoping he would provide a last name.

He looked back into the caravan, flicked his eyes around the room, and then returned his attention to them.

"Probably not a good idea," he said with a smile, ignoring her request to learn his name.

"Okay, we'll get straight to the point," Freya said. "Can you tell us where you were on Friday night?"

"Friday night?" he repeated, then stared up into the air in thought. "I was here, I think. Why do you want to know?"

"We're investigating a serious crime. We're appealing for witnesses," Freya said, at which he gave a laugh. "Has something I've said amused you?"

"You want my help?"

"We want the help of anybody who can provide information, not you specifically."

"Right," he replied. "I was here all night."

"Can anybody vouch for you?"

"I can," a voice said from in the caravan.

Vaughan rolled his eyes and stepped to one side to allow a young woman to come into view. She had a duvet wrapped around her, and her hair was, as Freya called it, styled like a professional woman of the night. "He were here with me."

"Was," Freya said out of habit.

"Eh?"

"Never mind," she said. "So, you were both here all night. Were you alone?"

Another of those wry grins crept across Vaughan's face.

"All night," he said.

"Is that about that girl?" the girl asked. "The one they found?"

"I'm afraid I'm not at liberty–"

"It is, isn't it?" she said, reading between the lines. "Was it... You know?"

"No, I'm afraid I do not know."

"Murder," the girl replied, wide-eyed with awe. "Oh, come on. Everyone knows they found a girl out there."

"At this stage of the investigation, we are simply collecting information. If you have nothing to offer, then I'd like to thank you for your time."

Freya turned away, beckoning for Ben to follow.

"It was Hayley, wasn't it?" the young woman said, her local accent strong and clear, and they stopped almost immediately. "Hayley Donovan. It were her, weren't it? She's missing. I know she is."

"Are you acquainted with Hayley Donovan?" Freya asked.

"I'm not," the girl replied, and then cautiously glanced at Vaughan.

"But you are?" Freya said to him, and he sucked in a deep breath of regret, giving the girl a look that said, 'Nice one, idiot'. "Tell me how you know Hayley Donovan."

"I used to know her," he replied. "That's all."

"That's funny, because her sister told us you two were an item."

"I used to see her," he said. "We had something once. Look, do we have to do this now?"

"Would you prefer it if I booked an interview room at the station?" Freya asked. "It can be arranged."

He huffed and closed his eyes like he was stopping himself from saying something he might regret.

"There's nothing to say," he said at last. "We had a thing. She liked someone else more than she liked me, so I called it off."

"She cheated on you?"

"We weren't exactly exclusive," he replied.

"When was this?" Freya asked.

"Is it really her then?" he said, changing the line of questioning. "You wouldn't be asking all these questions if—"

"I understand Hayley Donovan is missing. If you know anything that could help us."

"We don't," he said.

"I'll be sure to pass that information on," Freya said. "But I don't think we can eliminate you entirely from our investigation. Not yet, anyway."

"What? I've got nothing to do with it. We don't even speak anymore."

"Out of interest, when did you see her last?"

"I don't know," he said, which, judging by the way he folded his arms, was an outright lie.

"Oh, come on," Freya said. "She's a pretty girl. You must know when you saw her last."

He looked nervously at the girl beside him.

"Ah," Freya said knowingly. "Well, the truth will out. Might as well be now. You could save yourself a lot of embarrassment."

"A few weeks ago," he said, finally, and the girl glared at him, pulling the duvet tight around her chest.

"You told me you hadn't seen her," she began.

"It wasn't like that. It was at the seafront in Mablethorpe."

"In Mablethorpe?" the girl said. "What were you doing there?"

He looked guilty. There was no denying it. But he ignored her and spoke to Freya.

"She was with someone. An older bloke."

"Hayley was?" Freya asked. "Just to be clear, Hayley Donovan was with an older man?"

"Yeah," he replied.

"Do you have any idea who he was? Did she ever mention anybody?"

"Listen, I have no idea who he is or what she sees in him. Looked like he needed a bloody good bath if you ask me. Know what I mean?"

"As it happens, I do," Freya said, running her eyes over his sweaty, tattooed torso. "Would you recognise this man if you saw him again?"

"I suppose so. I mean, he had tattoos on his hands, and I suppose it was him who convinced Hayley to get hers done."

"Oh, so you know about Hayley's tattoos?"

He took a final drag on his cigarette and flicked it onto the grass near Ben's foot, then blew the smoke out in a thick cloud.

"She got them just before we split up. She'd been acting odd, distant, you know? She wouldn't get undressed in front of me," he said, and the girl shook her head and turned her face away from him. "I grabbed her and hurt her."

"You did what?" Freya said.

"Not like that. I just reached for her. The tattoo was still sore. That's what started the argument which led to us splitting up, if you must know."

"I see," Freya said, and she stared at Ben, who was making notes as fast as he could. "Do me a favour, Vaughan and Stella..."

She waited for the girl to provide her name.

"Green," she said. "Stella Green."

"Okay, then do me a favour, both of you. Don't go anywhere. I have a feeling we're going to need to speak to you again."

"Is that it?" Vaughan said. "Are we done here?"

"You can go back to doing what you were doing," Ben said, to which the girl puffed her cheeks and gave a look that said, 'Don't even try it'.

"Thanks for your help," Freya said, and she gestured for Ben to follow.

Vaughan and Green watched them leave, and it wasn't until Freya and Ben were out of earshot that Ben spoke.

"Well?" he said.

"Well, what?"

"What do you think?"

She stopped at the little road that ran around the caravan park and watched a woman in a pair of shorts, which were far too small for her substantial frame, dump an overflowing rubbish bag on the ground beside the communal bin outside number ninety-eight.

"He has guilt written all over his face. I'm just not sure what it is he's guilty of," she said, disgusted at the woman's absolute disregard for others. "Not yet anyway."

CHAPTER SIXTEEN

Dinner was mushroom risotto in a rich, creamy sauce, a scatter of broccoli heads, and a dusting of fine parmesan cheese served on a nineteen-seventies Pyrex plate accompanied by a bent fork and a tumbler of Chianti.

While Freya had been showering, Ben had changed into a pair of loose jogging bottoms and a t-shirt and had taken the time to open every window in the caravan to try and coax some kind of breeze through. Sadly, being the corner plot with tall hedges surrounding it on two sides, the breeze was weaker than baby's breath.

"This is astonishing," Ben said after just one mouthful of the risotto. He was sprawled across one section of the U-shaped couch, propped up with a couple of old cushions. Freya was on the opposite part of the couch with her plate on the table. She sat cross-legged wearing a pair of sports shorts and a sleeveless top, an odd combination that she somehow managed to make work.

"So, you're not going to run for the boil in the bag rice then?" Freya said.

"I'll see how I get on with this," he said, as Freya leaned across to the unused part of the U-shaped couch to grab her bag, from which she took out her notebook and pen and opened it to a clean page.

She forked a broccoli head into her mouth and began to write.

"Let's see what we've got," she said. "We have Hayley Donovan stuck in the mud, very likely chased by somebody."

"We don't actually know it's Hayley yet," Ben replied.

"We do know it, Ben. We just have to prove it, and we'll do that first thing tomorrow," she replied. "What I'd like to know is, why was she was barefoot? And where are her shoes?"

"Well, if Pip was right about the suffocation, then we know the killer was wearing boots, at least."

"Yes, but how long will it be before CSI come back to us with any details of the boot print?"

"Michaela is on the case. She'll make a call tomorrow," Ben said, taking a bite of risotto and covering his mouth to finish his point. "If she hasn't done already."

"I prefer not to place all my hopes in one basket. Especially if the basket has holes in."

"You mean, you prefer not to rely on Michaela?" Ben said.

"That's not what I said," she replied, bringing her knees up to her chest, which as far as Ben could see was a defence mechanism.

"But that is what you meant," he said.

"What else do we have?" Freya said, changing the subject as she often did when she was losing an argument.

"It's interesting that he took the bag," Ben said. "That is if he did use a bag to suffocate her."

"I don't see how he did it," Freya said. "I don't see how, if Hayley was stuck and trapped..."

She stopped mid-sentence, looking confused.

"What is it?" Ben asked.

She froze for a few moments like she was putting her thoughts in order.

"What would you do if you were stuck in a marsh?"

Ben laughed but Freya didn't, and he stopped.

"Call for help," he said.

"And then what?"

"I don't know. If I had no chance of pulling myself out?"

"No chance at all."

"Well, I'd stay still for a start," he said. "Struggling makes you sink further."

"True," Freya said. "But let's say somebody was trying to kill you while you were stuck?"

"Well, I'm under the impression my hands are free, just as hers would have been?"

"Your hands are free," she replied.

"I'd fight," Ben said flatly. "It's human instinct, isn't it? Fight or flight. She can't run."

"So why is there only one footprint beside the body? I would imagine there would have been some kind of scuffle."

It struck Ben that she had picked up on something he should have seen clearly. Faceless dummies re-enacted various hypothetical versions of events in his mind as his sense of logic demanded rewrites and rewrites from his vivid imagination. But only one alternate ending seemed plausible.

"Unless he didn't kill her," he said finally. "She killed herself and he stepped in to remove the bag?"

"Or he didn't kill her *there*," Freya suggested. "Maybe he carried her across the beach and dumped her in there?"

"No, there were two sets of footprints in the sand. CSI marked them. The second set was barefoot, remember?"

"That's right. There were two. But who's to say it wasn't more than one person who killed Hayley?" Freya said.

"So, we either have her killing herself and one killer stepping in to remove the bag, or whatever it was she used. Or we have two people carrying her, already dead, and one of them dumping her in the mud."

"Maybe they were trying to make it look like she got stuck and died there?" Freya suggested.

"I think both options are a bit weak," Ben replied. He took the last mouthful of risotto, shoved the plate onto the table, and leaned back, checking his phone for messages. There were none. "What about the bloke Vaughan saw her with?"

"Well, he's influential," Freya said. "Enough at least for Hayley to get tattoos."

"So, what do we do? Walk around Mablethorpe looking for a man with tattoos on his hands?"

"Vaughan said he saw them in Mablethorpe, but that doesn't mean he lives there. Ideally, we'd be in a position to check her mobile phone for messages, but we don't have it. We don't have anything."

"DS Hart said she had no possessions on her," Ben said. "And she had no shoes. Doesn't that strike you as a bit odd?"

"Nope," Freya replied. "In fact, it makes perfect sense. She met her killer, or killers, somewhere else. Maybe she escaped?"

"Hence the chase," Ben said. "We need to find her possessions."

"They could be anywhere. We need to narrow it down. But before that, we need to confirm it is actually Hayley," Freya said, as she too pushed her plate to one side and stretched out on the couch, so she faced Ben, then smiled when she caught his roving eye admiring her body.

"Do we need to go and see the Donovans again?" Ben said, and to distract himself from Freya's stretching legs, he stood and held his phone up to the door to see if he could get a signal.

"Yes," she replied. "But there's something we should do first. I need to think."

"I can't get a bloody signal," Ben said. "Have you got anything on your phone?"

She reached for her phone, gave it a cursory glance, then put it back down.

"Nothing," she said. "And to be quite honest, I'm rather glad of it. A little peace and quiet might help us focus on what's important."

"I said I'd call Michaela."

"I'm sure she'll understand."

"How are we supposed to work without the bloody internet? We're not exactly drowning in evidence here. It's impossible."

"Impossible?" Freya said, and her head cocked to one side as she pondered the word.

"What?" Ben said.

"Impossible," she replied. "That's it. That's why Standing volunteered us."

"What are saying? You think he set us up?"

"Not you, Ben. Me," she said. "You're just collateral. Think about it. Larson mentions to Granger that he has a ton of unsolved investigations that he doesn't have the resources for. Granger puts him in touch with Standing who then, when he hears about the girl in the marsh and the lack of evidence, volunteers us, knowing we'll likely fail."

"That's a bit of a tall order," Ben said. "I mean, Standing isn't the nicest bloke but even he wouldn't do that. He's not going to jeopardise a murder investigation just to get his own way."

"Wouldn't he?" Freya said. "You heard him tell us not to use the team. He said we need to use local resources. Besides, he's not jeopardising the investigation. He's made an impossible task harder, that's all."

"But Larson said he couldn't spare them. I mean, Hart said she could help out here and there, but it's not exactly like having a full team."

"Standing is pushing me out," Freya said. "Why else would they both refuse us resources?"

"Larson hasn't exactly refused us," Ben said. "He just hasn't any to give."

"Ah, but Standing has, and he knows Larson's position," Freya said. "He knows this will be damn near impossible without help of some kind."

From the doorway, Ben stared at her. She looked despondent. Not beaten, but unhappy.

"I won't go down without a fight," she said at last, although her voice lacked conviction. "I won't let that bastard beat me. We need to make progress, and fast."

"I need to call Michaela," he replied and stepped from the doorway. "I'll be back in a bit."

He walked the twenty or so steps to the next caravan then looked back in time to see Freya drop her head into her hands. He considered calling out or going back to make sure she was okay, but the prospect of talking to Michaela was too great, and he tore himself away to make the call.

CHAPTER SEVENTEEN

If Freya's choice of evening outfit had been geared towards getting some kind of reaction from Ben, then her morning attire was provocative, distracting, and downright indecent. She emerged from the tiny bathroom with a towel wrapped around her head and a gown so thin that when she made herself a coffee at the little kitchenette, the glorious morning light framed her in a magical silhouette, leaving very little to the imagination. She was a picture of femininity.

"Come on, Ben," she said, "I thought you'd be up by now. Do you want a coffee?"

She turned to face him, waiting for a reply, and caught his wandering eye for the second time in less than twenty-four hours.

"Coffee?" she said, and he nodded.

"Please."

She set to work making a second cup of coffee, leaving Ben to ponder two things. The first was the alluring shape before his eyes, and the second was how exactly how he was going to get to the bathroom from the couch, where he was partially covered by an old blanket.

"Come on," she said, as she placed his coffee on the table and checked her watch. "It's six-thirty. I want to be out in an hour."

"So, you're not content with conventional methods of upsetting everyone you talk to, you now want to take it up a notch by waking them up?"

To anybody else, the statement might have struck a few chords and caused upset or even anger. But he knew her better than that and the smile that followed was confirmation.

"I told you," she said, plopping down on the opposite couch and crossing her legs. "I'm not here to make friends. I'm here to solve a crime, and if a few noses are put out of joint in the process, then so be it. I won't be beaten by Standing."

Ben stretched, sipped his coffee, and then, clutching the blanket to his chest, he stared at her.

"I don't suppose you could close your eyes or something, could you?" he said and flicked his eyes downward.

"What?" she said.

"Oh, for God's sake, Freya. I haven't got any clothes on."

"You're naked?"

"I'm in bed."

"Again, naked?"

"Do you realise how hot and humid it was last night? I'm surprised I haven't photo-bloody-synthesised."

He waited for a reaction from her, but none came.

"Well?" he said.

"Well, what?"

"Are you going to close your eyes?"

"Oh, come on, Ben. I've seen it all before. What's the matter with you?"

"That was different," he began to argue, then gave up. "Oh, forget it."

Holding the blanket around him as carefully as he could, he stood, and made his way across the room, dodging Freya's attempts to grab the thin fabric.

"Just let me have a shower in peace," he said.

"You're such a prude," she laughed, which struck a chord and gained the reaction she was looking for.

"What would happen if I tried to pull your blanket off you?" he said. "I'd be up on a charge, and I'd probably lose my job."

"Only if I reported the offence."

"Well, what if I reported the offence?"

"Oh, Ben, what's wrong with you? I'm not exactly fully dressed."

"Yes, I did notice, thanks."

"That's a benefit of us having slept together. We don't need to be shy, and let's face it, in this heat, the more flesh we can bare the more comfortable we'll be."

"It's not about being shy, Freya. It's about having some respect for Michaela."

She quieted for a moment then sank the remains of her coffee before standing before him.

"You really like her, don't you?" she said, holding his gaze for a sign of untruth.

"Yes," he replied. "Actually, I do. She told me she missed me when I spoke to her last night. Do you know how long it's been since anybody said that to me?"

Freya shook her head.

"Forever," Ben said in reply to her silence. "Nobody has ever said that to me before. I had to walk off the holiday park to get a signal, but it was worth it. It really was. We spoke about the future and what we might do, where we might be. Don't you see, Freya? I have a real chance at something good here."

"Wow," Freya said. "There's nothing quite like rejection in the morning to whet one's appetite."

"Don't do this," Ben said.

"Do what?"

"We had our chance. We, or rather you, decided we should focus on our careers."

"You mean I had my chance and I blew it?"

"You had more chances than anybody I ever met," Ben said. "But that doesn't mean there's no room for you. I want you to like her. She even said last night that she'd love to have you over for dinner, so you two can–"

"Talk about you," Freya said, flicking her eyes down to his navel and back again.

"Build a relationship," he said, correcting her. "She's lovely and she's educated. I would have thought the prospect of having somebody to discuss current affairs with would appeal to you."

"She wants to be friends, does she?"

"Yes," Ben said. "We both do. Bloody hell, Freya. I love you to bits. You're like my best mate."

"I believe they call that the friend zone," Freya said eventually.

"I don't care what they call it. I just know that I've got a good mate in you and a real chance of happiness with Michaela."

Slowly, Freya nodded, and for a moment, Ben thought he'd really managed to break through her thick skin.

"I understand," she said, turning on her heels to walk towards her bedroom. She stopped at the door with her back to him, then fiddled with her belt, and let the silk robe fall from her shoulders to land at her feet. Ben forced his eyes closed.

"That's just bloody childish, Freya."

He was waiting for the door to close before opening them again, adamant that he could look Michaela in the eye and tell her nothing had happened.

But Freya spoke, and he opened his eyes to find her with one leg seductively stretching out from behind the door, and a mischievous grin on her face. "You'd better go and have a shower to cool off."

And with that, she closed the door, leaving him breathless and clammy but, most of all, confused.

CHAPTER EIGHTEEN

"Right, listen up," Standing said, as he burst into the incident room clapping his hands once, loud and obnoxious for a Monday morning. Chapman sipped her coffee, removed her glasses to let them hang around her neck, and watched as the rest of the team dealt with the intrusion in their own ways.

Nillson rolled her eyes at Anderson, and the two of them leaned back in their chairs with obvious reluctance. DC Gold, a mild-mannered female officer who a few months previously had become the team's family liaison officer, a role that seemed to have been designed for her exact personality, looked around the room, slightly startled, as if they were all in trouble and were going to start the week with a dressing down. Standing shoved Gillespie's feet off the desk to the amusement of DC Cruz. But that amusement was cut short.

"Is something funny, Cruz?"

"Funny, Guv?" he replied. "No, why?"

But Standing was in no mood for conversation. Without even looking in Cruz's direction, he slapped a pile of files on Freya's desk and turned to address the room.

"I've got some good news and some bad news," he began. "I'll start with the good, shall I? DI Bloom and DS Savage will be helping out our friends in Mablethorpe this week, so they won't be in the office, which means that one or some of you lot will have the opportunity to step up, demonstrate some competence, or just plain old impress me."

"Mablethorpe?" Gold said, although Chapman figured she hadn't intended on voicing the thought.

"That's right, Gold. Mablethorpe," Standing said. "Before I get inundated with questions, let me tell you the bad news, and then I'll explain. Detective Superintendent Granger has put us forward to help Mablethorpe with a few open investigations."

"Cold cases?" Nillson said.

"This isn't the LAPD, Nillson," Standing replied. "This is rural Lincolnshire. They aren't closed, in which case, they are open investigations."

"Same thing," she mumbled.

"As a result," Standing said, raising his voice to emphasise his desire to move on, "I had a call with a DI Larson who heads up the Major Crimes Team in Mablethorpe. He's having some serious resourcing issues over there, and as if to prove a point, while I was on the phone to him, he had a call come through to report a suspicious death."

"So, you sent the boss and Ben?" Nillson said.

"I did," he replied. "I want this team to be the number one Major Crimes unit in Lincolnshire. To get there, we need to demonstrate our capabilities. So, while DI Bloom and Ben are playing on the beach, we'll be working through the *open investigations*."

He over-enunciated the words to make a point, but Nillson's feathers weren't easy to ruffle. She stared him in the eye, refusing to back down, and Gold, being the most timid member of the team, turned away to pull a concerned face at Chapman.

Standing picked up the pile of folders, which, from where Chapman was seated, appeared to consist of two files, or three open investigations as Standing would have called them. He slapped them down in front of Nillson.

"There," he said. "You're running the show in Bloom's absence."

"Me? What about Jim? He has more experience than me–"

"DS Gillespie is working on a private project for me," Standing explained, at which Gillespie reddened and looked as unpleased as anybody in the room.

"A private project?" she said. "Such as?"

"A project that I personally asked him to undertake."

"He's doing an audit," Cruz blurted out, and he looked up at a very unimpressed Standing, as usual not picking up on social cues. "Isn't that right, Guv?"

"An audit?" Nillson said, and Gillespie just stared at his hands in embarrassment, or worse, shame.

"Thank you, Cruz," Standing said, with a sharp intake of breath. He turned to Nillson in defiance. "That's right. DS Gillespie is helping me with an audit. As the newly appointed DCI, I'm keen to make sure any investigations carried out before my promotion were carried out with the necessary due diligence and in accordance with standards. The last thing I want is for some dirty, low-life scumbag to drag up a past I am yet to familiarise myself with and make a claim that this team acted improperly."

"Misconduct, then?" Nillson said, cutting through the jargon to get to the point. "You're looking for evidence of misconduct?"

"I'm covering all of our backsides, Anna, if you must know. What would you have me do? Sit on my backside and trust that you lot haven't cut corners? Because I guarantee at least one of you has. If I know in advance what corners may or may not have been cut, then I can formulate a plan."

"Such as?"

"Well, that will depend on the specific corner that is being cut, won't it?" he replied. "And, of course, who it was that did the cutting. Now, why don't you have a look at the files and tell us where you'd like to start? Seeing as you're leading these investigations."

The room was silent. Even Chapman, who deplored the man, could see he had a reasonable argument to make the request, and as they had no live investigations of their own, now was an ideal time to carry out such a task.

Nillson flipped open the first file and read the brief summary.

"Aggravated assault," she said aloud for the team to hear. "No DNA, no fingerprints, no CCTV, and no evidence whatsoever."

"And?" Standing asked. "It wasn't just an assault, was it?"

"The victim suffered internal injuries and died on the spot," Nillson read and summarised for the team. She looked up from the file. "She was just picking up some tea bags for her mum."

"Does that count as manslaughter?" Cruz asked.

"It sounds like it," Chapman replied. "With a decent legal team anyway."

"A challenge is what it sounds like," Standing said, clearly trying to bring a little motivation to the team.

"It's twenty years old," Nillson said, suddenly showing some emotion in her voice. "What do you want us to do, drive around Lincolnshire asking people where they were two decades ago?"

"If that's what it takes," Standing said with a smile. "I'm sure you'll find your resourcefulness when push comes to shove."

Holding his stare, Nillson tossed the first file to one side and opened the second.

"It's a murder," she told the team. "The victim was a teenage girl, but it looks like the primary suspect took his own life before he was charged."

She looked up at Standing with a look of utter contempt on her face.

"The family would like some closure," he explained. Then quietly, he added, "I imagine."

"You imagine."

"Start distributing tasks, Anna. I don't care which of them you work on, I just want to see progress."

Nillson, ever the team player, looked around the room for support, but nobody dared say a word.

"Alright," she said finally. "Leave it with us. I'll keep you updated on how we're getting on."

"As you wish," Standing said. He strode toward the door, opened it, and then turned to face them all. "One last thing."

Everybody except Gillespie looked his way. It was as if Gillespie knew what was coming and dreaded seeing the team's reaction.

"Go on, Guv," Nillson said, living up to her newly appointed leadership position.

"Should anybody receive any requests for assistance from DI Bloom or DS Savage, I'd prefer if you deferred the request to the team at Mablethorpe. I don't mind lending a hand and sharing resources, but I want you all focused on scoring us some goals. I want to make an impact, and for that, I need some quick wins," he explained. "I'm sure those of you who also want the best for this team will understand."

CHAPTER NINETEEN

It was eight forty-five in the morning when Freya rapped on the door of the shop named *Vagabond – Skin Artists*.

"Freya it's not even nine o'clock yet," Ben said. "I doubt very much a tattooist will be open."

"I'm not looking for a tattoo," she replied. "I'm looking for answers, and for that, the shop doesn't need to be open. I simply need the proprietor to be awake."

She banged again on the door, stepped back, and gazed up to the windows of the upstairs flat.

"How do you know they live up there?" Ben said. "That could just be rented out."

"I'm sure if that's the case, then they can point us in the right direction, Ben," she replied. "What's the matter with you anyway? It's not like you to worry about waking people up."

"Oh, I don't know," he replied. "Maybe I got out of my bed on the wrong side this morning? That's if you can call a narrow couch in a caravan a bed or somebody rather selfishly flashing me before I'd even had a chance to wake up properly on the wrong side. I don't know."

"I thought you'd like that."

"Oh, I'm not complaining about the view," he replied. "It was quite nice if I'm honest."

"Quite nice?" she said.

He knew that would get her.

"Yeah, it was quite nice."

"Which suggests there's room for improvement," Freya said. "Shame. I thought I'd just show you what you're missing."

"Freya, I am not standing here on somebody's doorstep discussing your sex appeal at…" He checked his watch. "Eight-fifty a.m. As much as I'd love the opportunity to discuss it, now is not the time."

A bolt slid back inside the door, and through the Venetian blind that had been pulled down, appeared a single tired eye. Then the door was yanked open.

"Now then," the man said, although it wasn't with the same cheerful enthusiasm that usually accompanies the Lincolnshire greeting. This man had managed to apply a bored veneer to the expression as if he knew who Freya and Ben were and what they were going to say.

"DI Bloom," Freya said, flashing her warrant card to support the claim. "This is DS Savage. We wondered if we might have a word."

"Can it wait?" the man asked.

"No, I'm afraid not."

"Are you going to arrest me?" he asked.

"I wasn't planning on doing so," Freya said. "Do we have reason to?"

"I've been awake for a minute and a half, give me half a chance," he replied, and then stepped out of the way. "You'd better come in then."

Freya entered first and Ben followed, allowing the man to close the door behind them. He wore a pair of loose-fitting shorts, flip-flops, and a Metallica t-shirt that had seen better days. The lack of hair on his head was made up for with a full beard, much like Uncle Albert's in the Only Fools and Horses sitcom, only it was a vivid strawberry blond.

"Brew?" he said.

"Love one," Ben replied, much to Freya's annoyance. "White, no sugar."

"You?"

Freya stared at him, and Ben silently willed her not to start upsetting him any more than she had done so by waking him up.

"Just water," she said. "If it's not too much trouble."

The man nodded towards the corner of the room, where a small wine fridge had been filled with bottled beers, ciders, and water.

"Are you licensed to sell that?" Freya asked.

"You only need to be licensed if you sell alcohol. I don't sell it. I give it away."

"You give it away? Is that wise?"

"It seems to keep the punters happy," he said. "I'll just be a sec."

He exited the room by a back door, which Ben presumed led to where the tattooing was done.

"This is nice," he said quietly to Freya, and she stared at him, a little alarmed. "By nice I mean it's nicer than a nineteen-seventies caravan."

He began perusing the artwork on the walls, much of which were the standard types of tattoos seen on men's biceps, such as the tribal band, a single rose, and even the scroll bearing the word Mother. There were also the tattoos Ben had seen on the lower backs of numerous women, such as Chinese lettering, floral patterns, and even cherubs, which always made him wonder why such an angelic figure would be placed there specifically.

Another wall had photos of customers pinned to a board. For the most part, the tattooist was the same individual who was making Ben his tea, but the customers ranged from old men with scraggly beards to young women, one of whom was lying on her front with her skirt hitched up, smiling as the tattooist drew something on her buttocks.

"Do you have any?" he asked as Freya helped herself to a water.

"You know I don't," she replied. "You've seen practically every inch of me."

"True," he said, remembering the view from that morning. "Ever considered it?"

"Maybe, when I was a rebel teenager," she said. "But not since. Not that I can remember anyway. I'm afraid I'd feel rather a fool if I did. Like I was trying to be someone that I'm not."

"I do wonder what it's like. Not to have one, just the feeling of getting tattooed."

"I imagine it feels very much like being stabbed a thousand times with a tiny needle very fast."

"It does at first," a voice said, and Ben turned to find the man re-entering the room holding two mugs of tea. He handed one of them to Ben and then suggested they sit on a nearby couch while he took an armchair.

"This is cosy," Ben said.

"It has to be. People wait here for hours while their friend or partner is in with me."

"Hours?"

"Sometimes," he said.

"I'm sorry," Freya began. "I'm afraid we're getting distracted, and we haven't really had a chance to explain ourselves. We're working with the local police investigating a serious crime that took place recently."

"The girl?" the man said, and he jabbed a thumb over his shoulder. "In Saltfleet. Is that the one?"

"I'm afraid it is, yes," Freya replied.

"Heard about that. Shocking news. Do you know who it was?"

He sipped at his tea louder than even Gillespie sipped his drinks, which ordinarily would have irritated Freya. But to Ben's surprise, she either hadn't heard it, which was unlikely, or she had chosen to ignore it.

"The victim had some tattoos," Freya explained. "Recent tattoos. I'm sorry, I didn't get your name."

"Gene," the man replied. "Gene Finch. Sorry, I should have introduced myself."

"That's okay, people rarely give up information without being asked, at least not to us."

"And you thought that seeing as I'm the only legit artist around here, it might be me who did her tats."

"Precisely that," Ben said, and he fished his phone from his pocket, searched for the image Gillespie sent, then handed the phone to Finch.

"Do you know when they were done?" he asked.

"At least three weeks ago, but no more than three months."

"Yeah, I'd agree with that," Finch said, as he zoomed in on the image. "It looks like my work."

"You can tell?" Ben asked.

"I'm an artist, most of us have a style." He flicked from one image to the next, zooming in on the images to see details. "I do remember this."

"You do?" Freya said, and Ben had to stifle a laugh as she sounded like the man on the old Yellow Pages advert when the bookshop owner tells him he has a copy of J. R. Hartley's book.

"Yeah. Young girl, about eighteen or so."

"Do you remember her name?" Freya asked hopefully.

"Oh, come on. I have dozens of people in and out of here–"

"Anything," Freya said, cutting him off.

But Finch shook his head. "Sorry. She was quite plain really. Not the type to have those tattoos anyway. If anything, I'd have said she'd go for a butterfly on her foot or some type of memorable date. But she had the angel and the devil thing."

"So, you just gave it to her?" Ben asked. "She doesn't have to fill in a form?"

"No forms here, fella."

"Right, so she just walked in and said what, exactly?" He looked around the room. "Do you have some kind of catalogue customers can choose from?"

"I do have a portfolio," Finch said. "But you won't find those tattoos in there."

"Why not?"

"Why? Because she drew them. Had them in a sketchbook."

"A sketchbook?" Freya said. "Can you describe it?"

"Yeah, it had drawings in it," Finch said, then immediately apologised. "Look, sorry. I'm still waking up, and all this is a bit much, you know?"

"That's fine, Mr Finch," Freya said, as she stood from the couch. She fished a card from her wallet and handed it to him. "You've been a great help, but if you happen to remember anything."

"Right," he said, giving the card a brief look, then slipping it into his pocket. "I'm pretty sure that's all I can tell you, but if by some miracle I get a knock on the head and relive the moment, I'll let you know."

"One more thing," Freya said, as she and Ben moved towards the door. "Was she with anyone?"

Finch stared at the images on the wall as if they might help him recall.

"No," he replied and sipped at his tea. "No, she was alone."

"And how can you be so sure, if you barely remember any other details?"

"Because she was tense," he replied. "It was like she didn't want the tattoo, but it meant a lot for her to have it. Does that make sense?" He scratched his beard and then rubbed his bald head before cradling his tea in both hands and gazing at Freya, waiting for a response.

"No," Freya replied. "But I'm sure things will become clearer in the not-too-distant future."

CHAPTER TWENTY

"I can't believe he sent DI Bloom away," Gold muttered when Standing had left the room. "He could have sent you, Anna, or Gillespie even."

"Well, let's face it. After the way she got everyone's hopes up about promotions a few weeks ago, it hasn't exactly been happy families here, has it?"

"It wasn't her fault Standing was brought in to replace Granger," Gold said, hearing the whine in her own voice and cringing inwardly.

"I know it wasn't," Nillson replied. "But she didn't have to get everyone's hopes up about getting promoted, and all that talk of positive change in the team."

"Oh, come on, that's not fair," Chapman said.

"What's not fair? She was adamant that she would be promoted to DCI, which meant that Ben would move up to DI, and then all of us would have opportunities to progress," Nillson explained. "And look what happened. Standing is brought back in from HQ to take the DCI job, and if anything, we're in a worse position than we were before. The only saving grace is that Granger was made superintendent, so at least we have a safe pair of hands to keep Standing in some sort of order."

"I don't see how any of it's Freya's fault," Gold said.

"It's not her fault," Nillson said. "It's just the way she manipulated us all to work even bloody harder than we already do to support her case for promotion. If she hadn't said anything, we'd have achieved the same result with far less tension in the room. What do you reckon, Jim?"

"Eh?" Gillespie said, snapping out of a daydream.

"Did you hear any of that?"

"Not really," he replied.

"What's the matter with you?" Nillson asked.

"Me? Nothing. It's just this bloody audit. It's like reading a book you've already read and didn't particularly enjoy."

"Why don't you give it to Cruz?" Gold suggested.

"Oh, leave me out of this," the young constable said defensively. "I don't want to read through old reports and statements. I'd rather work on something new."

"How about a nine-year-old murder-suicide?" Nillson said. "Or a manslaughter case from two decades ago?"

"Anything but read through old statements," Cruz said. "Just give me something to do."

"Alright," Nillson replied, and she tossed him one of the files. "Do some digging on the murder-suicide. See if you can trace any of the witnesses and find out if they're still local. If they are, we'll make a plan to go and talk to them. Build us a detailed timeline from the statements and list any evidence we have, if any. That should give us a line of questioning. Got that?"

"Jesus," Cruz said. "So basically, you want me to do everything?"

"That's right," she replied. "Unless, of course, you'd prefer to investigate a manslaughter case with no evidence."

"I'm guessing whichever investigation I work on I'll be on my own?"

"You got it," she replied. "To start with anyway. Standing wants quick wins, so we'll work on whichever investigation we have the best chance of progressing. You take the murder, I'll take the manslaughter case. Anderson and Gold, can you back us up as and when we need it?"

"What about me?" Chapman asked.

"How do you feel about accommodating all of us?" Nillson asked. "We're all going to need research at some point, and that's your bag."

"Alright," she replied. "I can do that."

"I'll just be a minute," Gold said, and slipped out of the room, taking her bag with her to make it look as if she was heading to the ladies. But instead of turning left out of the door, she turned right. Then, slowly and cautiously, she approached Detective Superintendent Granger's office. She gave a little knock and held her breath in anticipation.

"Come in," he called, and she pushed open the door, still unsure of what she was going to say. "Ah, Gold. How are you getting on?"

"I'm fine thanks, Guv, I mean, sir."

"Guv will do," he replied, in that warm tone of his that could have belonged to a favourite uncle. "You seem to have taken to the family liaison role very well."

"Yes, Guv. I really enjoy it. Don't get me wrong, I still enjoy the other stuff. You know, the research and the questioning and all. But there's something about sitting with a victim and really helping them come to terms with what they're going through. I can't really explain it."

"I think what you just told me, and how you said it, explains it well enough," Granger said. He had larger-than-average ears, which suited his larger-than-average hands and feet, and although Gold had never met his wife, she imagined her to have rosy cheeks, an apron, and a bosom just ready to comfort anybody in need of a hug. "And how's the boy? Charlie, isn't it?"

"That's right, Guv. He's doing well, thanks. He loves school, so he's already ahead of me. Teacher says he's bright, and from what I can tell, he's working hard."

"Well, that's the main thing, isn't it? Hard work. If you're ready to work hard, then you'll get to wherever you want to go eventually."

"That's what my mum says."

"And my father too," he said. "Of course, some of us have to work harder than others for what we want, but that's by the by. Was there something in particular you wanted to discuss?"

"No," she said. "Well actually, yes. You see..."

"Go on," he said, sitting back in his chair and removing his glasses.

"It's DCI Standing, Guv."

"What about him?" Granger replied, his brow furrowing slowly, in line with his intrigue.

"I don't know," she said. "I don't know how to say it. But something's off. He's sent DI Bloom and Ben to Mablethorpe, or Saltfleet, or something."

"That's right."

"And he's given us a load of old investigations to work on."

"Yes, he did mention that."

"It's like he's keeping something from us. Everything's changed."

"I see," Granger said, and his brow relaxed as a gentle, understanding smile took form. He took a deep breath as if he was preparing what to say. "When I made DCI, it was the biggest thing that had ever happened to me. I'd gone from being DI, running investigations, managing the team with my finger on the pulse to being desk-bound, with nothing but reports to read, and the only gauge I had to read – the atmosphere within the team – was all hearsay. Little comments here and there, a few nuggets overheard in the kitchen or the bathroom. It's a tough move for someone like DCI Standing."

"But I don't understand why he's keeping us at arm's length, Guv. And why he's split us all up. He doesn't even want us to help DI Bloom out if she calls. Or Ben."

"Tell me, Gold, when you perform as an FLO, what's going through your mind?"

"I just want to do a good job, I suppose."

"But do you feel disconnected in any way?"

"I guess so," she said.

"So, you want to make a difference while keeping your hand in, as it were, with the interviews and building cases?"

"Yes," she said, seeing where he was taking her.

"Do you think it's any different for DCI Standing?" he said. "He's a young DCI who wants to make an impact while keeping his ear to the ground."

"But–"

"As for sending DI Bloom and DS Savage to Mablethorpe, it makes perfect sense. His team gets noticed within the region and he has the opportunity to see who in the team, if any, is ready to move up. Tell me, who has he got to lead the open investigations? Gillespie?"

"No, Anna, I mean, DS Nillson, Guv."

"Oh, I would have thought Gillespie would be well suited to that."

"He's doing an audit. He's going through all the investigations the team have worked on the past year or so."

"Ah, yes. He mentioned that too," Granger said. "And if I'm honest, while things are quiet, it's not a bad exercise to undertake. Quite proactive, in fact."

"So, you think I'm overreacting?" Gold said.

"Listen," Granger replied, leaning forward in his seat, "I've watched every one of you come up through the ranks, except for DI Bloom and DC Anderson, of course. But I feel very much the same way about them as I do you, and I can assure you, DCI

Standing has only the best interests of the team. Just give him a bit of elbow room. You'll see."

"You mean let him change things?"

"I'm afraid, just like the rest of us, Gold, DCI Standing will soon realise that making a good impression is not as important as retaining good police officers. Let him burn the energy off, things will settle down."

"If you're sure, Guv," she said, at which he smiled again, as a grandfather might smile at his grandchild. In fact, she wouldn't have been surprised if he'd offered her a Werther's Original.

"I'm sure," he replied.

"I'm sorry to have bothered you."

"Oh, you haven't bothered me, Gold," he said. "In fact, keep me posted on this, would you? It's good for me to keep my ear close to the ground."

She stood and made her way to the door then turned to face him.

"Thank you," she said. "Like you said, I'm sure it'll all be okay in the end."

CHAPTER TWENTY-ONE

Freya pulled the car to a stop outside the address they had visited the previous day. She peered past Ben through the passenger window to see if there was any movement in the windows. But she saw nothing, not even the twitch of a curtain.

"Do you have the images Gillespie sent through?" she asked.

Ben fished his phone from his pocket and opened the images of the newish tattoos on the girl's bare and pale skin.

"If you're wrong about this..." he began, but Freya was ready for it.

"If I'm wrong, then it'll be me who's wrong, not you," she replied. She shoved open the car door and stepped down to the road before finishing. "And right now, given Standing's behaviour, I don't really have too much to lose."

It took a full minute for the doorbell to be answered, and it was just as Freya was peering through the little window that the chain on the inside was disengaged. She stepped back and glanced behind her to find Ben looking as casual as ever.

She had expected it to be Deborah Donovan who answered, but instead it was a man who Freya gauged to be in his late twenties or early thirties; a similar age to Deborah.

"Help you?" he said, peering at each of them with a scrutinising eye and making no effort to open the door any wider than
necessary.

"We're looking for Deborah," Freya explained, and she held
her warrant card up for him to see. His expression seemed to
morph from slight alarm to nonchalance, briefly passing through
resentment before he took stock of his reactions. "DI Bloom.
This is DS Savage. We spoke to her yesterday."

"Oh right. She said you lot had been round."

"We'd like to ask her a few more questions, if we may?"

"Now's not really a good time," he said and peered over his
shoulder. "What with the way things are right now."

"Can we presume that Hayley still hasn't been home?"

"If she'd come home, don't you think we'd have told you?"

"You must be Trevor," Ben said, and Freya had a sense that he
had interrupted him to stop her from reacting to the man's lack of
manners. "Is that right?"

He stared at Ben but said nothing.

"We've had some developments," Ben continued. "It would be
easier if we came inside."

"Well, like I said, now's not a great time."

He had barely finished speaking but Freya had heard enough.
She pushed the door open, catching him off guard, and then
marched into the lounge where she found Deborah sitting on the
couch, her red eyes staring up at Freya.

"Excuse me, don't you need some kind of warrant?" Trevor
said. He reached out for Freya's shoulder but stopped when Ben
placed his hand on his arm.

"I wouldn't," he said.

Even if Deborah had wanted to protest, there was no fight left
in her. Three days of worry had taken its toll.

Freya stepped over to the bookshelf, praying that her hunch
was right. She grabbed the notepad she had seen and began
flicking through the pages.

"What the bloody hell do you think you're doing?" Trevor said, just as Freya caught a glimpse of the page she was looking for. She turned the book over in her hands to show Ben more than anybody else at that stage.

His face softened and he slowly turned to Deborah.

"What?" she said. "What is that?"

"Did Hayley draw this?" Freya said, showing her the sketches of an angel and a devil, which had been neatly coloured in with red and black pens to give a pop art feel.

"I suppose so," Deborah said. "That's her book. She's always drawing something or other."

"What does that even matter?" Trevor said, growing irate. "This isn't helping. Can't you see she's upset enough already?"

Freya ignored him and set the book down on the coffee table, open at the right pages so Deborah could see the angel and devil on opposing sides.

"The girl we found had these tattoos," Freya said.

"It's quite a common theme," Trevor said. "I'll bet nearly every tattoo artist in a five-mile radius does them at least once a month."

"These exact tattoos," Freya stated. "And they were fresh, maybe three weeks old or more."

"Fresh?" Deborah said.

"Oh, come on," Trevor cut in. "You're not saying Hayley went and had a tattoo done. We'd have known. She's been wearing little vest tops for the past month."

Deborah turned to look at him with an accusing stare.

"No, she hasn't," she said. "In fact, now you come to mention it, she's been covered up. Yes, she's been wearing vest tops, but usually with a baggy shirt over the top."

"Debs–"

"No, Trevor," she said, averting her eyes to the photo on the mantle. She spoke quietly to Freya, though she didn't look her way. "You're sure they're the same?"

"We have photos," Freya replied.

"Can I see?"

"I wouldn't recommend it," she said, and Deborah inhaled and sniffed, holding back what was to be a meltdown of epic proportions. "But there is something you could do to help us."

"And what's that?" Trevor asked, his tone spiteful and bitter.

Freya waited for Deborah to look her in the eye before she spoke again.

"You could identify her."

"Go and see her?" Deborah said.

"Are you mental?" Trevor said.

"Oh, shut up, Trevor," Deborah said. "Just shut up for once. Can't you see she's trying to help us?"

"Technically, we can't make any progress with an investigation until we obtain a positive ID from a family member or close friend. Family is preferred."

"So, you haven't done anything about it yet?"

"We've made initial enquiries. But if it is Hayley, then we'll have more avenues to investigate."

"Where?" Deborah asked. "I mean, where do I need to go?"

"Lincoln County Hospital," Freya replied. "I know it's a long way. I can arrange transport if it helps. I'd suggest you take us up on that offer."

"This is ridiculous," Trevor said. "So, we're supposed to go all the way to Lincoln? What if Hayley comes home in the meantime? What if it's not her?"

"Then I suggest you stay here," Freya said, politely shutting him down before turning back to Deborah. "I have a family liaison officer in Lincoln. I'll ask her to meet you. She's very experienced, and trust me, she'll help you through it."

Slowly, Deborah nodded, much to Trevor's annoyance.

"Oh, for crying out loud," he said, which was apparently the last straw for Ben, who coerced him from the room to have a private word, leaving Freya and Deborah alone.

"I know this is hard to hear," Freya said, dropping to crouch in front of Deborah. "I promise you I wouldn't put you through this without being certain."

"I know," Deborah mumbled, still managing to hold back the tears.

"Deborah, is there somebody that might have wanted to hurt Hayley?" Freya asked, but Deborah shook her head. "What about the tattoos? Do you recognise them?"

"No," she said. "No, I've never seen them before."

"Deborah, I'm sorry to ask this, but we spoke to Vaughan. He mentioned seeing Hayley with an older man a few weeks ago."

"An older man?"

"An older man with tattoos on his hands, which, if it is Hayley, might explain why she had them done."

"I don't understand," Deborah said softly, and Freya braced herself to deliver even more bad news.

"He said they were close. Hayley and the man, they were..."

"I get it," Deborah said before Freya had to go into detail.

"Do you know who it might be?" Freya asked, and of all the questions she had asked and could have asked, it was that single, innocent enquiry that broke the dam.

Looking around the room, Freya spied a box of tissues, which she reached for and handed to Deborah before taking the seat next to her. There were protocols to follow in situations such as the one Freya found herself in, but no deskbound administrator tasked with developing those guidelines could empathise with officers in those scenarios. The rules were clear. Don't touch. Don't comfort physically in any way shape or form. But Freya placed her hand on the grieving woman's shoulder and gave a light squeeze.

"It's just us," Deborah said finally, her voice thick with emotion. "Ever since..."

She stopped, closed her eyes, and let her head fall back as if she was willing the whole thing to just go away.

"Ever since what?" Freya asked gently, and Deborah sniffed hard and sighed, letting her body slump into a slouch and her head fall into her hands. Seconds passed like minutes, but Freya held fast. It was coming, and she knew it.

Eventually, Deborah looked up at her, wiped her eyes, and sniffed again.

"I'll do it," she said. "I'll go and see her. We're all she's got, after all."

"I'll make the arrangements," Freya said, sure that Deborah was going to say something completely different. "Be ready in an hour."

She left Deborah on the couch, staring at the tissue in her hands. At the door, Freya wanted to say something else, something to coax out some more of the truth she knew was yet to be aired.

But she thought better of it. There would be plenty of time for that in the coming days. She opened the door and, taking one last look at Deborah, stepped out into the hallway, then gasped at the figure standing there.

It was a young man in his mid-twenties, Freya guessed, with a vacant expression on his face and hair that looked as if it hadn't been washed in weeks or cut in months.

"You must be Justin," Freya said. But the young man said nothing. He hadn't blinked once in the past twenty seconds or so and made no effort to move out of the way.

It was clear he'd heard everything, but he neither looked sad nor angry at the news. Cautiously, Freya slipped past him and moved towards the front door, turning in the hope that Ben would follow, wherever he was.

"Inspector Bloom," Deborah said, as she carefully manoeuvred her brother from the doorway and stepped into the hallway. Freya stopped and watched as Hayley's sister walked slowly with her arms folded and swiped at her nose before speaking.

"I'm sorry," she started, and Freya's interest was pricked. It was either shame or embarrassment that caused her to avoid Freya's stare, finding solace in the patterned carpet before resting her gaze on her brother. "There's something you should know. Something I should have told you."

CHAPTER TWENTY-TWO

Mablethorpe Police Station was exactly how Ben imagined it might be at eleven a.m. on a Monday morning. The uniform on the front desk was occupied with a young woman holding her child, telling him, in no uncertain terms, that something or other was an absolute outrage and that she'd be making a complaint.

The complaining woman was almost textbook, and in Ben's mind, the uniform was handling it with a practised calm, not rising to her threats and not deviating from protocol.

The distraction worked well for Freya, as all she needed to do was flash her warrant card and he hit the button under the desk to unlock the side door, giving them access to the corridor.

"It's funny, isn't it?" Ben remarked. "It doesn't matter where you are, the job is pretty much the same. The complainers are the same and the routine is the same."

"I'd add a caveat to that," Freya said, more out of politeness than willingness to engage in a conversation. "City police and rural police. Sure, the complainers complain about similar things, but at this time of the morning in London, or Manchester, or even Glasgow, that front desk is heaving."

"Right," Ben said, as he followed her along the corridor.

"I'd have to agree with you on one thing though," she said, as she came to stop outside the room where DI Larson, DS Hart, and their colleagues had been the day before. "People anywhere can be rude, unhelpful, and downright selfish. Everybody thinks the world owes them a favour, I'm afraid."

She left the statement hanging there open-ended and pushed into the room.

"Ah, DI Bloom," Larson said. 'I wondered if we'd see you today—"

"When exactly were you going to tell me?" Freya said, her tone bordering on unacceptable and igniting a fire in Larson's eyes, which he controlled by removing his glasses and sucking in a deep breath.

"Tell you what, exactly?" he said, as the rest of the room stopped typing, writing, and talking, and watched in anticipation.

"That Hayley Donovan isn't the first girl to be found in the marshes?"

"Ah," Larson said.

"Ah, indeed," Freya began, and Ben heard the tell-tale intonations in her voice that signified a rant of epic proportions was imminent. "And not only did a young girl die in the marshes in exactly the same manner as Hayley but it was Hayley's bloody father who was sent down for it?"

"So, you've identified the body?" Larson said coolly.

"Yes," she said. "Well, nearly. She's being identified this morning, for which I'll need a uniform to pick Deborah Donovan up and escort her to Lincoln County Hospital. And before you give me some cock and bull about resourcing, I'd think long and hard about the time you've wasted by not giving me this information and how that will look when I submit my report."

He sighed, pinched the bridge of his nose, and then glanced across at Hart.

"Is this true?" he asked, then glanced up at Freya. "I'm also new here."

"There was a girl," Hart replied. "I was in uniform at the time. But we didn't see the connection."

'And why not?" Freya asked. "Surely it's obvious?"

"Not really. In fact, over the past two decades, the marshes have been responsible for at least four deaths in one way or another."

"But you didn't think of telling me that the missing girl's father is locked up for one of them?"

"Hayley Donovan was reported missing, not dead. There was no reason for me to investigate her family, especially when I was instructed to leave the investigation to you."

Freya's wrath had been met with reasoned arguments, which did little to calm her down.

"I'll have a uniform collect Deborah Donovan," Hart said. "But as for withholding information, I'm afraid you're grossly misinformed."

"Grossly misinformed?" Freya said.

"Okay, okay. Thank you, DS Hart. I'll take it from here," Larson said, then addressed Freya. "It seems to me we should perhaps have a sit down and see what you've got. With the information you've just provided, we might be able to add a little more insight."

"Oh, that would be helpful, but I wouldn't want to disrupt your resourcing," Freya said with more than a hint of sarcasm.

"You won't be," Larson replied, and he pushed himself from his chair slowly, as an old man might, then collected his glasses, his notebook, and his phone, which he took one look at then tossed back onto the desk. "Shall we?"

Ben backed out of the door and waited for Freya and Larson to follow. He was an odd-looking chap with inquisitive eyes who Ben figured was coming to the winter years of his career. He wore a woollen pullover, the type without sleeves, under which he wore a plain white shirt. His trousers were a grey tweed that hung over his brown, leather shoes with ample material to spare. If anything,

Ben would have said he looked less like a police officer and more like a retired gentleman pottering around in his garden.

He held the door as it closed and called to Hart, "Join us in a few minutes, would you?"

"Boss," she replied without looking up, as if she had been expecting the request.

"Through here," he said, as he led them through another set of doors and into a breakout space. A round table dominated the room, around which were half a dozen blue, plastic chairs that Ben had seen in nearly every police station he had ever visited. The walls were adorned with the usual posters and flyers that decorated police stations – information on drug abuse, domestic abuse, burglaries, and so forth, plus, in between the array of information, a large whiteboard, which Ben wagered silently to himself that Freya would be utilising before the meeting was over.

Larson picked a chair and seemed not to be fussy about which one he selected. He set his things down, folded his hands, and waited for them to follow suit.

"We're going to need some help here," Freya said. "If this is linked to a previous crime, we're going to need some kind of history, access to the records, and someone who worked the crime, if we can."

"Let's just stop there," Larson said, his ageing voice cracked and tired. "I think, before we get into that, I should explain a few things, specifically, why you're here."

"We've been over that–"

"Oh, we've discussed my conversation with DCI Standing," Larson said. "But you should know that, as of Monday next week, this team will be disbanded."

"Disbanded?"

"Transferred, relocated, diluted," Larson said. "Pick one, any one will do."

"But you're not exactly twiddling your thumbs."

"Not now," he replied. "Because it's summertime, and summer

is when the tourists come, and when there are tourists in the numbers we see, there is crime. The fact of the matter is that we're down fifty per cent of our team. They've either been transferred, left or taken the opportunity to find a new career."

"You're being wound down?" Freya said.

"Merged is the word my superior used," Larson replied. "With the Wolds."

"The Wolds?"

"Lincolnshire Wolds, which I must say is a beautiful place, but not somewhere I ever saw myself moving back to. I've become more of a coastal man of late. I love the water and the sea air."

"So, instead of busying your team with a murder investigation, we were brought in so you could focus on the move?" Ben said.

"That's right. Hart and I will be going over to start with. Samson will follow."

"Samson?"

"The pretty one. Spends more time combing his hair than the evidence," Larson explained.

"But you said you were new here."

"I am. To this station at least. I've worked in the area my entire career," he replied.

"So, who'll look after this place?"

"Me," he said. "The major crimes team will be merged with a team near Louth. They've built a new facility there. We'll cover the coast down to Skegness and the Wolds all the way out to Market Rasen."

"That's a huge area," Ben said.

"I'll have a larger team," he explained, though he seemed to not be overly enthused at the prospect.

"Did you have a choice in the matter?" Ben asked, suddenly finding himself empathising with the man who, by all accounts, had dedicated his entire life to policing the Lincolnshire coast.

"Oh, yes," he said. "They said I can take early retirement if I wish, but I don't think I'm quite ready for the scrapyard just yet.

The job keeps me active, keeps my mind going. Does that make sense?"

"It makes perfect sense," Freya said, then sighed audibly. "Listen, I'm sorry if I was..."

He held up his hand to stop her and shook his head.

"No need. I can see why you're a little disgruntled. I'd be the same. To be honest, I would have thought your boss... What was his name?"

"DCI Standing?" Freya said.

"Standing. That's it. I would have thought he'd have given you a few more resources. I told him the situation."

"So, he knows about the move?" Freya said.

"Oh, yes. I mean, after all, we'll be neighbours. I'm sure we'll be working alongside each other in the not-too-distant future."

Freya smiled, and from where Ben was sitting, the old man's gentle nature had won her over. There appeared not to be a bad bone in his body. He was calm, collected, and compassionate, all the traits of both a seasoned detective inspector and a warm, wise, and friendly grandpa.

The door opened and DS Hart entered, taking a seat beside Larson. She set a file down on the table, then waited for some kind of sign they were ready for her.

"When you're ready, please, Hart," Larson said, and the young sergeant pushed one of the files across the desk to Freya.

"This is the Frank Donovan investigation," she said. "Sentenced to eighteen years for the murder of Skye Green, an eighteen-year-old girl from Saltfleet. It seems he abused his position of authority."

Freya opened the file and moved it across the desk for Ben to see.

"He was a reverend?" Freya said. "As in a vicar? A man of the cloth?"

"It takes all sorts," Larson added. "It's a sad world we live in."

"Deborah Donovan gave me the impression her parents were dead," Freya said. "Where are they both now?"

"The mother died in a car accident years ago. You'll find a copy of her death certificate in the file," Hart said.

"And the father?" Freya asked.

"He was paroled three months ago," Hart said. "He's out there somewhere."

"What do you mean somewhere?" Ben said as Freya turned a page showing a photo of a clean-cut, middle-aged man with kind but tired eyes.

"There's a note on the central database," she replied. "Frank Donovan hasn't checked in with his parole officer for the last four days."

CHAPTER TWENTY-THREE

"Right," Cruz said to Nillson, without any kind of precursor or indication that he wanted to speak with her. "So, this is what I've got."

Nillson continued to read the record she was reading, hoping that either some kind of revelation might jump out at her or that Cruz would at least ask if she could spare a moment.

Neither happened.

"Anna?" he said. "Did you hear what I said?"

"I did," she replied, again without looking up.

"Do you want to hear what I've got so far?"

"Have you somehow managed to confirm that the suspect killed the girl before committing suicide?"

"Well, no, not really," he replied, "but I just thought—"

"You thought you'd interrupt me with a banal summary of everything of note in that file," Nillson said, spying a grin creep onto Anderson's face opposite her.

"I just thought—"

"Do you have a list of witnesses that A, might be of significance, and B, are still alive?"

"Yes," he said, and Anna looked up at him to find him holding his notebook up for her to see.

"And do you have a line enquiry you'd like to follow?"

"No," he replied, which was just as Nillson had presumed. "I've kind of started it but I was wondering if you could help me. I've never really done it before."

Suddenly, the irritation that had been building in Nillson's chest subsided, and she found herself viewing him not as the rude, lazy, and immature constable he was but as somebody who respected her opinion and was asking for her guidance.

"How could anybody refuse that?" she said and cleared a space on her desk. "Come on then. Let's see what you've got."

Excitedly, Cruz jumped from his seat, grabbed his files, and then took the seat beside Nillson, spreading his findings across the desk before she'd even had a chance to move her coffee.

Chapman interrupted them by calling out to Gold, "Jackie, Ben's on the phone. He's asking for you."

"Oh," Gold replied. "Do you think I should?"

"There's no harm in talking to him."

She hesitated a few moments longer, then gave Chapman the nod for her to transfer the call.

"Right then," Cruz began, clearly keen not to lose momentum, "ten years ago, Charlotte Rimmell, eighteen years of age, was found dead in a forest in Kirkby."

"How did she die?"

"Hanged," Cruz said, glazing over the subject as if she had asked for the weather. "But what's interesting—"

"Hang on, hang on," Nillson said, before he got too carried away. "Hanged?"

"Yeah. That's what it says."

"You do realise our job is to question the findings?"

"Right?"

"So, could she have hanged herself?"

"Ah, see, now that's what I thought, and that's what the investigating officer thought at the time. But there were footprints on the ground nearby and there was no way Charlotte Rimmell could have done it to herself. There was no ladder and the tree... Look," he said, extracting a photo of the tree from the file. "It has no branches for her to climb up it."

"She still could have climbed it."

"The tree was analysed for signs of her DNA and her hands were analysed for traces of bark."

"Don't tell me, both negative?"

"Exactly. So, it was definitely a murder," Cruz said.

"Okay, talk to me about the killer."

"Neil Barrow, fifty-six years old, reverend at the Church of Saint Peter near Kirkby."

"A reverend? As in a vicar?"

"That's what it says," Cruz said. "He left a note before he did what he did, describing how he'd abused his position and was sorry to Charlotte's family for failing her. He also stated that he hoped the tragic event would not deter them from the church and they should seek solace with God."

"Christ," Nillson said.

"No, his dad," Cruz said, and for a moment, she thought he was joking, but the look on his face said otherwise. "The problem is that there is almost no evidence at all to suggest it was him other than the note, a few witness statements saying they saw him with the victim during the days leading up to the event, and some photos of the victim on his computer, which to be honest, I dread to think of."

"So, the truth died with him, did it?" Nillson said.

"Let's hope not," Cruz replied. "The good news is that his son is still alive. The bad news is that he's not registered anywhere. He disappeared shortly after the event and is either sleeping rough or going by a different name."

"It must have been hard for Barrow's family," Nillson said.

"Still, ten years is a long time to be sleeping rough. I'd say he's assumed another name, wouldn't you?"

"The question is, how do we find him?" Cruz said. "He could be anywhere."

"Is there anybody else? Charlotte Rimmell's family, maybe?"

"A mother," he said. "Still at the same address in Kirkby."

"Good, we'll go and see her. I'd be interested to know if she can shed some light on Barrow's son. Hopefully, that will open a few more doors."

"Is that it?"

"Is there anybody else? Any other suspects?" Nillson said.

"No, it was just Neil Barrow."

"Then all we really need to do is prove without a doubt that Barrow was actually responsible."

"And how do we do that?" Cruz asked. "I mean, if the investigating officer couldn't do it ten years ago when all the evidence was fresh, what chance do we stand?"

"That's a very good point," Nillson replied. "We do, however, have the benefit of time on our side."

"What do you mean?"

"Think of it this way," Nillson said. "Neil Barrow was a vicar. So, why would his son run away and hide if he had nothing to be ashamed of?"

During the silence that followed, Gold finished her call with Ben and stared at each of them, obviously looking for some kind of help.

"He wants me to escort somebody to ID a body," she said, and Gillespie's head rose slowly from the records he was reading through.

"He asked for your help?" he said.

"Yes, but you heard what Standing said. We're not supposed to help them."

"What does your gut tell you?" Anderson asked.

"My gut?" Gold replied, then gave it some thought. "I owe him and DI Bloom a lot. I feel like I should help them out."

"Well, I won't say anything," Cruz said, surprisingly the first to voice his allegiance.

"Nor me," Anderson replied.

"We'll tell him you've had to pop out," Chapman suggested. "We'll say the school phoned. Something to do with Charlie."

Gold nodded at the idea then looked to Gillespie and Nillson, the two most senior officers in the room.

"Jim?" she said.

"Keep me out of it," he replied. "I'm having a hard enough time trying to justify all the corners we cut as it is. If he asks me, I'll just plead ignorance."

"That won't be hard," Cruz said, then laughed at his own joke but stopped when he realised that nobody else was laughing. They were all focused on Nillson.

"Anna?" Gold said.

"In my opinion, DI Bloom let us down," she began. "But we're a team. I think if we're going to stand a chance against Standing, and whatever else he has planned for us, then we need to stick together."

"So, you won't say anything?" Gold said.

"The school phoned, and you had to pop out," Nillson said. "That's all there is to it."

CHAPTER TWENTY-FOUR

"The ANPR data," Freya said. "I could do with a resource to put names to the vehicles."

"In the hope that Frank Donovan is one of them?" Larson asked.

"Possibly," she said. "But I'd also like to run the list by the guest list from the holiday park."

"Is that all you need?" Larson said.

The mood had altered significantly since Larson had explained about the team merging with another. Freya had spent long periods at various stations, and in the end, familiarity always provided a strange kind of comfort, and new stations were a breeding ground for toxic behaviour.

"For the time being," Freya said. "My main priority right now is locating Frank Donovan. If Deborah Donovan gives us a positive ID, then we'll move in immediately."

"There is something else," Ben said, raising his hand to interrupt the meeting before it ended. He checked his notes quickly. "Frank Donovan was put away for the murder of Skye Green."

"That's right," Hart said.

"Where's her family? I think if the two murders are linked,

then we'd better have an understanding of everybody involved in the first crime."

"I'll check the records," Hart said, making a quick note.

"Can you call us when you have something?" Freya asked, keen to get moving, at which, and after a cursory glance at her boss, Hart agreed with a nod.

"I'm also going to need Frank Donovan's address," Freya said. "I know it's an ask, but..."

"That's fine," Larson said, which was a one-hundred-and-eighty-degree turn on his attitude prior to the meeting. "Listen, I hope you understand why I was hesitant to help yesterday?"

"I do," Freya said.

"If this is to be our last investigation here, then let's knock it out of the park," he said. "I have a feeling my next move will be my last. I'd like to leave a legacy and not a stack of open investigations."

"I understand," Freya remarked. "We're only happy to help."

"Oh, you won't be helping us," Larson said with a laugh. "We'll be helping you, where we can, of course. We still have a list as long as my arm of things to close down."

"Then, we'll bear that in mind," Freya said and took a deep breath before turning to Ben. "Shall we get to it?"

"What are you going to do?" Larson asked. "I mean, until Deborah Donovan confirms the ID, I don't want you digging up the past or creating some kind of media frenzy."

"I have a few lines of enquiry we can make a start with," she replied, and he stared at her, eyebrows raised expectantly. "I'd like to talk to CSI, to begin with. Maybe they can help us start to build a picture here. Hayley Donovan–"

"If it is Hayley Donovan," Larson said.

"Okay then, the victim didn't have a mobile phone or any ID on her, and neither did she have any shoes. We know that the soles of her feet were lacerated as if she'd run through the marshes."

"I would imagine a fair few people run barefoot along the beach," Larson said.

"Not in the dark," Freya said, ready for him to make the argument.

"What makes you so sure it was dark when she was running? From what I understand, the FME said she'd been out there for at least a day."

"True, but then, if she had been alive in the daytime in this heat, she'd have sunburn," Freya said, and Larson made a show of understanding, even agreeing. "I'd love to claim that little insight as my own, but I'm afraid the forensic pathologist at Lincoln has staked her claim."

"And it's well deserved, too," Larson said. "Dead bodies don't get sunburn."

"Exactly," Freya said, and the movement in the investigation took at least five years off the old man's face. "Our victim was running from something, or someone. Not only that but her shoes and belongings must be somewhere too."

"They could be anywhere by now," Hart said.

"I know. I'm not asking for a search to be conducted at this stage, but I'll be taking a walk around the crime scene. Aside from caravans and mobile homes, where else could she have been running from?"

"There's a few houses down Sea Lane," Hart said. "Not many, but–"

"No," Freya said. "Put yourself in her shoes. If you ran from a house in fear of your life, what would you do?"

"Scream and shout," Hart replied.

"Precisely. We'll give the neighbours a knock to see what they have to say, but I'm not hopeful. I'm thinking she was running from somewhere remote or secluded."

"Frank Donovan was a reverend," Larson said. "What about the church?"

"He worked at All Saints church in Saltfleet," Hart said. "As far as I know that's the only one."

"No, I mean St Botolph's," Larson said, and a grave expression washed over him.

Hart, however, looked confused.

"It's abandoned," she said. "It's been abandoned for as long as I've been alive."

"An abandoned church? Is it far?" Freya asked.

"Skidbrooke," Larson said. "A two-minute drive from Saltfleet."

"A two-minute drive?" Ben said. "What's that, a five-minute run?"

"Ten if you don't have any shoes on," Hart suggested. "Maybe more."

"We'll take a look," Freya said, gathering her things. "So, to recap, Hart, you're going to call us with details of the first victim's family."

"Yep," she said, short and sweet, just the way Freya liked to work.

"And you, DI Larson, will ask somebody to put names to the owners of every vehicle on the ANPR report so we can cross reference them with the guest list from the caravan park."

"Consider it done," he replied.

"Thank you," she said. "We should have a response from Deborah Donovan in an hour or so. We've asked one of our colleagues to meet her and help her through it."

"Is that wise?" Larson asked.

"If I was asked to ID my sister, and have the past dragged up, as you put it, DC Gold is exactly the person I'd want by my side."

He stared at her, reading into her expressions the way Freya might have, had the tables been turned.

"I'll take your judgement on that one," he said. "But..."

He stopped, and for a moment, he glanced across at Hart, as if she needed to hear what he had to say more than anybody else. "If you're heading down to St Botolph's, then I'd better come with you."

"I'm sure we can handle an old church," Freya said, doing her best to let him down lightly.

"No," he replied. "No, I would be remiss if I let you go there on your own."

"Please don't tell me it's haunted," Freya said. "I'm not sure I can let local myths hinder an already complex investigation."

"Oh, it's haunted, alright. As far as local legends go anyway. But it's not the dead inhabitants you need to be wary of," he said, and his eyes widened with mystery. "It's the ones who are still very much alive."

CHAPTER TWENTY-FIVE

Freya pulled the car into a space at the foot of the concrete ramp that led up from the road and down into the marshes.

"It's bloody freezing," Larson said, as he climbed from the car in a hurry. "For once, I can't wait to get out into the sunshine."

"It's air conditioning," Freya replied. "It's a lifesaver in heat like this."

"It's not for me," he replied, and closed the door, leaving Ben and Freya to share a bewildered look. "Whatever happened to good old fresh air? Seems to me there's a gadget these days for everything."

"Each to their own," Ben said, as he climbed from the car to join Larson.

Ben chose to keep his distance as the three of them walked over the ramp, listening to Freya and Larson engage in very stilted conversation, as they each strived to understand the other. It was clear the two of them shared views on developing theories and the importance of understanding why somebody commits a crime in order to get to the truth, but there were so many gaps in their personalities, Ben wondered if a clash was imminent, and for that, he'd keep well out of the way.

At the top of the ramp, they stopped to survey the area. The view was beautiful. The marshes ran from left to right as far as the eye could see. The wild grasses, hardy and as brutal as the place, rose up in clumps between trodden paths and the waterways that, from above, resembled a river delta with its artery-like fingers seeking the low areas throughout. Beyond the marsh was a glorious beach, glimpsed only through a gap in the single sand dune that ran parallel to the coast. It was through this gap that water fed the marsh, and from where they were standing, Ben could see that each of the pathways had been formed by locals and tourists seeking a dry and safe path to the beach.

Often, a path was broken, cut through by a fresh stream at high tide, forcing walkers to jump across or find a new route through.

"This place would be deadly in the dark," he said aloud.

"That it is," Larson agreed, his tone low and thoughtful. "Most people use their common sense, but we do get the odd one or two that have very little appreciation for the wild."

The crime scene was marked only by the remains of the police cordon that fluttered in the hot breeze, and now that he had time to stop and take in the scene, Ben saw that the spot where the body had been found was nowhere near any of the little pathways.

"Where do you think she ran from?" Ben asked nobody in particular. "Which direction? Her footprints suggest she ran from the trodden path a hundred metres from where she was found. But that doesn't help us. At all."

"Well, the Donovans' house is inland, due west from here, as is St Botolph's, I might add," Larson said.

"What about north and south along the coast?" Freya asked.

"Marshes and beach," Larson said. "Mostly beach all the way up to the Humber. So, if you're looking for a remote property, you'll find a fair few."

"Within running distance?" Ben asked.

"Within shouting distance," Larson said. "It's mostly farmland up here."

"So, plenty of outbuildings and barns," he said.

"Yep. Plenty of them, alright. For what we lack in population, we make up for in land."

"That's very cryptic," Freya mused.

"What I mean is that we're very rural up here, even more so than you, I imagine. Plenty goes on away from prying eyes, and folk don't like to talk much. Makes for a variety of challenges."

"I can imagine," Freya replied, and she eyed Ben with a little humour in the glint of her eyes.

"As for which direction she came from, that's anybody's guess," Larson said. "If you're looking at running distance, you've got a holiday park to the south and another to the north."

"Yes, that's the one we're staying at," Freya said.

"You're in a static home?" Larson said. "I thought Standing would have put his best detectives up in one of those Air Whatsits."

"Airbnb?" Ben said.

"Yeah, one of them. There's plenty of them around here."

"Unfortunately, our killer didn't allow us the benefit of warning," Freya said. "It's the height of summer. Everywhere is fully booked. We were lucky to get the one we've got."

"Well I never," he said, and shook his head in astonishment. "Who'd ever heard of two detectives sharing a caravan in the middle of an investigation?" Then something dawned on him, and he looked from Ben to Freya and back again. "Hold up, you're not..."

"No," Ben said. "We're not together."

"And you're sharing a caravan? Isn't that a bit..."

"Intimate?" Freya suggested. "It's okay. We're comfortable with it. Besides, the warm summer evenings will give us a chance to go over the facts."

"Oh, right. You're one of them, are you?"

"One of what?" Freya said.

"Live to work, do you? Can't switch off?"

"When there's a job to be done—"

"Save it," he said, grinning to himself. "I've heard it all before, from these lips too. It catches up with you in the end. You mark my words."

"For your information, I happen to enjoy what I do."

"I used to say that as well," he said. "I've got the grey hair to prove it, look."

"Shall we focus on the job at hand?" Ben suggested, sensing Freya was going to cause an argument out of nothing once again. "So, if she ran from the north, then we can assume she came from the caravan park or the farm, and if she ran from the south, there's another caravan park, is there?"

"That's right," Larson said.

"But if she ran from this church you've been talking about. St Botolph's, was it?"

"That's right."

"Then she would have come down the road that we parked on. Sea Lane?"

"That's right."

"But if she did that, we'd expect the pathologist to have found stones in the lacerations in her feet," Freya said. "Or tar, or something. From what I understand, she only found sand and mud."

"Let's double-check. She wouldn't have been looking for a difference in debris. If there's no sign of road material, then we can assume she came from the north or the south," Ben said. "Which means we can rule out the church."

"Can we?" Larson said, as if he knew better, and he left his question open for them both to answer.

"I'd like to rule it out," Freya said. "How far is the church from here?"

"A mile, give or take," Larson replied.

"A mile?" Ben said. "Why would she run *here*? Surely in the space of that mile, she would have had plenty of opportunity to knock on somebody's door, or scream for help?"

"Unless of course, she wasn't killed here," Freya said, then turned to Larson. "Let's see this church. I'm very aware you have a list as long as your arm of things you need to close off before next week."

CHAPTER TWENTY-SIX

In the space of nine months, DC Jackie Gold had become well-acquainted with grief and the effects of tragedy on individuals. She could spot the signs a mile off. It wasn't just the often haggard and dishevelled appearance that marked an individual out as grieving. There was something far more intangible to it. Something Jackie couldn't put her finger on or find a word to describe other than the word *aura*.

From the moment Deborah Donovan stepped from the liveried car, her aura was quite apparent. She looked lost, forlorn, and downright scared, and when Jackie approached, she thought the grieving sister might jump from her skin.

"Deborah Donovan?" Jackie said.

"Yes," came the reply, almost instantly, but not without trepidation.

"I'm Jackie. DI Bloom asked me to meet you," she said.

"Oh. Oh, I see."

Jackie studied the woman, as she, in turn, studied the hospital before them, no doubt contemplating the thought that her sister's body was inside somewhere, and she was about to go and see it.

"Do you have any questions?" Jackie asked, to which Deborah shook her head.

"We can grab a coffee if you like. It might settle your nerves a little."

"No," she said, summoning some inner strength. "No, we should do this before I change my mind."

"Okay. Well, let me just talk to the driver a second," Jackie said, and she opened the passenger door and found a uniform waiting patiently. "I don't know how long we'll be. Do you want to park up in the car park, and I'll come find you?"

The uniform nodded and thankfully didn't offer any kind of complaint or moan about the wait. It was an easy shift for him, Jackie supposed – three or four hours driving with a lengthy wait in between.

She closed the door and turned to find Deborah marching towards the hospital entrance, but she didn't call out. Instead, she hurriedly caught up with her as she reached the main doors, and then guided her towards the morgue.

"The pathologist is nice," Jackie said eventually when they were following the painted lines on the floor. "She'll take good care of you."

Deborah stopped.

"Aren't you coming in with me?"

"Well, I can do. But if you wanted some privacy–"

"No. I was told you just needed me to identify her."

"Yes, but sometimes–"

"If it is her, then maybe. But to start with, would you?"

"Of course," Jackie said. "Pip will be there too."

"Pip?"

"The pathologist," Jackie explained. "Most people call her Doctor Bell, but she's so friendly."

"I see," Deborah said, closing the line of conversation down.

"Do you have any other siblings?" Jackie asked, looking for somebody who might be able to help the woman later on.

"A brother," she replied. "Justin."

"That's nice. I always wanted a brother. Are you close?"

"Kind of," she said. "But not really. He doesn't say much. He's got a few issues."

"Oh, don't we all."

"No, I mean he's incapable of interacting with people. He lives in his own world. Like a recluse, but in our house."

"I see. So, you care for him, do you?" Jackie asked as she pushed through the double doors that led into the long corridor before the morgue.

"As much as I can. It's hard, you know? I feed him. I clean his clothes. I fetch his medication. But it's like there's nothing inside. No heart or soul. Just a shell."

"Does he suffer from a condition?"

"Trauma," she replied, as they reached the double doors, and Jackie hesitated to push the button to alert Pip.

"What kind of trauma?"

"I don't know. Nobody can work it out, even the doctors. He suffers from severe depression. I suppose your boss told you about our father, did she?"

"No, she told me nothing about anything, only that you might need somebody to lean on while you're here."

The faintest of smiles touched Deborah's lips, then faded in an instant.

"Mum died when were young. Dad did his best. But as the eldest, he relied on me quite a lot. I didn't mind, really. It's not like I was into partying or anything, and what with Dad's work taking up so much of his time..."

"What does he do?" Jackie asked.

"Did," Deborah said. "What *did* he do?"

"Oh, I'm so sorry,"

"No, it's okay. He's not dead. He was the vicar at our local parish."

"He's a vicar?"

"Was," she said. "Which meant, of course, that the three of us were involved in the church. I sang in the choir when I was younger, and we were always helping out where we could. It was nice. Despite Mum being gone, we were still close, the four of us. He did a good job, before..."

She stopped, as if she was unable to say the words and suddenly regretted everything that she had told Jackie.

"It's okay, you don't have to–"

"No. No, it's fine," she said, then sighed and prepared to say the words. "Dad was convicted of murder. He killed someone."

"Oh, Deborah," Jackie said. She wanted to reach out and hug her, or touch her, just to comfort her somehow.

"So, I took on the house. I took on Hayley and Justin. And Justin has never been the same," she said.

"It hit him hard, did it?" Jackie asked.

"I don't know. He was close to Dad. Closer than Hayley or me, anyway. But I think he feels like it's his fault somehow."

"What makes you say that?"

Deborah stared at the button indicating the conversation was coming to an end, and Jackie raised her hand again but first waited for her to answer.

"The suicide attempts."

"Oh God, I'm so sorry–"

"It's only the Sertraline that keeps him alive," she said flatly. "If that is Hayley inside here, it'll destroy him. And if I lose him, I really don't know how I'll cope. I'll be the only one left."

CHAPTER TWENTY-SEVEN

St Botolph's sat at the end of a pretty lane a mile inland from the coast where the body had been discovered. It appeared to be an ordinary church from the outside, a little run down, and the grounds were not exactly a comfortable place for mourners to visit the graves of loved ones.

But as they drew closer, Ben began to see the signs of ruin and neglect. A few empty bottles dotted the pathway, almost lost to the long grass, which in the church's heyday would have been kept neat and tidy. On one wall, Ben caught sight of some graffiti; although inevitable, it was still sad to see on such an historic building.

"This is St Botolph's," Larson said from the back seat, as Freya brought the car to a standstill.

"Should we lock the doors?" Freya asked, catching Ben's eye to see if he had caught the joke at Larson's apparent fear of the place.

Apparently, Larson did.

"There's been some strange goings-on at this place, let me tell you," he said. "You might mock me, but you wouldn't want to be here on your own in the dark. Now that I do know."

"It's a church," Freya said, shoving open the door with her usual, casual nonchalance. "Come on. Let's have a look around."

They walked through the kissing gate and Ben caught up with Freya, noting that Larson was staying a few steps behind, keeping his distance.

"Bloody graffiti," Ben said, and he pointed out the red paint-work on the old stone walls.

"That's not graffiti," Larson said, with a knowing tone. "Look closer."

"Oh, for crying out loud," Freya said. "Is this what you're scared of?"

Ben studied the wall, tracing his finger around the old paint that formed a star within a circle.

"It's the Star of David," Ben said.

"Wrong," Freya said, sounding bored with the mystery. "It's a pentagram."

"A what?"

"A pentagram," she said again, as she tried the nearest door, which was locked. "Devil worshippers. Satanists. Call them what you like, they're all bloody nut jobs."

"They might be nut jobs," Larson agreed. "But they've caused more than their fair share of rumour and upset around here."

"Don't tell me," Freya replied, as she led them further around the old gothic building. "They light fires and chant into the early hours?"

She marched off around the corner, leaving Ben and a weary-looking Larson to follow.

"What kind of trouble?" Ben asked quietly, as the two men strolled around the grounds.

"They break in, which is to be expected, but still, it's a thir-teenth-century building. You'd think they'd have some respect."

"Is that it?"

"No, but you'll see," he replied, as they turned the corner and saw Freya up ahead trying another door and finding it locked.

She marched on, clearly keen to prove that every door was locked and that the church was of no significance to the investigation.

But when Ben and Larson reached the door, the older man stopped to try it for himself. Out of politeness, Ben waited, watching as Larson ran his hand around the doorframe, feeling the little brackets that he assumed the council or somebody had screwed in place to prevent break-ins.

"I wonder," Larson mumbled to himself, which pricked Ben's attention. He fumbled in his pockets and withdrew an old, well-used Swiss Army knife. He pulled open the little screwdriver component, but before he began to use it, he waved Ben over. "See here?"

Ben leaned in to see where the old man was pointing at the rusty screws, and there was clearly a sign of fresh, bare metal showing through the corrosion.

"Somebody's been here," Larson said quietly, and he indicated the rest of the brackets around the door, some of which had no screws at all holding the door in place. He unscrewed the first of the screws, and just as Ben's father would have done, he blew the dust from the head, then held it up to the light to study. It was old and had been painted over with red-oxide paint, the same as the door. He pocketed it before setting to work on the rest of them.

Ben had to hand it to Larson, he was clearly methodical in his ways. When the last of the screws had been blown and pocketed, he took the time to close the screwdriver, and then, with a quick glance at Ben, as if to say, 'Are you ready for this?' he pushed opened the door.

Light spread across the ancient, stone floor as the door creaked open, as if the designer back in the thirteenth century had wanted to add a touch of macabre intrigue.

Even their breath seemed to echo in the empty vault-like space. They were at the east porch, and as Ben stepped inside, dead ahead, he could see the piers of the old, stone arches on either side of a central aisle. No pews filled the space and no hymn boards displayed the order of events for a sermon either last week or next. The air smelled damp and dusty, and yet, despite its lack of furnishings or housekeeping, the space was a wonder to behold. Craning his neck, Ben studied the gothic ceiling, the beautiful, arched windows, and the octagonal stonework, which even with modern-day tools he, or anybody he knew, would be unable to match.

"Over here," Larson said quietly, his voice carrying through the empty space like a spirit. He was standing at one of the piers, on which another pentagram had been carved instead of painted. At its base though was a sight that Ben hadn't been expecting to find.

"How did you get in here?" a voice said, feminine, yet with authority and clarity.

Ben turned to find Freya silhouetted in the doorway, and he was immediately reminded of the sight he had witnessed that morning. But thoughts of her body were not going to distract him from the possibilities of what lay at his feet.

"Blood," he said, ignoring her question. "Plenty of it too."

"Dry?" Freya asked, stepping closer with caution.

"It's been there a while. You can see the layer of dust that's formed over it," Larson said. "Even still, we should tread carefully."

"I'll get CSI in here," Ben said, and he watched as Larson moved around the edges of the church as if the shadows provided some kind of sanctuary. And then he pointed to the centre of the room.

Three great shafts of sunlight spilled through the giant windows and lit the dust they had disturbed before spreading across the central aisle, where a single gravestone lay in the floor, then dispersing into the shadows.

"Are those..." Ben began.

"Bones," Larson finished for him, his voice dry and tinged with fear.

Moving as close as she could without disturbing the scene, Freya peered at the little pile atop the gravestone inlaid into the stone floor.

"Animals bones," she called out. "A dog, by the look of the skull."

"What?" Ben said.

"And that's why the neighbours don't like them here," Larson said.

"Who's them?" Ben asked to which Larson answered with a cold stare.

"The devil worshippers," he replied.

"If you believe in all that, DI Larson, then what chance do the rest of us stand?" she said, as she used the end of her pen to lift the remains of a dog collar for them to see.

"Jesus," Ben said, then stopped himself when he remembered where he was.

"I would go as far as to say the blood belongs to the animals, too," Freya said, as she rose, clearly not interested in the remains. But just as she stood, something darted into a shadow behind her.

"What was that?" Ben said.

"What was what?" she replied, turning to see what he was looking at.

"Something moved."

"It went into the south porch," Larson said, walking slowly over to the spot. He pulled a little pencil torch from his pocket and shone it into the corner of the space.

"You two watch too many horror films," Freya said, as she and Ben watched Larson step into the porch, which was a small area around ten feet by eight.

A silence followed but ambient noise still filled the space, as if the centuries that had passed lingered on, reverberating from the stone walls for eternity.

"You'll want to see this," Larson called out.

Freya rolled her eyes as if she thought the whole thing a waste of time, but she joined Ben and walked across the church to the doors Larson had disappeared through.

His torch illuminated a duffel bag, an old mess tin that needed cleaning, and a gas stove. The ensemble had been neatly tidied away beside a rolled-up sleeping bag.

"Rats don't eat old bones," Larson grumbled, and he turned to stare at Ben with a look that said. 'I told you so'.

"Frank Donovan?" Freya asked.

Larson dropped to a crouch, leaned forward, and was just about to grab the zip on the bag when Freya's phone sang out like the old bells.

"Ah, for God's sake," Ben said, clutching his chest. "You scared the bejesus out of me."

Larson grinned at the interruption which had given them all a jolt, and Freya, taking a deep breath, checked the caller ID then answered the call.

"Gold, how did it go?" she said, eyeing Ben as she spoke. She listened to what Jackie had to say then thanked her and ended the call. Freya, with her penchant for drama, pocketed her phone, making Ben and Larson wait for whatever news was to follow. Eventually, she licked her lips and steeled herself. "Deborah Donovan gave a positive ID. It's Hayley."

"And this is Frank Donovan's," Larson said, after he'd rummaged in the duffel bag and pulled out a small, well-thumbed pocket bible. He flicked through the pages, as somebody might scan the contents of a mail order catalogue, then nodded to himself and peered up at them gravely, holding the little book cover open in the dim light to reveal the initials *FD*. "He's back."

CHAPTER TWENTY-EIGHT

The address in Kirkby was a semi-detached cottage that had long since lost its rural charm. The ivy that had once decorated the walls was clearly out of control, covering more than half of the top-floor windows, and there was so much lichen on the roof that it was hard to see what colours the tiles had once been.

But there was life in the old house and movement through the windows when Nillson and Cruz walked up the garden path. The door opened before they had even knocked and before Nillson had a chance to retrieve her warrant card.

"Mrs Rimmell?" she said, still searching her pockets.

"It's okay. I know who you are," the woman replied. She had short cropped hair, wore sparse makeup, and had small pointed ears, which along with her snub nose gave her a pixie look.

"Were you expecting us?" Nillson asked, finally locating her warrant card. "DS Nillson. This is DC Cruz."

"I'd recognise a police officer anywhere," she replied. "Especially when they're walking up my garden path. It's not a sight you forget too easily."

Nillson offered an apologetic expression and waited for the lady to invite them in.

"I suppose you want to come in, do you?"

"Is it convenient? Nillson said. "We can come back–"

"Is this about my Charlotte?"

"It is, yes," Nillson said, and Mrs Rimmell seemed to stiffen at the mention of her daughter's name. "We just have a few questions."

"Well, then you'd better come in," she replied. "Although, I don't know what you're expecting to learn. I've been saying the same thing over and over again for years. Nothing seems to change."

She stepped back to allow Nillson and Cruz to enter, then closed the door behind them. Immediately, the smell of home baking hit them, and Cruz peered through into the kitchen.

"I'm just doing a batch of cakes for the church," she said, as she led them through to the kitchen.

"It's a lovely house," Nillson said as she followed her, noting how the inside was in a far better condition than the exterior.

"I'm afraid it's rather a sad house these days. Not like it used to be," she said, as she took her place behind the kitchen work-top, leaving Nillson and Cruz to stand opposite.

"I appreciate this must be hard to talk about," Nillson said. "We're hoping to close the investigation. We've read through the files of the previous investigation. It seems to me that due to a lack of evidence and the death of Neil Barrow, no decision was ever made."

"That's right," Mrs Rimmell said, a little harder than before as the memories of the past began to surface. "There's never been a conclusion. Do you know what that's like? Do you know how that feels?"

"I can't begin to imagine," Nillson said.

"No. Nobody can. He took her away from me and then, like a coward, he took his own life. Where does that leave me? Who pays for it?"

"I appreciate—"

"No. No, you don't. Nobody does. One day Charlotte was here, the next, she was gone. It's like this big open-ended question hangs over me that I know will never be answered. We all know it was Barrow who did it. He had all those pictures of her on his computer. Bloody disgusting, he was. What kind of man has photos of a young girl like that? And to think he was a man of God."

"Mrs Rimmell, I—"

"Listen, to me," she said, waving her index finger at Nillson. "I don't expect miracles, but I do expect some kind of recognition of the truth. Some kind of justice for my little girl."

"Well, we hope to bring some closure," Nillson said. "We hope to prove it was Neil Barrow, in a formal capacity."

"So, you can close your investigation?" she said. "Is that it? Was my Charlotte's file getting in the way?"

"That's not the way it works, I can assure you—"

"No. No, I don't suppose it is, and I don't suppose anybody will ever tell me, either."

"Mrs Rimmell, can you tell us a little bit about Charlotte? What was she like? What did she enjoy?"

She sniffed and wiped a lone tear from her eye, then snatched up a well-used oven glove and bent to open the oven door. A cloud of steam engulfed her, which she swiped away, and she emerged carrying a tray of cupcakes.

"She was a delight," she said eventually, and she set the tray down on a cooling rack. "An absolute delight. Never heard a bad word said about her, I never. Not one."

"Did she have many friends?"

"Yes, she had plenty of them. All sorts of kids came knocking for her. Some of them went to school with her, some she knew from the church. She was always there, you know? Always helping out with the kids club. She even used to serve drinks at the coffee

and cake mornings after the sermon. That's what these are for."
She gestured at the tray of cooling cakes that Nillson had noticed
Cruz eyeing greedily.

"So, she was comfortable in the church?" Nillson said. "Is that
fair to say?"

"Oh, yes. We all are. It's like a family., and to be honest, I don't
know what I'd do without them."

"You still attend the same church?" Nillson asked.

"Of course. I mean, it took me a while to go back. But when
he did himself in, well, there was nothing stopping me. And I'm
glad I did. He was replaced by Miss Greaves. She's still there now.
Lovely lady, she is. That's what this place needed. A female
rector. Somebody who can empathise with what we've all been
through."

"Well, I'm glad you managed to keep your faith, at least,"
Nillson said.

"He took my daughter from me," she said clearly, leaning on
the kitchen worktop for support. "All I have left is God. He can't
take Him from me."

The statement was said with such vigour that Nillson was left
searching for a new line of questioning to keep the momentum
going.

"Do you mind telling me what happened?" she said, and the
elder of the women closed her eyes, like she had been expecting
her to ask, and dreading it. "I'm sorry to ask, but sometimes
things can be missed. Details that might be important."

"I can assure you no detail was missed–"

"Even so, it could help us, Mrs Rimmell. It could bring you
some kind of closure. And I know that's no consolation for what
you've been through, or who you've lost, but that's all I can give. I
wouldn't ask if it wasn't important. And if we didn't think we
stand a chance of bringing Charlotte justice, then we wouldn't
have knocked in the first place. We'd have just tossed the file onto
the pile with all the other grieving families living with open-ended

questions. But we do, Mrs Rimmell. We do think we have a chance. But we need your help."

She turned the cooker off, laid an old tea towel over the cakes, and untied her pinny, hanging it on the kitchen door before taking a seat at a small kitchen table.

Nillson and Cruz remained standing and kept their distance until invited to come closer.

"I suppose you're right," Mrs Rimmell said softly. "I suppose I should be grateful you're here."

Nillson gestured for Cruz to take notes then moved into Mrs Rimmell's eye line.

"Charlotte was helping out at the Fun Run, kind of like a marathon, but just around the local villages. You know? Never a day goes by when the church isn't in need of donations."

"I see," Nillson said, watching as Mrs Rimmell stared out of the window into the overgrown garden, perhaps remembering the days when Charlotte was a young girl playing out there, with a skipping rope maybe, or even on her first bike.

"It was a beautiful day. I remember it, of course. Not hot like today, but the sky was clear blue and the breeze off the sea was cool. Perfect weather for a running race, I imagine," she said thoughtfully. "Charlotte was one of the crew helping behind the scenes, as she always was. She guided cars into the little car park then, when the race was underway, she and her friends got on their bikes and raced to various positions around the course."

"Marshalls?" Nillson said. "To guide the runners?"

"Yes, that's right. Marshalls. Anyway, the race finished. I can't even remember who won now. But I remember Charlotte's friends coming back without her. I asked them why Charlotte wasn't with them, and they just said she wasn't at her station, so they thought she'd already come back."

"But she hadn't?" Nillson said, and for a moment she thought she saw Mrs Rimmell's lower lip tremble.

"I knew something was wrong. I knew it. I don't know if it

was mother's instinct or what, but I knew something had happened. But nobody seemed to want to help. I kept asking people where she was, Neil in particular, and he just said that she was probably on her way back, and not to worry."

A silence filled the room and even the aroma of freshly baked cupcakes had waned, leaving Nillson with a sickly feeling in her stomach.

"They found her later that day, hanging from a tree not ten feet from where she was positioned. My baby. My poor, poor baby."

"Mrs Rimmell, I'm sorry–"

"You can't shake it, you know? You shake yourself out of it. You can't force yourself not to wonder how she suffered. You can't force your mind to think of something else, happier times. It doesn't work like that."

"How did Neil Barrow become a suspect?" Nillson asked, hoping to move the still grieving mother away from memories of that awful event.

"It was after he'd done what he did to himself, thankfully. Heaven knows what I might have done, not to mention the others in the village."

"Did they find something on his person?"

"No, not on his person," she replied, shaking her head. "He was seen with her. With my little girl."

"What were they doing?" Nillson asked. "Sorry, I know this is difficult."

"No, it's fine. I can talk about it. I have to," she said. "It helps, you know?"

"I think so," Nillson said, unable to imagine the agony she must have been living with.

"She was seen coming out of his office a few days before, and given that nobody could find him when the race had ended, well, even I could have worked that out," she said. "Then they found some photos on his computer."

"But the photos weren't enough to charge him, I suppose?" Nillson said. "I mean, he obviously shouldn't have had photos, but from the perspective of the CPS, they wouldn't prove he was responsible for her death."

Mrs Rimmell had clearly heard it all before and held a bitter resentment towards the force and all it stood for as a result. She continued her monologue, lost in her own little world of hurt.

"They couldn't pin him down. He was nowhere to be seen at the end of the race, but again, that doesn't prove he was with Charlotte. There was nothing definitive placing him there, only reasons to be suspicious. That's how the last detective framed it for me to understand. That was nearly ten years ago, now. He should have been found guilty for the photos alone. Photos of my Charlotte. Makes me sick, it does."

It was Nillson's experience that told her the clock had struck on the interview, some kind of intuition that develops only after years of service and experience, witnessing grief being relived.

"Mrs Rimmell, I have one more question, and I'm sorry to ask," Nillson began, and Mrs Rimmell looked up from the kitchen table and wiped the flood of tears now converging, ready to break free. "Neil Barrow had a son. We need to find him. There's no record of him anywhere since..."

She hesitated.

"It's okay, you can say it," Mrs Rimmell said.

"Since Charlotte was killed."

"He left shortly after, I believe, and who can blame him?" she said. "There was no way he'd have survived a day here after what his father did. He would have been lynched."

"Do you have a name for him?" Nillson asked. "There's no mention of it anywhere, only that Neil Barrow had a son."

"It still amazes me to this day that Neil Barrow was even allowed to conceive when so many good people struggle. But I suppose He knows best," she said, with a flick of her eyes upwards to indicate that she was referring to God and not Neil

Barrow. "The boy had an unusual name. Queer sort of fellow, he was."

"Do you remember it?" Nillson asked.

"Ah, yes," she said, content she had found him amongst the mass of memories she had stored during what must have been the hardest thing any parent has to go through. "Vaughan. Vaughan Barrow."

CHAPTER TWENTY-NINE

The three marched into Mablethorpe Police Station through the rear entrance. It was the DI who had given Freya a hard time who saw them first, and Ben admired the way Freya breezed past him with no sign of retaliation when he offered a backhanded insult.

"Look what the tide washed up. Have you been dredging the coastline again, George?"

They strode past him, stopping momentarily for Larson to poke his head through his office doorway.

"Hart, Samson, meeting room in two minutes, and bring whatever we have on Frank Donovan," he said. "The rest of you, carry on."

He closed the door without waiting for any kind of response from any of them and led them back to the room with the round table. There were no friendly gestures of offering seats or suggesting tea or coffee. It was strictly business.

"Frank Donovan," he muttered, scrawling the name on the whiteboard and underlining it a little overzealously. He drew a line to the side and then scribbled Hayley Donovan's name, circling it like the pentagrams they had seen graffitied onto the church walls. "Any other names so far?"

"Deborah Donovan," Ben suggested. "That's Hayley's sister."

"And Justin," Freya added. "Her brother."

"I know Deborah is still alive and kicking, but what about the brother?"

"Alive, but not quite all there," Ben said, much to the annoyance of Freya who scowled at him. "What?"

"You can't say that. You can't describe somebody like that, just because they're..."

She paused, searching for the right word.

"Because they're what?" Ben asked. "Disabled? Is that the right word?"

"No, he's not disabled. At least, he didn't look disabled."

"Well, what then?"

"Slow?" Larson suggested. "That's what we might have called somebody back in the day. Back when you could do your job and go home without worrying about offending anybody."

"I just think he's a bit challenged, that's all," Freya said. "Let's not offend anybody here. We've got enough on our plates. I don't want us going out there and making off-hand comments that could offend anyone."

"Justin, you say?" Larson said, ready to write the name on the board.

"Yes, Justin Donovan, and there was Deborah's boyfriend too. Trevor."

"Trevor what?"

"Trevor Starr," Ben said. "Two Rs."

"Have you spoken to him?" Larson asked. "Either of you?"

"Me. Only briefly though," Ben said. "He's an overprotective boyfriend, which, to be completely honest, doesn't surprise me when you consider what that family has been through."

Larson added the name to the board and then replaced the cap on the pen.

"Right, then. First things first, let's eliminate the immediate family. Where were they when Hayley died, and can they prove it? Once we're done there, we can move on to Frank Donovan."

They were joined by DS Hart and DC Samson, who dropped a fat file in front of Larson. They took seats on either side of Larson and waited patiently to be brought into the conversation. Larson leaned back in his chair.

"Would you like to take over, DI Bloom?" Larson said. "I get the feeling I've rather hijacked your investigation."

"Okay, I'll run through the facts, so listen carefully. If you have any questions, please wait for me to finish," Freya said. "Deborah Donovan has confirmed the body is that of her sister, Hayley Donovan. The forensic pathologist in Lincoln has also confirmed the cause of death as suffocation. Hayley was found in the marshes at the end of Sea Lane in Saltfleet, fully dressed except for her feet which were bare and badly lacerated. We're led to believe the lacerations were caused by running from her assailant. Finally, there is no evidence of sexual interference, so whatever the motive, at this stage, it is not sexual."

"Any suspects?" Samson asked.

"One so far. Her father, Frank Donovan," Freya said. "He was released from prison a few weeks ago and hasn't checked in with his parole officer for four days. DI Larson, DS Savage, and I managed to locate his belongings in St Botolph's. It seems he's been roughing it in the old church."

"What made you look in there?" Samson asked. "That's at least a mile from the marshes."

"We checked there for two reasons," Freya said. "First of all, Hayley Donovan was found without any belongings – no phone, no purse, no house keys. Nothing."

"So, you figure her belongings are in an old church?"

"No, I figure her belongings are somewhere close to where she was discovered, and the first place to check would be any disused properties, outbuildings, or barns."

"There are two caravan parks close by," Samson said. "What if that's where her belongings are?"

"They might be, and we'll close in on them as we narrow our search," Freya advised.

"So, what next?" Larson said. "How can we help?"

The three locals stared at Freya, waiting for instructions, a far cry from the previous day when she had been met with a solid wall of turned backs.

"Frank Donovan's address," she said. "I presume he was put up in a bedsit when he was released."

"I'll find it," Hart said, in what Ben was soon learning to be her usual no-nonsense way. She reminded him of Nillson.

"If he was hiding out at St Botolph's, he must also have a vehicle of some kind. I mean, it's only a mile or so, but in this heat? Plus, of course, he'd run the risk of being seen."

"Leave it with me," Hart said.

"No need," Samson cut in, and he fished a sheet of paper from his folder. "Before you went out, DI Larson asked me to put names to the vehicle registrations on your ANPR report."

He handed the sheet of paper to Freya, and Ben leaned in to see it. There were three columns, the first of which was the vehicle registrations, the second was the registered owners, and the third was the registered address.

"There he is," Ben said, pointing to the row fourth from the bottom. "Frank Donovan."

Freya slipped the sheet of paper inside her folder.

"You have another copy, I presume?" she said to Samson.

"Of course."

"Good. Can you get me a description of that vehicle?" she said, then turned to Larson. "When we know what he's driving, can we ask uniform to look out for it?"

"Easy enough," he replied.

"Good, that's Frank Donovan dealt with. I'd like to focus on what happened the night Hayley was killed. I've asked the caravan park manager to provide any CCTV footage from the front gate. Ben, can you talk to Pip? Ask her to check the debris found in the lacerations on Hayley's feet. I want to know if Hayley ran bare-foot on the road or not. If there is no road debris, then our search will be narrowed down to the caravan parks. If there is road debris, however, we have a larger problem."

"And what's that?" Samson asked. He leaned back in his chair, smoothed his hair, and stared at Freya the way Ben had seen more than one man stare at her, usually in a bar or a restaurant.

"Well, if Hayley ran along the road, she would have had ample opportunity to knock on one of the neighbours' doors for help."

"So?" he said.

"So, that means she was running to the marsh," Freya said. "Why else would she forego help from countless houses?"

"What else can we do?" Larson asked.

Freya studied the whiteboard for a moment.

"I'd like to add another couple of names to the board," she said. "Vaughan, for one."

"Vaughan?" Larson said.

"Any surname?"

"Not yet," Freya said. "We were hoping one of you might recognise it."

"Why do I know that name?" Larson said.

"Do you have a daughter?" Ben said, at which Larson appeared perplexed.

"No. No, I do not," he replied. "Why?"

"I believe my colleague is referring to the man's promiscuity," Freya said. "Although, I can't see it myself. He looks like he needs a good bath."

"Should I make a note of that?" Samson asked with a grin, clearly to win Freya's affection.

"Who else?" Larson said, standing by the board, and with enough experience of Freya to recognise when she was about to bite. He held the pen up ready to note down a name.

"Stella," Freya said. "Stella Green."

"Stella Green?" Hart said, almost in disbelief. She snatched the Frank Donovan file from Larson's desk and began flicking through the pages. Then she stopped and stabbed her finger at the page. "Here. Stella Green."

"Should that be significant?" Freya asked.

"I would have thought so," Hart replied. "Given that Frank Donovan was charged with her sister's murder."

"Skye Green. Of course," Freya said, looking to one side to focus on an area of wall not adorned with police posters and flyers. "I want to speak to her."

"Stella Green?" Larson said.

"Yes. I want to speak to her," she replied. "I need her address. Can we locate it?"

"Perhaps we should consider more of a strategic approach," Larson said.

"I have considered an approach," she replied, gathering her things. "And my conclusion is that we found Stella Green in Vaughan's caravan earlier today."

"So?"

"So, I gave her ample opportunity to make her identity known, but she withheld information. She even asked about the body," Freya said, jabbing her index finger at him. "And if there's one thing I hate, it's bloody liars."

CHAPTER THIRTY

"That's just bloody weird," Nillson said, as she and Cruz entered the incident room and the doors closed silently behind them. Anderson looked up from her laptop, and Chapman, who was on yet another call, nodded a greeting.

Gillespie, however, remained with his head down and his lank, greasy hair hanging over his face as he pored over printed documents.

"What is?" Cruz said, searching around the room for something out of the ordinary.

"The doors. Where's the bloody squeak?"

"Standing fixed it," Gillespie said. "Get used to it."

"Can't we undo it? Can't we make it squeak again?"

"Trust me," he replied. "If I could make those doors squeal again, I would."

"Were they your early warning for when the boss was coming?"

"Aye, they were," Gillespie said, looking from his document and sweeping his hair over his head.

"Is that why you're actually working and not sitting with your feet up like you normally are?"

"You, Anna," he said, and a grin emerged on his troubled face, "you'll make a fine detective one of these days."

"Such praise from Lincolnshire's finest," Nillson replied, as she took her seat opposite Anderson.

"Finest what?" Gillespie asked.

"Finest slacker," she said. "If ever I feel the need to improve my ability to do absolutely bugger all, and get away with it, trust me, you'll be the first person I call."

"We've all got to be good at something, Jim," Cruz said.

"Aye, that's rich, coming from the shortest detective in Lincolnshire."

"That's what I like to see," Chapman said, as she replaced the handset onto her phone. "A bit of life back in this place."

"I'm not the shortest detective in Lincolnshire," Cruz said eventually, as if the words had only just penetrated his brain.

"Aye, you are," Gillespie said. "You're what? Five foot nothing?"

"I'm five foot six, I'll have you know."

"And how tall is the lovely Hermione?"

"I don't know," he said. "Five foot something."

"Taller than you, though," Gillespie said.

"So? She happens to like shorter men."

"Aye, right," Gillespie mocked. "Chapman? How tall are you?"

"Oh, I don't know," she said. "Five foot seven or eight."

"Depends on what shoes you have on, right?" Anderson said.

"Of course," Chapman said, who famously never wore heels, makeup, or anything more provocative than a thick cardigan in the winter, which she was somehow able to look cute in, Nillson thought.

"Don't even ask me how tall I am," Nillson said. "But Cruz, I'm afraid I might have to agree with Jim on this one."

"Eh?"

"I can't think of a single person shorter than you," she replied. "Aside from Jackie's son."

"Charlie? He's ten years old," Cruz said, which sent Gillespie into a roar of laughter.

"Aye, give it a year or two and he'll be patting you on the head and sending you down to the sweetshop with a twenty-pence piece."

"I'm going to find someone shorter," Cruz said. "Then I'll bloody show you."

"Instead of spending your time scanning through the database," Nillson said, "why don't you scan through the Neil Barrow file and then get down to the evidence locker? I'd like to see the laptop Mrs Rimmell was talking about. The one that belonged to Neil Barrow."

Cruz appeared utterly disgusted at the idea.

"Is there a problem?" Nillson asked, and Gillespie leaned closer to her desk.

"He doesn't like the evidence room," he said.

"You don't have to go inside. Just present the file and tell the duty officer what you're looking for."

"It's not that," Gillespie said, and Nillson could see he was about to burst with laughter. "He can't see over the counter down there. Last time I sent him, he was gone all day. Duty officer didn't even know he was there."

Chapman stifled a laugh, but Anderson didn't hold back, flicking her head backwards in hysterics.

"Oh, right. Very funny," Cruz said. "I'll go and get it. I have absolutely no problem at all, if you must know, Jim. I'm just not looking forward to seeing the images on the laptop."

"Yeah, yeah," Gillespie replied.

"Yeah, yeah, what?" a voice with a deep East Midlands accent said, and Gillespie snapped upright and turned to find DCI Standing in the doorway. "I heard laughter. I was just checking this was still an incident room and not a playgroup."

"It's still an incident room, Guv," Nillson said, feeling the joy get sucked from the room.

"Good. Well then, let's get to work," he replied. "What do we have so far?"

"We've got a ten-year-old murder, a woman who's still grieving her daughter, and the son of a murderer who's been missing since the day his father killed himself."

"Is that it?"

"So far, yes," Nillson said.

Standing looked around the room at everyone, seeming to squint with one eye in a look of confusion.

"Who's missing? Where's Gold?"

"Charlie," Cruz said, almost immediately.

"Charlie who?"

"Her son, Guv. The school phoned, or something. She had to rush out."

"Will she be back today?"

"I'll call her," Chapman said.

"No. No, don't bother. I'll do it myself," Standing said, as he turned to leave the room. "And next time somebody has to go home early, I'd like to know about it. We do have a fire register to maintain, you know, and this is not a turn up when you feel like it bloody playgroup."

He left the room in silence and Gillespie turned around to make sure the doors had actually closed.

"In case anybody was left in any uncertainty, I think what he means is no more smiling or laughing," he said.

"Well, if he's trying to make an impact, he's succeeding," Nillson replied.

"Do you think I should give Gold a heads-up that he might call?" Chapman asked nervously but already reaching for her phone.

"Text her," Nillson replied. "With any luck, she'll be on her way back anyway."

She checked the doors to make sure Standing wasn't peering

through the windows, then caught Anderson wearing a glum expression.

"What's up?" she said.

"Oh, nothing much," Anderson replied. "It's just that I moved here from London and really thought I'd landed on my feet. It's been brilliant. I'm involved in real investigations, not just doing admin behind the scenes while senior officers are out there. It's changing though, isn't it? Even DI Bloom is behaving weird, and she was the one I followed up here. She's the one I wanted to work with, and she isn't even working for this station right now."

"She'll be back," Nillson said.

"I don't know if I can do it," Anderson said. "I worked for someone like him in London. DI Bloom did too. I don't know if I can put myself through it again."

"Do you want to know what I think?" Gillespie said.

"Not really," Nillson replied. "But I suppose you'll tell us anyway."

"I think change happens. It's the natural course of things," he said, which did little to raise a smile on Anderson's face. "It's like a river. The water will find its natural course downhill and out to sea."

"If you have a point to make, Jim, I suggest you make it clearer," Nillson said. "Before the beast from the East Midlands comes back in."

"The point I'm trying to make, Anna, is that by carefully placing a few wee rocks here and there, we can change the course of the river."

"I haven't got a bloody clue what you're talking about, Jim," Cruz said, shaking his head.

"I do," Nillson said, and she lowered her voice and checked the whole team was listening. "He's talking about subterfuge."

"Aye," Gillespie said proudly. "That I am."

"You mean we should deliberately go against Standing's wishes?" Cruz said. "Can you imagine what he'd do? And anyway, how are we going to get away with that? We can't even bloody smile."

"I hate to say it," Nillson said. "But what we need is someone on our side who knows how to manipulate people, a master of manipulation. We need a bitch on our side."

"We need DI Bloom," Anderson said.

"It pains me to admit it, Jenny, but yes."

"I thought you were mad at her?"

"I'm mad at her, yes," Nillson said. "But I still admire her."

"Can't we just have a word with Granger?" Cruz said. "Surely he can have a word with Standing and ask him to go easy?"

"Jackie tried that this morning," Chapman said. "I spoke to her in the ladies. Apparently, Granger said he's just trying to make his mark and that we should do what he asks until told otherwise."

"Then we're on our own," Nillson said as Chapman's phone began to ring. "It's down to us to change the course of the river."

"What's happening?" a voice said from the doorway, and Nillson turned to find Jackie Gold standing there with her phone in her hand. "I feel like I've just walked into the headquarters of the resistance with all the whispering."

"Fun has been banned," Cruz said.

"Standing put his foot down," Nillson explained.

"Plus, DI Bloom and Ben have been sent away," Anderson said. "And Gillespie's been tasked with pointing out all our mistakes."

"So, we're altering the path of the river," Gillespie added.

"You're altering what?" Gold said. "What river?"

"The natural course of things," Nillson added, enjoying the confusion the analogy was causing. "And we're the rocks."

"Anna," Chapman called, and Nillson turned to find her pointing at her desk phone, "DI Bloom is on the line."

"And there's the hand that places the rocks," Nillson said to Gold. "Transfer her to me."

CHAPTER THIRTY-ONE

"Nillson," Freya said, as she accelerated away from Mablethorpe Police Station. "You're on loudspeaker, so be careful what you say about Ben."

"Thanks for the heads-up," she replied, "You're also on loudspeaker, but we'll have to be quick. Standing is on the warpath."

"Oh, how's it going with him?" Freya asked.

"Well, you two have been sent away, Gillespie's been put into an impossible position, the rest of us are working on investigations from decades ago, and to top it off, we're not allowed to smile anymore."

"He's definitely making his mark, isn't he?" Freya said. "Is everyone there?"

"Yes. All of us," Nillson replied. "When are you both due back?"

"As soon as we can close this investigation. We'll be a few days the way things are going, maybe more. It's an impossible task. Thankfully, we've managed to get the local team on our side and even that was like pulling teeth."

The call was silent for a moment and Ben glanced across at Freya, suspicious of the silence.

"Is everything alright?" Freya said.

"Sorry, boss. Listen, what are you doing tonight?"

"Tonight? Nothing. We're not exactly living the dream up here."

"Do you think you could make a call, at seven p.m.?" Nillson asked. "There's something we need to ask you."

"We?" she said. "As in—"

"As in the whole team, boss," Nillson said. "We'll head to the pub or something. Maybe we can find a booth."

"This has the hallmarks of a conspiracy," Freya said, not needing a response. "We'll call you at seven. We'll have to call from the car. Our accommodation has been parked in nineteen seventy-five for some reason."

"Brilliant. Speak then," Nillson said. "Was there something you needed?"

"No," Freya said. "Nothing specific. I was just calling to see how everyone was getting on. You've answered my question. Speak to you later."

She ended the call and ignored Ben's stare.

"Sounds like we're missing all the fun," he said, hoping to tease her into a debate.

"Let's just wait and see what they have to say," she replied.

"Secret phone calls, Freya? What the bloody hell is he doing?"

"He's doing exactly what I said he was doing," she said. "He's managed to get us out of the picture, he's isolated Gillespie who is, believe it or not, his biggest ally, and he's whipped out his iron rod to let them know he's the boss, and before you make a joke about his iron rod, Ben, I am not in the mood for a double entendre."

"I wasn't going to say anything," he said with a laugh. "But I don't envy them. You didn't get to see it much, but when Standing was a DI, he was a right piece of work."

"I've heard the horror stories," Freya said, as they entered Saltfleet. "But like I said, I'd like to see what they have in mind. Hopefully, they're not relying on me to formulate a plan."

"Oh, if I know Anna Nillson like I think I do," Ben said, "she'll have it all worked out."

They turned into Sea Lane and Freya gunned the engine to the end, pulling into the caravan park and slowing to meet the five-miles-per-hour speed limit. A few moments later, they stopped outside Vaughan's caravan.

"He's a full-timer," Ben said, and when Freya looked this way, he explained. "This is his permanent address."

"I didn't think you could live in a holiday home for more than eleven months in a year?"

"Does Vaughan look like the type of man who would worry about that?" Ben said, as he pushed open his door and stepped into the stifling afternoon sun. Freya killed the engine and joined him as he rapped on the door. "Vaughan? Vaughan, open up."

Ben was tall enough to peer through the windows, and he made his way around the caravan searching for movement inside. Eventually, he rejoined Freya at the door.

"Anything?" she asked.

"No, but he's not far away. The TV is on," he said. "I think he might be going somewhere though. There's a bag is on the couch. Looks like he's been packing."

"It's not him we're looking for," Freya said, pulling her phone from her pocket. "She found her recently dialled numbers and hit the green button to make a call, which was followed by a series of beeps announcing she had no service. "Oh, for Christ's sake."

"No signal?" Ben said. "I thought you said it would be nice not to have any signal. Time to think about the investigation, you said."

"Your rhetoric is not endearing, Ben," she said. "She's a local girl. She must have an address nearby. Let's go to the gate. I want to talk to the manager anyway."

They drove to the main gate and parked outside the clubhouse, where a few families were enjoying some afternoon refreshments on some wooden benches – ice creams for the three kids and bottles of beer for the adults. Ben made to leave the car again when Freya stopped him.

"Let's just sit here a while," she said, basking in the air conditioning. "Call Hart, will you? See if she can get us Stella Green's address."

Ben put the call on loudspeaker then set his phone on his knee while Freya watched the holidaymakers toing and froing.

"DS Hart," the voice said when the ringing stopped.

"Hart, it's Ben and Freya."

"Did you find her?"

"No. We're at the caravan park, but she's not at Vaughan's place. We're thinking that she's a local. In which case she must have a house somewhere, or her parents' home."

"Sit tight," Hart said, and the sound of her tapping away at a keyboard followed. Freya caught his attention and pointed to the site manager's office, where Vaughan Barrow was emerging. Ben covered the phone's mouthpiece and was about to say something when Vaughan hugged Mrs Robinson, then turned and made his way into the caravan park carrying a plastic bag which appeared to be straining under the weight of some loose beer cans. "Got it. I've sent it to your email."

Neither Freya nor Ben said anything.

"Hello?" Hart said.

"Sorry, Hart," Ben replied. "Something's just come up. We'll check the address and let you know how we get on."

He ended the call and pocketed his phone.

"That was odd," Freya said.

"Are we going after him?"

"No. No, I think I want a word with our resident site manager," Freya said. "There's more to her than meets the eye, that's for sure."

A few moments later, they were at the door to the site office.

Freya knocked once then entered and found Mrs Robinson behind her desk about to make a phone call. The look on her face when she saw Freya and Ben said it all, and she replaced the handset with a heavy sigh.

"You again?" she said.

"I was wondering if you had the CCTV footage yet?"

"As it happens, I have," she replied. "It's just been sent from our security company."

"May we see it?" Freya asked, as innocently as she could.

"Now?"

"Now seems like a good time."

"For whom? You or me?" Mrs Robinson said.

"That rather depends on the contents, doesn't it?" Freya said, and she strolled over to the desk, pulled up a chair, and crossed her legs.

Ben came to stand beside her and waved the reluctant offer of a chair from Mrs Robinson away. She located the file on a USB stick, clicked a few buttons, and a media player appeared in the corner of the screen. She turned it to face Freya and Ben, then busied herself with the pile of papers on her desk.

Ben leaned forward and clicked the button to make the media player full screen, then dropped to a crouch. The timestamp read eight-thirty p.m on the previous Friday evening.

"Can we speed this up?" Freya asked, and Ben leaned forward to adjust the playback just as somebody knocked on the door behind them. Freya turned to find a man in his forties wearing shorts and a casual, button-down shirt with dark patches under his arms.

"Are you the site manager?" he asked in a gruff tone with an unmistakable London accent, which Freya placed as more East London than West.

"No, I'm a police officer," Freya replied.

"Well, you can help me then," he said.

"Excuse me, can I help?" Mrs Robinson said. "*I'm* the site manager."

"We've had a break-in," he said. "Bloody laptop's gone, and some cash, and they even took a bottle of vodka off the sideboard. I thought this was a family place. Safe and secure, the website says. I only popped down to the shop. I was gone literally five minutes."

Mrs Robinson looked alarmed and ushered him inside.

"Let's sit down, shall we?" she said. "I'll need to take your details and we'll make a formal report to the police."

"The police are here already," he said.

"We're working on a different investigation," Ben said. "But Mrs Robinson is right, a separate report will need to be made."

"Surely you can come and have a look?"

"Look at what?" Freya said. "The space where your laptop was? Or the sideboard where your bottle of vodka used to be?"

"I don't know. Can't you dust for fingerprints or something?"

"I'm sure this can all be resolved quite easily," Mrs Robinson said, trying to stop the conversation from getting heated.

"If you're suggesting we notify our Scene of Crime officers of the event and request they travel down from Hull to fingerprint a caravan all for a missing bottle of vodka, you are gravely mistaken."

"And my laptop," he added.

"There was no laptop," Freya said, turning back to the footage.

"You what?"

"There was no laptop," she replied. "If there had been a laptop, you wouldn't have left it lying around. The same goes for the cash. Forgive me for making a judgement, but you look like an intelligent man. Am I right?"

"What are you saying?" he said. "Are you calling me a liar?"

"No, I'm calling you an opportunist, much the same as the individual who saw your caravan window open, reached in, and snatched the bottle of vodka. You wanted to complain but you realised that asking Mrs Robinson here to act on such an insignificant crime would be both unrealistic and a waste of time. However, adding weight to the claim that your caravan was broken into and robbed of a laptop and some cash would provide your request for action much more plausible."

"Eh?"

"What make was your laptop?" Freya said as she watched the footage scroll by.

"I don't know. It's just a laptop."

"How much cash was there and where did you hide it?" she asked.

"Two hundred quid, give or take," he said. "I stuffed it in my suitcase under my clothes."

"And the TV is still there?"

"Yeah, I suppose so."

"As is the microwave, I presume."

"Well, yeah."

"Then I maintain that you are an opportunist," she said. "Any individual with the gumption to break into a property will do so for one of two reasons – to feed a habit, be that drink or drugs, or because they are a full-time thief. The individuals who are looking to feed a habit are usually opportunists who will not spend time rifling through bags and cupboards. They are magpies. They see something shiny, and they take it. Gone in a matter of seconds. Professional thieves, however, will watch a victim over a period of time to understand their behaviours and routines in an effort to assess their vulnerabilities."

"Their what?"

"How vulnerable they are, sir," Freya said. "For instance, would you prefer to be caught in the act by a frail, old lady, or by my colleague here?"

"The old lady," he said, looking perplexed.

"Precisely. Therefore, given that you are at least six foot two inches tall, weighing somewhere in the region of fifteen stone, and that you were out of the caravan for a matter of minutes, I can only assume the perpetrator was the former," she said. "The opportunist looking to feed a habit who aims to be in and out in a matter of seconds. Thus, my claim that you did not lose a laptop or any cash, but you may have left a window open to keep the caravan cool, while you popped to the shop to buy some kind of mixer to go with said vodka, seems the most likely order of events."

He stared at her, suddenly worried.

"Am I right?" she asked.

He looked up at Mrs Robinson, who appeared as dumb-founded as he did.

"I'll pop back later," he said, backing out of the office. "I'll just double check I haven't misplaced the cash."

"And the laptop," Freya said. "Don't forget that."

"Yeah. And that," he said, as he backed into the doorframe.

Freya hit the button to stop the playback and inhaled the stale air, sensing both Mrs Robinson and Ben were staring at her.

"Let's take a copy of this," she said to Ben. "It'll give us something to do tonight. It's not like this place has any internet to keep us amused."

CHAPTER THIRTY-TWO

With the CCTV footage on a USB stick in Ben's pocket, they climbed back into the car, but when Freya pulled out of the holiday park and sped along Sea Lane, Ben began to question where they were going.

"I thought you wanted to see Vaughan?" he said.

"I do."

"He's in his caravan. We just saw him heading that way with a bag full of beer."

"I know."

"Right," he said, more than a little perplexed and growing increasingly agitated with Freya's attitude. "I guess we're going the long way round then? Unless, of course, there's something else on your mind."

It was only when Freya pulled into a side street that Ben understood.

"We're going to see Deborah then, are we?"

"Correct," she said.

"Great. As long as we're on the same page. I mean, I'd hate to be in a position where I'm guessing what happens next."

"Heaven forbid," she replied, bringing the car to a stop outside the Donovan house.

Ben stared at her and marvelled at how she could keep a straight face.

"Because that could seriously affect my ability to play a key role in this investigation, couldn't it?" he said.

"We now have a confirmed ID," she said. "And we have a suspect. But what we haven't done, due to the way this investigation has played out, is eliminate the immediate family. Deborah Donovan should be home by now, so that's what we'll do."

"You're going to go in there a few hours after she's just seen her sister's dead body and ask where she was on Friday night?"

"Not I, Ben, we," Freya said. "And her boyfriend. And the weird brother. *We* are going to ask them all where they were, what they were doing, and who can corroborate their stories."

"Brilliant," Ben replied, as he shoved open the door. "You know, this day just keeps getting better and better. And what about Stella Green? An hour ago, you were ready to rip her throat out for not being honest with you."

"I should imagine that by the time we're done here," Freya said, speaking to him across the bonnet of her car, "Hart will have sent you the address. Which means that we can go and pay her parents, or whoever it is, a visit before going home, cooking a nice meal, and settling down to watch the latest episode of Beachview Holiday Park."

"I hear this week's episode is quite dull. Nothing more than a load of tourists coming and going through the front gate," Ben said.

"That's what I heard, too," she replied, as she walked toward the front gate. "Still, it would be a shame to miss it. Come on, chop chop."

"Yep, chop chop indeed. So many lives to ruin and so little time to do it in," Ben said.

The door opened before they had knocked and Trevor Starr stared down at them, his face a picture of disquiet.

"You again?" he said. "Don't you think you've done enough damage for one day?"

"Actually, no," Freya said, as she walked straight past him before he could complain. "The day is still young, and I still have plenty of questions to ask."

He watched her enter the living room where they had spoken to Deborah earlier, and then he turned back to Ben.

"Is she always like this?" he said. "Does she ever wait to be invited into a house?"

"If she waited, I'm afraid she'd spend a lot of time standing on doorsteps," Ben said.

"And some of my questions are for you," Freya said from the living room door with a finger pointed directly at Trevor. "So don't run away just yet."

"May I?" Ben said, with one foot on the welcome mat.

Trevor stepped out of the way, shaking his head in dismay.

"Does she even know what Deborah is going through?"

"I often wonder if she has empathy at all," Ben told him flatly. "But then she has a proven track record of catching killers, so I find myself asking which is more important, people's feelings or justice for the families of the killer's victims?"

Trevor stared up at him, processing the statement and searching for an answer in Ben's eyes.

"She's bloody rude," he said, closing the front door and leaving Ben alone in the hallway to find his own way.

He entered the living room and found Deborah as he had left her, sitting with her head in her hands being comforted by Freya.

"Ben, could you take Mr Starr into the kitchen, please?" Freya said.

"What's this about?" Starr asked, placing a hand on Deborah's shoulder.

"You'll be making a statement," Freya told him, as she

prepared her notepad with total indifference to his tone. "My colleague will explain."

"A statement?" he said.

"That's right," Freya replied, and Deborah looked at her, horrified that her ordeal must continue. "It's a formality, I'm afraid. We have to understand where you all were when Hayley died so we can eliminate you from our investigation."

"I was at the church," Starr said.

"So, you should be okay, then," Ben said, coaxing him away with a tug on his arm. "Like she said, it's just a formality."

"Deborah?" he cried, holding onto her shoulder. "Do you need me to stay?"

"Deborah will be just fine," Freya told him.

"Why can't we stay? I want to make sure she's okay."

"Because I want to make sure that each of your responses to our questions is not influenced in any way by the actions or words of other parties, Mr Starr. Like I said, it's a formality, and if you're going make this difficult, we can always do this down at the station."

"The station? The bloody police station? She's just lost her sister. What's the matter with you, you heartless—"

"That's enough," Ben said, and he gave the man a hard shove into the hallway.

"You're treating us like bloody criminals, mate."

"No, you're treating us like we're the enemy," Ben explained, as he closed the kitchen door behind them. "And what's more, you're making it harder for us to do our jobs, namely, find the individual responsible for killing Hayley and building a case to prosecute them. Now, we can do this the easy way, or we can do this the hard way, and quite frankly, the mood she's in, if I were you—"

"Yeah, yeah, I get it," Starr said with obvious reluctance. "She's not going to upset her even more though, is she? I feel like I should be in there, you know? Supporting Debs."

"She's a detective inspector with decades of experience. I'm guessing this is your first experience in a murder enquiry?"

He shrugged.

"Good," Ben said. "So, let's just take it easy. Less of the shouting, less of the aggression, and we'll be out of here in no time."

"I just don't get why you have to ask us where we were," Starr said. "It's not like we had anything to do with it, is it? We're family. We love her. Loved her... You know what I mean."

"You'd be amazed at how many murders are carried out by family members," Ben told him calmly. "And as for why we need to do this, can you imagine if we identified a suspect that had a motive, the means, and the opportunity, and even confessed to the crime, and then when it went to court, the defence argued that nobody had even asked where the victim's close family were at the time of the murder? Can you imagine how that would go down?"

Starr stared at the floor, red-faced.

"Like a lead balloon," finished Ben. "The case would be dismissed in a heartbeat, and all that work, all those hours invested into bringing you and Deborah justice..." he said, as he mimed a popping balloon, making a gentle popping sound for effect. "Gone. Wasted. Over. Poor old Deborah would have to spend the rest of her years knowing that the man responsible for killing her sister is out there somewhere, and all because her bigmouthed boyfriend couldn't keep his trap shut for long enough to let the detectives do their jobs."

"You sound just like her," Starr said, and he nodded at the door.

"I've worked with her long enough," Ben said. "Besides, we do this every day. How many people like you do you think I've met? How many people try to stand in our way, and then complain when progress is slow?"

Starr said nothing. Instead, he pulled a stool from beneath the breakfast bar and made himself comfortable.

"You said you were at church," Ben said. "Which one?"

"All Saints," he replied. "Just down the road."

"Was this a regular service?" Ben asked. "It was late on a Friday night."

"No, it's not a regular thing. I mean, I go there a lot. It's not unusual for me to be there. But this wasn't a service. A few of us are getting ready for a fundraiser. It's a sponsored bike ride. You know? Setting tables up and preparing leaflets and stuff."

"And can I have the name of somebody who can corroborate that?" Ben asked.

"Sure," he said, with a casual shrug. "Jessica. Jessica Hunt. She was there. So was her mate, Dawn. I'm not sure of her last name."

"Where can I find Jessica? Do you have her address?"

"Not to hand. But it's the big house on the right as you come into the village. The one with all the trees."

"I know it," Ben said, recalling being impressed by the property on more than one occasion. He made the notes and slapped his notebook closed, listening for the hum of voices in the next room. "How did you two meet, anyway?"

"Debs and me?"

Ben nodded. "She seems like a nice girl."

"She is," Starr said with genuine affection. "So was Hayley. Justin too. They're all nice. They've just been through it, that's all."

"So?" Ben said. "How did you meet?"

"At the church," he replied. "I don't seem to have much time for anything else."

Ben stared at him, purposefully saying nothing to encourage him to give a little more.

"She told you about her dad, right?" Starr said, and Ben nodded. "Well, he was our vicar."

"He was your vicar?" Ben said, then quieted his voice in case Freya and Deborah could hear. "So, you knew Skye Green?"

"Kind of. I'd only been in the parish a few months. It took me a while to build up the courage to..." He paused. "You know?"

Ben shook his head.

"Join a new church," Starr said. "I was terrified."

"Of going to church?"

"It's not just that," Starr explained. "We moved from Kirkby. Lived there my whole life up until then, but Mum was keen for us to get away. Her and Dad split, see."

"Divorced?" Ben asked.

"Not really. Dad just disappeared. Went to work one day and never came home."

"And you've never heard from him?" Ben said, imagining what life would have been like had his father done the same to him.

"Nothing. They weren't *happy* happy," Starr said. "You know? I mean, they argued. It was never a nice place to be. Home, like."

"That must have been awful," Ben said quietly, hoping to coax more from the man and mildly amused at something his own father had once told him about the people who shout the loudest often being the ones with something to hide.

"That's when I started going to church," Starr said. "I just went there once to get away from the shouting, you know? That was when I first discovered what God is about. For me, anyway. I suppose everyone has a different version. We all have reasons for faith."

"Or reasons not to have a faith," Ben added.

"Right," Starr said, with a sympathetic smile. "I got talking to somebody. It was nice, you know? To talk to someone without shouting. Not to have to worry that somebody was going to burst through the doors in a fit of rage. It was calming, and I found my reason for God."

"Which is?" Ben asked, and Starr looked at the floor, as if he was ashamed of disclosing his views.

"I believe," he began, "that our religion began with Jesus and Mary, and all the things the Bible tells us, and slowly, we began to visualise God, you know? Like the pictures you see of Him in the heavens and us mortals below, sinning and repenting."

"Right," Ben said, intrigued as to where he was going.

"And through the ages, that picture of God, an almighty being looking over us, has kept us on the straight and narrow, given us purpose, something to believe in, and quite frankly, kept us sane. But in this day and age, with so many opinions flaunted on the internet, it's hard to maintain that image. For me, anyway. But that doesn't mean I don't believe. I believe more than ever. I believe, not that God is a being, a singular entity, but a mass. A mass of collective good. Does that make sense?"

"Honestly?" Ben said. "No. You've lost me."

"Okay..."

"I'm sorry. I'm not religious."

"It's fine. Seriously," he said. "It's hard to explain but think of it like this. I believe that there is so much evil in this world, so many bad people doing terrible things, that simply to be a good person just isn't enough. I mean, you're a good bloke. I bet you'd help an old lady across the street, right?"

"Yeah, of course."

"But you wouldn't push one down the stairs?"

"What? No, of course not."

"Which one of those two scenarios stand out as unusual?" Starr asked. There was a confidence to his posture, and Ben felt his clutches on the upper hand begin to slip.

"The second one," he said. "Pushing the old lady over."

"Right. So, to be a good person, to do what society expects of us, just isn't enough, is it? Being a good person is the baseline of how we *should* behave. Which makes it passive behaviour. Being good isn't going out of your way to be good or bad, it's just the norm. So that means that when these terrorists and whatnot do evil things, or sin, as some might call it, they stand out. They *actively* make a point. They're doing the devil's work, and everyone knows it."

"And being a good person isn't making a point?"

"No. Of course not. Nobody blinks an eye at it, do they? Being good is not enough to make a stand against those doing the devil's work. And that's where the Church comes in."

"The Church?"

"Yes, exactly," he said, his gestures growing in excitement. "For me, God is not a single entity, it's all of us. It's our congregation, our families, our society, and the more of us who take a stand and actively do good things, actively do God's work, the larger our God becomes, and the stronger we'll be to fight the evil in this world."

Ben gave the man's perspective some thought. He was entitled to an opinion, of course, but Ben doubted if altering the image of God would go down well with those for whom *that* image had helped them through hard times.

"I'm going to need to talk to Justin," Ben said, and after a few awkward seconds, he jabbed his thumb over his shoulder. "We'll need his statement."

"I didn't mean to scare you," Starr said. "I know my views aren't orthodox. But I believe. That's the main thing. I have faith, and after all, it's faith that gets us through each day."

"I'm in no position to judge," Ben said, as he opened the kitchen door. "Where can I find him?"

There was a disappointment in Starr's eyes like he had failed to convince Ben but was sure that, given more time, he could have.

"I'll get him," he said softly. "He's easily frightened."

CHAPTER THIRTY-THREE

Justin Donovan was, from his appearance, an ordinary young man. But when Ben looked closer, there was a suffering in his eyes that he recognised as the long-term endurance of pain or anguish. He likened the look to a particular boy that had been in Ben's year at school who was the brunt of every joke, tease, and taunt the bullies cared to voice. There hadn't been a day that went by in those days when the poor boy hadn't received at least three punches to deaden his arms, and at least twice that of verbal abuse, mostly about the boy's mother or some slant against his sexuality.

Boys can be cruel, as can girls, Ben had learnt. But nothing compared to the harsh realities people like Justin had to suffer when those tormented few ventured into the workplace, not filled with confidence and ambition, as they should have been, but subdued, forlorn, and, often, cowering wrecks.

"My name's Ben," Ben said gently when Trevor brought him into the kitchen. "I just need to ask you a few questions, but don't worry. This is just a formality, a process we have to follow. You have nothing to worry about, okay?"

Justin nodded, averting his gaze to a cracked floor tile as if he hadn't noticed it before.

"Now, Justin, can you tell me where you were last weekend? In particular, on Friday night?"

He glanced once at Trevor, who was on the far side of the broad kitchen filling the kettle.

"Here," Justin said, in a robotic monotone not too dissimilar to that of a teenage boy.

"You didn't go out at all?" Ben asked.

"He doesn't go out. We told you," Trevor said, and Ben caught himself from shutting the man down and potentially scaring Justin.

"Perhaps Justin and I could have a few moments alone?" Ben said, in a way that left very little room for argument.

"I think it's best if I stay. Justin doesn't do well with strangers," Trevor said, then turned to the young man. "Do you, mate?"

"I'm not surprised," Ben said, then he turned to the young man and gave his shoulder a squeeze. "We'll be alright on our own, won't we? You and me?"

The boy looked absolutely terrified and turned to Trevor for some kind of support.

"Look, he doesn't go out," Trevor said. "He's scared of his own shadow. If you need some sort of proof he was here, then you can ask Deborah. She was here too."

"She told us she was working nights," Ben said. "At the local supermarket."

"Well, yeah. But that's not until nine o'clock. She was here until then, and he's hardly likely to have gone out at nine o'clock, is he? Besides, I got home around midnight, and you were in then, weren't you?"

"Is that right, Justin?" Ben asked. "You were here with Deborah until nine o'clock?"

"I was in my room," Justin said.

"All night?" Ben asked, and the lad nodded.

"What were you doing in your room all night? Do you play video games?"

"He's got fish," Trevor said, and Ben sighed.

"Is that right, Justin? Do you have a fish tank?"

"It's an aquarium," Trevor said. "Huge, it is."

"Really? I like fish, too," Ben said. "Could you show me it?"

Justin glanced sideways again, looking for help from Trevor, but Ben leaned forward, just slightly, and made contact with those sad eyes.

"Can I see your fish?"

Eventually, the boy nodded, and Ben seized the opportunity to lead him from the room.

"I think it's best if you stay here," Ben said to Trevor. "You've been a great help."

Justin was already in his room by the time Ben had climbed the stairs. He made no attempt to tidy up or pull the bedsheets into place. Instead, he just stood beside a six-foot-long aquarium that covered half of one of the walls.

"Wow," Ben heard himself mutter, and for the first time, he saw something other than fear in the boy's eyes. He saw pride. "This is incredible. Did you do all this?"

Ben dropped to a crouch to study the aquascape Justin had created using mangrove roots, red and green leafed plants, the names of which Ben hadn't a clue, and different shades of sand. Red Cherry shrimp dotted the grassy areas and tiny fish with brightly coloured stripes meandered through the maze of roots and plant life, brazen in the absence of predators.

"It's what I do," Justin said.

"Well, you're very good at it," Ben said. "This is one of the nicest aquariums I've seen. Where did you get all the stuff?"

Justin looked at him, wide-eyed.

"I mean, if you don't like leaving the house, how did you get all of this?"

"Online, mostly. Trevor sometimes brings me stuff too."

There seemed to be something different to watch everywhere in the tank. It was full of life.

"And this is what you do is it? You tinker with this?"

Justin shrugged.

"I like to watch them."

"And that's what you did on Friday night, is it? When your sister had gone to work?"

"I suppose," he mumbled.

"And when Trevor came home? Were you still awake?"

"I don't know."

"Sorry?" Ben said.

"I'm not sure," Justin said. "I was here. I didn't go downstairs."

"So, you didn't hear Trevor come home?"

"I don't think so."

"And you just sat in here, all night, watching your fish, did you?" Ben asked.

"I like it," he replied. "It calms me down."

"Okay," Ben said, taking the opportunity to take in the rest of the room. There was very little other than a desk with a laptop, an unmade single bed, a bookshelf, and the aquarium. The wardrobes were built-in, and closed, and the walls were painted an off-white without a single picture, poster, or photo on any of them.

"Tell me about your relationship with Hayley?" Ben asked.

Again, he shrugged. "I suppose. She was nice. She..." He paused like he was frightened to finish the sentence.

"She what?" Ben pressed, and Justin stared back at him, the fear draining back into his eyes.

"She understood me. I could talk to her."

Ben listened, digested, then found nothing to say that would add, only takeaway.

"Thanks for showing me your aquarium," he said finally. "I'll leave you to it."

Justin smiled graciously, the type of smile somebody pulls when they just want the interaction to end.

"If you do want to talk about her," Ben said, "about Hayley, you can call me. I'll always listen."

He offered the lad a card, but when Justin kept his hands in his pockets, Ben placed it on the desk. That was when he saw Hayley's sketchbook. He hadn't noticed it before as it was atop a small pile of books.

He caught Justin staring at him, as if merely possessing the sketchbook was a crime.

"I just wanted to be close to her," he said finally.

"That's okay," Ben replied. "We all have our own ways of dealing with grief."

He left the room and descended the stairs. In the hallway, he put his ear to the living room door and heard faint sobbing from inside, so he returned to the kitchen and found Trevor leaning on the kitchen worktop cradling his cup of tea. He watched Ben carefully, seeming to study him as he walked.

"Alright?" he said.

"He's fine," Ben replied.

Trevor sipped his tea and then placed it on the worktop.

"We just worry about him, that's all," he said. "He's fragile."

"Deborah mentioned," Ben replied, then checked over his shoulder to make sure Justin hadn't followed. "She said he's tried to harm himself a few times."

"That's right. That's why we worry about him."

"Why?" Ben said. "I mean, what made him do that?"

"Who knows? I've tried taking him to church a few times, but ever since..." He stopped mid-sentence, letting the silence speak for itself. "Well, it's understandable, isn't it? With a dad like that, it's impossible for him to trust in God, whichever image of him you hold dear."

"Has he always been like that?" Ben asked.

"As long as I've known him," he said, then saw the next question in Ben's face. "Which isn't that long, really. I got to know Deborah at the church. Then, after what happened, I wanted to help. She lost all interest in the place. So, me, being me, brought the church to her. Not through sermons or anything like that. But I could see she was hurting and, well, I couldn't just walk away. I just showed her some kindness. That's where it all starts, isn't it? Being kind? Besides, the church didn't walk away from me when I needed help the most."

"She's lucky to have you," Ben said. "So is Justin, for that matter."

"Well, they help me as much as I help them," he replied, then laughed a little. "We're all a bit messed up here. More so now."

"She'll need you," Ben said. "This has hit her hard."

"Yeah. Yeah, I know," he said. "Sometimes, time is the greatest healer. Faith is there just to ease the pain. To hold our hands on the journey."

The living room door opened in the hallway and Ben leaned out of the kitchen to make sure it was Freya. It was, and she gave him the nod that they were leaving.

"Look after her, Trevor," he said. "And call me if you need anything. We have people that can help."

"And you'll talk to Jessica, will you?"

"Jessica?"

"Hunt," Trevor said. "I was with her and Dawn on Friday night."

"Oh, yes," he replied. "What was it you were doing anyway?"

"Just planning something," he replied. "Church stuff."

Ben nodded and felt Freya's impatience the way somebody might sense a presence in the room, like a weight on the mood.

"I'll be in touch," Ben said.

"Thank you," Trevor said. "I think we have all the help we need right now. We're tight. We like to keep it that way."

CHAPTER THIRTY-FOUR

"Well?" Freya said when they were in the car and heading away from the Donovan house. "What did you learn?"

The question went unanswered, and Freya glanced across at Ben only to find him engrossed in his phone.

"Deborah was telling me about her job," she said. "She's a vampire. She sucks the blood out of late-night customers."

"Eh?" Ben said dozily. Then, when what Freya had said was finally digested, "What are you talking about?"

"I was just trying to get your attention," she replied.

"Sorry. Hart sent through Stella Green's address. I was trying to find it on the map."

"Am I going in the right direction?" Freya asked, and Ben looked up, checked their surroundings, and then sighed.

"Sea Lane," he replied.

"As in, the same Sea Lane—"

"That leads to the marsh, yes," he said. "And the same one the holiday park is on."

"Well, that makes things easier, doesn't it? Let's pay her a visit, and then, with any luck we can go and enjoy a dinner and a movie."

"Oh, don't remind me," Ben said. "I bet, if you added up all the hours I've spent watching CCTV footage of one description or another, it would amount to actual days of my life. Not hours. Days."

"Ditto," she said. "But it's all we've got so far. From what we saw earlier, we should see anybody who either left the park or walked passed it towards the marshes."

"Yeah, right, about fifty dog walkers and some joggers. Not to mention the odd couple heading over there in search of a private moment under the stars."

"Those are the ones we want," she said. "The late-nighters. The people out there in the dark who might have seen something, or somebody."

"Right, and how many of those are involved in affairs? They're hardly likely to hold their hands up and risk everything. You know what they're like. How many times do we come across affairs? It's always the same."

"You're looking at it the wrong way," she told him. "If we can identify someone who has no good reason for being there other than to meet their lover, then we have leverage."

"And there it is," Ben said, slapping his thigh for good measure. "The low blow. Destroyer of lives."

"I prefer catcher of killers," she said, setting free the smirk that was dying to spread across her face. "Whatever it takes."

"Here it is," Ben said, pointing at a bungalow set back from the road. Freya pulled to one side, checked her mirror, and then reversed the thirty yards until they stopped outside the house. "No upsetting anybody. Just see if you can do it. You might even feel good about it."

Freya unclipped her seat belt and let it slide across her body, watching his eyes follow its path.

"One day," he said, "I'd love to get inside your head. Just one day. That's all I need."

"You wouldn't want to go there," she told him as they climbed from the car and met over the bonnet. "The truth is, I don't think you'd ever look me in the eye again if you knew what my sordid little mind is capable of conjuring."

The front garden was plain but tidy, like the owner had invested the least amount of effort to ensure their house wasn't letting the street down but had little interest in winning garden of the year.

Freya pressed the doorbell, then stood back to glance at Ben, who was still smirking, either at what Freya had said or the idea of being inside her head. She couldn't tell which.

"One day, Ben. One day you'll understand me."

"And I hope that day never comes," he replied, then caught her intrigued expression. "It'll spoil the fun."

The door was opened by a large woman with lank, greasy hair. She wore a long, flowery dress down to her knees with a necklace of coloured, wooden blocks, not unlike the chunks of fudge Freya remembered buying while holidaying in Devon.

"Mrs Green?" she said, and she held her warrant card for the woman to read. "I'm Detective Inspector Bloom. This is Detective Sergeant Savage. I wondered if we might have a word."

"What about?" she asked with the same trepidation many people adopted on hearing those words. "Is it Stella?"

"Partly," Freya said. "Is she in?"

"No," she replied. "No, she's not here much. What's she done? Is it that fella she's been knocking about with?"

"What fellow might that be?" Freya asked, as innocently as she could.

But the woman said nothing, realising her mistake.

"Might we come in?" Freya said.

"Is she okay? You can tell me. Just tell me what's happened."

"Perhaps it's best if we talk inside," Freya explained. "I can assure you; you have nothing to worry about."

She glanced back over her shoulder as if contemplating an excuse to deny them entry. But then the idea of her daughter being in trouble tipped the balance, and she opened the door for them.

"It's a bit of a mess," she said, as if she might follow up with a statement to suggest she was just cleaning, but didn't. It was a blanket statement designed to forewarn them both that this was how she lived.

There was no hallway as such, just a large, open-plan area that Freya thought would be nice after a few hours of tidying and cleaning.

Mrs Green followed them in, limping and breathing heavily, then made a fuss of shoving a pile of clothes to one side for them to sit on the couch. Eventually, she sank into an armchair and caught her breath.

"Mrs Green, I'm sorry to visit you like this. We'll be as brief as possible, only there's been a serious incident and we think Stella might be able to help us with our enquiries."

"How? I mean, she's no angel but–"

"I'm not suggesting she was involved in any way, Mrs Green–"

"Dorothy. It's Dorothy."

"Thank you."

"What makes you think she might know something? Have you spoken to her?"

"Briefly," Freya said. "She happened to be in somebody's residence when we spoke to them."

"Him? Was it him?"

"I'm afraid I can't–"

"It was, wasn't it? That bloody man. I've told her. I've told her he's no good. He only wants one thing. I know his type. Met plenty of them in my day, believe it or not."

"We're not here to judge people, Dorothy."

"No, of course you're not. But mark my words," she said, sweeping her lank fringe back over her head. "Vaughan. That's him, isn't it?"

"Like I said, we're–"

"Yeah, yeah, you're not here to judge anyone, I know. So, she said something, did she? Protecting him, no doubt. She was such a good girl, she was. What was it she said? Is this about the girl they found?"

"I'm afraid–"

"It is. I know it is. Why else would you be here? What did she say?"

"She just made a comment that suggests she wasn't being one hundred per cent truthful with us."

"Go on," Dorothy said.

"She asked questions about the incident," Freya said. "But it was more what she didn't say that I'm interested in."

"What she didn't say? Sorry, I don't understand."

"She failed to tell me she was Skye's sister," Freya said. "Despite us discussing a similar incident."

Dorothy went rigid at the mention of her daughter's name.

"I'm afraid I got the feeling she was playing on her anonymity. There was no surprise."

"No what?"

"No surprise. People are usually surprised to learn that a murder has taken place in their community."

"So, it *was* a murder?" Dorothy said, and her hand shot to her heart, empathising with the family of the deceased. "Oh no. How dreadful for the family."

"Do you see what I mean?" Freya said. "She didn't have that kind of reaction. It was like she already knew what had happened, but for some reason didn't tell me who she was."

Dorothy shook her head in dismay.

"What are you saying?"

"I'm saying there are some striking similarities between the way in which Hayley Donovan and Skye were killed, Dorothy."

"Hayley Donovan?" she said. "*His* daughter? That bloody man's daughter?"

"I thought you should find out from us, rather than through

less informed channels," Freya said. "Is there anything you could tell us that might help us?"

"No," she said softly. "No, I told them everything I know way back when. He had images, didn't he? Frank Donovan. He had images of my Skye on his computer. That's what did it. That's what they said in the trial. That's what put him away."

Freya stared at her, hoping she saw what was coming next in Freya's expression.

Slowly, Dorothy's mouth fell open, and her eyes grew large in a terrible combination of disbelief and horror.

"No," she said, providing her own narrative during Freya's silence. "He's out? Frank Donovan is out?"

"You should have received a letter or some form of communication," Freya said. "That's usually what happens."

Dorothy glanced across at a small telephone table that stood beside the front door, which, aside from a modern, cordless telephone, was home to a stack of unopened letters at least three inches high. It was clear that, should Dorothy have been sent a letter, it was very likely lost in the pile.

She seemed lost, staring from the floor to Freya and Ben, and then to a wilting potted plant in the corner of the room that was in desperate need of some water.

"But why?" she said. "It doesn't make sense. Why would he do that to his own daughter?"

"That little piece of information," Freya began, as she stood and beckoned for Ben to follow suit, "is exactly what has been puzzling me."

They made their way to the front door, and Freya took the opportunity to leave her card beside the telephone.

"In case you want to talk to somebody," she said, receiving a grateful smile in return.

Ben opened the door and stepped outside, and Freya was about to follow him into the late afternoon heat when a hand on her arm stopped her. Dorothy had a pleading look etched into her eyes.

"She's not a bad girl," she said. "My Stella. She's not bad. She just hasn't been right since... Well, you know? I guess she fell off the rails, a little."

"I'm sure," Freya replied.

"If she comes home, I'll call you. I'll make sure she talks to you."

"I'd be very grateful," Freya replied. "And if you do happen to see Frank Donovan–"

"I'll keep my distance. I won't go near him, I promise."

"And?" Freya said, hoping to end on a friendly note.

"And then I'll let you know," she replied. "I dare say if he shows his face around here again, the whole neighbourhood will pounce on him."

"In that case, we'd better find him first," Freya said. "Thank you for your time, Dorothy. You've been a great help. Out of interest, what is it about Vaughan that you're so against? Has he upset you in any way?"

"Upset me? No. I've never met him. Couldn't even point him out if he were standing right here."

"So, what is it?" Freya asked.

"It's just..." she began then faltered. "I've heard things. Things that turn a mother off somebody, if you know what I mean?"

"I think so," Freya said, deciphering the cryptic response as best she could. "I think I know exactly what you mean."

CHAPTER THIRTY-FIVE

"Cruz, talk to me," Nillson said, as she closed her laptop. She pulled her hair grip to release the ponytail she wore, and then set free her hair to release the tension in her scalp that had been slowly building over the course of the day. "What have you found?"

Cruz's face had turned a pale white and the joyous grin he usually bore had somehow dulled.

"It took me an hour just to get Neil Barrow's laptop charged," he said. "It's been sitting in storage for nearly a decade."

"And?"

"And I wish I hadn't bothered. I wish I'd just read the statements and taken the word of the arresting officer."

"Are the images bad?"

"They're not indecent, thankfully," he said. "But these are definitely not images you'd expect to find on a vicar's laptop."

"What do you mean?" Chapman asked, stopping her typing in an instant.

"Well, there's a whole folder here dedicated to Charlotte Rimmell. It's just her doing normal stuff." He turned the laptop for the others to see and clicked through the images. "Look, here she's with a bunch of other girls playing. Here she's drawing or something. In this one, she looks like she's in her choir gown or whatever it's called. They're not indecent."

"But why would he have them on his laptop?" Nillson said.

"And why does he have all those images of her in a single folder?" Chapman added.

Cruz flicked through a few more photos.

"There are dozens of them. It's like he was obsessed."

"What a creep," Nillson muttered. "No wonder he ended his own life. Men like that don't have a particularly nice time in prison; worse so than others."

"There's no suggestion of anything indecent taking place," Cruz said.

"No, there's not. But can you imagine what a jury must have thought? Charlotte is found dead at a church fundraiser, the vicar can't explain where he was, and then they find those images on his laptop. It doesn't look good, does it? Was there a DNA match? What else did they have on him?"

Cruz opened the file and spread the documents out looking for something in particular.

"Here it is," he said, holding up a witness statement. "It reads like somebody saw them both a few days before, a Jane Barker. Said she saw Charlotte coming out of Neil Barrow's office looking upset."

"Right, but was there anything on the body?" Nillson asked.

"No DNA. She wasn't..." he began, then hesitated. "You know?"

"Assaulted?" Chapman said, and he nodded.

"Right. But they did find his footprints in the mud where she was found," he said, holding up the image of Neil Barrow's boot side by side with a cast of a print found in the mud. "And his fingerprints were on her arm."

"On her arm?" Nillson said.

"Yeah. Kind of on her shoulder," he replied and then held up the lab report showing an outline of a human body with the shoulder encircled in red pen. "And then, to top it off, he was nowhere to be seen at the end of the race. All the witness statements from the organisers and the crowd say they didn't see him. Most of them assumed he was just doing something. According to at least three witnesses, he arrived a few minutes after the race had ended looking worried or, as one lady put it, ruffled."

"Ruffled?" Nillson repeated.

"Yeah, his clothes and that," Cruz said. "When the police questioned him, he couldn't say where he was at the end of the race. Then, when the other statements came in suggesting he was nowhere to be seen, the investigating officers looked a little deeper. That's when Jane Barker said she saw Charlotte leaving his office a few days earlier."

"So, they seized his laptop?" Chapman said.

"And his phone. I suppose they were looking into evidence of grooming."

"But she wasn't assaulted?" Nillson said.

"Nope. There's no evidence to suggest so anyway," Cruz said. "He was taken in for questioning but he couldn't explain the photos on his laptop, he couldn't provide an alibi, and he failed to provide a reason for Charlotte being in his office, or why she was upset."

"Yet he managed to end his own life?" Nillson said, seeing a huge flaw in the narrative. "Surely that would have been enough to hold him?"

"Ah," Cruz said, raising his index finger in a manner not unlike that of a TV detective pleased to have captured the imagination of his audience. "That's where the pathologist report comes in. The report states that Charlotte was murdered at or around ten-thirty in the morning."

"So?" Nillson said, looking for some kind of context.

"The race didn't start until ten, and it finished around eleven.

A few stragglers came in afterwards apparently, but for the most part, the race ended at eleven."

"During which time, Neil Barrow was where?" Nillson asked.

"At the start line. He was there at the beginning of the race, he stayed for a while talking to people, then, when they started gearing up for the runners to return, he was nowhere to be seen."

"So why did they investigate him if had an alibi at ten-thirty?"

"Because the pathology report didn't come in until a few days after the statements. They had him bang to rights until the report provided a time of death."

"That's enough to cause reasonable doubt," Nillson said. "So, they bailed him until they could secure a conviction?"

Cruz shrugged and sat back. "Looks that way. But they didn't get a chance to rearrest him. He took his own life hours after being released."

"Hence the open investigation," Nillson said with a sigh. "So, we need to prove that either Neil Barrow killed or didn't kill Charlotte. What we need is to talk to someone who actually ran the race."

"Aha," Cruz said, and he did that annoying thing with his index finger again. "I'm one step ahead of you. The investigating officers interviewed everyone who ran the race. But what they didn't do was analyse that data."

"And I suppose you have?" Nillson said.

"I have indeed," he replied, clearly enjoying the freedom to demonstrate his capabilities without Gillespie picking him apart. "A man named Simon O'Hara won the race, and when he passed Charlotte's spot, she offered him a bottle of water. He remembered it clearly. It's the same story for the first forty-odd runners. They all remembered seeing her there."

"How many runners were there?" Chapman asked.

"Ninety. Not bad for a local church event."

"So at least half of them *didn't* see her at her spot, and I suppose they weren't offered water when they passed?" Nillson said.

"Exactly. I've got a map of the route," he said, holding up an old, photocopied sheet of paper and using a pen to point out the relevant spots. "This is the start and finish line, and this is where Charlotte was positioned. Two-thirds of the way around the course. Bear with me, this is where it gets complicated. Simon O'Hara finished in forty-five minutes, which, when you work out his average speed, means he passed Charlotte at around twenty-seven minutes past ten. But the last person to remember seeing Charlotte at her post would have passed her at around ten thirty-nine, if you use the same calculation."

"That's fine. Pathologists can't determine an exact time of death, even today. There's always an allowable tolerance."

"That's fair enough," Cruz said. "But that means the next people to pass her spot would have passed at around ten forty-something, and they didn't see her."

"But at that time, Neil Barrow was still talking to the crowd at the start line."

"Exactly," Cruz said. "I can't prove Neil Barrow killed her, but I think I can prove he didn't."

"What about the photos?" Chapman asked. "And the prints? And the witness saying she'd been in his office alone?"

"An unhealthy obsession?" Cruz suggested. "But if Charlotte was murdered between ten thirty-nine and ten forty-five and given that her post was at least fifteen minutes away on foot, then it certainly wasn't Neil Barrow who murdered her."

"Oh, for God's sake," Nillson said, tossing her pen onto her desk. "So now we have an even bigger job to do."

"Sorry," Cruz said, as he gathered up the papers into a neat pile and reorganised the file.

"Don't apologise," Nillson told him. "You've done a good job. You might just have saved the reputation of a man. The trouble is, we're going to need to interview everyone involved in an event that took place a decade ago."

"That's ninety runners plus however many people organised it," Cruz said.

"I know. It's a mammoth task, and I expect we're going to have plenty of doors slammed in our faces. But it needs to be done. Pull together a list of the event organisers. We'll start with them."

"Right," Cruz said with a heavy sigh. He flipped open the file again and puffed out his cheeks as he fingered his way to the relevant documents.

"I'd also be keen to talk to the last person who saw her alive," Nillson said. "Do we have a name?"

"Ah, yes," Cruz said with a little excitement, scanning the document before him. "He had an unusual name. Vince something."

"Vaughan?" Nillson said, the name ringing alarm bells in her mind.

"That's it."

"Last name?" Nillson asked.

"Barrow," Cruz said finally, pointing at the sheet of paper. "Vaughan Barrow."

Nillson stared at him, waiting for his brain to connect the two pieces of information.

Then it happened like the flicking of a switch.

"The bloody vicar's son?" he said loudly. "Vaughan Barrow? Mrs Rimmell mentioned him."

"Exactly," Nillson said. "We need to find Vaughan Barrow."

"Something doesn't make sense," Chapman said. "If you can prove it wasn't Neil Barrow, then why did he kill himself?"

"I have a feeling the son will be able to answer that," Nillson said. "And when we find him, that's going to be one of the first things I ask him."

CHAPTER THIRTY-SIX

There had been many an occasion when Ben and Freya had returned to one of their homes after a hard day, flopped into some armchairs, and demolished a bottle of wine, discussing the case with their feet up and eyes closed to the world.

But somehow Buttercup didn't quite offer that same level of comfort. Ben tossed his keys onto the dining table and fell into one arm of the U-shaped sofa, just as he might have done at home. But the old furniture didn't provide the same flex as his armchair, and he groaned at the bruise that was sure to develop on his backside.

"You're like an old man," Freya told him, while she opened a bottle of white wine. She raised the bottle, offering him a glass, at which he nodded, but only after twisting around to inspect his bruise.

"Aren't we going to pay Vaughan a visit?" he asked when she handed him a glass. "I expect he'll be working his way through those beers by now."

"Vaughan can wait," she replied, checking her watch. "We've got to be at the front gate to call the team soon. Just enough time for dinner and some of that movie."

"Oh, bloody hell," he said. "I'd forgotten about that."

"Get it set up," she said. "I'll start dinner. Just go through it and mark the timestamps when there's movement. We can go through each one later."

"It's okay, this isn't my first CCTV playback," he replied. "What's for dinner anyway?"

"Nothing if you don't have the video set up," she said and gave him a teasing wink over her shoulder.

"And if I do?"

"Seared salmon fillet with couscous, asparagus, and garlic mushrooms," she replied, taking a sip of her wine. "I'd like to go over what we know."

"Again?"

"Yes, again. So, we know that nine years ago, Frank Donovan was convicted of murdering Skye Green. Much like Hayley Donovan, she was found asphyxiated in the marshes. Let's look at the similarities between the two murders. DNA wasn't found on either of the bodies, but in both cases, boot prints were found in the mud."

"So, we've got the same MO," Ben said. "Both asphyxiated, and both times the murderer reached in to use the plastic bag, or whatever it was he used."

"Right. The only difference I can see is that Frank Donovan gave himself up the first time around. If you check the file notes, you'll see that he walked into the police station at Mablethorpe two days after Skye's death and surrendered."

"What are you saying?" Ben asked. "Are you expecting him to do a nine-year stretch inside, come out, murder his own daughter, then hand himself in?"

"No. See, here's my problem—"

"Only one problem?"

"Check the boot print from the Skye Green murder against the Hayley Donovan murder."

"Hold on, I downloaded the original lab report while we were in Mablethorpe," he said, then waited for the file to open on his computer and browsed the summary. "Here we go. Right, yes, I can confirm that no DNA was found on Hayley Donovan's body, and no fingerprints either."

"Boot print," she said.

"Alright, alright. Keep your hair on."

He scanned through the file until he found the image of the cast print in the sand. Then he did the same with the old investigation DS Hart had sent.

"They're the same," he said. "Identical boot prints."

Freya poured a healthy glug of olive oil into the pan and held her hand over it to check the heat.

"Are you sure about that?" she asked, busying herself with the preparation of the salmon.

"Positive."

"How can that be?" she said, placing one of the fillets skin-side-down into the pan. "Frank Donovan was in prison for nine years. Unless he wore the same boots that he murdered Skye Green in on his court appearance? And then, surely, the investigating team would have held them as evidence?"

"I'm not following. We've got Frank Donovan, a convicted murderer who left a boot print at the first murder, just released from prison, and now a second body with the same boot print beside it."

"Right, so how has he got those boots? Those exact boots, Ben. The first thing the SIO would have done is confiscate them as evidence. The chances of him getting them back are slim to none."

"So, he didn't kill his daughter? Despite him just being released from prison, breaking his parole duties, and violating his restraining order?"

"Yes," Freya said. "Think about it. Why would he kill his own daughter?"

"I don't know."

"He's hiding in a disused church, Freya. If he wasn't up to no good, you'd think he would find somewhere better to hang out. It's not like this place doesn't have enough bloody caravans. He could have had this one. I'll bet it's only about twenty quid per night, and if it's not then Standing is being ripped off."

"So, tell me why he killed his own daughter," Freya said, as she flipped the fillet.

"Well, I don't know. We need to talk to him."

"Give me some hypothetical reasons," she said. "What could she have possibly done, or threatened to do, to make him do that?"

"Maybe she knew something?" he suggested.

"Maybe, but he's just served nine years for murder. What could she possibly know that would be worse than that?"

He shrugged and felt the balance of the argument tip in her favour.

"So, what's he doing here?" Ben said.

"He's here to see his family, those that will talk to him anyway, and there was only one of them, wasn't there? I mean, Deborah made it pretty clear she didn't want anything to do with him, and as for the brother, Justin, he's in no fit state for clandestine meetings with his ex-convict father."

"Hayley was the only one," he said. All the pieces of information were there, they just needed to be assembled in his mind and aligned with Freya's poor attempt at nonchalance. "But Hayley was killed."

"And now we're beginning to get somewhere," Freya said. "What if she was killed because she knew something? Or more realistically, what if she was killed *because* Frank Donovan was released?"

"That doesn't make sense."

"No. No, it doesn't," she replied. "But it will. I'm sure of it. How are you getting on?"

Ben had increased the playback speed to four times, and every time there was a hint of movement on the screen, he was noting down the timestamps.

"Nearly done for Friday night," he said. "There seems to be a lot of activity in the early evening, then it dwindles. The clubhouse closes at eleven-thirty p.m. and there's a fair amount of activity then. But after that, it's just been one or two. Mostly people standing outside the gate trying to get a phone signal."

"What time are you at now?"

Ben glanced down at the screen then hit pause to read the time.

"One o'clock," he said.

"Take it to three a.m. and we'll work back from there," she said, as she gave the mushrooms a quick flick in the pan to ensure they were suitably covered in the olive oil and garlic. She gave them a quick sprinkle with rock salt before rolling them around the pan and then deftly shared them on the two plates. "Are you ready for this? You haven't touched your wine."

"No, sadly my attention has been hijacked by the world's worst movie and a housemate who dreams up whacky theories on murder suspects, despite the obvious staring her in the face.

"We could always have another bet," she said, as she set the plate down before him, along with a knife and fork.

"No way. Every time I bet with you, I end up either making myself look like a fool, or..." He stopped and shook his head, unable to bring himself to say the words.

"Or what?"

"Or in Paris having my hopes raised to great heights only to come crashing to the ground on my return."

She stared at him with her head cocked to one side, as a Border Collie might wait patiently for its master's command.

"You haven't called Michaela," she said.

"And you haven't called lover boy," he replied. "Whatever his name is."

"I messaged him earlier and told him I'd be in touch when I'm home," she said. "I don't want to set expectations too high, do I?"

"And who said romance was dead? I'll call Michaela tonight," Ben said. "Probably once we're done talking to the team."

"Oh goody," Freya said. "And then I can have you all to myself, can I?"

"You're unbelievable," he said, and the smallest of laughs spilled from his lips.

"Am I? Am I really unbelievable, Ben? Or are you just in denial? Are you just telling yourself that Michaela is the one for you and that you've wasted too much time on me?"

Ben took a forkful of salmon. The skin was perfect, lightly salted and crisp in contrast to the zesty, soft, pink flesh. For a moment, he likened it to Freya, who beneath that hard and arrogant shell was as fragile as the crystal champagne flutes her kind sipped from, with the pinkie finger raised, of course.

The world that moulded her was a far cry from the one in which Ben had been raised, where work involved blood and sweat, and the future was always uncertain regardless of a healthy yield. Although that difference had never been an issue when he had lusted after her, when he had wanted her so badly that he would have sacrificed everything he had worked for, now, the fall from his lofty dreams had knocked some sense into him and the differences were as vivid as the sickly green, nineteen-seventies decor the caravan boasted.

He glanced at his watch then set his knife and fork down just as the video passed the three a.m. point, taking his time to lick any remnants of the salmon from his teeth. He finished with a puck, smacking his lips as if to underline his decision. He let the video roll on a little further, making one last entry before he stopped it, made a note of the time, and then snapped the laptop closed.

"It's time to go and talk to our team," he said. "And then, when we're done, I'm going to call my girlfriend to see how her day has been and to thank her for giving CSI a professional nudge. If you don't want to grow old and lonely, Freya, I suggest you do something similar."

CHAPTER THIRTY-SEVEN

If anything, the evening air was stickier than during the day. It was close, as if a thunderstorm loomed, although the clear sky belied any hopes of a quenching downfall.

"Are we all here?" Freya asked, her eyes closed with the driver's seat headrest taking the weight from her shoulders; the burden of rejection and loss, she masked with casual indifference.

"We are," Nilsson said. "Can you hear us okay? We've had to come to the pub."

"I'm sure Jim put up a fight on that one," Ben added by way of a greeting to his teammates.

"Aye, Ben," came the gruff tones of the big Glaswegian. "I had to get here early just to claim a little booth, you know?"

"And I suppose it was out of the question to pass the time with a lemonade?" Freya said.

"Well, you know how it is. When in Rome, and all that."

"Or the Red Lion," Cruz added.

It was good to hear their voices. Even though it had been just a few days since she had seen them, Freya felt a warmth talking to them, similar to the days when she had been married and away on various courses. From the confines of her hotel room, or the hotel bar, she would video call her husband each night as promised, and his son, Billy, would pop his head into the camera view to offer a big, toothy grin and bellow a whiny, *'When are you coming home?'*

"How's it going up there?" Nillson asked.

"It's hot and sweaty, but we're making slow progress," said Freya. "How about you lot? What's the news?"

A silence followed, long enough for Freya to raise her head and offer Ben a questioning stare.

"Pretty bad," Nillson said. It pleased Freya that Nillson had assumed a leadership role in her absence. The young and feisty woman would go far. Being the only girl with three brothers had given her a competitive edge and a tenacity that had, on occasion, taken a fleeing suspect by surprise. "Something's going on. You two are up there and we're not allowed to contact you. Jim has been tasked with auditing previous investigations to highlight any corners we've cut. And we're working on open investigations from decades ago, which by the way, don't even belong to us."

"Has anyone spoken to Granger?" Freya asked. "I know Gold has, but has anyone else brought his attention to this?"

"No, should we?" Nillson said.

"No. Let's keep it between us. If we flag this to Granger, we'll have eyes on us. For the time being, we're only being watched by Standing, and I can handle him."

"He gave us a mouthful earlier for having a laugh in the incident room, boss," Cruz said. "I mean, if we can't have a laugh, then what's the point? The bloody job's hard enough. I spoke to DI Forest earlier. He said there's room on the CID squad, but I'd still be under Standing."

"You didn't mention that," Nillson said.

"I know, well... It was nothing really. I asked how he was doing, and he just mentioned having a hard time with resourcing."

"Ah, Christ, Gabby," Gillespie said, loud enough for the entire pub to hear. "If you transfer, we'll have nobody to bloody laugh *at*, so we won't even need to be told not to laugh."

"Nobody is transferring," Freya said. "I need you to trust me."

"With all due respect, boss," Nillson said, and Freya felt a pang of regret at her choice of words, "you told us to trust you before. You told us you'd be promoted, and we'd all have opportunities to move up."

"I know," she said. "And I'm sorry. I didn't see that coming. I didn't see Standing coming back. It was never an option when I spoke to Granger about it."

"Yeah, well, we need to do something," Nillson said. "We need him off our backs."

"That's right," Freya said. "That's exactly what we need, and there's only one way to get a man like that off your back."

A few moments of near silence followed, filled only by the background noise of the pub and Nillson's exhale. Freya rested her head on the headrest, picturing the team in a booth in the pub and Nillson's attitude dominating the mood.

"I get the feeling I've lost your confidence, Anna," she said finally, to which nobody said anything for a few seconds.

Another of those long exhales followed, rattling the phone speaker.

"You can't blame me for feeling a little disillusioned, boss."

"No, I can't," Freya said. "May I ask you to trust me on this? Give me a chance to make amends."

"I wouldn't be here if I thought otherwise," Nillson said. "We need all the help we can get, and we need to work together. What we can't have right now is empty promises."

"I can't promise it'll work, Anna, but I do know how we can get Standing off our backs."

"How?"

"Is Jenny there?" Freya asked.

"I'm here, boss," she said, her flat, southern accent prominent among the mix of voices.

"Do you remember DCI Ball from the Met?"

"How can I forget?" she replied.

"Did he ever call you into his office on a reprimand?"

"Of course. I thought he did that to everyone?"

"He did," Freya said. "How did he make you feel?"

"About two inches tall with no hope of promotion unless I grew a pair of testicles and joined his golf club."

"But you did get promoted, didn't you?"

"Barely. I got through my probation and made DC, and I'm still a DC three years later."

"You survived, though, Jenny, and that's the point I'm trying to make. DCI Ball, for all his flaws, was, and probably still is, an outstanding officer. You don't get that far in the Met without having something special about you; the competition is too fierce. Standing, however, is not an outstanding officer. He has somehow managed to make DCI by the skin of his teeth. He's lazy, he's arrogant, and he's not afraid to tread on a few toes to get what he wants."

"Where are you going with this, boss?" Nillson said. "Jim's finishing his third pint and wants to know if he should get another."

"Oy, come on," he said.

"Listen," Freya said, almost laughing at the camaraderie between them. She stared sideways at Ben who stared back with intrigue. "I never thought I'd admit this to you all, but the reason Standing made DCI is because of me. It's because I'm not ready. It's because I have too many flaws. And I'm working on them. I'll admit, I'm not the nicest person. But I am a damn good officer, and I will never tread on my friends' toes to get what I want. There. I said it. Now you know. I accept that I am far from perfect. I accept that sometimes I can be a bitch. But you can rely on me, as a friend, and if one day we all go our separate ways, you should know that my door will always be open."

"Wow," Gillespie said. "Is this like alcoholics anonymous when we all have to admit to our addictions in front of the rest of the group?"

"No, Jim," Nillson said. "We already know you're a lazy oaf."

"Jenny," Freya said, trying to bring them back to the conversation. She continued to stare at Ben, hoping that her sincerity was reflected in her solemn expression. "How did you get through your probation with DCI Ball?"

"I don't know," she said. "By the skin of my teeth?"

"No, have a little more confidence."

"I suppose I just got my head down and did my job," she said, slightly unsure of herself but voicing the only obvious answer.

"You performed," Freya told her. "You didn't just do your job. You did your job so well that even a conniving bastard like Ball couldn't find a fault in what you did. And if Ball couldn't find a fault, then Standing has no chance. The man can barely find his way to the station. Do you know what I'm saying?"

"We do," Nillson said. "But it doesn't help us. We're already doing the best we can, but the investigation we're working on is ten years old, and Gillespie is clearly between a rock and hard place."

"And a few pint glasses," Cruz added.

"Right," Freya said, and she took a deep breath while she thought. "Gillespie, what investigations are you auditing?"

The sound of a pint glass being placed on the pub table was loud over the call, and as he spoke, Freya could have sworn he was stifling a burp.

"Pretty much all of them since you arrived, boss," he said. "The wee lass out on the beach at Anderby—"

"Jessica Hudson," Freya said.

"Aye, her. Then there's the Woodhall Spa one, the lunatic in Wasp's Nest, the bloke at Tupholme Abbey, the girl from Dunston—"

"Alright, I get it," Freya said. "So basically, you're being asked to audit my work so Standing can bring my shortcomings to Granger's attention?"

"That's about the size of it, boss, aye," he said. "I'm sorry. I've been trying to cover them up—"

"No, don't do that. He'll have been through them already."

"Eh?"

"He'll have read them all and will know every corner I cut already."

"So, why's he asking me to go through them?"

"Because he wants to know if he can trust you. When he was DI, you were his closest ally. He wants to know if that's still the case. If you try to cover my mistakes up, he'll know you're a team player."

"Aye, just not *his* team."

"But if you flag every one of my mistakes to him, he'll trust you, and that's what we need."

"I don't get it, boss."

"I know my mistakes," she told him. "I know where I went wrong. Trust me, these are the things that keep me awake at night hoping that they never come to light. We all have them. We all replay the things we should have done differently or handled better. I'll send you them. I'll break them down into the investigations and send you them. I'll start with the Jessica Hudson investigation. You can submit those to him to keep him happy."

"But, boss, you'll be pulled into his office," Cruz said.

"I can handle Standing, and I probably deserve a dressing down. They are my mistakes, after all."

"Are you sure about this, boss?" Gillespie asked.

"Positive. You'll have them tomorrow," Freya said. "Tell me about these cold cases."

"Standing is calling them open investigations, boss," Nillson said. "He said we're not the LAPD or something."

"It's all the same thing," Freya said. "They're just instances of the police force either not putting the resources in or not using the resources they do have effectively."

"That's a bit strong," Ben said.

"That may be, Ben, and I'm sure there are cases where the evidence is just not there, but nine times out of ten it's a lack of resourcing or being restricted by protocols that hinder us."

"I can't argue with that," Gillespie said.

"Nillson?" Freya said. "What are you working on?"

"Oh, boss. It's a fifteen-year-old mugging that seemingly went nowhere," Nillson said. "The victim was female, aged twenty-three, who died from her injuries a couple of days after the event."

"Did she give a statement?" Freya asked.

"No, she never regained consciousness. The pathology reports indicate a single stab wound to the abdomen, and then a series of stab wounds to her back."

"And what's your theory?" Freya asked.

"My theory? Well, it looks to me like the attacker demanded her money and she put up a fight. He stabbed her in the gut, after which she dropped to her knees and he finished her off."

"That sounds plausible," Freya said. "What does that tell you?"

"Well, considering this happened on her way home from the shops, I would rule out this being a family member or friend for the time being. This was an opportunist, who for one reason or another lost control of his emotions when she put up a fight. He was desperate."

"And which type of individuals are desperate?"

"Junkies," Nillson said. "Maybe someone living on the streets with a habit to feed? Although, that sounds unlikely in Kirkby."

"I think you're on the right track," Freya said. "Leave it with me to mull over and see what else you can find."

"Will do," Nillson said, then added. "Thanks, boss."

"Right, Cruz, tell me about this ten-year-old investigation."

Another silence ensued, giving Freya time to read the new expression on Ben's face. It was one of renewed confidence, or at least that's what she hoped it was. She imagined Cruz silently asking Nillson if it was okay to share the details despite Standing's instruction.

"I'm waiting, Cruz," she said.

"Alright," he began. "I don't really know where to start."

"At the beginning."

"Charlotte Rimmell," he said. "A teenage girl found dead in Kirkby ten years ago."

"Okay, any suspects?"

"Yes, one. But he died while out on bail," Cruz said. "He took his own life, boss."

"Sounds pretty guilty to me. Why was he out on bail?"

"Just to add to that," Nillson said. "They had him bang to rights, but the time of death and his whereabouts gave reasonable doubt. It looks like the investigating team was trying to eliminate any doubt but ran out of time."

"Alright, so he took his own life before they could charge him, and as the investigation was never closed, I'm assuming nobody else was suspected?"

"No, just him, boss," Cruz said.

"And you need to prove it was him to close the investigation?"

"Well, I can prove it *wasn't* him," Cruz replied. "And I think I have another suspect. Somebody the original SIO overlooked."

"Oh, good. Nice work, Cruz," Freya said, and both she and Ben shared impressed expressions. "Who are they?"

"The thing is, the suspect who took his own life was a vicar."

"A vicar?" Freya said, for clarity, and those shared expressions turned almost immediately to intrigue. "Did you say a vicar? A man of the cloth?"

"Yes. Neil Barrow," Cruz said. "We're trying to locate his son. He moved away with his mother shortly after his dad killed himself."

"I suppose the shame was unbearable," Ben said. "And the locals wouldn't have gone easy on them. Do we know where they went?"

"Not a clue," Cruz said. "It's like they disappeared."

"Do we have a name?" Freya asked.

"Vaughan, boss."

"Did you say, Vaughan?"

"Yeah. Vaughan Barrow."

It was as if somebody had turned on a light, but somehow the details were even harder to make out.

She looked across at Ben, unsure if the news was good or if they were now in an even worse position.

Ben looked as if he was still trying to place the information into some kind of order. But Freya could see the big picture. It was as if everything they had been through those past couple of days had been a challenge, a test of patience, and now they had been presented with a solution to nearly all their problems.

"I need to know every little detail about this investigation, Cruz," she said. "I think we might all be able to help each other."

"We can't, boss. He specifically told us not to contact you," Cruz whined.

"Well, when you hear what I have to say you might change your mind," Freya told him. "I think I can give you Vaughan Barrow I know where he is."

CHAPTER THIRTY-EIGHT

It was eight-thirty by the time Cruz had given Ben and Freya a rundown of his investigation. The holiday park clubhouse was in full flow with families coming and going. Kids were running riot and the dull thrum of holidaymakers seemed to fill the air.

Ben watched Freya ignore the five-miles-per-hour speed limit as she headed back to their corner plot and then ended his unanswered call to Michaela. She was probably in the shower or something, he thought. Or maybe she was in the kitchen. He'd found a spot by the side of the road with the clubhouse behind him where the signal was the strongest, yet the second attempt also ended with a recorded apology.

He waited a minute or so, hoping she would check her phone and call him back, and as he stood there, leaning against the brickwork, a man wearing shorts and flip-flops ambled by with a tiny dog who seemed even less happy about going for a walk than he did.

Ben watched him pass, nodding a greeting as the man stared quizzically at the trousers and shirt Ben was wearing. He hadn't really considered it before, but he must have stuck out like a sore thumb amongst the relaxed holidaymakers.

It was as he watched the man walk up the concrete ramp towards the marshes that Ben recognised the view as being almost identical to the CCTV footage, and he sighed at the prospect of going through it with Freya when he returned.

He redialled Michaela and prayed she would answer. He needed normality, something that was neither police business nor Freya-related. He wanted to hear Michaela's voice. He wanted to be reminded of who was waiting for him when he got home, whenever that might be.

But the call ended with the same recorded message of consolation, and he resorted to sending her a message, which took him longer than it should have to type due to his sweaty hands. He watched the message send, waited a few moments longer, then pocketed his phone, thrust his hands in his pockets, and ambled back to paradise, which was a nineteen-seventies caravan positioned in the far corner of the site, beside the bins, with a temperamental housemate who could transition from seductive and teasing to cold and bitter in a heartbeat.

The thought of returning was not one he relished. A month ago, he might have jumped at the prospect of sharing the old caravan with her, knowing full well that the seductive and sensual Freya was never far away.

But now, the idea of meeting the cold and bitter Freya dampened his spirits and did little to stir anything but dread.

He took a slow walk, choosing to venture off the main road through the park to navigate the edges, where the dog owners let their dogs cock their legs, and where he was as far from the shouting and laughter of holidaying families as he could be. He checked his phone every now and then, hoping that, by some good fortune, his phone might discover a bar of signal, which typically ended in bitter disappointment.

But that disappointment waned when he heard shouting from the next caravan he passed. The voices were familiar, their tones heated, and the majority of the argument was coming from the woman of the pair. Using a neighbouring static home for cover, Ben stopped and listened.

"Don't go," the man said. "Just bloody calm down, will you?"

"Calm down, Vaughan? Calm down? Do you know what I've been doing today while you've been sitting here getting drunk?"

"Of course, I bloody well know. It's all you've been harping on about—"

"Harping on about it? Do you even know what this means to me?"

"I should think the whole county will know if you don't keep your voice down, Stella."

"Don't give me that. Don't try to shut me up. This was your idea. If it wasn't for you, we wouldn't be in this bloody mess. If I hadn't have met you—"

"You'd what?" Vaughan said, his tone suddenly far more threatening than before. "You'd what, Stella? Tell me what you'd be doing."

"Let me go, Vaughan," she said, and Ben resisted the urge to intervene. "Let me go or I'll scream. Those coppers are in the next field. They'd be here in a heartbeat. You don't want them sniffing round here, do you?"

"You wouldn't," he said.

"Let me go," she said, the quiver in her voice denying her hopes of sounding calm. "Just get your hands off me. I'm out. I'm not having anything to do with this."

"You're going nowhere," he said, in a deep, hushed tone. "We're going to see this through. You and me. You're in this up to your eyeballs just as much as I am."

A silence followed, and then a small whimper, as Ben imagined him shoving the much smaller Stella back onto the bed or the couch.

"From now on, we do things my way," he said.

"Oh, because that's worked well so far, hasn't it?" she said, and

Ben heard a heavy footstep on the thin floor. "Alright, alright. We do things your way."

He imagined them both coming to an agreement, with Vaughan looming over Stella. He'd seen the victims of domestic abuse a hundred times over, both female and male, and every time was as hard as the previous one.

"No more going solo on this," Vaughan said. "We've got a plan and we're going to stick to it. Look how far we've come. We're close, Stella, so bloody close. Don't cock it up now or do you know those coppers over there will do? They'll be slamming the door on both of us, alright?"

"Alright," she said, agreeing to whatever plan they had devised.

"Right. You're going nowhere. While those two are here, you are a liability."

"You can't lock me up—"

"I can do what the bloody hell I like when it comes to my freedom, Stella. Do you hear me? Whatever I bloody like. You take one step out of that door and you're on your own. You can go back to your loser mum and see if she can put her bottle of vodka down for long enough to help you."

"Don't talk about her like that," she said.

"Do you understand?" Vaughan replied, ignoring her plight. "You stay in here. I don't care how hot it gets or how uncomfortable you are. Don't go out and don't answer the door."

The conversation quietened and Ben risked a peek around the corner of the caravan to get a glimpse through the window. But all he caught was Vaughan leaning over the couch to close the open window, shutting Ben out of the conversation.

Navigating his way through the maze of vans, he found the road and walked briskly to the nineteen-seventies, where he found Freya at his laptop watching the video, wearing a long t-shirt and those shorts. A glass of wine was in her hand, naturally, and when he walked in, she watched him, trying to read his expression.

"How is she?" she asked.

"She's okay," he replied.

"Really? Miss you, does she?"

Ben loosened his shirt and tossed his tie onto the couch.

"What about lover boy?" he asked. "Have you spoken to him?"

"I couldn't get a signal," she replied.

"And you didn't think of calling him while we were out on the main road?"

"No," she said. "In fact, I can see him now, sitting by his phone, waiting for me to call. And that's the way I shall keep it."

"You're something else, you are, Freya Bloom."

"It's funny. That's what he said," she replied.

"You'll never guess what I just heard," Ben said, moving the conversation on.

"And you'll never guess what I've just *seen*," she replied, turning the laptop so he could see the screen. She'd paused the video at a point when somebody, a girl, from what Ben could see, was standing exactly where he'd been standing, clearly trying to get a phone signal.

"You first," Ben said.

"Stella Green," Freya replied, sipping at her wine. "And that's not even the best bit."

She hit the space bar to play the footage in normal time, and Ben watched as the girl he'd just heard arguing with Vaughan Barrow lit up as a small, white van passed her and parked at the foot of the concrete ramp. From where Stella was leaning against the clubhouse wall, she watched the van stop and reverse into a parking space at the side of the road. But there was something about the way the van had caught her attention that seemed out of place. She took a small step forward like she was trying to get a better view.

And when the driver's door opened and a man climbed out, the two seemed to lock stares for a moment, as if time had stopped.

Then, quick as a flash, Stella turned and ran into the caravan park. The man, who, from the camera angle, was little more than a dark silhouette, jumped back into his little van and sped back up Sea Lane, leaving a cloud of diesel fumes in his wake.

"What just happened there?" Ben asked.

"Your guess is as good as mine," Freya said. "But this was twenty-seven minutes past four on Saturday morning. Right about the time Hayley Donovan was killed."

"We need to find out who was driving that van," Ben said. "It's lucky I didn't stop at three a.m."

"What was your news?" Freya asked, taking a long sip of her wine and drawing her knees up to her chin, ignoring his victory as minor as it was.

He stared at her, feeling the confused expression fade from his face as the tide might slowly wear away a child's footprints in the sand.

"Like I said," he replied, "we need to find out who was driving that van. I have a feeling Stella and Vaughan are planning something."

"Like what?"

"Something bad," he said. "Something very bad."

Freya looked as if she was about to press him to be clearer. She had a look in her eyes that Ben recognised, the look that accompanied every critical moment in every investigation they had worked on together.

But there was a knock on the door behind Ben and the moment dissipated like a bad smell.

"Are you expecting anybody?" he said, and Freya shook her head, then quickly closed the laptop.

Ben stepped over to the door, but the frosted glass disguised the visitor's identity.

Slowly, he opened the door and peered through the gap, feeling his jaw drop at the sight before him.

"Hello," the visitor said, holding up a bottle of cheap white wine. She smiled that smile he had missed so much and bit down on her lower lip in anticipation. "Aren't you going to invite me in?"

"What are you doing here?" he asked.

"I thought you might like some company," she replied, as she stepped up into the caravan and gave him a kiss on the cheek. She held a small holdall up for him to see. "Which one is your room?"

"It's the big one at the end of the corridor," Freya said, as she stepped into the little kitchenette. Then she surprised Ben with an overly polite, "Hello, Michaela, what a lovely surprise."

Michaela smiled awkwardly and gave Ben's waistline a squeeze.

"Hope you don't mind?" she said, to which Freya shook her head sadly.

"Why should I mind?"

Ben jabbed his thumb over his shoulder.

"That's your room," he reminded her.

"You take it," she replied. "I'll take the couch."

"But there's a bedroom here," Michaela said, reaching for the handle to what would have been Ben's room had the mattress not looked as if somebody had been murdered on it.

"No," he said, beating her to the door handle and holding it firmly closed. "It's probably best not to look in there."

Michaela looked quizzically between them both, then settled on Freya who had reached for another glass from the little cupboard above the sink.

"Wine?" she said. "You must be thirsty after that long drive."

CHAPTER THIRTY-NINE

Freya was already awake when Ben emerged from what had been her bedroom. He wandered through to the kitchenette and then felt the warm kettle before poking his head around the corner into the little living room.

"You're awake," he whispered, as he slid sideways into the tiny washroom.

"I promised Gillespie that email," she said.

"At seven a.m.?" he replied, doing his best to disguise the noise he was making.

"I've been going over what we know," she called out to him.

He pushed open the bathroom door and squeezed out, leaning back inside to push the flush, then he washed his hands at the kitchen sink, which offered far more elbow room for his six-foot-something frame.

"I want to bring Vaughan Barrow in for questioning," she told him.

"Have I got time for a coffee beforehand?" he replied and turned to reveal a sarcastic grin.

"I was going to make eggs Benedict."

"Is that the one with the yellow sauce?"

"Hollandaise," she told him, and she peered at him disbelievingly. "Ben, how old are you?"

"Old enough that I need a strong coffee before I engage in conversation."

"I often wonder how on earth you've managed to live this long and still retain the palette of an eight-year-old," she said. "Honestly, there are tribes in the middle of the Amazon with a broader culinary knowledge than you."

"Do they have yellow sauce on their eggs then?"

"Should I just make you boiled eggs and soldiers?"

"That's my dad's favourite," he said, as he prepared two mugs of coffee. "He has it every morning."

"Well, tough. We don't have any egg cups, so it's eggs Benedict or nothing."

"Am I making extra?" she asked, clutching her coffee with both hands and offering a saucy wink.

"Michaela?" he yelled, then made a show of listening for an immediate response. "Michaela?"

"Did you keep her up all night?" Freya asked, at which Ben rolled his eyes. He was about to say something when the bedroom door opened and Michaela walked out of the bedroom pulling her long, blonde hair into a ponytail.

"Coffee?" Ben said.

"Strong," she replied.

"Breakfast?" Freya offered, as she and Ben both watched his tired girlfriend stumble across the living room floor and collapse onto the couch, puffing at the already warm morning.

"I could eat," she replied.

"It's eggs with yellow sauce," Ben said. "On toast."

"It's what?"

"Eggs Benedict," Freya said. "And I'll be using English muffins in lieu of Ben's toast."

"You're going to make eggs Benedict in that kitchen?" Michaela said, slightly in awe.

"Sure," Freya replied. "Why don't you two get showered and dressed while I make breakfast?"

"I'll shower while you're both at work," Michaela said. "Or maybe when I've been for a walk."

"Oh, really? Where will you go?" Freya asked.

"The marshes, and then the beach, I suppose. We used to come here when I was younger. A little trip down memory lane might be nice. There's a seal sanctuary around here too. I'd like to pay it a visit."

"Sounds like a fun day," Freya told her. "Aren't you working?"

"Nope. I have some time to take, and it seemed like an opportunity to take a break," she said. "I don't want to get under your feet. I realise you're here to work."

"You won't," Ben said. "It's fine."

"We try to spend as little time here as we can," Freya added, at which Michaela studied the decor.

"I can see why. It's a bit dated, isn't it? It's probably the same caravan we stayed in when I was nine years old."

"There's also no internet," Ben said. "Which is why I had to walk out to the gate to call."

"Then it's perfect," Michaela exclaimed. "I'll cook dinner."

"No, it's fine," Freya said. "I've got a meal plan—"

"I won't hear of it," Michaela said. "It's the least I can do. What about you two? Have you made much progress?"

"We've gathered plenty of information," Ben said. "But putting it into some sort of order is proving to be a challenge."

"No suspects?" she asked.

"Two," Ben told her. "One convicted murderer recently released from prison and one person of interest whose father was suspected of killing a girl around Hayley Donovan's age ten years ago."

Michaela seemed impressed as Ben handed her a coffee. She tucked her legs beneath her, so that she sat cross-legged, and took a sip of the coffee.

"It's funny, isn't it? It doesn't matter how beautiful or rural the place is, people always clash. There's always conflict, isn't there? There's always somebody who is willing to take it too far."

"Would it shock you to learn that both of the men that Ben just mentioned were vicars?" Freya said, and Michaela coughed into her coffee in surprise. "I'll take that as a yes."

"Vicars?"

"The first was in Kirkby ten years ago. The suspect took his own life before he was charged, but the son relocated here."

"I imagine it would have been difficult to stay when your father was a murderer," Michaela said.

"Exactly. It's a little coincidental, though, that the second murder happened one year later in similar circumstances."

"Was the son involved in the second murder?"

"No. But he was local, and if I'm honest, of all the murder investigations I've worked, there have been only two involving religious leaders."

"These two investigations?" Michaela asked.

"Exactly," Freya said. "He's involved somehow. He has to be."

"He's also up to something," Ben added, and Michaela switched her attention to him. He took a sip of his coffee and leaned back on the kitchen worktop. "I walked past his caravan yesterday and heard him arguing with his girlfriend."

"Who, by the way, is the sister of the second victim," Freya added.

"What?" Michaela said, setting her coffee down on the table. "So, ten years ago, a vicar killed a girl in Kirkby then took his own life. You think the son moved to Saltfleet where presumably nobody knows him. Then one year later, another girl dies at the hands of another vicar in Saltlfeet? But this time, the suspect didn't take his own life and was sentenced to eighteen years, I'm guessing, if he was paroled after nine?"

"Correct," Ben said.

"So, the son of the original killer is now hooked up with the sister of the second victim?"

"Yep," Freya said, and she jabbed a finger at the window. "They're about twenty caravans away."

"What?" Michaela said, staring at the window as if by chance she might glimpse a potential murder suspect. "And what about the man who was released? Where is he? Don't tell me he's living next door?"

"No, he's hiding in a disused church about a mile away from here," Ben said.

"But why has he come back?" Michaela asked. "Surely in a place like this, somebody who murdered a local girl wouldn't be welcomed?"

"Well, that's where it gets even more interesting," Freya said. "His daughter was murdered last Friday."

"Out in the marshes," Ben added before Michaela could offer any kind of reaction. "That's why we're here."

"Bloody hell," she said quietly. "I'm having second thoughts about going for that stroll now."

"You're perfectly safe," Freya told her. "These weren't random attacks. They were calculated and personal."

"What makes you say that?"

"The links. Every one of these murders is linked somehow, either through Vaughan Barrow, the first vicar's son, or through Frank Donovan, the second vicar."

"The man who went to prison?"

"That's right," Freya said. "Something, or someone, connects the three murders. That's how we're going to close this one. By finding that connection."

The three of them mulled over what Freya had said, each lost in their own thoughts. But it was Michaela who broke the silence.

"I want to help," she said.

"You don't need to do that—" Ben began before he was cut off.

"I mean it. I can help," Michaela said.

"I'm not sure if it's a good idea," Freya said. "You're supposed to be on leave."

"Get me the CSI reports from the first two murders," she said. "It makes sense. I'll work from here. I can compare the reports. I might see something you or the previous SIO hasn't."

Ben took a deep breath then puffed out his cheeks as he exhaled. "She's got the clearance," he said, at which Michaela nodded.

"But you couldn't testify," Freya said.

"That's okay. If I do happen to find something, we can bring it to the attention of the local CSI team," she said. "Come on, you know it makes sense. Give me something to do."

"It's not exactly the R and R you were looking for," Ben said, which she palmed off with a wave of her hand.

"This is what I do," she said. "I analyse data."

"You'd have to walk down to the clubhouse to get an internet connection. You could download the files onto your laptop then come back here."

"That's fine," she said, and she stared at them both, daring them to throw another obstacle in her path.

"Alright," Freya said, with a heavy sigh. "Alright, let's do this. We're already breaking nearly every rule DCI Standing has put in place. What difference will one more make?"

CHAPTER FORTY

Much like the rest of the static homes in the park, there were three steps up to the front door of Vaughan Barrow's. However, unlike the other hundred or so sets of steps, Vaughan's were littered with five empty cans of Stella Artois, crushed and discarded for somebody else to deal with.

"Ready?" Freya asked as she caught Ben glancing over his shoulder in the direction of Buttercup. "Head in the game, Ben."

"Don't worry about me," he told her, and he reached past her to rap on the door. He gave three hard knocks then stepped back to watch for movement through the windows.

There was nothing. Not a single twitch of a curtain, not a single thud of a footstep or a hissed curse could be heard.

Freya knocked again, slightly harder than Ben, which he assumed was just to prove a point.

"Vaughan Barrow. Open up," she called out, then gave Ben a nod, which he interpreted as an instruction to check around the back. He left her there and checked the windows as he circled the static home. He found only one unlocked window, beneath which at least thirty dog ends littered the grass. Carefully, he prised open the window.

"Vaughan," he said loud enough for anybody inside to hear but not loud enough to disturb the neighbours. There was no movement at all. He could hear Freya banging on the door again, which in turn woke up a neighbour's dog who began yapping loudly.

"Vaughan Barrow, we know you're in there," she called out, while Ben listened for movement.

But there was none.

He completed his walk around the unit and found Freya testing the door to see how strong the lock was.

"There's an open window," he told her, but he was too late. She gave a sharp yank on the handle, and then another, and the door popped open, shuddering as it opened in her hand.

"There's an open door too," she said with a smile. "And before you tell me we need a warrant, I think you'll find we have reason to believe he's involved in at least three murders, which negates the need for a warrant."

"You're the boss," he said with a sigh, and followed her inside where he was hit by the stench of old cigarettes, sweat, and beer. "Crikey, and we thought Buttercup was bad."

"Buttercup is bad," Freya said quietly, as she nosed into one of the bedrooms. "This place is just worse, that's all."

He laughed to himself then caught her waving at him, nodding at the only closed door in the home. Ben stepped closer and put his ear to the wood, hearing nothing. He shook his head at her, then slowly turned the handle, easing the door open for her to peer inside.

"It's empty," she said, and he let the door fall back against the thin wall, taking a look inside. The covers looked as if they had been tossed onto the bed instead of any attempt at making the bed. He lifted the covers to check beneath them, then, seeing a cup on the little built-in side table, he felt it with the back of his hand.

"Warm," he said, and he smelled the contents. "Bad coffee."

"Says the connoisseur," Freya remarked with no attempt at

hiding her sarcasm. She left him to investigate the rest of the unit, leaving a trail of her perfume in her wake that did little to quell the stench of stale tobacco. "I remember when you lived on cheap coffee."

"I remember when you used to say nice things," he replied as a retort. A moment later, she appeared at the bedroom door.

"No, you do not," she said, sternly but with a hint of humour.

"No, you're right. You've never said anything nice."

"That's better," she told him. "By the way, I think I've found something."

He followed her out of the bedroom and into what, in any other static home, would have been called a lounge, but in this instance was no more than a mass of drinks bottles, mixers, and beer cans, along with clothes, including a women's bra which was hanging from the TV.

"How does anybody live in this mess?" Freya said with a judgemental tut.

"I don't know. Maybe we should call Gillespie and ask," Ben replied.

"Even that neanderthal has higher standards than this," she said, then drew his attention to a little handwritten note beneath the TV. "Read that."

Ben pulled a latex glove from his pocket, slipped it on with a snap, and picked up the post-it note, peeling it from the veneered wood.

Vaughan,
Come and see me in the office this morning. I have some news for you.
Aunt Sandy.

"Aunt Sandy?"

"Sandy Robinson," Freya said. "My new best friend."

"His aunt?"

"It would explain the hugging," she said. "Think about it. Vaughan's father takes his own life. Vaughan needs somewhere to stay. Where better to go than an aunt with a few hundred bedrooms at her disposal?"

Ben gazed around the room while he contemplated the relationship between Vaughan and the site manager, until something caught his eye, and he gave a little laugh.

"What?" Freya said, trying to follow his gaze.

He nodded at the mess in the corner of the room, where, beside an overflowing bin, an empty bottle of Vodka lay on its side.

"Remember the man who claimed to have been robbed?"

"You don't think it was Vaughan?" Freya said.

"I wouldn't put it past him," he said, and he stepped over to the bottle, feeling the heel of his shoe catch something, which then scattered across the linoleum floor. He followed the sound and then crouched in the corner to pick it up. "Well, well, well."

"What's that?" Freya said.

He held his hand out to pass it to her and she turned her hand palm-up for him to drop it in.

"A screw?" she said, a little confused.

"Not just any screw," he replied, pleased to have found something that actually took the investigation forward and not just sideways. "Look closely, what do you see?"

"It's a rusty, old screw," she said. "Forgive me for not getting as excited about ironmongery as you, Ben."

"What else do you see?" he said, savouring the tease.

She held it up to the light, squinting to find something she might have missed.

"There's some red paint on the end."

"That's the head," he corrected her. "And that's not red, it's burgundy. I thought you of all people would recognise that colour seeing as you drink so much of it. Actually, to be precise it's red-oxide paint. It's used to protect metal."

"So what?" she said. "Just spit it out."

"That, Freya," he said, reluctant to put her out of her misery, "is the missing screw from the lock on the door to the disused church."

"St Botolph's?"

"I'd have money on it," he said, then saw her face light up at the mention of a wager. "Figuratively, at least."

"Why would he have a screw to a disused church door?" Freya said, voicing her thoughts rather than seeking an immediate answer.

But they both came to the same conclusion at precisely the same time, and they inhaled the same foul air as if the pair were synchronised.

"He must know Frank Donovan is staying there," Ben said. "The note. That's why Sandy Robinson needed to talk to him. His bloody aunt told him Frank Donovan was out."

"They would have known he was out," Freya said. "We saw Stella in the CCTV footage. She clearly saw him and ran back inside the holiday park."

Ben took the screw from her, holding it up to the light to make sure he hadn't been quick to make assumptions. But the screw was identical to the ones he saw Larson removing with his multitool.

"She must have seen him," he agreed. "Where did Sandy say her house was?"

"In a nearby village," Freya said.

"Not Skidbrooke, by any chance? The same bloody village the church is in? If it is, she might have seen Frank Donovan."

"What if Sandy knows what they're up to? Whatever that is," Freya said, reading the little note. "What if she told him where to find Frank Donovan?"

"Well, then it's not Vaughan we need to worry about," Ben mused, remembering the argument he'd overheard. "He said they were in something up to their eyeballs. He made it clear Stella wasn't to leave here. So where is she?"

"Well, if somebody told me where the man who killed my sister was hiding, I know where I'd be," Freya said. "She's going after Frank Donovan."

CHAPTER FORTY-ONE

The large Range Rover slewed into the old church grounds, and Freya eased off the accelerator to quieten the engine noise. The car slowed, and she brought it to a stop at the end of the little driveway to block the exit. Ahead of them, the large church loomed tall and proud from the mass of trees and overgrown shrubs that had taken over the grounds. But before it, parked in a space between two old Elm trees was a small, white van.

"Do me a favour," she said to Ben, handing him the piece of paper Samson had provided. "Check the registration against that."

It took a few moments for Ben to locate the row with Donovan's name on it.

"It's him," he said. "That's his registration."

"Let's just double-check the make and model of the van with Hart. I don't want to jump to conclusions, not at this stage."

Ben did as he was instructed, dialling Hart's number and setting the call to loudspeaker.

"DS Hart," the voice said when the call was answered.

"Hart, it's Ben Savage."

"Oh, good morning. Did you manage to catch up with Stella

Green?" she asked, to which Freya shook her head and put her finger to her lips.

"Erm, no. Not yet. But we're hopeful we'll find her today," he said. "I was wondering if you had a chance to look into Frank Donovan's vehicle?"

"I did. Sorry, I was meant to call you, but you know how it is."

Ben recited the number plate of the van in front of them.

"That's it," she said. "It's a white Ford van. Have you found it?"

"Oh, just a sighting, that's all," he said. "I don't suppose you could run that through the original ANPR report, could you? It would be handy to know if he was in the area on Friday night."

"Already done," she said. "Samson did it. The vehicle passed through on Thursday and hasn't been seen on ANPR since, so I presume he's either still in the area or, if he's not, then he used a route without ANPR cameras."

"Right," Ben said, flicking his eyes up to see if Freya had anything to add. "Just out of curiosity, does your custody sergeant need a warning if we were to bring somebody in?"

"I usually let him know, just out of courtesy, but we've got plenty of room. It was a quiet weekend. Who have you got?"

"Oh, nobody yet," Ben said. "But I have a feeling today is going to be busy."

"I'll head down there now and let him know to keep a cell free for you."

"Make that two," Freya said, then added her manners as an afterthought. "If you wouldn't mind, please, Hart."

"Two cells," she repeated. "Got it. I'll let George know. I'm sure he'll be pleased. We could do with some good news at the moment."

"I'd rather you didn't," Freya said. "Let's not count our chickens just yet."

"What about support? I might be able to get you a couple of uniforms. Where are you? I'll send them now."

"No need," Freya said. "But thanks. We'll let you know if we need anything else. Thanks, Ivy, you've been a great help."

Ben ended the call and slipped his phone into his pocket.

"I didn't realise you were on first-name terms with her," he said.

"I'm not. But it doesn't hurt to treat people like human beings once in a while," she replied as she pushed open her car door. "Oh, would you look at that? I *can* say nice things once in a while. You walk that way, I'll go this way. We'll meet at the door. If you see anyone, shout."

"Likewise," he said, and any sign of the humour they had shared vanished.

Keeping close to the old church walls, Freya walked with care so as not to announce their presence. She ventured into the shady area behind the church, feeling the temperature drop almost instantly, and then, with the door in sight up ahead, she waited for Ben to come around the corner to arrive at the doors at the same time. Regardless of her confidence, if a convicted murderer was to spring from the old, wooden door, she would stand little chance of stopping him on her own.

They closed in on the door as Freya had planned, and it was clear, even from ten steps away, that the lock had been unscrewed, with the hasp and staple hanging uselessly in the air.

"Head in the game, Freya," he said quietly, mimicking what she had told him earlier.

"My head hasn't been out of it," she replied, then slowly pulled the door open. Sunlight spewed through the doorway and reached across the ancient floor, bringing the coloured, decorative tiles to life, just as it had for hundreds of years.

Both of them stared directly across the void into the shadowy porch where Donovan's possessions had been stored. They searched for movement but found none. So, cautiously, they entered.

"Donovan?" Freya called. "Frank Donovan, we know you're here."

The great pillars that formed the huge archways along the length of the interior cast deep shadows along the far wall, and as their eyes adjusted to the brightness, it became clear the main area of the church was devoid of life.

"Come out, Frank," Freya said. "Don't make us look for you."

She nodded for Ben to approach the south porch from one side while she took the other side. Together, they could cover any eventuality.

It was times like this she wished she carried a torch like Larson had, or at least knew how to use the torch on her phone without having to ask Ben for help. The shadows seemed to play tricks on her mind, suggesting movement when there was none and causing her to doubt the reality of what she had or hadn't seen.

With both of them positioned on either side of the porch, Freya stepped into the entrance. The dark space where Donovan's possessions had been before was now clearly an empty space, and her eyes slowly became accustomed to the darkness.

"He's not here," she said, and she turned to Ben, just as a shape passed through a shaft of light from the windows, darting towards the door they'd entered through. Despite the tricks her mind had played, this time there was no doubt at all, and she screamed for him to stop. "Frank! Don't move."

Ben sprang into life, bolting for the door, just in time to slam it closed and trap the three of them inside. The figure realised there was no escape. He backed away as if to defend himself.

"Frank Donovan?" Freya said, calmly striding across the ornate and ancient floor. She pulled her warrant card from her pocket and held it up for him to see. "Detective Inspector Bloom. This is DS Savage. We've been looking for you."

He was a large man, not formidable like the ex-cons that Hollywood movies portray, but he was large in the shoulders and chest and tall like Ben, and the sight of the warrant card seemed to confuse him more than anything.

Then, as if the fight had gone from him, he dropped to his knees with a heavy sigh.

"Are you alone, Frank?" Freya said, to which he nodded. "Do you know why we're here?"

"Yes," he said, softly, letting his head fall back so he was staring up at the huge, vaulted ceiling above. "She's dead. My girl. My beautiful baby girl."

"You need to come with us," Ben told him, and he fell forward onto his hands and knees revealing the tattoos Vaughan Barrow had mentioned, that even in the low light Freya could make out; an angel on one hand and the devil on the other. He began to pant heavily like he was struggling to breathe. "Frank?"

But the big man said nothing. He lowered his head as if building up the energy to stand.

"Am I under arrest?" he asked in a gentle voice, and he let out a sob. The tender tone that had once preached to his flock broke into a whine. "It wasn't me. I couldn't kill my own daughter. I couldn't."

"I know, Frank," Freya said, and she stepped closer, dropping to a crouch beside him. She placed her hand on his shoulder, to which he responded with a jolt as if he wasn't used to somebody daring to touch a convicted murderer with such confidence. "But there are some people who think it was you. We need to keep you safe."

CHAPTER FORTY-TWO

"We need a cell and an interview room," Freya told Hart, who was waiting by the custody desk.

At the mention of the cell, Frank stiffened in Ben's grip.

"It's okay, Frank," he told him. "You're not under arrest."

"What's this?" the custody sergeant asked. "Am I processing him or what?"

"No," Freya said. "We need him kept safe."

"In a cell?"

"Can you think of anywhere safer?" Freya asked.

The custody sergeant appraised Donovan with a trained eye while he processed the information.

"I know you," he said. He was a slight man who took pride in his uniform and his appearance. "You're–"

"We all know who he is, Sergeant," Freya said, clearly doing her best to prevent embarrassment. "And whatever mistakes he may or may not have made in the past have been paid for. I need Mr Donovan kept safe in a cell, and when an interview room becomes available, I'd like to book it, if you don't mind. Is there a process you'd like me to follow?"

"Is he staying the night?" the sergeant asked.

"That all depends on how soon you can find me an interview room," she said, and Ben felt the usual awkwardness that followed Freya's direct approach.

"Room three," he said, checking his watch. "Should be available in ten minutes or so."

"Good. That gives us time to go through our findings with DI Larson. We'll be in the meeting room," Freya told him, then turned to Donovan. "It's alright, Frank. I know it's not exactly the Ritz, but it's dry and warm, and the only rodents you'll find here wear uniforms."

The comment raised a feeble grin that faded with his next breath. The custody sergeant held open the door to the cells, and Donovan looked to Ben for some kind of support.

"Keep the door open, Sergeant, please," Ben said. "Don't lock him in."

"You what?" he said. "He's a bloody convicted murderer. What do you want me to do, make him tea and toast as well?"

"Frank?" Freya said, ignoring the sergeant's plight. "When did you last eat?"

"Hey now," the sergeant complained. "That wasn't an offer—"

"Frank?" she said, to which he shrugged.

"Last night. There's a cafe out near Anderby."

"Thank you, Sergeant. I'm sure Mr Donovan would appreciate a hot drink and something in his stomach."

She pulled open the door leaving Ben to pick up the pieces, as usual.

"Best not to rile her," he whispered to the bemused sergeant as he followed her and Hart through the door. The sergeant inhaled a long breath, and then gave in, presenting Donovan with the corridor to the cells like he was royalty.

"Fifteen years I've been in this job," he said, as Donovan passed him. "Thought I'd seen it all."

"Every day is a school day," Ben said with a smile. "Oh, and by the way, thanks for your help."

He caught up with Freya in the break room a minute later, a few moments before Hart arrived with Larson and Samson.

"Well, you certainly know how to make waves," Larson said, shielding his judgement with a well-practised tone of indifference. "What next? Will you be putting an advert up on Airbnb?"

"Here, you could open a chain of them," Samson said, revealing that whiter than white smile.

"If you're referring to Frank Donovan, George, perhaps it's best if you hear what we have to say before we enter into the practicalities of housing him in one of your cells."

Larson grinned. He had a warm smile, friendly, like that of a favourite uncle, to which Ben was drawn. Maybe it was the fact that he made no effort to adhere to fashion trends, choosing instead to wear a plain shirt and trousers that could have been five, ten, or even twenty years old. Or perhaps it was the knitted tank top he wore even in the height of summer. Whichever it was, he had a manner about him that was as endearing as it was competent.

"I'll start, shall I?" he said, nudging his reading glasses onto the bridge of his nose. He held his notes out before him. "Before we move on, let's recap on yesterday's meeting. Have we given you everything you asked for?"

"Everything aside from the address of Frank Donovan's bedsit, or wherever it is he calls home. But seeing as we have him downstairs, that's rather a moot point."

"I have it here," Hart said, sliding a note from her file. "It's in Hull. Might be worth sending the local uniform round there to have a look. We're still missing Hayley Donovan's possessions, aren't we?"

"We are," Freya said. "And I agree. Can you arrange that, please? I don't suppose they'll find anything, but we might get lucky."

"Has he said anything?" Larson asked, to which Freya shook her head.

"He had a little breakdown, which is to be expected given his recent loss."

"Interesting," Larson said, and he nudged his glasses up onto his nose again, letting the silence speak for itself.

"What is?" Freya asked. "What's interesting?"

He removed his glasses this time, taking a moment to rub the bridge of his nose.

"You found him in the church, did you? St Botolph's?"

"That's right."

"And out of interest, did you arrest him?"

"I had no need. We've had a development which doesn't necessarily give him an alibi, but it does raise questions as to whether or not he was guilty of murdering Skye Green."

Larson stared at her across the table, as if he was trying to understand if there was some kind of joke hidden within her statement.

"You're not planning an enquiry, are you?" he said.

"Not right now," she replied. "But what if he was innocent?"

"If he was innocent, then that's somebody else's problem," Larson said. "Don't make it mine. Not right now."

Freya closed her notes, linked her fingers, and placed her hands on her lap, sitting back in her seat. A familiar sense of dread washed over Ben.

"Ten years ago, a girl named Charlotte Rimmell, about the same age as Hayley and Skye, was murdered."

"You're really going to town on this, aren't you?" Larson said.

"The only suspect the investigating officers were working on was a man named Neil Barrow. Mr Barrow was released on bail while the SIO built his case, but there was one flaw that would have caused the CPS to throw the case out. A timing issue between the inaccuracy of our ability to determine the time of a victim's death and the length of time it would have taken Mr Barrow to get to the crime scene on foot."

"Right?" Larson said. He appeared to have more to say but

was polite enough to let Freya finish, and he made a show of his patience, which Ben recognised as something Detective Superintendent Granger would do. It must have been an old-school thing.

"Barrow took his own life before they were able to press charges," Freya said.

"Why does this sound familiar?" Larson asked.

"Because it's one of the open investigations our team is working on in our absence."

"Where did you say this first murder took place?"

"Kirkby," Freya said. "Your new stomping ground. I'm assuming the team there is undergoing a similar process as yourselves. Trying to close down whatever investigations they can before they are merged with you."

"And you think there's some kind of connection to the death of Hayley Donovan, do you?"

"I know there's a connection," she said. "Neil Barrow was a vicar."

"A vicar?" Samson cried out. "What are you saying, we have a bunch of rogue priests in the area?"

"I said vicar, not priest, Samson, and please pay attention. Frank Donovan is in a cell downstairs with the door unlocked. I imagine right now your duty sergeant is bringing him a nice cup of tea."

"Don't count on it," Samson replied. "On it being nice, that is."

"Does that seem odd to you, George?" Freya asked. "That two religious men in positions of authority should stoop so low as to both commit murders?"

"These are strange times," he replied. "But I can see why you've flagged it. How do we connect them?"

"That's where we have to use our imaginations," she said, and she pointed a finger at the whiteboard. "Neil Barrow had a son."

Larson turned to the board on which he'd written the names

of everyone involved so far and slid his glasses on, scrunching his nose to read his own writing.

Then Freya added the surname to Vaughan's forename.

"Vaughan Barrow," he said. "Is it the same man—"

"If he was called John Smith, then I might have questioned it," Freya told him, then turned to Hart. "Can we get a background check on Barrow, please?"

"You'll have it by this afternoon," she said.

Freya gave her a nod of thanks, then continued.

"We know Vaughan moved to Saltfleet shortly after his father ended his life. We think he has an aunt here, a Sandy Robinson. She's the site manager at the holiday park where we're staying."

"You're kidding?" Larson said.

"I wish I was," she replied, again turning to Hart. "Another background check please, Ivy?"

"Shouldn't be too hard," Hart said.

"She stays in a static home on-site during peak times, but we think she has a house nearby. Can we get the address, please? No action needed, but I want it ready in case we need it. At the moment, we have no idea if Vaughan uses the house at all. So, if he goes on our missing list, then we might find him there."

"Got it," Hart said, and she rattled her pen between her teeth while she thought. "What about Stella Green?"

"That's an interesting one," Ben said, sensing now was the time for him to join the discussion. "I walked past Vaughan's unit last night and overheard him and Stella Green."

"If you're going to raise the topic of his promiscuity, Ben—" Larson said.

"Not on this occasion," Ben replied. "But emotions were running high. I got the feeling they were both up to something. Stella Green told him she was out."

"Out of what?" Samson said.

"We don't know. But whatever it was, Barrow made it clear she wasn't."

"Was he violent?"

"Aggressive, yes. Violent, no, not on this occasion at least. But if I can pick up from what Freya was saying," he said, "we know Vaughan Barrow was either involved in the death of Charlotte Rimmell, or at least in the area. We're faced with a decision to make. If Barrow's father took his own life through guilt, then we can assume Vaughan moved here to start again."

"Small communities do tend to stick together when tragedies strike," Larson agreed. "The son of a murderer wouldn't have had a particularly pleasant experience in the days that followed."

"That's what we thought," Ben said. "But what if his father was innocent, just like we believe Frank Donovan is innocent? Vaughan is the only one who links all three murders. He was Neil Barrow's son, he was in Saltfleet when Skye Green was murdered, and we know he had a relationship with Hayley Donovan that ended recently."

"How is he linked to Skye Green?" Larson asked.

"We don't know," Ben said, with his hands held up. "We've only really just eliminated Frank Donovan."

"So, you have eliminated him entirely?" Larson said. "Despite him confessing to the murder of Skye Green?"

"We all know how unreliable confessions are, George. Convenient? Yes. Irrefutable proof of guilt? No."

"But you have proof that all these crimes are linked, I hope?"

"No, but we don't have proof they're not linked either," Freya said. "And we'd be remiss if we discounted the first two murders to focus on Hayley Donovan when so much evidence points to them being linked and Frank Donovan being innocent. For starters, Hayley Donovan was his daughter, and from what we can tell, the two were either rebuilding a relationship or spending time together, at least."

"What makes you say that?" Larson asked.

"The tattoos on Hayley's back are identical to those on Donovan's hands."

"That doesn't mean anything," Larson said.

"The pair were also seen in Mablethorpe together," Freya said. "Apparently they were quite familiar."

"Who saw them?" Hart asked.

"Vaughan Barrow," he replied. "According to him, that was the reason they split up. I think she was keeping the relationship with her father a secret from her siblings, Deborah and Justin."

"So, you want to take the word of the primary suspect?" Larson asked. "I don't want to be the one to tell you this, but criminals tend to bend the truth a little."

"Vaughan wasn't a suspect when he told us," Freya added. "And he was standing beside his current girlfriend, which must have been a difficult conversation for him to have."

"Okay," Larson said, clearly sensing how determined they were to build on the theory. "So, what do we do now?"

"We talk to Frank Donovan," Freya said. "I want to know exactly what happened the night Skye Green died. I want to eliminate him entirely so we can focus on Vaughan."

"And us?" Larson said.

"Find me the link between Vaughan Barrow and Skye Green," Freya said. "He's clearly in some kind of relationship with Stella Green, but that's now. I need to know if they were close when Skye was murdered."

"Failing that?" Larson said, as Freya closed her notes and gave Ben the signal they were finished.

"Find me Stella Green," she said. "I do not want Vaughan brought in until we have our ducks in a row. We'll have thirty-six hours with him at the most. When we eventually bring him in, I don't want him to have anywhere to turn."

"You don't want to question him first, perhaps? Give him the opportunity to tell his side of the story?"

"This morning, that's exactly what I wanted to do," Freya said. "But now I've seen Frank Donovan and we've linked Barrow to the murder of Charlotte Rimmell, I'd consider him a flight risk."

Larson exhaled heavily and removed his glasses again, folding them carefully and setting them down on the table.

"Okay," he said. "I've asked you to help us and helping us you are. I suppose I have to give you some slack."

"Thanks for the vote of confidence," Freya said, as she stood and replaced her chair beneath the table. Ben held the door for her, and she was almost out of the room when Larson called out.

"Bloom?" he said, and Freya stopped, leaving Ben to inhale her perfume. "Please don't let me down," he said. "I don't like leaving open ends."

CHAPTER FORTY-THREE

On first appearances, Frank Donovan sat with a straight back, calm and still, with his hands on his knees, as if he was waiting for a bus to arrive or attending a job interview.

But on closer inspection, Freya saw the cracks in his shell, which seemed to emanate from his red eyes and furrowed brow.

Freya studied the tattoos in the bright light. They were good for prison tattoos, which she presumed they were due to the limited colour palette and almost childlike finishing touches.

"Shall we?" she said from the doorway. "I think you'll find the interview room a little more comfortable."

"I do have some experience of interview rooms," he replied. "Not ones I wish to recollect."

"Naturally," she replied. "Have you eaten?"

"The custody sergeant has been more than accommodating. A far cry from how he treated me once years ago."

"You remember him then?"

"Oh, I remember him. I remember them all. I remember the journey in the back of the transit vehicle, I remember my first day in prison, I remember my last day with my family, everything. I remember it all."

"You've been through it, haven't you?" she said, to which he offered no response other than a polite smile, albeit as brief as a flash of lightning. "Perhaps we can right some wrongs along the way? Come on."

She waved him past, gesturing that he should follow Ben. They passed the custody desk, and before they went through into the main corridor, Freya touched the custody sergeant's arm.

"Thank you for taking care of him. I realise it was out of the ordinary."

He stared down at her hand on his arm and then at her, wide-eyed.

"No need," he said.

"It's just…" she began, then stopped herself.

"It's just what?"

"It's just that I'm trying to be a good person," she said, realising she was talking to a stranger. "It's not something that comes naturally, so apologies if my manner was a little abrupt."

It took a lot for Freya to voice that statement, and she checked over her shoulder to make sure Ben wasn't within earshot. But the sergeant seemed to brush it off, returning to working on the computer.

"You're not the first and you're not the last," he said. Then he saw the intrigued expression on Freya's face and explained a little more. "Stressed police officers. You should take a leaf out of George's book. He's made of Teflon, I swear. Everything just washes off. It'll be a sad day when that man hangs his cuffs up."

Freya pondered that comment thoughtfully.

"You're not the first person to speak highly of him," she said.

"And I won't be the last. The man has the patience of a saint and the heart of a lion."

"I'll bear that in mind," she told him, and slipped through the doorway, seeing Ben wave to her from the interview room door.

"Right then, Frank," she began when she entered the room and tossed her file onto the table. "How are you feeling?"

He stared at his hands with a look of utter misery on his face.

"Been better," he replied, then he pulled himself together and took a deep breath. "I'm getting there. It's a hard one to get my head around."

"I understand," Freya replied softly. "I'll try to make this as painless as I can, but first and foremost, I have a duty of care to ensure your safety, Frank. I have to make sure you're okay."

"I'm fine," he said.

"You might feel fine, but..."

"But what?" he asked, and Freya considered how she might phrase what she had to say to release the information in the right order.

"Frank, I want to tell you something," she began.

"Shouldn't you be recording this?" he asked. "They recorded me before. Hours of it, there was."

"It's really not necessary," Freya explained.

"I should have a brief, shouldn't I?" he said. "What is this?"

"This is an informal discussion, Frank. I'll be making notes, but as for using what you say in court, I don't think it's the best idea right now."

"And why's that?" he asked. "Surely you have a protocol to follow?"

"I do," she said. "But you know what? I'll just come right out and say what I have to say. If I hit record on that machine, I'll need to log a file along with a statement, all of which is tied to you within our central database. Do you know what will happen then?"

"No," he said.

"Hull Police will see the record and your parole officer will be knocking on our door in under a day, and they won't be bringing bloody tea and toast," she said. "They'll nick you for breaking the terms of your parole, and you'll be back inside before you know it. Is that what you want?"

His chest deflated as he exhaled, and his nostrils flared.

"No, of course not," he said.

"Which is why this is informal."

"Why are you helping me? Why bother with all this? Why leave the cell open? Why make sure I was fed?"

"Because, Frank, believe it or not, you're sitting in front of the only two police officers in Britain that believe you're innocent."

"You believe what?" he said quietly.

"I don't believe you killed Skye Green, and I certainly don't believe you had anything to do with Hayley's murder."

"Of course, I didn't murder Hayley. She's my daughter."

"And Skye Green?" Freya asked, to which his body seemed to slump.

"I pleaded guilty, didn't I?" he said dryly.

"There are people out there who believe you had something to do with Hayley's death, Frank," she said. "And it's not hard to see why. I mean, you were released from prison three months ago and you showed up here despite what happened."

"I had to do something—"

"I'm not questioning the time you spent with Hayley. I'm not questioning anything you've done. But the fact remains that Skye Green was murdered, and if it wasn't you, then who was it?"

He stiffened at the statement and sucked his lips thin.

"If I knew that..." he said eventually.

"Tell me about those tattoos," Freya said, changing tack, and he immediately lowered his hands beneath the table and adopted a shameful expression. "Do they have any significance, Frank? They look like prison tattoos. Is that where you had them done?"

"They remind me," he said suddenly. "That's all."

"Remind you of what exactly? It seems odd to me that a man who once held a very prestigious position in society would even consider a tattoo. It's not unheard of, of course, but it's not often one sees it."

He held up the hand with the angel. "That reminds me of who

I once was," he started, then held up the hand with the devil's head in muted red. "And this reminds me of who I am now."

"Are you saying you no longer believe in God?" Freya asked. "Sorry, you'll have to help me here. I must admit I'm not well-versed in religious matters."

"I believe. Of course, I believe," he said, staring at the hand with the angel and flexing his fingers to see the image distort. Then he stared hard at Freya with a sadness in his eyes. "I'm just no longer worthy, and if I'm no longer worthy, then I must walk a different path."

He held up the hand with the devil again, then lowered them both to his lap, out of sight.

"Surely God forgives?" Freya said. "I thought that was at the very heart of faith? Forgiveness. Repent."

"For some, maybe," he replied. "But I can never return to God's side. Not now. I can never do God's work."

"Does that mean you must do the devil's work?" Ben asked, then he caught Freya's stare and explained. "It was just something somebody said once, that's all."

"I once did God's work by choice," Donovan said. "I'm no longer worthy to do His work or anybody's. I'm forced to live in purgatory, which, for a man like me, might as well be hell."

"Frank, tell me about your relationship with Hayley," Freya said.

"My relationship?" he replied, with a shake of his head, as if he didn't understand the question. "She was my daughter."

"So is Deborah," Freya said.

"Deborah is different," he began, and the tiniest of laughs escaped. "She's like her mother. Strong and unforgiving. She made her opinion of me quite clear before I was sentenced."

"She didn't visit you?" Ben asked, to which he shook his head.

"Only Hayley ever came," he said. "She was like you."

"She believed you to be innocent?" Ben asked. "Despite your guilty plea?"

"Speaking of which," Freya said. "The file on Skye Green's investigation says you confessed and then pleaded guilty. Why exactly did you confess?"

"Why do you think?" he said.

"The obvious answer is that you *were* guilty," Freya said. "But I don't believe that for a second, and if Hayley did, then I must be missing something."

"Tell me what would have happened if I hadn't confessed," he said. "Come on, you know the process. What would have happened?"

"If you were the primary suspect in a murder enquiry, Frank, your life and that of your family would have been turned upside down until they had enough on you."

"Right," he replied. "Don't you think they've been through enough? Debs and Hayley?"

"And Justin?" Ben said.

"Him too," Frank replied. "They all have, what with them losing their mum."

"So you just confessed? Just like that?"

"What was I supposed to do? Have the police tear us apart? Have their private lives opened up for the world to see?"

"That's very noble of you."

"I wouldn't call it noble," Frank said. "Debs certainly wouldn't. She hasn't spoken to me since. Didn't even come to my hearing."

"But Hayley did?" Ben said. "Why did Hayley believe you were innocent when Deborah didn't?"

"I think they call it being in denial," he explained.

"So you maintain that you're guilty?" Freya asked. "Why don't you tell us what happened?"

"I explained it all to the officers nine years ago," he said, and he nodded at the file. "It should be in there."

"I'd like to hear it in your own words," Freya replied. "Straight from the horse's mouth, if you please."

He stared at her, and then down at the file, and brought his hands up to rest on the desk as if the two images tattooed onto his skin were a reminder.

"It was summertime," he started. "Not as hot as it is now, but still nice. We'd arranged a night walk for the younger members of our congregation."

"We?"

"The church," he said. "The community. There was a comet due over us. Pan something or other."

"Pan-Starrs?" Ben asked. "I remember that."

"That's it," Frank replied. "A few of us wanted to see it, and it's not really safe for the younger members to stay out to see it, so we arranged a walk."

"And did you see it?" Ben asked, to which he nodded.

"We did. We saw it in all its glory, streaking across the sky," he said. "It was a night to remember, in more ways than one."

"And that's it, is it?" Freya asked.

"That's when it happened."

"Tell me what you did then, Frank," she said. "Tell me exactly how you managed to coax Skye Green away from the group, and exactly how you murdered her."

"I didn't have to coax her," he said, then looked away, casting his eyes to the floor. "She managed to get herself stuck in the mud. All I had to do was put my hands around her neck."

"Is that right?" Freya said.

"It's the truth."

"It's one version of the truth," Freya told him. "But if you expect me to believe it, I'm afraid you're going to have to try harder than that. For a start, Skye Green wasn't strangled, she suffocated. Similar, but the symptoms are slightly different. For example, her trachea was intact."

"Her what?"

"Her trachea," Freya said, indicating the area to the front of her throat. "Just like Hayley's."

"You're mistaken."

"Who else was there?" Freya asked.

"A few of us went," he explained, and he held Freya's gaze like he was trying to convince himself of his guilt. "About a dozen, I think."

"And your family?"

"Of course," he said. "I took them all."

"And what happened when the comet had passed?" Ben asked. "Surely somebody noticed she was missing?"

"You've got the statement I made nine years ago," he said. "Don't make me relive it. Please?"

"So shall we agree to disagree?" Freya said. "You say you killed Skye Green. I say you're lying."

"I've got a criminal record that proves I'm not a liar."

They met eye to eye, each one digging their heels in, refusing to budge.

"Talk to me about your relationship with Hayley," Freya said.

The change of topic seemed like a relief to him and he settled back into his seat, the tension falling from his shoulders.

"When I was released, it took me a while to adjust to life on the outside. They arranged a little bedsit for me and I even found work, shifting boxes in a factory."

"You were lucky," Freya said. "Many people in your situation find it hard to gain employment."

"Maybe it was because I kept my nose clean while I was inside. They give you references, you know? The screws. The good ones do, anyway," he said, and he held up his angel. "I saved what money I could and bought a little van. My thinking was that if push came to shove, I'd always have somewhere to sleep. But mostly, I needed the means to visit Hayley. She was my lifeline."

"You must have been close," Freya said.

"We were. I only wish I could've done more with her. Maybe if Deborah had seen how close we were, she might have come around. She might have learned to love me again."

"Did you know Hayley had those tattoos?' Freya said, flicking her eyes down to his hands, to which he appeared surprised.

"My Hayley?" he said, and Freya nodded. "She didn't tell me that."

"On her back," she said, nodding. "She must have thought highly of you. But do you know what I find interesting, Frank? You haven't once mentioned your son, Justin. Why is that?"

"Do you mind if we don't?" he asked, although he was clearly pained at the mention of his son's name.

"We will need to discuss him at some point, Frank."

"I can't," he replied, his voice thicker than it had been a few moments before, and his breathing had grown heavy.

"Very well. Have you ever heard of a man named Vaughan Barrow?" Freya said.

"Vaughan Barrow? Should I?"

"He was living in Saltfleet nine years ago when Skye Green died."

"And you think it was this Vaughan chap? Despite me pleading guilty?"

"Frank, there's something I have to say. I want you to listen very carefully, okay? If you continue to help me, I'll do everything I can to keep the parole officers off your back. But I need you to listen, and I need you to be honest with me. If you're not honest with me, then I'll be on the phone in a heartbeat."

"Okay," he said, and he sat forward in his chair, linking his tattooed hands together. "But I should warn you, I've just been released from a nine-year prison stretch, during which time I lost my home, my family, and everything I owned. Now, three months later, I've lost my daughter. So, you'll forgive me if I seem a little keen to get to the point here."

"The point is, Frank," Freya said, "ten years ago, a girl around the same age as Hayley and Skye was killed over in Kirkby."

"Are you trying to make me feel better?"

"There are several similarities in the MO, Frank," she said. Then explained, "The way in which the girls died."

"Okay, sorry, you're going to have to explain a little more. I'm not sure what you're saying—"

"The primary suspect in the murder was a man named Neil Barrow," Freya said. "He was a vicar."

The words seemed to register almost immediately, but the meaning took a little longer.

"A vicar?" he said, mulling it over. "Was he convicted?"

"No, Frank. Sadly, he ended his life before the investigating officers could charge him."

"Something I never had the chance to do," he said, which took Freya by surprise. But she chose not to dig deeper into the topic, given the man's fragile emotional state. "If you had any idea of what it's like in there, you'd understand."

"Oh, I do understand," Freya said. "And I know exactly what it's like in there. I also know what happens to individuals charged with murdering young girls."

"First-hand experience?"

"I haven't had a front-row seat, but I've been close enough," she said. "The point is that Neil Barrow's circumstances were similar to your own, and you, Frank, are still alive."

"And you think I know something about this Barrow chap? Vaughan, was it?"

"Not necessarily," she replied, and she set her pen down on the table. "But before you leave here, you're going to tell me every single thing you can. I want every name of every individual, and every conceivable possibility you thought of while you were locked up, and before you tell me you pleaded guilty, I'd recommend you give it some serious thought. One phone call from me, and you're back inside to complete your sentence."

He shook his head as if she was crazy to suggest he might know something. He spoke slowly and softly, but his tone carried with a defiant tone, a tired growl.

"What's left of my family doesn't want to know me. The only person who did is now dead. I have no house, no friends, and I spend more time looking over my shoulder than I do looking forward," he said. "So, go ahead. Make that call, Inspector. Do us all a favour."

CHAPTER FORTY-FOUR

Ben held the door to the public entrance open, then stood back to allow Frank Donovan to pass.

"You're free to go," he said.

"I'd suggest you find somewhere else to stay," Freya told him. "Maybe it's time you used that van of yours? Find somewhere quiet and out of the way."

"Aren't you going to take me back to Saltfleet?" he said.

"We're not a taxi service," Freya said. "Like I said at the beginning of our chat, you help me, and I'll help you."

"I've told you everything—"

"All you've given me is a vague description of what happened the night Skye was murdered, which anybody who read the newspaper might know, and that you pleaded guilty to Skye Green's murder, yet you deny murdering Hayley, despite there being so many similarities," she said. "When you've been in this game for as long as I have, you get to learn there is no such thing as coincidences. Two murderous vicars in one county, one year apart?" She shook her head at the prospect. "I don't think so, Frank."

"So, who is it?" he replied. "You said I was in danger. Who from? Who's this Vaughan you spoke of? Is it him?"

"I'm afraid I can't compromise our investigation," she said. "Of course, if you were willing to give us a little more..."

"I've told you—"

"Then I'd be willing to take measures to ensure your safety," she said, cutting him off to finish her sentence before he lied again. "But as you're hellbent on continuing your ridiculous claim of being responsible for Skye Green's murder, I'm afraid there's very little I can do. Now, I won't be calling your parole officer and I won't be filing a statement of any kind. But please don't expect me to help you in any way. If you want to continue your lie, then you're on your own."

"This is rid—"

"You know where we are if you change your mind, Mr Donovan," Freya said, and she nodded for Ben to let the door close. They watched him through the little window as he left the station. He fished an old baseball cap from his pocket and pulled it down onto his head, then disappeared from view.

"Is that wise, Freya?" Ben said, as she stared into space. He recognised her expression as the one she wore when she doubted her own actions. "If anything happens to him—"

"If anything happens to him, it'll be me in the firing line," Freya said, then turned away from the window to meet Ben face to face. "And quite frankly, that's a risk I'm willing to take right now. Now, let's talk to Hart before we get back out there."

Ben reached and grabbed her arm to hold her there, and she stared down at his hand in utter disgust.

"Wait a minute," he said.

"Let go, Ben."

"No. Listen. That man is in real danger."

"I'm warning you, Ben—"

"Not to mention your career," he continued, gripping her arm as tight as he dared without actually hurting her. "He's a convicted murderer who is the only one we know of who might help us identify his daughter's murderer. We know Stella Green and Vaughan Barrow have been to the church, and we know they're up to something."

He dropped his voice to a low whisper and pulled her closer.

"Every officer in this building knows we've spoken to him, Freya. If something happens to him, all it would take is for somebody to mention us and we'll be up before the board before you know it. Not just you, but me too. And what do you think will happen? I hope you don't think Standing will step in and support us because he won't. You'll have given him everything he needs to palm you off."

"Let go of my arm, Ben," she said, her voice low and threatening, and he did as she asked but was reluctant to break her stare. "What do you suggest?"

"I suggest we keep him safe," he replied. "I suggest we lean on him. We both know he's not telling us everything. We can't just let him go. What if we're wrong? What if he *did* murder Skye Green? And what if he was even responsible for Charlotte Rimmell's death? And, come to think of it, Hayley, too? We could have just let a killer walk free."

"He's not a killer," Freya said, more to silence him than any other reason. "And trust me, none of this will come back on you."

"Freya—"

"No, wait. Hear me out," she said, holding her hand up to give her some time to compose her temper. "I don't believe Frank Donovan murdered Charlotte, Skye, or his own daughter. I think he's hiding something though. I think he knows who it was and he's going after them."

"Oh, well, that's okay then," Ben said. "That makes it totally acceptable to let him go free."

"It does, as it happens," Freya told him.

"So, what now? We follow him and hope he leads us to the killer?"

"Don't be ridiculous, Ben. This isn't the movies," she said.

"Besides, we know where he's going. All we have to do is beat him there."

"For God's sake. Could you be any more cryptic?"

"Yes, if you want me to," she said, turning to leave him standing there at one end of the corridor.

"So, where are you going?" he called, hearing the frustration in his own voice.

She turned the corner, forcing him to run a few steps to catch her as she pushed through the double doors and burst into the Major Crimes room.

"Hart?" she said. "How are you getting on?"

"Bloody hell, Freya. Give her a chance, she's only had an hour," Ben said.

"Actually, I have something," Hart said and looked to Larson for his approval. He glanced up from his laptop, then at Freya, and gave a curt nod before returning to whatever he was doing. Hart produced a few printouts and handed them to Freya, who, without reading them, slipped them inside her folder. "You were right about Sandy Robinson. She's Vaughan Barrow's aunt. His mother's sister. She has a house in Scupholme."

"Where's that?" Ben asked.

"Put it this way, she'd drive past St Botolph's on the way to Saltfleet," Hart said. "No criminal record, no history at all, to be honest."

"So, it's a dead end?" Freya said.

"Not quite. There's another name on the electoral register for her address."

"Another name? Who?"

"Gloria Barrow," Hart said. "Her sister. Vaughan's mother."

"And Neil Barrow's wife," Freya muttered. "The address?"

"On page one," Hart said, nodding at the file.

"Excellent. Let's pay her a visit to see what she has to say. Anything else?"

"Maybe, I'm not sure," Hart replied, this time with a little less confidence. "Vaughan Barrow has a few offences to his name. Mostly small-time stuff, breaking and entering, TDA, and some driving offences."

"Standard for someone like him," Ben said.

"That's what I thought," Hart continued. "So, I ran an internet search for him. It's getting harder with all the data protection rules, but I did find something interesting. There's a community group on Facebook, some kind of grief counselling sessions. He's a member, or at least he used to be. The post was old, and he was tagged, which for some reason wasn't picked up by GDPR."

"He lost his dad," Freya said. "Therapists often steer people suffering with grief down that route."

"Especially if Vaughan Barrow had something to do with Charlotte Rimmell's death," Ben said. "Imagine the guilt."

"I thought that too," Hart said, again nodding at the file Freya was holding. "Check page two."

Freya flipped open the file and found the document, and Ben leaned over her shoulder to read it, finding a list of names that appeared to be associated with the grief counselling group.

Freya stabbed a well-manicured fingernail at a name halfway down, and Hart smiled.

"Stella Green," Ben said. "Of course, she lost her sister."

"Maybe that's where they met," Freya mumbled, voicing her thoughts. Larson looked up from his laptop, removed his glasses, and cocked his head with interest as Freya deciphered the information. "Two individuals, both suffering from grief."

"Yes, but if we're right about Vaughan Barrow, Freya," Ben said, "then he's the reason Stella Green is there in the first place. You're not suggesting he's creepy enough to actually help the sister of one of his victims through the grieving process, are you?"

"What if he's not who we think he is?" Freya said. "What if he's innocent but knows who the real killer is?"

"You don't think he and Stella Green have been hunting the

killer, do you?" Ben said. "You know? Working together? It would make sense, given that Frank Donovan is out there walking the streets."

Freya slipped the piece of paper back into the file and licked her lips.

"Well done, Hart. This is excellent," she said. "I need one more favour."

Hart waited for the instruction, and again, Larson nodded his approval.

"I need uniform on standby," she said.

"Do you think Frank Donovan is in danger?" Larson asked, still listening for Freya's response to Ben's question. "I understand you've just let him go."

"Possibly," Freya said, glancing back at Ben. "Either that or he's about to make a very big mistake."

CHAPTER FORTY-FIVE

"Where are we going?" Ben asked as he watched Freya from the passenger seat, but as expected, he received no reply. She had slipped into one of those almost catatonic states of thought, during which the facts they had to work with, and her emotions wrestled for her attention. "Well, I'm glad we cleared that one up," he said, hoping a touch of sarcasm might snap her out of it.

She turned onto the main road towards Saltfleet, which did little to narrow down the possible destinations she had in mind, so Ben resorted to staring out of the window to let the peaceful surroundings provide some kind of clarity in which the facts could be laid out and, more importantly, the gaps become evident.

"So Frank Donovan was released from prison three months ago. In that time, he saved up, got himself a little van, and rebuilt a relationship with Hayley, which, as we understand it, was kept secret from Deborah and Justin. However, her boyfriend, Vaughan, saw them together and thought something was going on. She denied it and he broke it off. That gives Vaughan a motive, albeit on the weak side." He looked across at her to see if what he had said had stirred any kind of reaction from Freya, but there was nothing. She stared ahead, lost in her own thought process. "Feel free to join in."

"Feel free to continue voicing your thoughts," she said. "I'm just trying to work something out."

He stared back out of the window again, spying a farmer tending a hedge in a nearby field, which made him think of his father and his brothers. But the distraction lasted seconds, and soon the serenity the scenery provided took effect.

"Then, Friday night, we saw Stella Green outside the holiday park until she spotted Frank Donovan, and then she ran back inside, presumably to the caravan. What was Frank doing there? Why was she out there? And why did she run back to the caravan?" he said. "We didn't ask Frank why he was there?"

"No, I chose not to reveal that particular piece of information," she said. "I wanted to see if he brought it up, which he didn't."

"Which adds weight to the fact that he's hiding something," Ben said.

"Carry on," Freya muttered, sounding disinterested but clearly paying attention.

"Where did Frank go when Stella Green spotted him on Sea Lane? He drove off, but where did he go?" Ben said, pulling his phone from his pocket to check for messages from Michaela. There were none. "Then we have Vaughan Barrow, which is where this gets complicated. We know his father was accused of murdering Charlotte Rimmell and subsequently took his own life. We know the investigating team found photos of her on his laptop and he can't account for his whereabouts during the window the murder took place, despite him being seen at the start line when the race began."

"But we also can't prove he was at the scene," Freya said. "Which is why he was bailed in the first place."

"Right," Ben said, pleased to have caught a thread of her

attention. "And now Cruz is working on trying to prove it *was* Neil Barrow who killed Charlotte."

"Which he won't do," Freya said, and she glanced his way for the first time during the journey, placing one of her expensive heels on the verge of interaction. "He won't prove it, because it wasn't Neil Barrow."

"You think it was Vaughan, still?" Ben asked, coaxing her towards a shared thought process.

"We know Vaughan left Kirkby shortly after Neil Barrow died, presumably with his distraught mother," she said. "A year later, another girl dies in a similar circumstance and another vicar pays the price."

"But Frank Donovan hadn't even heard of Vaughan."

"So he says," Freya said, as they entered Saltfleet and slowed as they passed another church. She glanced in the mirror at the sound of the driver behind them honking his horn, then accelerated back up to forty miles per hour. "But we now know that Vaughan attended some kind of group grief counselling where he met Stella, and that's where the two troubled individuals bonded. Which leads me to two potential theories."

"Oh, so we do actually have theories, then?" Ben said, and Freya glared at him. "Sorry, it's just that up until now we've been chasing people who you claim to be innocent."

"The first," she said, continuing her monologue before she lost her focus, "is that Stella and Vaughan believe Frank to be guilty of the murder of Skye Green, and that they murdered Hayley by way of revenge."

"Nine years later?" Ben said. "Why wait?"

"Because if Frank Donovan was still in prison when the murder took place, he couldn't be accused, which would lead the police, or you and I, to investigate them further."

"Right," Ben said. "Which would explain why Stella Green was outside the holiday park in the early hours of Saturday morning. She was keeping watch."

"Correct," Freya said. "And if that is true, then Frank somehow knew about it and realised they were on to him."

"How do we prove that?" Ben said.

"Well, that's going to be difficult," she replied. "Which leads me to my other theory."

"Which is?"

"Far simpler. Vaughan Barrow is a psychopath," she said flatly. "Revenge has nothing to do with it. He's a coercive, manipulative psycho who enjoys destroying lives."

"Which is where our investigation links to Cruz's cold case," Ben agreed. "It's a lot more plausible than your first theory."

"I've been mulling it over," she said. "His father's laptop had images of Charlotte Rimmell on the hard drive. I wonder if anybody considered that it wasn't him who put them there?"

"You think Vaughan could have done it? But why?"

"That's what we're about to find out," Freya said, as she passed St Botolph's, heading inland.

"Are we going to Sandy Robinson's house? You want to talk to Vaughan's mother?" Ben said. "Well, thanks for the guessing game. That was fun."

"I wasn't sure at first," she said. "But the more we discuss him, the more I'm certain. And as for why he would have positioned his father as the murderer, perhaps his mother can explain? Get Cruz on the line, will you?"

Following the instruction blindly, he routed the call through the car's Bluetooth system and sat back as Freya took the narrow country lanes slowly. "Cruz?" Ben said.

"Ben?" Cruz's tinny voice replied. "How's it going?"

"Apart from being baked in the sun like a potato?" Ben replied. "Not bad. How's it going there?"

"Ah, you know," Cruz said. "I'm keeping my head down, trying to stay out of it."

"Best way," Ben said.

"Cruz, it's DI Bloom," Freya said, cutting their little chat short. "I need you to do something for me."

"Morning, boss," he said cheerfully. "How can I help?"

"You mentioned some photos on Neil Barrow's laptop," Freya said. "Have you seen them?"

"I have," he replied, the joy gone from his voice.

"You told me they were in a folder. Is that right?"

"Yes, boss. A folder named Charlotte."

"Do you have the laptop there?"

"I do, as it happens," he said. "I'm scared to turn it off. Took me an entire morning to get it charged and turned on."

"I want you to look at the details of the images, and by that, I mean the metadata."

"The what?"

"I want you to tell me if all the photos were added to the laptop at the same time, or if the little collection was built up over a period of time."

"Oh, right," he said, as he busied himself with the task. From the passenger seat, Ben watched with quiet admiration as Freya navigated the streets of Alvingham, a tiny village east of Saltfleet and St Botolph's. "Bloody hell. They were all added at the same time."

"That's what I thought you'd say," Freya said, as she came to a stop at the side of the road. "And without going into detail about the photos, does it look like they were taken at different times?"

"Definitely," Cruz said. "And don't worry, they aren't *those* types of photos. They aren't indecent. It's just that a vicar probably shouldn't have them on his laptop. It's a bit creepy."

"So, if all the images were added at the same time..." Freya said, leaving space for Cruz to fill in the blanks.

"Then he wasn't developing a library of photos over time," he replied. "They were copied onto the laptop all at once. But from where?"

"From somebody else's laptop, I would imagine," Freya said. "His son, to be more precise."

"Vaughan? Have you managed to talk to him yet?" Cruz asked.

"Briefly, but I don't want him spooked. He's transient, so we're keeping our cards close to our chests until we can be sure. When we bring him in, he's staying in."

"What do I tell the guv if he asks?"

"Tell him you're pretty sure Neil Barrow is innocent and you're following up on a lead," Freya told him. "When the time is right, I'll give you and DS Nillson everything you need to put him back in his box. Just keep him at bay. Can you do that?"

"I'll try, boss," Cruz replied. "But you know what he's like."

"Sadly, I do," Freya said. "Bear with me. If my theory is wrong, then I'll talk to him. I'll take the hit."

"No, boss—"

"I mean it," she said. "And I meant what I said last night. You all deserve better from me, and from now, you'll get it. Twenty-four hours, Cruz. Just keep him off your back for twenty-four hours. Can you do that for me?"

"I'll do my best, boss," he said, doing his best to sound positive.

"Good," she said. "I'll be in touch."

Ben ended the call and pocketed his phone, sensing Freya needed a moment of peace. She stared up at the house they were parked outside.

"Are you sure about this?" he asked.

"No," she replied, as she opened the door and climbed down. "But if I'm right, and Vaughan is a psychopath, then we have an even larger problem on our hands."

"Which is?"

She stared him in the eye, hesitating before committing to the added complexity.

"Vaughan met the sister of his second victim at grief counselling and befriended her."

The statement hit Ben like a hammer in the chest and he took a few moments to absorb it.

"Are you saying Stella is in danger?" Ben asked. "And if so, why now? Why wait?"

"We might not know too much about our murderer, Ben," she replied. "but we do know one thing. He likes to ensure there's somebody else to take the rap."

CHAPTER FORTY-SIX

"Mrs Barrow," Freya called, as she rapped on the door for the third time. "It's the police. I wondered if we could just have a quick word."

She studied Ben's face for some kind of idea of what he was thinking, then flicked her head at the little alleyway down the side of the detached cottage. He did as instructed and ventured out of sight, leaving Freya peering through the living room window.

The cottage was nice, not too dissimilar to the one she had been looking at when Ben had called at the weekend. The rooms were small but cosy enough to make homely, and not too much for a single person like Sandy Robinson to keep clean, even if her sister was on an extended stay.

"Mrs Barrow," she called out, "I know you're in. The TV is on and your sister is home."

Peering through the front window gave her a clear view through the house and into the back garden, from where Ben was staring back at her, pointing to his right.

He knocked gently on the glass and called to her, his voice a faint mumble from where Freya was standing.

Eventually, the door lock clicked and a woman pulled the door open.

"Mrs Barrow?" Freya said, presenting her warrant card. "I'm terribly sorry to bother you, but might we have a quick word?"

Ben re-joined her at the front of the house and showed his warrant card for good measure.

"I can assure you, you're not in any trouble," Freya told her.

She wore her grey hair tied back in a scraggly ponytail, and the extra pounds that filled her bosom and midriff were unnatural as if she wasn't designed to be overweight but circumstances had dictated her so.

"It's Vaughan, isn't it?" she said, finally and with the intuition of a mother. She sighed before Freya could even respond. "What's he done now? Stealing again?"

"I think it's best if we come inside," Freya said, which seemed to alarm the woman even more. "We just need to ask you a few questions."

"He's okay, isn't he?" she asked. "He's not hurt?"

"No, he's not hurt," Freya told her. "Not that we're aware of, anyway."

"How did you find me?" Barrow asked. "Nobody knows I'm here."

"The electoral register," Freya replied, taking a step into the house and waiting for her to make way. She stepped back, and immediately, Freya smelled alcohol, stale like an old pub in the morning. It was the type of smell that clung to skin and clothes.

Mrs Barrow offered no tea or coffee but led them through a small living room – where a jigsaw puzzle depicting an amusing image of a florist and a customer struggling with a dog and a cat lay on the coffee table – to the kitchen as picture-perfect as the one in the house Freya was keen on buying. A row of copper saucepans hung from a linen rack, suspended in the air for effect and, Freya thought, due to the lack of cupboard space the quaint little space offered.

"It's a nice place," Freya said. "Very charming."

"You can thank my sister for that," she replied, as she drew a clear, glass bottle from the cupboard. "Do you mind?"

"Gin?" Freya asked. "Don't let me stop you."

She poured a large measure into a glass tumbler, then with practised movements topped it up with tonic water and returned the mixer to the fridge. A single ice cube from the freezer followed, and she took a sip, which seemed to quench a fire inside her from the way her body relaxed.

"Sorry," she said, seeming embarrassed. "I just need it sometimes."

"We're not here to judge," Freya said, as warmly as she could, and the woman took a large mouthful, gulping it down greedily. "When was the last time you saw your son?"

She set the tumbler down on the wooden kitchen surface, but her grip remained tight against the glass.

"A few days," she said. "A week, maybe?"

"Does he visit often?" Freya asked.

"He doesn't have a schedule if that's what you mean. He comes and goes when he needs something. Money, usually."

"Mrs Barrow—"

"Gloria," she said. "Call me Gloria. I imagine now's the time when you announce what he's done. Might as well get straight to it."

She took another mouthful of her drink and prepared herself.

"Gloria, we think Vaughan is involved in a serious event that took place last Friday night."

"A serious event?"

"A murder, I'm afraid," Freya said. "I know that's not something any mother wants to hear."

"It's okay. You don't have to sugar-coat it," she said, and she stared down at the drink in her hand. "I suppose it was always going to escalate."

"First of all, can you confirm if you saw him last Friday

evening?" Freya said. "You said you saw him a few days to a week ago. Can you provide a little more clarity?"

Again, Gloria looked embarrassed and stared down at her drink.

"I don't think so. If I see him, it's normally around lunchtime. In fact, it was. I know it was. It was Thursday lunchtime."

"You're sure?"

"He's no fool, Inspector," she said. "He knows when I collect my pension."

"He borrowed money from you?"

"Borrowed? No, not Vaughan. He helps me out from time to time," she said with a weak smile. "He's not all bad, you know? There is a heart in there."

"I'm sure," Freya said.

"Who was it then? Who has he supposed to have hurt? Not that Donovan girl? Janice down the bakers said something about her. What's her name?" She clicked the fingers of her free hand to see through the alcohol-induced fog. "Helen? No. Hayley. Hayley Donovan. Is that right?"

Freya nodded once.

"Well, I doubt he had anything to do with that. He might go the wrong way about things, my Vaughan, but he's no murderer."

"Nobody is until they are," Freya said.

"I heard he was out. The dad. What's his name? Used to be the vicar up at All Saints. Clive? No, Fred–"

"Frank," Ben said.

"That's it," she said, seeming to come alive the more they spoke to her. "I heard he was released a while ago."

"Where did you hear that?" Freya asked.

"Oh, you know? Here and there. People talk, don't they?"

"They do indeed," Freya agreed.

"Bit of a coincidence, isn't it?" she said. "Him being out and that happening to his daughter. It was him who murdered that other girl. Green something."

"Skye Green," Ben said, clearly tired of her inability to recall names.

"That's her. Nice girl, she was, by all accounts."

"I'm afraid I can't discuss the details of the crime, Gloria," Freya said. "But we do have reason to believe that Vaughan is in a relationship with Skye Green's sister, Stella Green."

"In a relationship?" Gloria said, and she laughed for the first time. "My Vaughan in a relationship? That'll be the day."

"I'm afraid the pair of them do seem to be rather close, Gloria," Freya said. "And we've seen enough to be certain they are... Well, we're sure they're close."

"Oh, I'm sure they are," Gloria replied. "He never was one to shy away from doing what needed to be done to get what he wants. If there's one thing about Vaughan, he's not afraid to get his hands dirty, whether he likes it or not."

"What does that mean?"

"It means," Gloria said, taking another sip of her drink, which was, by now, nearly empty, "that she's not really his type if you know what I mean?"

"Not his type?" Ben said. "From what we've heard, he doesn't have a type."

"He might be promiscuous, but I can assure you he would not be in a relationship with her."

"Because of who she is?"

"No, because of what she is," Gloria said, and spoke over the rim of her glass. "Female."

"Vaughan?" Ben said disbelievingly. "He's—"

"He's not gay," Gloria said. "But he's not straight, either. I don't think he has a preference. But I do know that he doesn't like being tied down."

"But—"

"Like I said, he's more than happy to use his looks to get what he wants," she said, finishing her drink but holding onto her glass. "Whatever that might be."

"Are you saying he might be using Stella Green to get something?" Freya asked. "Is that something he would do?"

"I wouldn't put it past him," she replied, then began to make her second drink.

"Gloria, we know what happened to Neil," Freya said, starting a new thread as Gloria's back was turned and she was putting the gin back in the cupboard. She stiffened at the mention of his name, which, if Freya was correct, was the root cause of her drink problem; she froze with her hand on the bottle. "We need to know what happened to Vaughan during that time. Was he involved in any way?"

"No," she snapped. "No, Vaughan stayed away."

"Stayed away?" Ben said. "From the church or from your husband?"

"Both," she replied, turning with the bottle of tonic in her hand. "They had a difficult relationship. Neil was a good dad. He was a good man. Not a bad bone in his body. But I think the way Vaughan was, or is, was perhaps just a little too much for him."

"Do you mean the petty crime?" Ben asked. "That must have been difficult for your husband, given his position."

"I was referring to Vaughan's sexual preferences," Gloria said. "The crime didn't start until we moved here."

"Speaking of which, why doesn't he live here with you?" Freya said.

"Have you got children, Inspector?" Gloria asked.

For a moment, Freya nearly said yes, remembering with fondness her ex-husband's son.

"No," she said. "No, I don't."

"Well, when they get to a certain age, they become fiercely independent. They need their space, and who am I to stand in his way?"

"So, you do know where he lives?"

"Oh, I know, and if I'm honest, Neil and I shared certain views."

"You mean you're not exactly a fan of his sexual preference?" Freya asked.

"Was there anything else?" Gloria asked as she dropped a single ice cube into her tumbler.

"Yes, as it happens," Freya said. "I just wanted to warn you that covering for your son could lead to serious consequences for you, if he is involved."

She held Freya's stare while taking a large mouthful. Any shame in her habit she had demonstrated earlier had dissipated. It was as if she was daring Freya to comment on her drinking.

"Vaughan is many things, Inspector," she said. "But he's not in a relationship with that girl's sister, and he is certainly not a murderer. So, warn me until your heart is content. I'll never betray my little boy."

For somebody who clearly drank regularly, the two glasses of gin had taken effect with relative ease, and the silence that followed was cold and hostile.

"Let's go," Freya said to Ben. "That's pretty much all we needed to know."

CHAPTER FORTY-SEVEN

"Get Hart on the phone," Freya said to Ben before he'd even pulled his seat belt on. He clicked the belt into place and fished his phone from his pocket, setting the call to loudspeaker rather than routing it through the car's Bluetooth system. "She's as bad as her bloody son is. It's not even midday and she's already on the sauce."

"I thought we weren't there to judge?" Ben said.

"Not publicly," she said. "I'm glad we got here when we did. Another hour and she'll be sloshed."

"Hart," the voice on the end of the call said.

"Ivy, it's Freya Bloom. I need a favour."

"Okay," she replied, and the sound of the call shifted, which Ben interpreted as her setting her phone to loudspeaker for Larson's benefit.

"I need Donovan's laptop," Freya said.

"His what?"

"His laptop. From the original Skye Green investigation. His laptop was taken as evidence, so I imagine it'll still be in the archives somewhere. Can you get it?"

Her tone and abruptness caused Ben a little discomfort, and

he glanced across at her, which must have resonated, as she then offered a curt, "Sorry, can you get it, please?"

"I can try," Hart said.

"I can get it," a male voice said, which Ben thought sounded like Samson. "I can head down there now."

"How long do you need?" Freya asked, as she pulled away from Gloria Barrow's house and sped back towards Saltfleet.

"Half an hour," he said. "Anything else?"

"Yes, as it happens. Am I right in thinking that you're investigating a spate of burglaries?"

There was a short silence, and Ben imagined the three of them sharing confused expressions.

"Erm, yes," he replied.

"When was the last one?"

"Last night," he replied.

"And before that?"

"One sec," he said, as he shuffled through some papers. "Friday night. Sometime between eleven p.m. and two a.m. according to the victim."

"What was taken?" Freya asked.

"Whatever they can get their hands on," Samson said. "It's usually the same things that are stolen. TVs, microwaves, cash if there's any lying around, alcohol."

"Location?" Freya asked, and she stared across at Ben, clearly enjoying his blank expression. "Where was Friday night's robbery?"

"Sea View Holiday Park," Samson said. "In Mablethorpe. It's–"

"On the seafront," Freya finished for him. "Yes, I worked that out, thank you. Can you give me a call when you've got the laptop charged and functioning?" She caught Ben's stare again, then added a second, "Please."

"Will do," he said, then handed the phone back to Hart.

"Anything else I can do?" she asked.

"Yes, are uniform on standby?" Freya asked.

"Ready to go on your command."

"Good, I want St Botolph's searched. The building, the grounds, and everything in between."

"What are we looking for?"

"You'll know when you find it and call me when you do," Freya replied, and she nodded for Ben to end the call.

"What the bloody hell are you doing?" he asked.

"It's not Vaughan," she said with a sigh.

"But I thought you said—"

"I know what I said, Ben. But you heard what Samson said. There was a burglary on Friday night in Mablethorpe. As wonderful as his mother thinks he is, even Vaughan Barrow can't be in two places at once."

"You think he did the burglary?"

"I'd have money on it," Freya said. "I just need to prove it."

"So where does that leave us?" Ben asked. "I mean, we've got a man convicted for one of the murders who you say is innocent. We've got another man who we can actually link to two of the murders who you're now saying is innocent."

"It leaves us," she said, leaving him hanging while she navigated a turn at high speed, "with Stella Green. The only person we know to be near the scene of the crime at the right time, other than Frank Donovan, of course."

"So why have you asked for his laptop?"

"Because, if there's a folder on his laptop named Skye, and all the photos have been copied onto it in one go, as the folder on Neil Barrow's laptop was, then perhaps whoever killed Charlotte Rimmell killed Skye Green."

"What about Hayley?"

"Ah, she's different," Freya said. "Whoever murdered the first two girls is a psychopath. They have no empathy and there's no limit to what they'll do to satisfy their desires. Both of them were attending church events when they were murdered. Hayley Donovan, however, was murdered for a different reason altogether. They're linked, of course, but the motive is different."

"Oh, great. So, we're looking for two murderers, are we?"

"No, we're looking for one murderer," she replied. "Hayley Donovan's. Frank Donovan has already paid the price for Skye Green's murder and as far as Standing is concerned, Cruz is working on the Charlotte Rimmell investigation. It just so happens that we'll need to understand Charlotte Rimmell's murder to progress."

"And how do you intend on doing that?" Ben asked as Freya eased the car into Sea Lane. She checked her watch, clearly processing some kind of internalised theory that she couldn't put into words, and as a result, Ben was left in the dark again.

"By doing what they train us to do," she replied cryptically. "We eliminate the suspects from the investigation."

Ahead of them, standing outside the holiday park holding her phone in the air, Michaela appeared to be doing some kind of dance as she sought a phone signal. She stopped when she recognised Freya's car and stepped to one side to allow her to park.

"I was trying to call you," she said, as soon as Ben climbed from the car. She waited for Freya to do the same and then began. "I've been on to the local CSI team regarding the debris found in the cuts in Hayley Donovan's feet. No road surface, I'm afraid. Just sand and dirt. Which seems to be consistent with what I found over there." She jabbed her thumb over her shoulder towards the ramp and the marsh.

"So can we assume she removed her shoes in the marsh?" Freya asked, leaning on her side of the car bonnet.

"It's a safe assumption to make," Michaela said, and Ben mused at how the two of them worked so well together yet clashed whenever he was involved. "I would hazard a guess that she removed her shoes to run faster."

"I'd agree with that," Freya said. "Which makes me wonder what she was doing out here in the first place."

"I also had a look at that single boot print," Michaela said.

"Oh, yes?" Freya replied, cocking her head as she did when her interest had been piqued.

"It's definitely the same boot with the same wear on the right-hand side of the sole," Michaela said. "But as far as I can tell that boot hasn't been used for nine years. If it had been used, I would expect to see the worn part eroded further. But there's no evidence of that."

"Which means the owner hasn't used it since Skye Green's murder," Ben said, looking across at Freya, who appeared not to be sold on that idea.

"Or it's been stored," she replied.

"Stored?"

"Kept, waiting for the day when Frank Donovan was released, and another murder could be pinned on him."

"Oh, come on, Freya. Everything points to him."

"Is that right?" she asked. "Tell me, Ben, in the original report on Skye Green's murder, did they mention the weather at all?'

"The weather?" he said, and glanced at Michaela who looked as dumbfounded as he was. "No."

"What time of year was it?"

"Summer, if I recall. That's what Donovan told us, anyway. Why?"

"He said it was hot, but not as hot as it is now. Which begs the question, why was he wearing a pair of boots? One wouldn't need the additional grip to handle any slippery mud. The paths are fine, it's only the boggy parts that are muddy."

"I see," Ben said, and he kicked himself for missing her point. "Why would anybody wear a big, heavy boot in this heat?"

"It's in the high twenties in the evenings," Freya said. "A pair of flip-flops would suffice."

"You're saying the killer stored the boot to implicate Frank Donovan for a second murder."

"Now who would do a thing like that?" she asked, not without a strong element of sarcasm to her tone.

"Somebody who held a grudge against him," Ben said. "Vaughan Barrow?"

"No, we know Vaughan Barrow was elsewhere," Freya said. "While Hayley was being murdered, Vaughan Barrow was conveniently busy robbing a caravan in Mablethorpe."

"We don't know that for sure," Ben said. "That's just a theory."

"And it's a theory I'm going to prove," she said, walking towards the holiday park.

"You have to admit, she's good," Michaela said when Freya was out of earshot.

"Oh, I'm not arguing her competence," Ben agreed. "But sometimes I just wish she'd go about things differently. You know? Apply a little more tact."

"I think that would be like removing the eggs from Hollandaise sauce," she replied, and that cute smile spread across her face. It was nice to have a moment with her. A few minutes to remind him that the world did not revolve around death, murder, and protocol. "Somehow it just wouldn't be the same."

"Are you coming, Ben?" Freya called out from the park entrance, loud enough to get the attention of a family walking their dog. "Come on. Put her down. There'll be plenty of time for you to whisper sweet nothings later on, no doubt."

And with that, she pushed open the door to the site office and disappeared from view, leaving Ben and Michaela under the scrutinising glares of the holidaying family.

CHAPTER FORTY-EIGHT

The site office was empty and compared to their last visit, was in an untidy state. Several coffee cups were dotted about the small space. Paperwork lay in piles, which presumably made sense to Sandy Robinson, just as Freya's own spread of paperwork made sense to her. The floor crunched under Freya's heel from a multitude of beachgoers stopping by on their way back to their caravans.

A toilet flushed somewhere from the back of the room and Freya stepped inside the office just as Ben joined her. She put her finger to her lips, gesturing for him to be quiet, and slowly made her way past the main desk, coming to a stop outside the first of two internal doors in the room.

Hearing the sound of running water as the occupant washed their hands, she stepped back to let the door open and smiled at Sandy Robinson's surprise when she saw her.

"You?" Sandy said, wide-eyed.

"Good afternoon, Sandy," Freya replied, adding a healthy amount of enthusiasm. "I thought we might have a little chat."

"A chat?" she replied, brushing past Freya and heading towards her desk, ignoring Ben who was still in the doorway. "Can we do it later when I'm not so busy?"

"Afraid not," Freya said, and Sandy gave her a reproachful look. "It's quite important, you see."

"Well, then you won't mind if I work while you talk," Sandy replied, leaning across to flick the switch on the kettle, and then collecting a pile of printed invoices from a nearby table.

"I think you might want to pay attention to what I have to say," Freya told her, and she poked her head inside the little wash-room, finding nothing but a surprisingly clean toilet, basin, and some cleaning products. "You see, while we've been looking into the murder of Hayley Donovan, we've had to overcome some rather difficult challenges."

Sandy wore the expression of a bored and disinterested teenager. She held the pile of invoices in one hand and waited for Freya to finish what she was about to say. But Freya savoured the spotlight, pacing the room slowly, peering into cupboards as she went.

"Such as?" Sandy said.

"Oh, you know?" Freya said, hoping her off-the-cuff tone would have an effect on the woman. "Incomplete truths, mostly, which, in my experience, is normal. You see, when somebody lies, they very often have tell-tale signs. They're unable to look me in the eye, they find interest in a wall or a picture, or they fiddle with their hands. Sometimes they waffle, purely to fill the void. But that's where individuals, such as yourself, I might add, have a tendency not to lie but to provide a half-truth. Like a puzzle with a missing piece, and as you know, a jigsaw puzzle with a missing piece can be extremely frustrating."

Sandy took the hint. She slapped the papers down on her desk and plopped into her seat, resigned to the fact that Freya was going to draw her agony out for as long as she needed to.

Freya watched her with a scrutinising eye, daring her to voice what she so wanted her to say. But there was doubt in her eyes, a fear that she might say too much. The mention of the jigsaw puzzle had caught her attention, but had it been a fluke? Or had Freya been to her house? In which case, she would know about the sister, and of course, Vaughan being her nephew.

"Is there something you'd like to tell me?" Freya asked. "I do prefer to offer people the chance to voluntarily divulge information before I pass judgement."

"What do you want to know?" she said.

"Oh, lots. All of it. Everything. I want to know why you failed to tell us that your sister lives with you in your house and that she's the widow of a man who was suspected of murdering Charlotte Rimmell ten years ago."

"I don't see why I should–"

"I'd also like to know why it is you failed you tell us that Vaughan Barrow is your nephew and that you let him stay here on your caravan site with the sister of Skye Green, the girl who was murdered here in Saltfleet nine years ago."

"Again, it's none of your business–"

"And finally, I'd like to know how long you've been at it."

"At what?" Sandy said, at which Freya simply smiled.

"Why does Vaughan stay here?" she asked and Sandy shrugged.

"He wants his own space, and space is something I'm not short of," she replied.

"And he pays rent, I presume."

"No, but he earns his keep."

"Oh, I'm sure he does."

"What's the supposed to mean–"

"I'll ask the questions at this stage," Freya said. "Tell me what happened ten years ago. Why did they come here?"

Sandy gave the exact response Freya had expected her to. She tutted and shook her head as if the whole thing was a charade. But Freya waited, maintaining her tantalising smile and enjoying every moment of the woman's discomfort.

"You obviously know about Neil," Sandy said, and Freya nodded. "Well, it wasn't easy for them after he did what he did. I gave them somewhere to stay."

"Your poor sister and her troubled nephew?" Freya said, coaxing her on.

"He is troubled," she said. "He hasn't had it easy, that boy."

"I imagine having a father with a strong sense of right and wrong would be difficult for somebody like Vaughan," Freya said. "Especially somebody in a position of local authority, keen to portray an image of perfection and purity. Vaughan must have been a disappointment."

"He can't help who he is."

"No, but I don't suppose Neil saw it like that, did he? I can only assume that seeing as Neil isn't around to defend himself, he made life quite difficult for Vaughan. And when Neil did what he did, he left in his wake a rebellious son with a chip on his shoulder."

"He's not a bad lad," Sandy said.

"I hear that a lot," Freya said, and she began her pacing again, stopping outside the closed second internal door. Sandy eyed her, forcing a neutral expression, which Freya saw through like it was sculpted from glass. "Do you know what I don't understand?"

"A lot by the sounds of things," Sandy muttered.

Freya ignored the offhand comment and continued.

"You agreed that Vaughan was a disappointment to his father and the impression you give is that the two didn't see eye to eye."

"Neil was a strict man," Sandy said. "He put a box around Vaughan when the boy needed to stretch. He needed to find himself."

"Yet Vaughan was so distraught when his father died that he attended grief counselling."

"He did what?"

"Oh, you didn't know?" Freya said. "I thought it was I who was in need of education?"

"Grief counselling?"

"That's where he met Stella Green," Freya said. "You see, I don't think Vaughan and his father had issues, not to the extent which you're implying anyway. I think the boy loved his father. I think he played some part in Charlotte Rimmell's death and his grief was in fact guilt."

"Are you calling him a–"

"I'm not accusing him of anything," Freya said. "I'm merely saying he had some part to play in it. The move from Kirkby gave him a fresh start, didn't it? His kind-hearted aunt provided homes for him and his troubled mother, where they live for free."

"What was I supposed to do?"

"But why did they come here? Why not move to a city where they could start again with no chance of anybody recognising them?"

"Vaughan always liked it here. He said he wanted to be near the sea," Sandy explained. "I suppose, back then, Gloria would have moved heaven and earth to give the boy what he wanted."

"Do you know what I think?" Freya asked. "I think Vaughan's residence here is one of convenience."

"Of what?"

"Convenience," Freya repeated, and she nodded at the closed internal door. "If I look behind this door, am I going to find anything I shouldn't, Sandy?"

"I don't know what you mean."

"Oh, I think you do," Freya said, sharpening her tone. "How many units do you have here?"

"Units?"

"Static caravans," Freya said. "How many? Two hundred?"

"Something like that."

"Of which, I imagine at least a third of those belong to you, with the rest of them being privately owned. Is that accurate?"

"More like a quarter," Sandy said.

"A quarter? Ah well, that makes the maths simpler. So, you

need to ensure that at least fifty of those static caravans are equipped with the facilities holidaymakers in this day and age expect. They'll need TVs, microwaves, bedding, kitchen appliances, and the rest. If I was to look through your accounts, would I find invoices for fifty of each of those items, Sandy?"

"I've had those units for years. How do I know when I fitted them out?"

"That man that came in here the other day, the one I kindly helped you out with. Do you remember him?"

"Of course, I do."

"He was telling the truth, wasn't he? You see, I think Vaughan targets other holiday parks, providing you with the equipment you need to keep your caravans in tiptop condition."

"That's rubbish," she said.

"So, if I look behind this door, what will find?"

"It's just a storage cupboard," Sandy said, her tone rising in pitch. "It's where I keep things under lock and key."

"Like TVs, et cetera," Freya said, her hand on the door handle.

Even from across the room, Freya could see the rise and fall of Sandy's chest.

"If I open this door, I'll wager I'd be marching you out of this room and down to the station," Freya said. "Handling stolen goods, at the very minimum."

"You can't arrest me. I've got this place to run–"

"So, help me, Sandy," Freya said. "Help me understand who Vaughan is and why his father took his own life."

The silence that followed was broken by a scream from a child outside, which then incited laughter and squealing from more children.

"Aiding and abetting a murder is a far more serious crime than handling stolen goods, Sandy," Freya said. "Make the right decision."

"What is it you want to know?" Sandy said flatly.

"Why did your brother-in-law take his own life?" Freya said, and she let go of the handle to lean on the door, maintaining the threat to ensure there were no more half-truths.

Sandy watched her, and when she saw there was no room to manoeuvre, she sighed and dropped her head into her hands.

"Neil was a good man. Of course, he was, he was a vicar," Sandy began. "He was a good husband, and yes, you're right, he adored his boy, regardless of who or what he was. But the day Charlotte Rimmell was murdered, something happened. I don't know what it was, but he refused to talk to Vaughan, wouldn't even look him in the eye. It was as if they had a secret so bad that even Gloria wasn't to know."

"Do you think Neil killed himself to protect Vaughan?" Freya said. "Is that why both you and Gloria have suggested Neil was a less-than-decent man?"

"I'm sorry," she said. "I just want the best for my sister. I just want her to be happy, instead of drinking her life away. I don't know what else I can do to help. I've given her a home and Vaughan a place to stay. I do what I can to find him work."

"And when there's no work, he keeps you in assets?" Freya said.

"It's not ideal, I know. But I can't keep funding their lives."

"Nobody is asking you to," Freya said. "But you can't keep protecting him either."

"He wouldn't have done it without reason. I know that. He's not a monster."

"Nobody has suggested he's anything of the sort," Freya said. "But I do need your help."

"My help?" Sandy said, as if the idea was utterly preposterous. "After this?"

"What if I were to tell you that I believe Vaughan to be innocent?"

"Excuse me?"

"I believe he's innocent," Freya repeated. "I don't believe Neil Barrow murdered Charlotte Rimmell and I don't believe Vaughan did either. But he's involved."

"But..."

"But what?"

"But why else would Neil..." She stopped, like her thought process hadn't caught up with her mouth.

"Vaughan did something," Freya said. "And Neil took the blame somehow. Where can I find him?"

Vaughan?" Sandy said. "I don't know."

Freya raised an eyebrow and moved her hand toward the door handle.

"Okay, okay," she said. "He's up to something. One of his schemes. I don't know what."

"Where?" Freya said.

"Mablethorpe. The sea front," Sandy said. "He borrowed my car. Said he had to meet somebody."

"Do you know who?" Freya asked.

"No," she replied, eyeing Freya's hand. "Honestly, I don't. That's everything. I don't know anything else."

Freya studied her face, then let go of the door handle and moved towards the door from where Ben had taken in the whole scene in silence.

"What happens now?" Sandy said, her head hanging low and her elbows leaning on her thighs. She glanced at the cupboard then back at Freya.

"That all rather depends on what it is Vaughan is planning, doesn't it?" Freya replied. "I suggest you make the necessary arrangements to undo whatever it is that has been done. Thanks for your help, Sandy. It's been an absolute pleasure."

CHAPTER FORTY-NINE

"What are you thinking?" Freya said, when they were back in the car and heading towards the main road. "I know that look. You're processing information."

"Well, for a start, I'm thinking that you missed a trick," Ben replied, settling into the passenger seat and turning the air conditioning down on his side.

"How so?"

"She would have told you anything back there," he said.

"And she did. She told us that Neil Barrow did not have a problem with Vaughan's sexual habits, and she confirmed, in one way or another, that he was protecting his son. What else were you hoping for her to tell us? The killer's name?"

"No, but you could have negotiated an upgrade," he replied. "Buttercup is okay, but one of those fancy static caravans with a balcony would have been nice."

"Even I wouldn't stoop that low, Ben," she said.

"I'm also extremely confused," he admitted, and he let out a long sigh to accompany his frustration. "First you say it's Vaughan then it's not, and now I don't know who's who and who did what."

"I do," she replied. "And right now, that's all that matters. Can you call Samson for me? I need an update on Donovan's laptop."

Ben's phone lit up as soon as he pulled it from his pocket, and a local number displayed on the screen.

"Ben Savage," he said, turning the call onto loudspeaker.

"Ben? It's Samson from the station here in Mablethorpe."

"I was just going to call you," he replied. "DI Bloom is looking for an update."

"It's not good, I'm afraid," Samson said. "The tech guys managed to get the laptop up and running for me, but if you're looking to prove Frank Donovan is innocent, then you'll be disappointed."

"Why's that?" Ben asked, and both he and Freya waited in anticipation.

"I'm not sure why it wasn't picked up during the first investigation, but we found a folder on here named Skye. It's full of photos of the victim. Sorry, mate. It looks like he's guilty as charged."

"Are any of the images indecent?" Freya called out.

"Well, not exactly indecent," he replied. "But if my local vicar had a folder full of images of my daughter, I'd be asking a few questions."

"Check the metadata," Ben said.

"The what?"

"The metadata. The date the images were copied to the laptop, specifically."

"If you sort the images by the date they were added, Samson," Freya said. "I want to know the date the first one was added and the date the last one was added."

"Oh right," Samson said. "Hang on."

In the short time it took Samson to do as requested, Freya and Ben shared a knowing nod. They were on the right track, and at least one of their theories was beginning to come to fruition.

"They're all the same," Samson said, sounding a little confused. "Have I done this right? I'm not really into computers."

"You've done it right," Ben told him. "What you've just done is prove Frank Donovan's innocence. Add that to your list of achievements for the day."

"My what?"

"Your list of achievements," Ben said.

"Do you want another?" Freya asked, smiling as they navigated the lanes.

"Another what?"

"Achievement," she said. "Do yourself a favour and get a few uniforms together. Head down to Mablethorpe seafront. Your light-fingered friend is there. He goes by the name of Vaughan Barrow and he's driving a car registered to Sandy Robinson, the site manager at the caravan park we're staying at."

"You what?"

"I'm sure you can fill in the blanks, Samson," Freya told him. "Nick him for burglary."

"On what basis?" he said. "I've got nothing on the bloke. I thought you were looking at him for the murder?"

"I am. But you'll have twenty-four hours to hold him, and that's all I need," she said. "You're welcome, by the way."

Ben ended the call and pocketed his phone, and then made a last ditch effort to work out where they were heading.

"That was a bit below the belt," he said. "You told Sandy you wouldn't say anything if she helped you."

"I didn't say anything," she replied. "Not about her, anyway. But this way, our slippery little friend, Vaughan Barrow, will be in custody for the next twenty-four hours, which means if we need to arrest him, we'll have a further twenty-four hours to do so. But if I'm honest, I don't think we'll need that."

"What are you planning on doing?" he said, recognising her tone as dangerous.

"Oh, not much," she replied, when it was clear they were heading back to Mablethorpe. "Except break him."

"He's being arrested for breaking and entering. You can't go in guns blazing and start questioning him about a murder, Freya. How's that going to look if and when he goes to trial? The case will be thrown out before it's begun."

"Who said anything about a murder?" she asked defensively. "I've got an angle I can work here, and I'm going to exploit it."

"An angle?" he said, as his phone began to vibrate in his pocket. "You'll need a bloody crowbar to get him to talk. If he's a career thief, he'll know the law inside and out. He'll probably be able to teach us a thing or two."

He drew his phone out and showed Freya the screen displaying Hart's mobile number.

"Well, let's hope so," Freya said, as she took the turning into Mablethorpe. "Because I'm all ears if someone has something to say."

"Ivy?" Ben said, setting the call to loudspeaker. "What's the news?"

"The news, Ben, is that I'd like to know exactly how your colleague does it?"

"Upset people, you mean?" Ben said, and Freya rolled her eyes.

"No, how is she always bloody right?"

"Oh, don't say that, Ivy. You're on loudspeaker. She'll never get her head through the car door."

"I'm at St Botolph's like she asked. We've only gone and found it," Hart said. "Mobile phone, flip-flops, and a front door key, all of which were covered in sand, stuffed in a plastic Tesco bag, and hidden in one of the drains."

"Does the phone turn on?" Freya called out. "Do we know if it's definitely Hayley's?"

"Not yet. It does turn on, but it's locked and we don't know the security code."

"Have you tried her birthday?" Ben asked, grabbing the file to find her details.

"Tried that," she said. "We can get it to the tech guys, but it'll take a while."

"When was Frank Donovan released?" Freya asked.

"Eh?" Ben said.

"When was he released? What date?"

"May something," Hart said. "The twelfth, I think."

"Try it," Freya said, as she pulled into the beach parking area.

The wait was just seconds but felt like an hour.

"How the bloody hell did you know that?" Hart said.

"Somebody who has tattoos to match her father's clearly loves him and clearly believes he is innocent," Freya said. "The question is, who put it there?"

"Well, surely that was Frank Donovan," Hart said. "He was staying there, right? We also found his boots inside. I'm going to run them by CSI to see if they're a match."

"They are a match," Freya said. "But it's still not him."

"Freya?" Ben said.

"It's not him, Ben. I'm telling you. Don't ask me why, because I can't tell you. All I know is that it's not him."

"Are you still pursuing Vaughan Barrow?" Hart asked.

"No," Ben said. "He's off the hit list too."

"I just spoke to Samson. He said you gave him a lead on the burglaries. He's just picked up Vaughan Barrow at the amusement arcades in Mablethorpe. Is he still a suspect?"

"That's a grey area," Ben said. "And don't worry, I don't understand, either."

"Everything will become clear," Freya said, as she nosed the car into a space in front of some little, wooden steps that led from the car park down to the beach. "Thank you, Ivy. Have those items checked in for me, will you? I'll see you back at the station this afternoon."

"Right," said Hart, sounding as confused as Ben was. "Speak soon."

Ben pocketed the phone and stared ahead.

"How do you do it?" he asked.

"I honestly don't know. Everything is in my head. The facts, the lies, the ideas, it's all there. But I just can't seem to put it in the right order. Something is missing, and the only way we're going to get to the bottom of this is to play harder."

"Play harder?"

"I've been soft," she said. "I was soft on Donovan, soft on Sandy Robinson, and soft on Vaughan. Now it's time to get harder with them."

"What happened to the Freya who was trying to be nice to people?" Ben asked.

"She didn't get anywhere," Freya replied, as she gazed out of the windscreen at the wooden steps.

"I was kind of getting to like the nice Freya," he said.

"That's a shame," she said, and she drew his attention to the car ahead of them parked beside the steps. It was a little, white van. "Do you recognise that?"

"Is that...?" Ben said, just as a figure emerged from the beach, climbing the steps with his shoes in his hand and looking back over his shoulder in a panic.

"Do you want to nick him?" she began. "Or should I?"

CHAPTER FIFTY

It was nearing three p.m. by the time Freya and Ben escorted Frank Donovan into the station for the second time.

"You again?" the custody sergeant said to him. "Don't tell me, tea, one sugar, and toast with butter?"

"Not this time, Sergeant," Freya said. "This time he's here on official business."

"Nicked?" he replied with far too much joy in his expression. "Oh, that is a surprise, Franky. What happened? Did the good inspector finally see through you?"

"No," Freya told him. "This good inspector finally had a reason to arrest him."

"Suspicion of murder, I presume," he said, as he navigated to a new page on his computer.

"As it happens, no," she said. "Not yet anyway. Aiding and abetting, conspiracy to murder, and breach of parole to start with. We'll see where we go from there."

"You've been a busy boy, Frank," the sergeant said. "I'll notify transport. You'll be back in your old cell before you know it."

"Not yet you won't," Freya said. "I have twenty-four hours

with him, and I intend on using them to their fullest. Process him and have him sent to an interview room for me."

"What about a legal representative?" Donovan said, his voice remaining pleasant and calm, a reflection of his previous career. "Am I to assume I need one now?"

"Do you have a solicitor you'd like to call?"

He turned his pockets inside out in response. "What do you think?"

Freya caught the amused sergeant's attention.

"Get him a duty solicitor. I'd like to start in thirty minutes," Freya told him. "Where's Barrow?"

"Room two," he replied, and she barged through the doors into the corridor. The sergeant turned to Ben. "What happened to her? She told me she was trying to be a nicer person."

"That didn't work out for her," Ben replied, as he caught the swinging door. "In fact, come to think of it, it didn't work out for any of us."

"Vaughan Barrow," he heard Freya say from inside the interview room as he approached. Ben closed the door behind him and took his seat beside the recorder, leaving Freya face to face with the light-fingered Vaughan. He hit record and announced the date, the time, and then introduced himself. Freya followed suit, who then introduced Vaughan on his behalf. "Do you have a solicitor?"

He shook his head slowly, refusing to be the first to break eye contact with Freya.

"Do you want a duty solicitor?" she asked. "I'm duty bound to provide one if you wish."

"Will it take long?" he asked.

"Not long enough for you to be bailed," she replied. "Ten minutes."

"Will they help me at all?"

"If you want to get out of here, Vaughan, then I'm afraid only you can help you."

"Then let's get it over with," he said, and he slumped back in his seat.

"Good," she said, closing her folder and shoving it towards Ben. "You've been arrested on suspicion of burglary, and I know from your record this is not your first offence. However, this is the first time you've been caught by me, so you'd better buckle up, because you are in for a rough ride, Mr Barrow."

She peered down her nose at the charge sheet in front of Ben, and read out a few instances of Barrow's colourful record.

"Breaking and entering, taking and driving away, demanding money with menaces, and of course, burglary. It's all much of the same, isn't it, Vaughan? Once a thief, always a thief."

"You're the wordsmith," he said.

"I'd like to start at the beginning," she began. "Way back when you were a wee lad back in Kirkby."

"What?"

"When your father was alive," Freya said, and the smarmy expression on his face faded to a scowl. "Why don't you tell me all about your relationship with your father?"

"What's that got to do with anything?"

"Oh, simple really," Freya said. "You see, I believe you were once a good boy. Then, when your father died, your rebellious side emerged. The Vaughan Barrow who sits before me now, was born."

"What does this have to do with me and the burglaries? You don't need to know about my history. You can either prove it was me or you can't."

"Oh, I do need to know," Freya said. "In fact, we've got the next twenty-three and a half hours to discuss your past, your present, and your future. So, get comfy, Vaughan. You are here for the duration."

"This is a joke. Where's the bloke who nicked me?" he said, suddenly seeming rather uncomfortable in his seat. He did what many guilty people did and found solace in the closed door.

"Let's start with your father, shall we?" Freya began. "He was the vicar at St Michael's Church, a highly respectable position. How did that make you feel?"

"Eh? I didn't feel anything."

"Not even pride, Vaughan? You didn't feel even the slightest bit proud of who he was and how highly the community regarded him?"

"I wasn't ashamed of him, if that's what you mean."

"That's good enough for me," Freya said. "So, you were close, were you?"

"He was my dad. Look, what are you getting at here? What are you trying to do? You know what he did, right?"

"No, actually," Freya said. "What did he do?"

It was clear from Vaughan's expression that he couldn't tell if Freya was being genuine or if she was trying to tease information out of him. He studied every inch of her face searching for a clue, then looked to Ben.

"She knows, right?"

Ben stopped writing his notes and gave a little shrug. It was usually best if he didn't meddle with Freya's techniques, not just for him, but for the suspect too.

Vaughan stared at Freya again.

"He murdered someone," Vaughan said.

"Did he?" Freya said, adding a touch of doubt to her words.

"You know he did."

"Do we?" she said, with that same doubt in her tone. "I don't believe you."

"He was missing, weren't he? He wasn't around when she was supposed to have been killed."

"I heard that much but it seems a little weak, Vaughan."

"He had the photos on his computer."

"Hmmm," she said. "Okay, but again, it's hardly a smoking gun, is it?"

Vaughan's chest rose and fell fast now. He had walked straight into Freya's ploy and found himself playing the prosecution, searching for the evidence against his father to protect the image he had lived with for so long.

"Then there was that woman who said she saw Charlotte coming out of his office a few days before," he said. "What kind of vicar has photos of a young girl on his laptop? He didn't have photos of anybody else, did he?"

"I don't know, Vaughan. Didn't he?" Freya said, and his face dropped. He'd tripped over his own lie and fell into her trap. "So, you've seen his laptop, have you? You had access to it?"

"No," he said, the frustration building now like a head of steam. "He kept his work in his office at the church."

"But you went to church?" Freya said. "So, you could have seen his laptop there—"

"No. No, you're wrong there. I never went to church. He wasn't like that. He didn't force me to do anything. He wasn't one of those preacher dads who drags their family along kicking and screaming to put on a good show. He was just like any other dad. He left for work in the morning and came home at night, and he left his work there. So no, you're wrong. I didn't have access to his laptop."

"So why then did both your mother and your aunt tell us a different story?"

"My mum? You've been to see my mum?" he said, and he threw himself back into his chair, aghast at the idea. "What has she got to do with this?"

"She's very fragile, Vaughan—"

"You don't have to tell me that. You're not the one who has to keep her in booze."

"How long has she been that way?"

"Can we just leave her out of this?"

"Actually, no, Vaughan, we can't. You see, I believe your mother is an alcoholic for one reason, and one reason alone."

"Because my dad killed himself—"

"No," she said, and she slammed her hand down on the table, which stunned him into silence. She softened her voice almost immediately, toying with the young man's emotions and fears. "No. Your mother is living a lie. Your father died because of some-thing *you* did, and your mother is doing her very best to join him."

"No—"

"Yes, Vaughan. She's drinking herself into oblivion. She might not have the courage to do what he did, but she's doing every-thing she can to kill herself."

"No," he shouted.

"Yes, Vaughan," Freya said, again softly. "And it's because of something you did. I honestly believe you caused your father's death, and it won't be long before you can add your mother's death to that too, especially when we bring her in for questioning."

Freya made a show of leaning across to read Ben's notes while she waited for Vaughan's response.

"You what?"

"We'll be bringing her in for questioning," Freya said matter-of-factly.

"Why? What's she done? She hasn't done anything wrong."

"She lied to us, Vaughan," Freya said. "She lied to us to cover for you. That's aiding and abetting in the eyes of the law. A serious crime, all things considered."

"You can't bring her in," he said. "It'll destroy her."

"When it comes to a murder enquiry, individuals charged with aiding and abetting can get what, DS Savage?"

He sucked in a breath through gritted teeth.

"Depends on the circumstances," he replied. "But I'd say they'd get at least five years, maybe more considering the age of this case and the money the state has invested into it."

"No way," Vaughan said. "Leave her out of it."

"I'm afraid we'd be remiss if we did, Vaughan," she said. "We'd be accused of all kinds of wrongdoings. Think about it, we know your father died because of something you did, which means that a crime has gone unpunished. Imagine what Charlotte Rimmell's family have been through–"

"You're wrong," he said, leaning forward to place his elbows on the table. He held his head up by his forehead as if the weight was too much for his neck to bear. Then he lifted his head and stared Freya in the eye, defeated. "It wasn't something I *did*. It was something I was accused of doing. Something terrible."

"Go on, Vaughan," she said softly, and a single tear formed in the corner of his eye.

He shook his head.

"Vaughan, this is your chance to clear your father's name."

"And sully mine," he said, his voice thick with emotion. "He's dead. What does he care?"

"Your mother cares," Freya said. "Your poor mother. She's had the love of her life snatched away from her. She's had to endure a life of lies and untruths. Everything she once knew to be good and pure is tainted. His memory, Vaughan. The memory of your father–"

"Rape," he said and blinked away the tears with resentment, the way men often do to hide their emotions. "I was accused of rape. That's why he was ashamed of me. That's why he killed himself. Because his only son could do such a thing."

"He thought you guilty?" Freya said.

"He would have thrown away the key if it wasn't for Mum," he said with a laugh. "There, I said it. You want to lock me up for stealing? Go ahead. I'll be back out in a year and my time will be a damn sight easier than if I get locked for anything you're suggesting."

"Are you saying you're innocent?" Freya said. "Because, if you are, we can help–"

"Are we done here?" he said, making it clear that was all they were going to get from him. "Are you going to charge me? I presume you do actually have evidence of my crimes, and this

hasn't just been a ruse to accuse me of murder? Because I know
for a fact that arresting me under false pretences would make for
a very weak case and put you in a very awkward position."

Just as Ben had suggested, he knew the law and his rights, and
he sat back in triumph, folding his arms, closing off.

"One last question," Freya said, and he huffed as if granting
her wish with reluctance. "Who accused you of rape?"

He leaned forward in his seat, interlocked his fingers, and
took a deep breath.

"Are we done?" he asked, drawing a line under the
conversation.

Freya studied him for a moment, feeling a pang of pity
towards the bitterness that had poisoned him.

"We're done," she said, and she retrieved one of her cards
from her pocket. "If ever you want to discuss what happened–"

"I won't," he replied. "That's something I never ever want to
discuss with anybody."

CHAPTER FIFTY-ONE

"He's all yours," Freya called out to Samson when they passed him in the corridor.

"What do you mean, he's all mine?" he replied. "I've got nothing on him."

"Talk to his aunt at the holiday park," she said, as she stopped in the doorway that led out to the car park. "If you're quick, you might even catch her hiding the evidence."

She left him there, dumbfounded and unsure what to do first, and she stepped out into, what only an hour before, had been blistering heat but was now a hot breeze with dark clouds rolling in from the coast.

"It's going to chuck it down," Ben said, as he followed her to the car. "The farmers will be happy."

"Right now, Ben," she said, "I couldn't care less about the farmers."

"Freya, stop," he said. "Just stop, will you?"

She paused with her hand on the door handle and saw the frustration in his face.

"What is it, Ben?"

"You're pulling me from pillar to post, Freya. Bloody talk to me, will you? I'm not some kid straight out of college. It's me. Surely by now you know I'm a safe pair of hands? You should be able to trust me enough to bounce ideas off me."

"I do," she said. "And of course, I know that. You're just being sensitive."

"And you're being a cow," he replied. "A bloody difficult, stubborn cow. Talk to me. What's going on in your head? Has it occurred to you that I might have ideas too?"

"A few times," she replied.

"So, why not ask me what they are?"

"Because, Ben, my head has all this information circling round and round. None of it makes sense. We're missing something. We're missing a link between Charlotte Rimmell's murder and Skye Green's murder, and all we've done by talking to Vaughan Barrow is muddy the water."

"Has it occurred to you there might not be a link?" he asked. "These could be two separate, unrelated crimes and we're trying to fit a round peg in a square hole. Have you thought of that?"

"Every second minute of the day, Ben," she snapped. "But there are just too many parts that line up. Two vicars, two murders."

"Three murders," Ben said. "Charlotte, Skye, and Hayley."

"Two," she replied. "I told you, the motive for killing Hayley was very different to the motive for killing the first two. Like I said, the information is in my head, I just can't put it in the right order, and if I'm honest, Ben, all I want to do is finish this job and get home. I'm tired of it already."

"You're tired of it?"

"This isn't our crime, Ben," she said, imploring him to see her point of view. "We don't belong here. We could be back home working on what's important to us instead of fannying about here, chasing our tails, making DCI bloody Standing look good. Every moment we're here, our team, our friends, are back there being harassed by that bloody imbecile. I've had enough of it. And what's more, every time we talk to someone, all we get are lies, and if it's not the public telling us lies, it's people like Standing making our jobs harder."

"You should be used to that–"

"I am used to it, but right now I just wish that somebody would tell us the bloody truth so we can do what we're paid to do," she said. "It's like the whole bloody town is working together to keep us from finding out who the killer is."

A cold breeze found the bare skin beneath her thin blouse and a carpet of goosebumps rose in response.

"What is it?" Ben said, sensing a shift in her demeanour. "What's wrong?"

"The screw," she said.

"Eh?"

"The screw. The bloody screw we found in Barrow's caravan."

"What about it?"

"Vaughan and Stella weren't out to get him," she said. "Donovan's in on it. They're bloody well working with him."

"They can't be. We saw Stella Green's reaction when he pulled up outside the holiday park."

"Yes, we saw her reaction then," Freya said, voicing her thoughts as, bit by bit, parts of the puzzle fell into place. "But then what did she do?"

"She ran back to the caravan in case he saw her," Ben said.

"No, she ran back to the caravan because she wasn't expecting to see him. She didn't know then that he'd been released."

"Right?" he said, clearly not following.

"Remember the note from Vaughan's aunt?" she said. "I have some news for you?"

"I thought she was referring to Frank Donovan?" he said. "We've already established that she must have seen him at the church when she passed on her way to work."

"She was referring to him, and the news she had was where he was staying. She bloody well told Vaughan and Stella where Frank was."

"I know," he said. "We worked that out already. Vaughan and Stella were going after Frank."

"No, they were not," Freya said. "She didn't tell them where Frank was so they could go down there and hurt him. She told him so they could collude."

"Why? He was convicted of murdering her sister for God's sake."

"Put yourself in Stella's shoes, Ben," she said. "Why would you go to the man who was convicted of murdering your sister?"

It took a few seconds while he composed his thoughts, but he got it, just as she knew he would.

"Because Stella doesn't believe he's guilty," he said.

"And why wouldn't Stella believe he's guilty?" Freya asked, taking a few steps from the car and turning on her heels. "Even if a jury found him to be so?"

He gave it some thought, then said the only plausible reason he could think of.

"Because she knows who the real killer is," he said finally and rolled his eyes at their mistake. "But Frank said he didn't know Vaughan."

Freya brushed past him, heading back to the station. She stopped at the door long enough for him to catch up, and so she didn't have to shout across the little car park.

"Exactly," she said. "And now do you see why I'm fed up with being bloody lied to?"

She shoved her way inside, ignored the custody sergeant's surprise, and burst into the corridor. A moment later, she pushed into interview room two, where she found Frank Donovan sitting beside a middle-aged woman, who, from her posture, dress, and bored expression, was the duty solicitor.

"You've got some explaining to do," Freya said, as Ben

followed her inside. She jabbed her index finger at Donovan, who, in Freya's opinion, had never looked so guilty. "Who?"

"Who what?" he said.

"Excuse me, my client is entitled to–" the duty solicitor began.

"Oh, shut up," Freya told her, daring her to speak again. She turned her attention back to Donovan. "Who is it, Frank? I know all about you, Vaughan Barrow, and Stella Green. It's quite the little revenge party, isn't it?"

"You don't have to say anything," the duty solicitor said, scratching away her notes, no doubt taking as much down as she could in preparation of a defence.

"Oh, he does," Freya said, not even giving the solicitor the satisfaction of looking at her, and instead choosing to grind Donovan down, leaning over him with all the hate she could muster. "He *does* have to talk. Vaughan Barrow lost his dad because of somebody, the same somebody who killed Skye Green, for which you were convicted, Frank. Nine years you were inside. Nine years? And I find myself asking why on earth you wouldn't want the help of a police officer who actually believes you?"

"And what conclusion did you come up with?" he asked, letting his mouth hang open to reveal a string of saliva in his mouth.

"All three of you have reason to want revenge," Freya said. "And that's why you've been sending us round on wild goose chases, giving us half-truths, buying time–"

"I have not–"

"You've been withholding information, Frank. You lied to me about not knowing Vaughan Barrow, yet you were at Mablethorpe meeting him when he was picked up. You've been playing us since day one, haven't you? Why, Frank? Why, when I said I'd do everything I can to help you clear your name?"

"I would recommend you adopt a no comment position," the solicitor said. "At least until the interview is formally initiated following the correct procedures."

"And I recommend you take your formal procedures," Freya began, "and shove them—"

"DI Bloom," a voice growled from behind them, and she turned to find Larson in the doorway. "This is not how we operate here. Might I have a word?"

"I'm not done yet," she said, and she cast her attention back to Donovan. "Who is it, Frank? Don't make this even harder on yourself."

"Bloom," Larson said, his voice booming in the small room.

But Freya held her ground, her sweaty palms planted on the table so that her face was just inches from Donovan's.

"Tell me, Frank. You're protecting someone, aren't you? Just like Vaughan's dad was protecting him. Who is it? Justin?"

"Freya, come on, let's do this properly," Ben said. He reached for her arm, but she shrugged it off in anger, refusing to break eye contact with Donovan, who sat bolt upright, revealing nothing but his guilt.

"DI Bloom, I won't ask again," Larson said, this time his voice much softer, just like the image of the favourite uncle she had aligned him with. "Do I need to have you removed? Because I will if I must."

It was a stalemate. Given a few more minutes, Freya was sure she could have broken Donovan, but it was four against one, and as much as she hated it, Freya knew when she was beat.

She nodded at Frank knowingly, sneered at the solicitor reproachfully, and ignored Ben completely. If anybody should have had her back, it was him. Larson, a picture of maturity, experience, and warmth, held the door for her. He'd probably just saved her career, and she acknowledged his actions by refusing to meet him eye-to-eye as she passed.

"Come on, Ben," she said. "Maybe we can find somebody who actually wants to find the murderer before another girl dies."

"It's over, you know?" Donovan called out, much to everybody's surprise.

Freya stepped back inside and stopped beside Larson, who by all accounts was as intrigued as she was.

"I'm sorry?" she said.

He stared down at the two images tattooed on his hands and then glanced across at the solicitor before meeting Freya eye-to-eye.

"It's over," Donovan repeated with a weak smile. "You're too late."

CHAPTER FIFTY-TWO

They drove fast, heading towards the dark skies, both physically, Ben thought, and metaphorically. Freya was silent, except for a few curses born of frustration that had escaped her mouth when she had started the car.

"I suppose you want to know where we're going?" she said in that haughty tone she adopted when her back was against the wall.

"I already know," Ben replied, and she looked his way, a little surprised. "Neil Barrow killed himself to protect his son. Frank is doing the same. He's protecting Justin Donovan."

"You're starting to understand me," she replied. "One day, we might even get through a day without falling out."

"Oh, I very much doubt that," he replied, pulling his phone from his pocket.

The journey to Saltfleet from Mablethorpe took fifteen minutes usually but much less the way Freya was driving, and there was something he needed from Cruz before they reached their destination.

"Ben?" Cruz said when he answered the call. his voice was light and weak like a schoolboy's, yet there was an echo on the call. "Thank God it's you. Standing's doing our heads in. I can't even go to the toilet without him pressing me for updates."

"Cruz, where are you now?" Ben asked, and Freya pulled a face.

"What, right now?" Cruz said.

"Actually, don't answer that. I need something," Ben said. "I need a list of every woman who gave a statement in the Neil Barrow investigation."

"Every woman?" he said. "There are loads of them. Most of them just say how nice he was and how surprised they were that he'd done such a thing."

"Vaughan Barrow was accused of rape," Ben said. "Neil Barrow was innocent."

"But there were no signs of sexual activity found on Charlotte Rimmell's body."

"I know it doesn't make sense, but it will do. We need to find out who he was accused of assaulting. I think that's the link we've been looking for. I think whoever accused him might have done the same thing here."

"A list of names?" Cruz said.

"That'll do. We'll run them against the list of names in the Frank Donovan investigation. One of them has to match."

"Give me twenty minutes," he said.

"Twenty minutes?" Ben replied, and then he remembered where Cruz was. "Call me back in ten, or better still, email the names to me."

He ended the call before the image of Cruz in the bathroom was forever imprinted onto his brain.

"Good shout," Freya said. "We've been trying to link Donovan or Vaughan to the murders. It stands to reason that somebody else is involved."

"You know who I'm thinking of?" Ben said, and being in a mood, Freya's patience was running far too thin for guessing games. "Stella Green."

"Me too," Freya said. "But we still can't link her to the Charlotte Rimmell murder. As far as we know, Stella doesn't become involved until her sister is killed a year after Charlotte Rimmell."

"Neither does Frank," Ben countered. "But we've been on his case since day one."

"But we've never been able to link him, which is why he hasn't been banged up again, until now, anyway," Freya said, as they drew up outside the Donovan house. "Looks quiet."

"What's your plan?" Ben asked.

"My plan," she said with a heavy sigh as she released her seat belt. "Is to make a plan when we get inside and talk to Justin. I have a hunch he hasn't always been the way he is."

She shoved open the car door before Ben could ask any more questions, then she strode up the footpath to knock on the door. None of the cars that had been there before were on the driveway, and through the window, Freya could see the TV was off.

Ben knocked the second time, with far more vigour than Freya's initial knock, but still, nobody answered.

"Round the back?" he suggested.

"No," she replied, quickly adapting to the situation. "Kick it through."

"Freya—"

"Kick it through, Ben," she said. "Or do I have to call uniform to help me?"

"Alright, alright," he said, holding his hands up defensively. "Step back."

It took three hard kicks, each one harder than the one before, but eventually, the door gave, slamming back into the wall behind and then shuddering to a stop.

"Justin?" Freya called out, leaning into the hallway. "Justin Donovan, are you in here?"

She nodded for Ben to enter then watched him go through to the kitchen, only to return seconds later shaking his head and glancing up the stairs.

"He doesn't leave the house," Ben whispered. "He must be upstairs."

"Go," she said, closing the door behind them as best she could. The lock was busted, and she had to use the security chain to keep it from swinging open. Then she followed Ben up the stairs, keeping the noise to a minimum.

Gently, Ben knocked on the door to the back bedroom.

"Justin," he said, and there was a comfort in his voice, Freya thought. He was a man of many sides with a rare gentle side that overshadowed his dominant masculine appearance. "Justin, do you remember me? It's Ben Savage. We spoke a few days ago. You showed me your fish. Do you remember that Justin?"

He glanced behind him, and Freya gave him the nod to enter, her heart pounding in her chest.

Gently, he nudged the door forward, and immediately Freya heard the sound of dripping water.

"Oh Christ," Ben said, suddenly coming to life.

He burst into the room and Freya followed to find him scooping the young man up from the floor and laying him on the single bed, holding a bloody right arm as high as he could get it.

"Ambulance," Ben said, searching around him for some kind of bandage.

He handed her his phone, and she found he'd already dialled Hart. With the phone to her ear, Freya threw him a clean t-shirt to wrap around the boy's wounded wrist, then stepped clear of the broken glass, searching for a dry piece of carpet to stand on but finding none. She squelched out of the room as soon as Hart answered.

"Hello Ben, I hear that stuck-up boss of yours has well and truly made her mark on this place," Hart said when she answered the call, clearly expecting to raise a laugh.

"I'm glad to hear it, Ivy," Freya replied.

"DI Bloom?"

"I need an ambulance at the Donovan house right now, and I

need uniforms on standby. Suicide attempt, plenty of lost blood, male, mid-twenties."

"How many uniforms?"

"Everyone you can spare."

"On it," Hart replied, and the call ended, leaving Freya to squelch back across the sodden carpet to inspect the damage.

"How is he?"

"Alive," Ben replied, and he gestured at the floor against the wall. "Unlike them."

She followed his gaze and found dozens of tiny dead fish strewn across the carpet and the small piece of glass Justin had used to hurt himself.

"What the bloody hell has happened here?" Freya mused aloud.

One side of an enormous aquarium had smashed, spilling the contents all over the carpet and leaving a three-sided aquatic scene devoid of life. It reminded her of the bombed-out houses she had seen in Second World War movies. On the floor of the tank, a tiny fish flapped once in the black substrate, then stilled, as if it had depleted its oxygen supply and finally given up.

"With all that water inside," Ben said, "that would have taken some doing to smash."

"Somebody did it on purpose?" Freya said, eyeing the young man in his arms.

"Not him," Ben said. "He loved those fish. They were all he had."

Just then, Justin stirred and groaned like he was coming out of a deep sleep, then screamed as the pain hit home.

"It's okay, Justin," Ben said, his knuckles white with the effort of applying pressure on his wrist. "Justin, do you remember me? It's Ben Savage. We spoke the other day."

His eyes opened slowly, and he struggled in Ben's grip. Helpless to do anything, Freya covered the doorway in case he made a run for it, but she needn't have bothered. The moment Justin's red eyes landed on the remains of his pride and joy, he stopped, and any fight in him drained like the water from his tank.

"My fish," he whined, in a pitch not dissimilar to that of the dozens of mothers she'd had to deliver bad news to over the years. And then he screamed in agony at the loss, springing into life. Tearing free from Ben's grip, Justin clawed his way through the glass and debris to the carpet of dead and dying fish, seemingly oblivious to his wound. And it was there, he crumpled, curling into a ball amidst the fish, the plants, and the stones.

"Justin, who did this?" Ben asked, firmly, but gently enough that he wouldn't scare the lad into submission. "Justin, come on, talk to me. Who did this?"

"What did I do to deserve this?" he cried. "I haven't done anything."

"Justin, listen to me," Ben said, a little more forcefully than before, which caught Justin's attention and clearly frightened him a little. "I'm not going to hurt you. There's an ambulance on its way, but I need you to talk to me, mate."

He stared back at Ben, then at Freya, as if seeing her for the first time, and he backed off, snatching his bleeding arm from Ben's grip again.

"Here," Ben said, tossing him the t-shirt. "Keep the pressure on. Don't take it off, Justin."

"What do you want from me?" he whined, then winced as he pressed the shirt against his wrist. "Where is everyone?"

"There's nobody home," Ben said, which seemed to alarm Justin even more. "It's just us. You're safe now, okay? You're safe. We're going to take care of you."

"I need Debs. Where is she?" His breathing became laboured like an asthma attack was taking hold of him.

"I don't know," Ben said. "But listen to me, okay? I need you to be calm. You're not in any trouble. We're not going to hurt you."

But Justin backed into the corner opposite the door, and

Freya, seizing her moment to win him over, stepped towards Ben, leaving Justin a clear run if he wanted.

"You're free to go," Freya said. "We're not going to hurt you."

"What do you want?" he said, studying the open doorway as if it was some kind of prize. "I don't know anything."

"About what?" Freya said. "What don't you know about, Justin?"

But he realised his mistake and he clammed up, looking between them as if one of them was readying to attack him. Slowly, and with her hands in the air, Freya stepped closer to Ben and sat beside him on the bed.

"We're not here to hurt you, Justin. Leave if you want."

"And go where?"

"I don't know. Where do you like to go?"

He shook his head. "I don't," he said finally.

"I'd like to tell you a story," Freya said, and she dropped to a crouch before him. "Is that okay? Can I tell you about somebody we know?"

Justin shrugged. "I suppose," he said, his lower lip trembling as he discovered more and more of his beloved fish scattered across the floor.

"His name is Vaughan," Freya said. "He's like you. He has difficulties dealing with people."

"I do," he said. "I don't like them."

"And that's okay," Freya said, finding herself using a tone reminiscent of that she used to use with her ex-husband's boy. "We don't have to like people if we don't want to. Not many people like me if I'm honest. That's fine. That's their choice."

"Why don't they like you?" Justin said, and he cocked his head, the first sign he'd given of true engagement.

"Because they don't understand me," she replied. "I'm not a bad person, and neither is Vaughan."

"Vaughan?" he said, as if hearing the name for the first time.

"Yes, Vaughan. The boy I was telling you about. My friend.

You see, once upon a time, somebody accused him of doing something terrible. They accused him of hurting somebody."

Justin stiffened at those words, and Freya caught Ben's sideways glance, confirming he too had seen it.

"Did he get into trouble?" Justin asked softly, in an almost childlike voice. "Your friend. Did he go away to prison?"

"No," Freya told him. "No, you see, somebody else took the blame for him. His father, in fact. A father would do almost anything for his children. He would die for them, if need be. Because that's what they do. It's what parents do. They protect their children. They keep them safe."

"My dad protected me once," Justin said, like he was recalling a distant memory. They waited a few moments for Justin to embellish the statement, but he said nothing more, choosing instead to stare at the floor like he was enjoying the memory he'd recalled.

"What did he do?" Freya asked. "He didn't die, did he? Did he die for you?"

"No," Justin said, snapping his head left to right. "No, he didn't die. He just went to prison for a very long time."

"He went to prison? Why? Did somebody accuse you of hurting somebody, Justin? Is that what happened?"

The young man nodded. There were no more tears and there was no sign he was going to run away. There was just Freya and Ben sat side by side on the single bed with Justin on the far side of the room standing like a weak, old man, and a riot of mess and carcasses on the floor.

"Somebody made some lies up about me."

"Some lies?" Freya said. "Who would do such a thing?"

"Somebody bad."

"Evil?" Ben added, at which Justin nodded.

"They said I hurt somebody too," he said slowly.

"And did you?" Freya asked. "You don't seem like a bad person."

"I'm not," he said defensively, which was the most animated he had been during the last few minutes. "And no, I didn't. They just said I did."

And there it was. The truth that set a few of those misaligned cogs into place.

"Justin, how did your dad protect you?" Freya asked. "You said he went to prison. Why?"

"Because of what I did," Justin whined, and as he stared at them both, the knuckle of his index finger in his mouth like a toddler. A dark patch appeared on his tracksuit bottoms. "Because of what Trevor said I did."

"Trevor?" Ben said, for clarity. "Trevor Starr?"

Justin nodded. He wore the expression of a small boy with a football in his arms explaining how the window was broken.

"What did he say you did?" Freya asked, as gently as she could to protect the fragile state before her.

"I killed her," he said softly. "He said I killed her."

"Killed who, Justin?" Freya said, just to be sure. "Who did he say you killed?"

"Skye," Justin said, and a faint smile emerged amidst the sorrow at the mention of her name. "But I didn't. I wouldn't. She was lovely. So lovely. She was my friend."

"Justin, where is Trevor now?" Freya asked, slowly rising to her feet.

"At the church, of course," he said. "Today's the day."

"What day, Justin? What's happening today?"

He stared at Freya as if she had been living on another planet.

"He's been working on it for weeks," he said. "It's the fundraiser. The charity bike ride."

CHAPTER FIFTY-THREE

It had taken a full minute to help Justin down the stairs, convincing him every step of the way that Ben meant no harm to him. On the floor below, Freya opened the door to the paramedics, who relieved Ben of his duties, laying the young man down on a gurney.

"Male, mid-twenties," Ben told the two women. "There's a deep gash to his right wrist."

"Got it," one of them replied.

"Get me Hart," Freya said, as they ran to the car and Ben felt the first drops of rain quench his skin. By the time they were belted up, the windscreen wipers were on full, washing away an almighty deluge, as if the heavens had opened.

Ben dialled the number and held onto the car door. He trusted Freya's driving, but in this downfall on the hot and oily tarmac, the large Range Rover would need some taming to keep it on the road.

"Is that you, Ben?" Hart asked, a little more carefully than before.

"Ivy, we need those uniforms," Freya said. "All Saints Church in Saltfleet."

"Got it," she replied. "Do you need us there?"

"I don't know. Probably," Freya called out, as a pair of oncoming headlights flashed brightly on the windscreen, dazzling them both for a moment with a thousand tiny stars. She swerved and leaned forward to gain a better view of the road, and Ben took over the call to let her concentrate.

"We think we've got him," Ben explained, finding himself shouting to be heard over the rain on the car roof. "We'll meet you there."

He ended the call and immediately called Cruz.

"Alright, alright," Cruz said, by way of a greeting. "I'm sending it now."

"Forget it," Ben said. "Have you got the file in front of you?"

"Of course," he said. "Bloody hell, where are you? Sounds like you're in the shower."

"It's chucking it down here," Ben replied. "We're looking for a man named Trevor Starr."

"A man?" Cruz said as if he hadn't quite heard Ben properly with all the racket.

"Yes, Cruz, a man. Trevor Starr."

"But I just got all the female names."

"Well, now we need a man's name."

"Bloody hell," Cruz said, muttering to himself the way he often did. "Trevor Starr, you say?"

"Two Rs," Ben said, then waited for a tense moment as Freya accelerated through Saltfleet.

"Got him," Cruz said. "He gave a statement in the Charlotte Rimmell investigation. Funnily enough, he was one of the only ones who said Neil Barrow could be guilty. Said he was a little too familiar with the young girls."

"We've got him," Ben said, shouting for Freya to hear. If anything, the news should have put Freya's mind at ease, but she seemed to put her foot down even more. "Nice one, Cruz. We'll call you when we've got him."

"Eh?"

"I said, we'll call you when we've got him."

"What do I tell Standing?" Cruz said.

"Tell him the local station is picking up your suspect," Ben told him. "Leave everything else to us."

He pocketed his phone just as Freya slewed the car into the little farm driveway opposite the church. The road was lined with parked cars and on the church grounds, a white marquee sagged under the weight of the rainfall as opposed to keeping the sun off the gathering.

They ran across the main road and into the grounds, where Ben scanned the area for Trevor Starr.

"Looks like the bike ride is underway," Freya said as she headed towards the marquee, and was immediately approached by a senior lady offering a tray of teas and coffees in delicate, white cups with saucers. "Not for me, thank you."

"There are some cakes on the table," the lady said. "They've only just got underway, so you've got half an hour or so until the first ones come back."

"We're actually looking for someone," Ben told her, and he discreetly showed his warrant card. "We're looking for Trevor Starr."

"Trevor?" she said, and she handed her tray to a passing girl. "Take these, dear, will you?"

The girl gave them both a cursory look and then busied herself with the drinks.

"It's okay," Ben said. "You don't have to take us. Just point us in the right direction. You can stay here in the dry,"

"Are you sure? He's here somewhere," she said. "I'm sure I've seen him."

"It's okay," Ben began, but it was too late. The kind lady had caught the attention of a friend. "Janice? Janice, have you seen Trevor?"

The second lady smiled at them both then approached, as if

time for her was standing still and they had driven for miles just to hear her voice.

"Trevor, you say?" Janice said.

"Yes, have you seen him?" the first lady said. "I thought he would be out here. After all, it was him who arranged it all."

"No, I saw him inside a few minutes ago. He said he would take a few moments before the fun begins."

"Before the fun begins?" Ben said, just to confirm that was what she had said.

"That's right. I imagine we'll be having a party when the riders return," Janice replied, and with that, she turned and left them to it.

"I can show you, if you like, dear," the first woman said.

"Thank you," Ben said. "We'll take it from here. Why don't you stay out here and enjoy yourself? We'll only be a minute. I might even take you up on one of those cakes."

"Ooh, I'll get one ready for you," she replied, and with an accompanying eye roll from Freya, he turned and began a brisk walk towards the church.

"Shall I go around the back?" he asked.

"No. No, we're staying together for this one," she replied when they reached the two arched main doors.

"I meant to say," Ben said, catching her arm before she entered the church. She looked down at his arm again and raised an eyebrow the way she often did. "I thought you handled Justin really well."

"Is that it?" she said.

"I just thought you were really nice, that's all," he said. "It was good to see."

"Yes, well, " she replied, "I told you. I'm done being nice. It doesn't seem to get me anywhere."

"Well, of all the places to denounce your soul, Freya, you couldn't have picked a better one."

She burst into the church leaving no room for a discreet entry.

But as the echoes of the old, wooden doors faded among the gothic eaves, their eyes adjusted to the dim light to reveal a bare space not too dissimilar to St Botolph's, only furnished and loved.

Freya's heels clicked loudly against the old, stone floor, and that dusty aroma common in old buildings gave way to her perfume, the way cold air permeates warmth.

"Trevor?" she called out, and her voice seem to hang in the air like her scent. "Trevor Starr?"

Nobody replied and they moved forward towards the pulpit, where an open door led out to the vestry.

"Ah, Maureen said we have visitors," a voice said from behind them, and they both turned on their heels in a flash, frightening a man in a wet cagoule. He had a bald head that shone with the wet and he stared wide-eyed, as if they might jump him. "Sorry, may I help you at all?"

"Who are you?" Freya asked.

"Me?" he replied, with a little laugh as if they should know who he was. He unzipped his cagoule and slid it from his arms, leaving it to drip-dry on a hook in the porch. He stepped into the main space of the church, where the dim light made everything clear. "My name is Jeremy Grantham. I'm the vicar here at All Saints."

"The vicar?" Freya said, and the look she gave Ben was one of absolute horror. She withdrew her warrant card and held it up for him to see. "I'm Detective Inspector Bloom. This is my colleague, Detective Sergeant Savage."

"Oh, well, I hope everything is in order," he said. "I believe one of our clergymen has completed the forms to close the lanes."

"I'm sure they have," Freya said, letting her demeanour take effect on his intrigue. "Tell me, Mr Grantham, do you keep a laptop here?"

"Of course," he said, with another of those carefree laughs. "I'm afraid even the church can't function without the internet these days."

"I need to see it," Freya said, and his smile faded. "I need to see it now."

"Well, I suppose–"

"Is it through here?" she said, jabbing a thumb at the open door behind them.

"Well, yes, but…" he began, but it was too late. Freya's heels were already clicking across the flagstones.

The two men caught up with her in a small room with a few tables and chairs, and where the smell of cheap coffee was strong enough to go head-to-head with Freya's perfume.

"In here?" she asked, hurrying them along.

"This is where the volunteers work," Grantham said, pointing to a door further on. "That's my office in there."

She burst through the door, and by the time Ben had caught up with her, she was already at an open laptop on the desk.

"I usually keep it locked," he said, with pride in his voice. But Freya turned the computer around for them both to see the plain blue desktop background. "How did you…?"

"Does anybody else have access to this room?" Ben asked.

"Well, of course, but nobody comes in here. We're all quite respectful of each other's property. Most of the clergy have a cupboard to keep their personal belongings and nobody would ever dare to touch…"

Freya coughed to get his attention and turned the laptop around for him to see again.

"What's that?" he asked, fishing a pair of frameless reading glasses from his breast pocket. He leaned in close and scrunched his nose to peer at the screen as Ben's father might do to read the instructions on the back of a pot noodle. "Oh, I say."

"Have you seen this folder before?" Freya asked him.

"I most certainly have not," he replied with more than a hint of indignance. "Are those photos of Jessica Hunt? She's one of our girls. What are they doing there?"

"Copied a few days ago," Freya said to Ben.

"What is this? What does this mean? I have never seen–"

"It means somebody has accessed your computer, Mr Grantham," Freya said, cutting him off before he began a defensive rant. "It also means Jessica Hunt is in danger."

"In danger?"

"Do you have a son, Mr Granthm?"

"A what?" he said, trying to keep up with the barrage of information.

"A son, Mr Grantham. Do you have a son?"

"Well, yes. James. Why? What does he have to do with this?"

"James is most likely involved somehow."

"Involved? Of course, he's not involved. He's out there."

"He's one of the riders?" Freya said.

"Of course, he is," Grantham said. "He's been looking forward to this. He even helped Trevor in setting it up."

"Helped? In what way?"

"He helped to plan the route and position the marshals."

"The marshals," Freya said. "Including Jessica Hunt?"

"Well, yes, of course. Listen, are you going to explain what's going on?"

"Where is she?" Ben asked.

"Who? Jessica?" he said. "She's out on the course."

"We need her exact location," Freya told him as she stormed from the room and called back over her shoulder. "And lock this building."

"I demand to know what all of this is about," Grantham said, in about as aggressive a tone as somebody in his position was ever likely to use. "Danger? What do you mean?"

Freya stopped halfway down the aisle and turned to face them both. The light from one of the large windows spilled across her face, casting the other half into shadow. She was as beautiful in rage as Ben had ever seen before.

"It means that if I find out anybody else has been in here, Mr Grantham," she said flatly, "there'll be hell to pay."

CHAPTER FIFTY-FOUR

The congregation spilled from the marquee, drawn like flies towards the flashing blue lights and melee of uniforms that filed from the transporter and squad cars in the pouring rain.

"You, you, and you, crowd control. Nobody leaves," Freya said, identifying three of the uniforms. She singled one of them out, an intelligent-looking female community support officer who appeared unfazed by the heavy rainfall that ran down her face. "What's your name?"

"Harris, ma'am," the girl replied.

"Good, take names, every one of them. I want to know if they're working here or just here to enjoy the day. If they are working or volunteering, I want to know what their responsibilities are and where we can find them for a statement later on."

"Ma'am," the young woman replied, by way of confirmation, and she set off to corral the flock back underneath the marquee.

"You two," Freya said, identifying two male officers. She jabbed her thumb over her shoulder at the church. "Guard that building. The next person to go through those doors are CSI. Speaking of which, where's DS Hart?"

"Here," she replied, and she stepped forward, her light frame concealed by a burly uniform.

"Good. Make the call to CSI then stay with us," Freya said. Then she addressed the remaining half a dozen uniforms who waited patiently for instructions. "The rest of you, we have a known murderer on the loose, and we believe he is about to strike again. Trevor Starr is in his late twenties to early thirties, and we believe his intended victim is Jessica Hunt, sixteen years old, currently positioned as a marshal on the sponsored bike ride taking place right now. That means we're already behind him. *That* means you'll need to move fast. I want one of you positioned with every marshal on the course. Mr Grantham, do we have maps?"

"I-I don't actually know," he said, killing the momentum Freya had built up. "Trevor normally does that sort of thing."

"Do we know who is stationed at which post?" she asked, to which he shook his head.

"Sorry–"

"Trevor and James took care of it, I suppose?"

He gave an apologetic look.

"It is signposted, if that helps?"

"How many marshals do we have, Mr Grantham?"

"At least nine," he replied. "It's a ten-mile race, and we usually-"

"Right," Freya said, cutting him off. "We don't have time to find maps. I want half of you in one van following the course and the other half following the course in reverse. As you pass a post, one of you gets out and stays with the volunteer. The first lot is team A, the second lot is team B. Keep your radios on, your eyes open, and don't be afraid to hit your emergency button if you need to. I don't want any heroes. Is that understood?"

"Ma'am," they chorused, enthused and ready to do their jobs.

"When you reach your post, I want you to radio in, identify your team and your post, and confirm the safety of the marshal. Clear?"

"Ma'am," they called out again.

"Do we have a radio?" she asked Hart, who tapped her pocket in response. "Right, get to it," Freya concluded, then turned to Ben once they had all set off. "I can't sit and wait. I've got to do something."

"We don't know where he's going to strike," Ben replied. "Ten miles is a huge area to cover. We can't be everywhere at once."

"I can't believe nobody has a bloody map except Trevor Starr," she said, racking her brains for some kind of starting thread to pull on. She pulled out her phone and ducked beneath a nearby tree. "Mr Grantham?"

The vicar, keen to make up for his shortcomings, quickly joined her, taking a moment to wipe the rain from his head. She navigated to the maps app on her phone and zoomed in on the area. The satellite view gave her an idea of the terrain and any nearby houses.

"Show me the route," she said.

"Well, I don't know for sure," he said. "But as I understand it, the riders will pass through Saltfleet towards Mablethorpe, circling round through Maltby towards Skidbrooke, then back along the main road. It's not a challenging route, but-," He paused, his soft index finger stopped tracing the approximate route on her phone, and then he stepped back, clearly worried. "I should have been more vigilant," he said.

"Don't blame yourself," she replied. "Nobody could have fore-seen this."

"Trevor always manages the events. He's so good at it."

"He's had a lot of practice," she replied. "Have you spoken to your son? If not, call him. Make sure he's okay and tell him not to worry about anything."

"I don't understand," he replied. "He hasn't got his phone on him. Not while he's riding."

"Well, then you'd better pray for him," Freya said, making her way back over to Hart, who had her radio held up for her, Ben, and Samson to listen to. She called over her shoulder to the vicar. "Call him, Mr Grantham. Make sure he's okay."

She approached the trio of detectives, straining to make out a garbled message on the radio.

"That was Brooks. Team A first drop is fine," Hart said. "The marshal is an Adrian Campbell."

"Thanks, Ivy. Keep calling them out."

"I've been thinking," Ben said. "Starr's car is parked over there on the road. He'll be on foot."

"Oh no," Grantham said, appearing a little guilty for listening in. "He has a push bike. He keeps it here sometimes."

"Brilliant," Freya muttered. "Just brilliant."

"The chances are that he's positioned Jessica Hunt near the start or the end," Ben said. "He'll have given himself time to get there."

"Speaking of time," Grantham said, again appearing quite sheepish. They turned to face him, waiting for another insight. But all he did was tap his watch. "I was wondering... I have to be somewhere."

"That's fine," Freya said, turning back to Ben. She was just about to continue their conversation when something struck her, and she called out to the vicar, "Out of curiosity, where is it you have to be?"

The vicar was a few steps away, pulling his hood onto his shiny head, squinting at the deluge that pounded them.

"I have to collect somebody. They called this morning to say their lift had let them down and they were keen not to miss the party."

"And who is this somebody?" Freya asked.

"It's one of our oldest parishioners. Dennis Hawes. We haven't seen him for a while. Hip trouble, you know?"

"And you spoke to him, did you?"

"Me? Well, no, but..."

"But?"

"Trevor passed the message on," he said doubtfully.

"Trevor Starr?"

The vicar nodded and seemed to wait for her to respond.

"How's that for a set-up?" she said quietly to Ben. "The vicar disappears to pick somebody up and Trevor denies all knowledge of it. Meanwhile, his son is out on the course, and I'll bet he's the last one to pass Jessica before Starr strikes."

"All part of his plan," Ben replied.

Then Freya called out to the vicar, "I wouldn't worry about the old man. If I were you, I'd stay close to somebody. Don't wander off."

"What? Why?"

"I don't have time to explain," she said, and then called for Hart. "Don't let him out of your sight, Ivy. I want his alibi rock solid."

"Ma'am," she replied, and for a moment, Freya saw Nillson in her – efficient, tough, and to the point.

"We should have some news any minute now," she said to Ben, as one of the ladies they'd spoken to before ambled over to them. "Can I ask you to stay beneath the marquee, Janice?"

"I just wondered if I could help," she said, holding a paper plate over her head to keep the rain off.

"You can help by returning to the marquee, please," Freya said, then called out to the uniforms assigned to crowd control. "Harris?"

The young uniform stood from where she was crouched in front of a pensioner with her notepad, and the look of horror on her face when she saw that one of her flock had broken free was enough of a reprimand.

"Sorry, ma'am," she said. "Excuse me. Janice, wasn't it? I need to ask you to come back to the marquee for me."

"I just want to help," she said.

"We have all the help we need right now," Harris said.

"I have the names of all the marshals," Janice offered, to which Freya stopped Harris and paid attention.

"Did you say you have a list?" she said.

"Of course," the old lady said. "I made them all a packed lunch. We can't have our volunteers out there with nothing to keep them going, can we?"

"No, we can't," Freya agreed. "Do you happen to have the list on you?"

"Ma'am?" Hart called out. "That was Barnes from Team B, first drop okay. He's with Jessica Hunt. She's safe."

It was as if somebody had punctured Freya's heart to relieve the pressure.

"Oh, thank God," she said, as she took the list from Janice. "Thank you. Can I take this?"

"Yes, please do," Janice said. "Is there anything else I can do?"

"Just follow my colleague here back to the marquee," Freya told her. "You should stay in the dry. We can't have you all getting colds now, can we?"

Freya left a sorry-looking Harris with the helpful lady and approached Hart, Samson, and Ben. Hart received another radio call, which she stepped away to hear clearly.

"It's like herding sheep," Freya muttered, watching one of Harris' team coax two elderly ladies back under the marquee from where they were appraising a rather large hydrangea nestled into one of the church borders.

"McPherson, team A," Hart announced. "All okay. The marshal is Helen Fielding."

"Helen Fielding?" Freya said, studying the list of marshals. She gestured for Ben to hand her a pen and then ticked off the names they had heard. "Helen Fielding, Adrian Campbell, and Jessica Hunt."

"Do you want me to stop them?" Hart said. "Now we know Hunt is safe, I mean?"

"No. He's still out there," Freya said. "And he's clearly been through a lot of effort to get this far."

Hart stepped away again, holding the radio to one ear and covering the other.

"I don't get it," Samson said. "Why is he doing this? I mean, what's she done to him?"

"That's just it," Freya said, and the officer she had dismissed as a vain pretty boy was actually paying attention, ready to gain some kind of insight into her mind. "She hasn't done a thing. The fact is that most murderers target family or friends. More than seventy per cent, in fact. The other twenty-five per cent of murders are usually gang-related or business-related of some sort, where the motive is money, control, or both. But every now and then, you come across a murderer who appears to have no motive at all. And they're the hardest to track down. Think of the Yorkshire Ripper or Ted Bundy. They took years to find, and they killed indiscriminately. They had no real motive. They were just psychopaths. That's exactly what we're dealing with here, Samson. And I hope to God you never have to deal with another one like this."

"How does it feel to be right?" a voice said, and she found George Larson making his way towards her holding a tartan umbrella over his head. "You were right when you said he'd done this before."

"Charlotte Rimmell, Skye Green, and very nearly Jessica Hunt," Freya replied. "The similarities are too striking to ignore. It's the same set-up every time. For him, it's tried and tested."

Larson gave a little laugh, which was more of a humph. But his expression gave Freya the impression he wasn't entirely convinced.

"What is it?" she asked.

"It's just..." he began, then paused, as if he was trying to put his thoughts into a cohesive sentence. "Your assessment of Starr is right, however, serial killers usually get better with each one he does."

"What do you mean?"

"Well, if Charlotte Rimmell was his first time, then he must have been very lucky to get it right first time. Not one mistake. He managed to get away with it for, what? Ten years?"

She tried to conceal the doubt he had planted and convey how grave the situation was through an expression born of experience, regret, and many sleepless nights. But the moment was broken by Hart's voice.

"That was Bright from team B, ma'am. Second drop," Hart called out, and her expression was sombre. "The post is empty. There's no marshal there."

"Bloody hell," Ben said, and Freya glanced down at the list. "It could be any one of them."

"No," she replied, and she slapped the list into Ben's chest for him to read then took the radio from Hart. Freya hit the push-to-talk button and took a breath.

"Team B, team B, this is DI Bloom," she said. "All units head to the second drop. Be on the lookout for an IC-one male. We have a missing marshal."

"Copy that. Do we have a description?" a voice said over the radio, and Freya closed her eyes, utterly convinced the whole thing was a set-up by Standing to make her look the fool.

She pushed the button on the radio.

"He'll be riding a bike," she said, and even Ben raised his eyebrows at the description that matched at least a dozen males participating in the ride, but he knew better than to say anything.

It was easy to imagine the two teams sharing exasperated expressions due to the radio silence that was broken by a rather stoic, final question that came across the airwaves. "Do we have a name for the missing individual?"

Ben stared hard at Freya with the list in his hand hanging heavily at his side.

"We're looking for a female, IC-one, mid-twenties," Freya said. "The marshal's name is Stella Green."

CHAPTER FIFTY-FIVE

The downpour did little to ease the weight of Freya's foot on the accelerator, and twice Ben braced for a collision as they rounded bends on tight country lanes seeming almost to defy the law of physics.

She needed no directions from him, and her determination was etched into the lines surrounding her eyes.

"I'm struggling to understand something," Ben said, almost as a distraction from the terror he was experiencing. "If he planted those images on Grantham's laptop a few days ago, why was the computer unlocked just now?"

It wasn't unusual for Freya not to reply, and her focused expression didn't alter in the slightest. But he knew the statement had permeated that mind of hers and the answer would come when he'd least expect it.

"Get Cruz on the phone," she said, as she overtook a car towing a caravan, the owners clearly reading the storm as a sign that the heatwave was coming to an end.

Ben knew better than to ask why. He found Cruz's number and hit the button to initiate a call. He held the phone on loud-speaker, hoping the fierce noise of the engine and the drumming rain wouldn't be too loud.

"Ben," Cruz said, and there was an echo to his voice, which Ben took to mean he was in the stairwell out of Standing's earshot. "I hope you've got something. He's just berated Nillson for not making any progress on her manslaughter case. I'm bloody terrified to go back in."

"Cruz, it's DI Bloom. I need you back in the incident room."

"Oh, God. Really?"

"I want you to check the list of people in the fun run, or whatever it was. I need to know if Vaughan Barrow was a participant."

"He was," Cruz said. "I know that for a fact. I read Trevor Starr's statement after our last call. Vaughan Barrow was out there when Charlotte was murdered."

Freya took the turning towards Skidbrooke, and although the news hadn't raised a smile, Ben could have sworn some of the tension around her eyes had eased.

"What does that mean?" Cruz said. "I need to give him something."

"It means that Neil Barrow was indeed innocent, and so was his son, Vaughan. What I need, though, is some kind of motive. Why did Trevor Starr set Neil Barrow and his son up?"

"I don't know," Cruz said. "I do know that Trevor was fairly new to the church. His statement talks about the church being his saviour. It gave him a purpose when he was on a downward spiral or something. I didn't really understand it. He said something about the church being his God, and that it was a way for him to actively be a good person, rather than passively. I don't know. It didn't really make any sense."

"He means that by attending the church, he's actively doing good, just like bad people actively do bad things," Ben said, remembering his chat in the Donovans' kitchen. "The rest of us are living a passive existence. We're not bad people, but we're not actively out there doing good."

"Sounds like a nut job," Cruz said.

"Well, it does take a certain type of crazy to do what he's doing," Ben said. "What's interesting is that he doesn't recognise God as a single entity. It didn't really make sense when he explained it to me, but it does now. He's like a trojan horse, infiltrating the church with evil and refusing to accept God in the way that we do."

"What Ben is trying to say, in a long-winded way," Freya said, "is that Trevor Starr is evil. Something made him that way. Something caused him to set Neil Barrow up. I need to know what that is, Ben. Once we have a motive, all of this will make sense."

"Bloody hell," Cruz said. "Where do I start?"

"Statements," Freya replied. "I don't believe for a second that he was always like this. I think something happened that turned him against the church."

"He's promiscuous," Ben said. "Vaughan Barrow. Even his mum said so. Start with that."

"Right," Cruz replied, sounding more unsure than ever. "Why does everything always revolve around sex? There's always a bloody affair of some sort going on."

"That's because we're a nation of greedy sexaholics fuelled in part by social media and our desire for the things we can't have. We want more money, we get it however we can. We want what somebody has, so we take it," Freya told him. "Get reading, Cruz. Call us when you have something."

Ben ended the call just as Freya stopped the car on the road beside a small patch of trees. Both the liveried transporters were there with the blue lights still flashing, and the uniforms were spread out, searching the nearby ditches and fields for Stella Green.

"Bloody hell," Ben said. "I didn't see this coming."

"Neither did I," Freya replied, as she climbed from the car. She called out to a uniform in a bright yellow jacket, "Is this where she was supposed to be?"

He pointed at a small, foldable chair, the type used by beachgoers the world over. Beside it was a cool box containing bottles of water, and a small rucksack.

Freya marched over to the chair and collected the rucksack from the ground. Rain dripped from her sodden hair which stuck to her face, and her coat seemed almost twice its weight.

"Apart from the packed lunch the old lady gave her, it's empty," she told Ben when he approached, and she tossed it to the ground. She glanced around at the spread of yellow jackets searching every nook and cranny in the area.

"Why would she have an empty bag?" Ben said. "Rain mac, maybe?"

"It's been raining all morning. She would have been wearing it before the race began. I would have thought, anyway. We can't be sure," Freya said. "It's not what's in the bag that bothers me, it's the fact that she felt the need to bring a bag at all."

"What do you mean?"

But she didn't answer, again internalising her thoughts. Freya turned on her heels, her head bobbing as if she was silently counting the yellow jackets.

"There are ten uniforms," she said.

Ben counted them, then agreed with her.

"Yep," he said.

"Ten, Ben. There should be nine."

"Why?" he asked. "Two teams of five. That makes ten the last time I checked."

"Ten, minus the officer with Jessica Hunt."

"Barnes?" Ben said, and a nearby uniform raised his head from the ditch.

"That's me," he said.

"You're Barnes?" Freya asked, to which he nodded.

"That's right, ma'am."

"Why are you here?"

He looked panic stricken, the way new officers often do when asked a straightforward question.

"It's not a trick question," said Freya. "What are you doing here?"

"Checking the ditch, ma'am."

"I mean, why aren't you with Jessica Hunt?"

His eyes were wide and he seemed to doubt his own reasons as he considered them.

"You called for all units, ma'am."

"Yes, but not you. I specifically asked for..." she began, then sighed. "Oh, forget it, I'll deal with you later. Where was she?"

"Eh?"

"Where did you leave her?"

"Up by the church, ma'am," he said innocently, and pointed due east. "St Botolph's. It's just—"

"I know where it is," she said, and marched back to the car, leaving Ben to run after her.

"Are you thinking what I'm thinking?" he said.

"I'm not thinking, Ben," she replied, as she started the car and put it into drive. She paused long enough to stare him in the eye. "I'm bloody praying."

CHAPTER FIFTY-SIX

The rain hadn't subsided one little bit by the time Freya and Ben reached the church, drawing up beside a foldable chair that lay on the ground as if somebody had discarded it along with the soft cool bag that presumably contained bottled water to hand out to the riders.

They said nothing but thought the same terrible thoughts, both of them itching to do something, to stop him. Freya released the footbrake and slewed the big Range Rover into the derelict church grounds at full speed.

If anything, the downfall was even heavier, bouncing from the ground before them and smothering the windscreen the moment the wipers had passed, rendering visibility almost impossible.

The ABS thrummed into life as soon as Freya slammed on the brakes, and the car eased to a stop beneath the overhanging and overgrown trees.

She switched off the engine and the pair of them scanned the grounds for movement, but found nothing.

"I know where I'd be," Ben said.

With the engine off, the windows wipers gave one last sweep, then settled into their little nook beneath the bonnet.

"Do you want to wait for back-up to arrive?" Ben asked.

"Not really," she replied. "Do you want go inside?"

"Not really," he said, shoving open his door. "But I can't sit here and hope we're wrong."

The tension was broken somewhat by Ben's ringing phone, and had anybody but Cruz been calling, he might have ignored it.

"Cruz, talk to me," he said. "What do you have?"

They strode side by side to take cover by the old church wall, then paused for Ben to hold the phone up.

"The statements are useless," Cruz replied. Again, the fire escape stairwell added an echo to his voice. "But I have found something. Well... I say I found it, but really it was–"

"Chapman found it, yes, yes, Cruz," Freya said, her impatience getting the better of her. "Just tell us what you found. We don't have time."

"Assault," he said, without thinking. "She found a sexual assault claim that was dropped. The officer attended St Michael's Church in Kirkby, but nobody was charged. The victim dropped all charges. Looks like they changed their mind sometime between making the call and the officer attending."

"Any idea why?" Ben asked.

"No, it's just a note against the church. She ran a search for St Michael's and that's all we could find."

"We need more details than that," Freya said, and she peered around the corner towards the door that Larson had opened with his multitool. "What about the victim? What was her name?"

"That's just it, that's why I'm calling," he replied. "It wasn't a *she*."

"Say that again, Cruz?" Freya said, using Ben's mass to protect her from the rain. "Did you say the victim was male?"

"The victim, boss," he said, "was none other than Trevor Starr."

"Starr was the victim?" Freya said.

"So who was the attacker?" Ben asked. "Does it say who attacked him, Cruz?"

"No, there's no name given-."

"It was Vaughan," Freya said. If Ben had heard the final cog clicking into place in Freya's mind, she wouldn't have been surprised. She glanced up at him, trying to read his thoughts to see if he had come to same conclusion as she had, but there was no time to ask. "It all makes sense."

"What makes sense?" Cruz said.

"Thanks, Cruz," she said, taking hold of Ben's hand with the phone in. "We'll get back to you."

She thumbed the button to end the call, then peered up into Ben's stunned eyes.

"That's the motive I was looking for." she said.

"Hold on, what?" Ben said. "How is Vaughan raping Trevor Starr a motive to kill a young girl?"

"It's not a motive to kill Charlotte Rimmell, Ben. It was never about Charlotte. He was getting back at the church. All of this," she said, staring into space. "He's getting back at the church."

It wasn't her words that roused him from his thoughts, it was a chilling scream that seemed to echo from every broken window like a choir of dying angels.

They both ran, with Ben leading the way, reaching the door before her. He stopped with his hand gripping the handle, eyeing Freya as she ran, silently questioning if she was sure, if they really wanted to do this.

Then he shoved it open, letting it slam against the wall.

There were no streaming beams of sunlight to bring the stained glass to life this time, only a gloom that seemed to have embedded itself into the core of the place. The open door made no real difference, banished no shadows from the dark corners, and no spreading fan of sunshine revealed the flagstones in all their ancient glory.

"Jessica?" Freya said, not quietly but not too loud. "Jessica, are you in here?"

She peered into the gloom, signing for Ben to hold fast. The scrape of a shoe on the stone floor seemed to come from all directions at once, reverberating off the hundreds of carved stone surfaces.

"Jessica, is that you?" Freya said, and she stepped inside, allowing her eyes to adjust to the impenetrable gloom. Before her, the huge, octagonal pillars stood like soldiers on parade, reaching up into the eaves to cross swords. But it wasn't the ceiling that had caught her attention. Something shone on the floor, lit briefly by a flash of distant lightning. She studied it, finding a dark familiar form, then another. Wet footprints.

"Trevor, I know you're here," she said. "I know everything."

"You know nothing," somebody said, deeper and colder than she remembered his voice to be, like somehow the adrenaline had roused some kind of demon inside of him.

"I just want to talk, Trevor."

"Don't lie to me," he replied, and in the grey gloom ahead of her, a dark shape sidestepped into view. It was more than just the vague figure of a man. He was carrying something – no, dragging something. Dragging it across the floor.

And then it crinkled, that unmistakeable sound of plastic so alien in the surroundings.

"Is she..."

"Dead?" he finished for Freya, and his form shifted as he lowered his head to listen. "Maybe?"

"Don't," she said. "Put her down. It's not too late."

"Too late for what?"

"Too late for help, Trevor," she said, just as the dark form he held onto kicked out and a muffled scream followed. He fought to maintain his grip, resorting to tightening the plastic bag over her head.

"What has she done to you, Trevor?" Freya asked, softening

her tone, trying to find the tiniest trace of empathy inside him. "Look at her. What has she done?"

"It's not what she's done," he replied, calling out over the girl's muffled struggles. "Tell your friend to get back. Stay outside."

"There's no escape," Freya told him. "If you do this, there's no way out. This is the only door that opens."

"Out of what?" he said. "I don't need doors to get to where I'm going."

"And where's that? Hell?" Freya said, holding her hand palm out for Ben to stay put.

Jessica's kicking feet slowed to a drunken scramble, her oxygen-starved brain releasing its control, and that infamous fight or flight reaction leaning more towards the latter, the less arduous of the choices.

"Let her go, Trevor. There's no excuse for this," she said, taking a step towards him, and for the first time being close enough to see the dark shapes of his eyes. "Not like Charlotte."

Beneath the dark holes that were his eyes another opened. His mouth. And Freya grinned inwardly like she had struck a magical chord.

He said nothing, but his grip relaxed on Jessica's body, and Freya took another step, daring him on, daring him to finish what he'd started before she struck another chord, a deeper chord that resonated through the building.

"I told you, I know," she said softly, forcing him to listen hard, to listen to her recount his tale, from the embryonic caterpillar gaining his first taste of blood to the moth he'd become, masquerading as a butterfly in the glorious light of God with the devil's work in his heart. "She wasn't the first, was she?"

"You don't know anything—"

"I know it all," she told him. "What was her name, Trevor? The first one. The one you didn't mean to kill. What was it?"

"Get away from me," he said, backing off, no longer able to hold onto Jessica and keep his distance. He dropped her and stepped backwards, back into the centre of the room, where long ago another deranged mind had defaced that sacred place with a star within a circle, where the dim light from the high windows seemed to meet, where the shadows were at their weakest.

"What was it? Drugs?" she said, closing the gap between herself and Starr so that Ben could drag Jessica to safety. She glanced behind her to find several uniforms in the rain outside, ready to help Ben as he pulled her form across the stone. "Is that it? What was so bad that you couldn't let her get away? Did she put up a fight? The girl you mugged, Trevor, did she put up a fight?" Freya said, her voice rising like the crescendo of a sermon, delivering the power of good to the room and letting the echoes drive it home. "Answer me," she yelled. "Was it drugs?"

"Yes," he screamed back at her, leaning into the effort so that the skin on his face pulled taut and his gargoyle-like features came at her from the gloom. Then his anger waned as fast as it had arrived, and his voice softened as his darkest of memories replayed. "Yes."

"She put up a fight, didn't she?" Freya said, matching his delicate tone, hoping to coax more from him.

"She shouldn't have. She should have just given it to me."

"But you didn't mean for her to die, did you?"

"No," he said, the pitch an octave higher than before.

"You needed her money, didn't you? You needed money to get your fix and she was an easy target."

"I didn't mean to hurt her," he said.

"But you did, Trevor. You did hurt her. You stabbed her."

"I didn't mean it—"

"You stabbed her, and you left her there to die, for somebody else to deal with," Freya said. "How long was it? How long was it before you realised what you had done? When you realised the thrill of it? How long? Seconds? Minutes? Hours?"

"Days," he said.

"Ah, there it is. Days. After the police had cleared her away, when they had mopped up her blood and stopped knocking on doors, am I right?"

Somebody cried from behind her, somewhere in the rain, and although she hadn't heard Jessica's voice, she knew it was her. Somehow, she knew the girl was alive.

"Tell me what it's like, Trevor," she said.

"What?"

"Tell me. I want to know. I want to know what it's like to take a life. I want to know what it's like to feel their pulse fade away, to watch as their kicks begin to wane, and to hold their lifeless body when it's done. When it's over."

He stared at the floor, as if he was contemplating those moments he had sought, savoured, and probably relived a thousand times over.

Then slowly, he raised his head to face her, and whatever pain he had felt, whatever emotions she had stirred had been buried, and the man that stared back at her was the monster they'd been hunting.

"Glorious," he said, in that tone she had heard once before.

"Charlotte Rimmell," she said. "That's where it began, wasn't it?"

"Glorious," he said again, and he took a step towards her, the balance suddenly shifting in his favour.

"It was Vaughan, wasn't it?" she said, hoping to find that magical chord that had stilled his demons before. "It was Vaughan. I know it was. What did he do, Trevor? What did he take from you? Your faith? No, that came later."

He took another step, and even in the half-light, she saw a curiosity in his expression.

"Your innocence?" she said, and that curiosity vanished to reveal an anger.

"Ah, it is, isn't it?" she said, striving to maintain the upper hand despite his advancement. "I need to know, Trevor. I need to know what happened. I need to understand."

"You need to know if you're right," he said, and that vague, dark oblong that was his mouth spread into a smile, grotesque and hungry for more. "That's what you are, isn't it? You're a narcissist. A psychopath. You're no better than me. I watched you in our house. I watched you control the room, and I envied you."

"You went to Neil, didn't you, Trevor?" she said, countering his verbal attack with her own. "You went to Vaughan's father to complain. To tell him about the monster he had raised. To tell him what his son had done, and how unholy his family was, his blood was–"

"You're an only child, aren't you? No doubt spoiled by a doting father–."

"He didn't listen, did he, Trevor? You had to convince him to call the police. To report his own son."

"How doting was he, Inspector Bloom?" Trevor said, closing the gap, forcing her to sidestep towards the altar. "Was he an attentive father? Or was it somebody else? Somebody close, I'll bet. An uncle, maybe. Yes, that's it. An uncle."

"So, you set him up," she told him. "You devised a sick plan to frame Neil Barrow, knowing that Vaughan would have to live the rest of his life with the knowledge of what he'd done."

"That's who you are, isn't it?" he said, seemingly ignoring her narrative. "You're a victim."

"You'd done it before, hadn't you? You'd killed before, and now you had a way to get away with it."

"I bet you're a devil in the sack," he replied. "All those nights you prayed to be left alone, those times you woke with his hot breath on your neck while your precious, doting daddy slept in the next room."

"Skye was perfect, wasn't she? She was everything Charlotte wasn't. You even wore Neil's boots, not to implicate him, no, of course not. I mean, he was long dead. But just for kicks. Just to tantalise the world, like a signature. It was me. I did this."

"How long did he get away with it, Inspector Bloom?" he said. "How long was it before you finally took control?"

"But Hayley?" Freya said, feeling the heat rise in her body as his words stung her eyes like a hundred tiny daggers. "She was different, wasn't she? Let me guess, you framed Justin just like you framed Vaughan. But Frank Donovan didn't die. He lived, Trevor. He lived. And that scared you, didn't it? It scared you so much you worked your evil little mind into their lives where you could control Justin and cast your dirty spell over them, turning them from their father, just like God had turned from you."

"How did you do it?" he asked. "You couldn't just walk away, no. That would never do, would it?"

"She defied you. She kept her faith, didn't she? She kept her faith in her father."

"You strangled him," he replied. "No, no, he was too strong for you. It was your first time, it was unplanned–"

"Poor Frank. He truly believed it was Justin who killed her. And what's a man like Frank Donovan going to do? A real man. A father."

"You hit him," he said. "Something close to hand. A lamp – no, too cumbersome. A statue. One of those expensive ornaments the rich enjoy so much, brass maybe. Something frivolous–"

"They worked it out, didn't they? Frank and Hayley. They worked it out. They worked out that it was you after all. And it was Vaughan, he was the link. It was Vaughan who told her what you did. It was Vaughan who roused the monster inside of you and it was Vaughan who threatened to destroy it."

"Did you lay there?" he said. "Afterwards? With his weight pressing down on you? His blood on your hands, in your hair–"

"But Hayley Donovan played you at your own game, didn't she?" Freya said, taking a final step backwards until she felt the solid presence of one of those stone statues behind her. "She lured you to the marshes. She knew you'd come. She knew you'd be

there. And she knew her father would come. In fact, she'd
arranged for him to be there."

"Ah, poor Frank," he said, finally acknowledging what Freya
had to say. "Imagine the guilt he must be feeling. He never did
make it, did he?"

They were face to face now, equal in height and well-matched
in argument, and Freya sought the blow that would bring him to
his knees.

"How long have you lived with it, Freya Bloom?" he said
quietly. "It's funny, isn't it? How one gets used to it. The guilt, that
is. The resentment. Somehow the motive seems stronger when
you recall that moment of betrayal, doesn't it?"

He was so close now, she could see his features, which were
somehow prominent in the gloom, like they belonged there, like
he belonged there.

He glanced to the side, to the door where Ben was holding
back the team of uniforms who were ready to pounce on Freya's
signal, then he turned back to Freya and leaned in close.

"You're just like me," he whispered. "Embrace it."

She closed her eyes, forcing the story he had told from her
mind, refusing the venom he had spewed that had twisted the
reality she had created.

Then she felt it. A jolt so subtle it could have been the breeze.
And he touched her, held her, gripped her, and coughed. Freya felt
the unmistakeable warmth of blood on her neck and smelled fear
in the stale air around her, and in his hot breath.

He dropped to his knees, his grip tugging at every inch of her
as he slumped.

She opened her eyes slowly, allowing her eyes to welcome the
gloom, not wishing to miss a single one of his final heartbeats.

But it wasn't his face she saw.

"Stella?" she said, and the church rang out with the clatter of
steel as the knife the girl had held slipped from her hand.

The girl watched Trevor slump into a heap at Freya's feet, her dark, bloody hands open in submission. Freya followed her gaze to the man that had destroyed so many lives. He peered up at her, eyes wide open as if welcoming the invitation to hell.

"I'm nothing like you," Freya told him, and she stepped away, allowing his dying body to fall to the flagstone, framed by a graffitied pentagon in the house of God.

CHAPTER FIFTY-SEVEN

The vestry at All Saints Church in Saltfleet was far more welcoming that the ancient, derelict building in which Trevor Starr's decades-long killing spree had come to an end.

As requested, a uniformed officer stood guard at the entrance while two crime scene investigators brushed every surface they could find, quietly working their way through the building.

Freya snapped on a pair of latex gloves, gaining the attention of the nearest investigator.

"Mind if I have a nose?" Freya said, flashing her warrant card, and he nodded before continuing with his work.

She sat down at the desk, opened the lid of Grantham's laptop, and then, finding the internet browser, she opened the history tab to reveal the list of recently browsed webpages.

But what she found was far more than the archives of a Kent newspaper. To her they were memories she had long ago buried; devilish birds she had kept caged in a dark corner of her mind which had been set free.

She didn't follow the links to the archives, the mere sight of the Kent and Sussex Courier was enough to hear the beating of those black wings.

"Ben said I'd find you in here," a voice said from the doorway, and she found Larson staring at her. "I believe congratulations are in order."

"I wouldn't call it a result, George. He bled out before the paramedics could get there."

"I was talking about Jessica Hunt," he replied. "She's safe."

"And the vicar's son?"

Larson smiled at her. "He came in fourth."

She gave a laugh. It was nice to find some humour at the end of a gruelling investigation, and it was nice to find a peer who understood her, even if the first day or so had been challenging.

"I owe you a thanks," he said, "and probably an apology."

"I'll settle for the gratitude."

"That's lucky, then," he said. "If it's any consolation, we managed to hit our deadline. We're all wrapped up, boxed up, and ready to start afresh next week. We'd never have done that without you."

"Well, when you're settling into your nice, new, shiny office, you can think of me."

"We still have a day or two left at Mablethorpe. Enough time to close down the paperwork if you'd like to get back. If anything needs your signature, I can always send it through."

"I'd like that," she said. "I have a feeling my team need us back there."

"What are you doing there, anyway?" he asked, and he nodded at the laptop.

Freya shrugged and shook her head, then, as smoothly as she could, she hit the delete button, watched the recent history file into the digital waste bin, and closed the lid.

"Just seeing if we'd missed anything, that's all."

"And did you?"

She shook her head.

"Neat as a pin."

Freya stood from the seat, tugged off the gloves, and then led him out into the main church. Thrusting her hands into her pockets, she ambled along, wondering, like he was, what her next adventure might entail. At least she had an idea. Unlike him, she knew she would be heading into the belly of the beast from the east, whereas Larson would be starting a new team on a new patch – not an easy task at his age or at any age.

"Give me a rundown, will you?" he said.

"Everything will be in my report."

"I imagine it will, but I dare say my super will want a debrief. You know what they're like."

"The short version?"

"Starting with the manslaughter case," he replied. "I don't recall you mentioning it before."

"I hadn't. It's one of the cold cases my team are working on for Kirkby," she replied, coming to a stop at the ornate doorway. "It was something you said, though. Something about Trevor Starr getting it right first time."

"It wasn't his first time."

"No, but it gave him a taste for it, even if he didn't realise it at the time. It was only when Vaughan Barrow assaulted him, and Neil Barrow let him down, that he tried it again, and this time he meant to kill her. The first time was just bad luck. Charlotte Rimmell was when he realised that he could get away with murder. Skye Green was his addiction coming to life. And Hayley Donovan, well...that was just him covering his tracks, hence her possessions planted at St Botolph's and the use of Neil Barrow's boots."

"Neil Barrow's boots? I thought you said they were Frank Donovan's."

"I didn't say that. The previous investigation presumed that. But the next time you see him, when you set him free, and I hope you do set him free, have a look at his feet. Size nine, ten at best. Far too small for those boots."

He gave a little laugh of amazement, of adoration or respect. She couldn't tell which it was. But it was friendly and genuine.

"And you managed to piece that together in three days?" he said.

"Not just me," she said. "I had a little help. Let's call it an interregional effort."

She felt the pull of her armchair and the promise of a good wine, all the things that home offered. Yet she found herself attracted to George Larson, not in the romantic sense, but he had a quality about him. She imagined that, had the timing been different, they could have whiled away the hours sharing anecdotes of long-closed cases, and even a few recent ones.

"I'll leave you to deal with Frank Donovan," she said.

"He broke his parole."

"He also served nine years for a crime he didn't commit," she said. "I know what I'd do."

"So you think Starr set Donovan and his boy up, do you?"

She leaned against the old, wooden doors and folded her arms, considering the young man they had seen.

"I think, if you dig a little deeper, you'll find that when Skye Green was killed, Justin was unable to tell you where he was, much like his father," she said. "The plan doesn't work unless the father has somebody to protect and that that the person he's protecting is vulnerable, of course. I like to think that Justin and Deborah are able to open their arms to Frank. He's a good man, deep down. Conflicted, but good."

"We don't always get it right, do we?" Larson mused.

"No, but so long as we choose to do the right thing when we can, we can't do any more than that, George."

She reached for the door handle, but Larson, being the oldschool gentleman he was, beat her to it and held it open.

The sky was a brilliant blue, almost as if the world was apologising for the break in summertime, or, Freya thought, happier now that the devil's plan had been foiled.

"I think it's going to clear up," she said, as cheerfully as she could.

"If there's anything I can do," he said, and he met her eye-to-eye. "I'd like to say thanks, somehow."

She smiled the gesture off and was about to step out into the sunshine, where Ben was waiting with Ivy Hart and Samson, when an idea struck her.

"Now I come to think of it," she said. "How close are you to the DCI at Kirkby? Are you on speaking terms?"

"Pretty close," he replied. "*She* happens to be one of the good ones."

"She?"

He nodded. "She's one of the reasons I took the job."

"Well in that case," Freya said, "there is something you could do, and if it comes off then we can call it quits."

CHAPTER FIFTY-EIGHT

It was nearing the end of the day when Ben and Freya climbed the fire escape staircase to the first floor. They heard no banter from the incident room, and none of Gillespie's roars of laughter rolled off the walls, as they so often did.

They peered through the little windows like children at the window of the sweet shop or toy store, but there was nothing inside to taunt their desires, only misery and silence broken by the shuffling of paperwork.

"Christ," Ben said. "I wouldn't be surprised if we saw Pip the pathologist in there pushing a body around."

He had expected to at least raise a smile on Freya's face, but when he looked at her, her eyes were saddened, as if she pitied them.

She shoved her way into the room saying nothing but gave Nillson's shoulder a squeeze as she passed. One by one, the heads rose from their work, until each of them stared at her and Ben like baby starlings in the nest, still in total silence.

Freya nodded for Ben to check the corridor, which he did, giving her the all clear.

"Listen up," she said, which Ben thought unnecessary as she had their undivided attention. "How are we doing?"

Cruz, Gold, and Chapman looked to Nillson for a response.

"Pretty bad, boss," she said. "He was in here a moment ago giving Cruz a hard time."

"Cruz? Are you okay?" she asked.

"Ah, well," he said, searching for a brave face and failing. "I don't know how much longer I can hold him off. If it wasn't for a phone call, he'd still be in here."

"You don't need to," she told him. "You too, Anna."

"That's easy for you to say," Nillson replied.

"I need you to trust me," Freya said, and looked to Ben for some support.

"She's right," he said. "Did you say he was on a call?"

"Yeah, but he'll be back in a minute," Cruz said. "He hadn't finished with us."

"What about you, Gillespie?" Freya asked. "Did you submit your report?"

"Aye, I did, and grim reading it was too."

"I'm sure it was," Freya said, clearly trying to lift the mood with a smile. "Did you include all the items I sent?"

"Aye, boss."

"Then you have nothing to worry about."

"But you do," he replied. "That's my problem. He has enough on that report to grill you for hours. There's cases of interviewing suspects without providing legal support, of entering homes without warrants, and even discharging suspects on what I can describe as gut instinct."

"Listen," she said. "What have the team been doing this week?"

"Eh?"

"It's a simple question, Gillespie. What has everyone been working on?"

"Those two cold cases," he said, unsure of where she was going.

"And what have Ben and I been working on?"

"Erm, a murder case," he said slowly, as if she had completely lost her mind. "In Saltfleet, remember? You just came back from there."

"Exactly," she said, folding her arms and sitting back on the desk. "Together, we've closed two cold cases that have been open for decades, we've proved a convicted man to be innocent, and we've helped to incarcerate a man who has been killing for nearly twenty years."

"Right?" Gillespie said.

"How many cold cases do we have here?" she asked him.

"Cold cases?"

"Major crimes only," she added. "How many do we, as a team, have?"

"None, as far as I'm aware."

"Right, and how many open investigations are we working on?"

"Erm, none," he said again, adopting that same bewildered tone.

"So, what the bloody hell is Standing going to say? As far as I can tell, we're the best performing team in the county. What's he going to do? Sack me?"

Just as she finished her sentence, Ben signalled that Standing was coming and moved back to his desk. He unpacked his laptop, making a show of only just returning.

"Ah, Bloom. I thought I smelled your perfume," Standing said. "Have you forgotten something?"

"Forgotten something, Guv?" she asked innocently.

"You're back early. I expected you to be away for at least a week, more if luck was on my side."

"I suppose you should have given us a harder investigation then," she said.

He stared at her, making no attempt to hide the fact that he was trying to gauge her sincerity. But he left it there, choosing instead to address the room. It was a sign of poor leadership, of a disconnect between leader and followers.

He paced, rather than strode, with his hands in his pockets and not out in a welcoming manner as Granger used to when he had been DCI. He avoided eye contact, choosing instead to look through the window down to the car park, no doubt eyeing Freya's brand-new Range Rover, which she had deliberately parked behind his five-year-old Mercedes.

Seizing his moment, Ben glanced across at Freya to watch how she reacted to his arrival.

She met his stare and offered nothing but a confident wink.

"I've just been on the telephone," Standing announced with his back to the room. "Can anybody guess who I was talking to?"

"Were you booking a table at a restaurant?" Freya asked.

"And why would I be booking a restaurant?" he replied still refusing to meet her eye-to-eye.

"Oh, I just thought you might like to show us your appreciation, that's all."

"When you've done something worthy of appreciation, DI Bloom, you shall be the first to know about it. No, I had two calls. Two rather similar calls, in fact. The first was from DI Larson in Mablethorpe."

"Ah, George," Freya said. "He's a good detective."

"Funnily enough, he said the same about you. I don't know what spell you cast over him, but I can assure you, I am not so easily won over."

"No spells, Guv. Just good old-fashioned police work."

"You got your man, did you?"

"We did. I'd like to report that he's in custody now, but that all rather depends."

"Depends on what?"

"On whether or not he pulls through."

"He didn't," Standing said. "DCI Larson told me he succumbed to his injuries before he reached the hospital."

"Well, either way, he won't be hurting anybody else."

"He also said you managed to find a convicted man innocent."

"That's right, Guv. Frank Donovan. Served nine years for murder."

"There's a hell of a lot of paperwork to right that wrong," Standing said.

"He's an innocent man. If George needs help, he knows where to find me."

"And for some bizarre reason, you also managed to help one of his team bring a spate of burglaries to an end. What on earth were you getting involved in that for?"

"Oh, you know, Guv. I just had a gut feeling and I went with it. The suspect was robbing local holiday parks to kit out his aunt's caravans. It wasn't a difficult one to work out."

"And I suppose you left the paperwork for DI Larson to finish, did you?"

"He knows where I am, Guv."

Standing glanced to his side to offer Freya a look of contempt, then returned his attention to the window.

"The second call I had was from a DCI Rose over at Kirkby," he announced. "Any ideas why she called me?"

"Does her incident room have a squeaky door that needs fixing, Guv?" Freya said, to which Standing's body tensed; he sucked in a deep breath to calm his temper.

"Nillson," he said.

"Guv?"

"The manslaughter case," he said. "She tells me you've provided everything she needs to close the case and charge the suspect. Is that right?"

Nillson's eye widened, and she looked to Freya who simply nodded in silence.

"Yes, Guv. That's right."

"How? It was nearly two decades old."

"Oh, it was nothing really. More of a paperwork exercise than anything. There were few details in the statements that nobody had picked up on. I would have done it sooner, but you know what cold cases are like, witnesses aren't always at the same address, phone numbers change—"

"I get it," he said, cutting her off. "Cruz?"

"Guv?" Cruz replied, sounding far more nervous than he needed to.

"DCI Rose reports that you somehow managed to prove the original suspect was innocent."

Again, Freya nodded behind Standing's back, and Cruz stammered into a ramble as an old car might stutter into life.

"Erm, yes, Guv. Erm, well...you see, I had to find the victim's mother, and that wasn't easy. Then there was the CSI report and the pathology report—"

"She tells me you also gave her enough to charge a new suspect," Standing said, not willing to listen to Cruz's verbal discharge. "Is that right?"

"Erm yes, Guv."

Standing turned to face the room and looked between the two of them for some kind of sign they were lying, but found only sincerity in their eyes.

"It seems to me they deserve some kind of recognition, Guv," Freya said, diverting his attention to her.

"Like I said, DI Bloom, when there is recognition to be given, I'll let you know."

"You're the boss," she replied.

"Yes," he said. "Yes, I am. And while I'm the boss, I intend to keep you all on a short leash. Especially you, DI Bloom. Do you know I have a report as thick as the bible on your investigations since you arrived here in Lincolnshire?"

"I didn't know you were a religious man, Guv," she said.

"I am not," he replied. "Which you will find out in our little party with Detective Superintendent Granger."

"Oh?" she said, sounding surprised enough to charm him into thinking he now had the upper hand.

"We'll be going through that report line by line. We'll be scrutinizing every single move you have made, every mistake you have made, and every rule you have broken. So why don't you save that smarmy smile of yours for when we're done? See if it still fits then."

"Sounds nice, Guv. I'll bring a bottle, shall I? A nice Chianti, I think."

"Save your rhetoric for when you're back in uniform," he told her, striding towards the doors. He pulled them open in anger and winced as one of them gave a gentle squeak, reminding Ben of how things used to be. He stared at every member of the team in turn, settling on Freya. "I don't know what's going on here, but something isn't right. You lot are up to something, and when I find out what it is, believe you me, heads will roll."

He let the doors close under their own weight and marched back up the corridor to the safety of his office, leaving the team to sigh collectively.

But nobody spoke. Nobody said a single word. They all looked between Ben and Freya wearing a mixture of relieved, amused, and bemused expressions.

"How?" Nillson said finally. "I thought I'd be working that manslaughter case until I retire."

Freya shoved herself off the desk and was clearly about to give one of those cryptic responses that raised more questions than it answered when Detective Superintendent Granger pushed the doors open.

"I just had a call from the Deputy Chief Constable. He's putting this team forward for an award," he announced, seemingly unable to contain the news. He was sure to look every one of the team in the eye for a moment or two. Then he shook his head, seemingly astounded by what he'd heard. "Bloody good work, everyone. Bloody good work indeed."

"Thanks, Guv," Freya said, and her smile was as genuine as they come. "That means a lot."

CHAPTER FIFTY-NINE

The events of the week played over on repeat in Freya's mind. From DI Larson, whom she had developed a healthy respect for, to Frank Donovan and Vaughan Barrow. Barrow, she was certain, would face some kind of prison sentence for his burglaries and if Larson is inclined, he might even get him on a rape charge for his attack on Starr. Either way, Freya thought, Vaughan Barrow's future was bleak, but she was doubtful if his conniving and manipulative aunt would even see inside a holding cell. Vaughan would take the blame, ensuring his mother was cared for. Of that Freya was sure.

She hoped Frank Donovan and his family were reunited and that Frank would now see that Justin was never guilty of anything but fragility. Maybe the young man she had seen writhing on the floor amongst his dead and dying fish would leave his depression behind him, safe in the knowledge that his father was there by his side.

There were so many *perhaps* that Freya caught herself staring through the living room window, wondering.

What if Michaela hadn't turned up? Perhaps she and Ben would have broken through those barriers. Perhaps Buttercup, with its soiled mattresses and seventies decor, would have gained an extra mark on its tally of infidelity?

Perhaps, she thought, as she unwrapped the old newspaper she'd used to protect her favourite wine glass. She set it down beside another on the mantlepiece then delved further into the box in search of the bottle she had brought back from Saltfleet.

Most prominent of all the scenes that replayed in her mind was her final interaction with Trevor Starr. The way his face seemed almost gargoyle-like in the gloom. The way he seemed to speak with such confidence. Like he actually understood her.

A knock at the door roused her from her daydream. She checked her watch, finding that three hours had passed and all she had done was unpack the kitchen boxes, most of which contained food. She still had her clothes to deal with, which was the lion's share of her belongings.

The visitor knocked again, harder this time and with the flat of his hand. She knew it was Ben; she recognised the knock.

"Afternoon," he said when she opened the door. He beamed up at her from the doorstep. She forced a smile when she saw Michaela at his side.

"What the–" she began, then remembered her manners. "How did you know I was here?"

"We just thought we'd swing by," he replied, turning to Michaela. "Didn't we, babe?"

"We did. We thought we'd bring you this." Freya glanced down to their feet, where a large box had been placed, wrapped in brown paper with a little blue bow affixed to the top.

Freya looked between them, then down at the box again.

"What's that?"

"Aren't you going to invite us in?" Ben asked.

"I was actually just in the middle of something," she replied. "What's in the box?"

"A gift," Ben said. And he stepped inside anyway, disappearing into the living room from where he called out, "A home warming present."

Michaela scooped up the box then gave a little shrug before they followed Ben.

"This is nice," he said, gesturing at the first space Freya could actually call her own in far too long.

"Well, I meant to tell you before, but..."

"But?"

She paused. There was something about his expression. It was almost as if he was toying with her.

"I couldn't find the right time."

"You couldn't find the right time?" he said. "Even though we just shared a caravan? Not to mention the two-hour journey to Mablethorpe and back?"

"I had other things on my mind."

"Ah," Ben said, and he winked at Michaela. "Lover boy, you mean?"

"His name is Greg."

"And how is Greg? Did he wait for you? Was he pining, as you thought he might be?" Ben said, then his eyes widened, the way he did when he felt playful. "He's not upstairs, is he?"

"No, Ben. He is not."

"Downstairs? You do have the dungeon you always wanted, don't you?" he said, opening the little cupboard under the stairs.

"No, Ben. I do not have a dungeon. And could you not be so nosy?"

He smiled, closed the cupboard door, and leaned against the wall, a sign he wasn't going anywhere fast.

"But he did miss you?" he said, teasing an answer from her the way a Victorian doctor might have lured a tapeworm from a patient's mouth with a morsel of rancid meat.

She chose her words well, opting to stay on the right side of a lie.

"He was pleased to hear from me, yes," she said.

"And you, erm...managed to seal the deal, did you?" he asked.

"Don't be vulgar, Ben," she said. "Now, what's all this about?"

"I was hoping you were going to tell us," Ben said, seeming to enjoy her frustration.

"What's in the box?" she said.

"Tell us about Greg, first," he replied. "Unless you don't want it, of course. I mean, we could see if we can get our money back."

She sighed. It was obvious she wasn't going to hold him off, not at this stage, at least. She fiddled with the flaps on a new box then ripped the seam of tape a tug.

"You've unpacked your wine glasses," he said. "Two of them? Seems a little odd–"

"Alright. Alright, I have a confession to make," she said, cutting him off.

"Yes?" he said, making a show of waiting just as the doorbell rang – far more polite than the pounding Ben had used to announce his arrival. "Oh, who could that be?"

Freya rushed to the front door, but Ben beat her there, his big hand covering the handle.

"It's okay, Freya. You can never be too careful in a new neighbourhood," he said. "I'll just see who it is."

"No, it's for me–" she said, but he held his free hand up to calm her down.

"Don't worry, I'll get it. What are friends for?"

He opened the door and Freya covered her face with her hands, waiting for the embarrassing conversation to begin.

"Oh, hello, Greg. Come in," Ben said, and Freya splayed her fingers as Greg, armed with a large bouquet of flowers, stepped inside. The men shook hands like old friends and Freya uncovered her face just in time to see Greg step across the room and give Michaela a peck on the cheek.

"Alright, sis," he said. "What are you two doing here?"

Then it hit her.

"Sis?" Freya said, hearing the disgust in her own voice. "As in, sister?"

"That's right," he replied.

"You two?" she said, pointing between Greg and Michaela. "Brother and–"

"Sister," Ben finished for her.

A very sheepish-looking Greg held out the bouquet of flowers and muttered, "Happy moving-in day."

"How long have you known?" she said to Ben, her voice a low growl.

"Oh, only a few days."

"A few days?"

"Pretty much since Sunday evening," he said.

"Sunday evening?" she said. "And you let me–"

"It was fun, watching you wiggle and squirm."

"And you?" she said, turning on Greg. "Haven't you ever heard about client confidentiality?"

"Don't look at me. I didn't bloody know you knew each other. I just mentioned to Michaela that..."

He paused, stopping himself from saying too much.

"That what?" she snapped. "That some posh tart from the police is buying one of your houses?"

"Well, I didn't call you posh."

"No?"

"He didn't," Michaela said. "In fact, he was quite complimentary."

"Complimentary?"

"He said you smelled nice and..." She stopped and glanced at her brother.

"And?" Freya said.

"And he wondered if we were able to a put a good word in for him," Michaela said. "So here we are."

"Why do I feel like I've been set up?" Freya said.

"I should go," Greg said, placing the flowers down and avoiding eye contact with Freya.

"No," she said. "No, stay. You're here now."

Ben and Michaela edged closer to the front door and Ben guided his new girlfriend out.

"Enjoy your gift," he told her. "We'll get out of your hair."

"It's a coffee machine," she replied, to which he cocked his head.

"How did you guess?"

"Because you have the imagination of a Brussels sprout, Ben Savage," she said. "And you know me better than anybody."

"Hope you like it."

"Thank you," she said, holding onto the front door, and glancing over her shoulder to make sure Greg wasn't listening. She grinned. "And thanks for that, too."

Michaela was waiting by his car, her head tilted back with the sun warming her face.

But Ben wasn't quite ready to go. He stopped halfway down the footpath and turned back to speak to her.

"Something's been bothering me," he said. "Well, a few things, really."

"Hayley Donovan isn't on the CCTV footage from the holiday park?" she said, and he nodded.

"She ran from the church," Freya said. "That's where she arranged to meet Trevor. Next?"

"Why did Frank go to Sea Lane at four a.m. in the morning?"

"Because she was supposed to lure Starr to him," Freya replied. "But we know now he didn't make it. He saw Stella and bolted. And now you're going to ask why Stella Green and Vaughan went to St Botolph's."

"I was, yes," he said, shaking his head at her ability to seemingly read his thoughts.

"There's no connection between Frank and Vaughan," she told him.

"No connection?" he said. "But what about—"

"They were going there for Trevor," she said. "If I'm right, and of course, we'll never know if I am, but if I'm right, then Vaughan's aunt saw Trevor at the church, probably while he was planting Hayley's belongings. She has to drive past St Botolph's to get home."

"But you don't think we'll ever know for sure?"

"I'm not Mystic bloody Meg, Ben," she said, sensing he had one further question he wanted an answer to, but it was unrelated to the investigation and would change everything. "Besides, we got our result. We freed a man, we reunited a family, we put Standing back in his box. And that's all that matters. Whatever else happened is in the past, it's irrelevant. To examine the past for every minute detail is a futile practice, if you ask me. I'd like to move forward, if I can," she said, glancing up at the house. "A fresh start."

He stared at her as if he was questioning all that he knew about her. A seed of doubt had been planted and it troubled him.

"What Starr said to you," he said. "In the church. I couldn't quite hear, but I thought he said—"

"Trevor Starr is a psychopath, Ben," she told him. "He was trying to find a crack in my armour, that's all."

He mulled it over, with a quick look back at Michaela. Then he smiled contemplatively.

"If you're sure," he said, and he nodded at the house, indicating that Greg would be waiting. "I'll see you in the office, Detective Inspector Bloom."

"Don't be late, Detective Sergeant Savage," she replied, and with that, she closed the door on him then turned and closed the door to her new house. Her house. Not a rental, not a motorhome, her own home.

Greg watched her, appraising her from her feet up. He'd found the bottle of wine, filled the glasses, and was holding one out for her.

"You read my mind," she told him.

"To friends," he said, holding his drink up in a toast. "New and old."

She studied him unabashed, admiring his blond hair and clear skin. His nails were trimmed, his hands were clean, and he dressed well.

She raised her own glass in response.

"To new beginnings," she said. Then to herself, she muttered, "And distant pasts."

The End

ALSO BY JACK CARTWRIGHT

Secrets In Blood

One For Sorrow

In Cold Blood

Suffer In Silence

Dying To Tell

Never To Return

Lie Beside Me

Dance With Death

In Dead Water

One Deadly Night

Join my VIP reader group to be among the first to hear about new release dates, discounts, and get a free Wild Fens Novella.

Visit www.jackcartwrightbooks.com for details.

VIP READER CLUB

Your FREE ebook is waiting for you now.

Get your FREE copy of the prequel story to the Wild Fens Murder Mystery series, and learn how DI Freya Bloom came to give up everything she had, to start a new life in Lincolnshire.

Visit www.jackcartwrightbooks.com to join the VIP Reader Club.

I'll see you there.

Jack Cartwright

AFTERWORD

Because reviews are critical to an author's career, if you have enjoyed this novel, you could do me a huge favour by leaving a review on Amazon.

Reviews allow other readers to find my books. Your help in leaving one would make a big difference to this author.

Thank you for taking the time to read *In Dead Water*.

COPYRIGHT

Printed in Great Britain
by Amazon

27082993R00229